DEAD MAN'S CHEST

Roger L. Johnson,
Commander U.S. Navy - Retired

Cover Design by Rob Johnson
Book Design by Neil Mazuelos

Printed in the United States of America
First Edition

ISBN 0-939837-45-5

Published by
Paradise Cay Publications
P.O. Box 29
Arcata, California 95521
800-736-4509
707-822-9163 Fax
paracay@humboldt1.com
www.paracay.com

Dedicated to my darling wife, Elizabeth, without whom this book would never have been possible.

About The Author

Commander Johnson retired from the United States Navy in 1985 after a 21-year career as a Naval Aviator, which took him to Vietnam on three separate aircraft carriers. He has recently completed a second career as a Fire Captain with the California Department of Forestry and Fire Protection in Northern California. Along with his writing endeavors, Roger has been a published cartoonist and illustrator for twelve years, working for three publishing companies and drawing gag cartoons for two magazines. He and his wife, Elizabeth, live in Hiouchi, a small hamlet on the outskirts of Crescent City, California where he continues to write and paint.

Preface

They say that the salt content of seawater is identical to that contained in our blood. Maybe that explains why so many of us are drawn to the sea and the wonderful stories it has spawned over the centuries. One of those stories fascinated most of us as children and still holds a special place in our hearts. If you share my love of adventure, then perhaps, like me, you've wondered after that classic three-some; the lice-infested maroon, Ben Gunn, the courageous Bristol lad, Jim Hawkins, and that most famous of all pirates, the softhearted cutthroat, Long John Silver. Did they really exist, and if so, what happened to them after their legendary eighteenth century adventure? I believe I found the answer to those questions during the summer of 1982, when I chanced upon the hand-written transcript of a 1777 Royal Navy Admiralty investigation that dealt with the attack and near-sinking of H.M.S King James, a fourth-rate British man-of-war near Andros Island in the Bahamas. There were dozens of similar investigations made by the Royal Navy, but none with the significance of the questioning of Lieutenant Desmond R. Roberts.

I was in London that summer to attend a NATO-sponsored leadership symposium for command-grade military officers. Since I had arrived early at Whitehall, three days before the first session, I had the entire weekend to collect gifts and keepsakes for my wife and three children. My eldest son, Stephen, had asked that I do some research for a term paper he was writing, so a few minutes before three in the afternoon, on Friday, I signed into the search room of the House of Lords Record Office in the southern section of old London.

Stephen was writing a term paper on relations between the United States and England following World War I, and had become frustrated at the lack of information contained in our local libraries. My search for the raw material he needed began with Parliamentary proceedings of December 1918; the month following the allied and central powers signing of the armistice.

The transcript of Lieutenant Roberts' testimony measured seventy pages and was misfiled between the February and March, 1919 Parliamentary records. The cover page was embossed with the Royal Navy seal and dated 5 April 1777. The knot in the thin blue ribbon which bound the neat stack of parchment was crushed in such a way that it was very probable that the transcript had not been disturbed since its writing. Naturally I became curious, but it wasn't until the fifth page that I began to realize what I had discovered. In his defense, Lieutenant Roberts had requested that a seaman's ballad be entered into evidence. The name of the song was "Fifteen Men on the Dead Man's Chest."

In the two hours available to me before the search room closed, I managed to read the entire document and make notes of the major events it described. The chief witness in the case was one Desmond R. Roberts, a Lieutenant and mid-grade officer on the ill-fated man-of-war H.M.S. King James. Although many of his fellow crew members survived the attack, Lieutenant Roberts was the only man able to identify the pirate captain who had attacked his warship.

What was most amazing about the document was that in a short section near the beginning, Lieutenant Roberts described a series of events which matched in nearly every detail, a pirate story I had read as a child. The transcript also provided a concise record of a great American naval hero's movements during a hitherto unknown twenty months of his life, and explained how he overcame several tremendous obstacles to obtain one of the very first Colonial Navy commissions. The man was John Paul Jones; a Scotsman and fugitive from King George III.

After comparing the dates, places and events Lieutenant Roberts had described, I became convinced that he was the very Jim Hawkins of Robert Louis Stevenson's novel, Treasure Island. This conclusion, however, was not based entirely upon the transcript. In my subsequent research, I discovered that retired Commander Desmond R. Roberts had married one Christiana Osbourne of Edinburgh, Scotland, the same town where Frances Osbourne was born nearly a hundred years later. In 1880, while Robert Louis Stevenson was in San Francisco, California, he met and married Frances. It was shortly after their marriage that he began writing his novel, Treasure Island.

As I checked out of the search room that Friday evening, I told the Clerk of the Records, a Mister Cobb, about the misfiled transcript and asked if I might borrow it for the weekend, promising to return it the following Monday after my first NATO session. He said that if it were up to him, he would be glad to oblige, but "...the '67 Public Records Act only allows for the reading of these older documents, not their removal or copying." He did, however, agree to hold the transcript aside for me. When I returned Monday afternoon, there was only a note from the clerk informing me that the transcript "...had been collected by two gentlemen from the Admiralty."

I can only speculate as to why the transcript was taken. It may have been the Royal Navy's desire to keep a certain questionable incident aboard the King James from becoming public. According to Lieutenant Roberts' testimony, two weeks prior to the attack on his ship, one of the midshipmen lost his life during some horseplay with several of his mates. The ship's Captain singled out two of the Ensigns who had been hazing the cadet and accused them of murder. After a quicker-than-normal court martial, they were hanged. Not only did this action violate Admiralty Law, but there was compelling evidence in Lieutenant Robert's testimony that the Captain had a personal vendetta against the two along with several of the other officers.

I have not seen the transcript since that Friday afternoon in London, and my letters of inquiry continue to elicit the same response. "The document you cite in your letter of 29 January 1983 is not available at this office, nor is there any record of it having been held by the Royal Navy at any time."

Unless I have been duped by a cleverly conceived hoax -- and I sincerely doubt that I have -- I present to you what I believe is the entire story of Long John Silver, and the only true account of John Paul Jones' movements during that missing twenty months; and this from the Royal Navy Lieutenant who walked the deck of the Scotsman's treasure ship and learned the tale from three of the pirates who manned it during it's final voyage.

I have included from memory a portion of the Admiralty transcript as my first and last chapters. Except for the historical persons involved, none of Mister Stevenson's characters were named in the transcript. I have, of course, changed their names as appropriate in my story so that they coincide with the characters in his novel, Treasure Island.

It is a complicated story of piracy, politics, greed, and lost love; and of how one man was able to manipulate the lives of hundreds of patriots and pirates in his attempt to attain a King's ransom in buried treasure. You may notice, as I did, that Lieutenant Roberts' testimony contains a great deal of coincidence. This disturbed me until I realized that the world was much smaller back in 1775, just prior to the American Revolution. Merchants knew every other merchant of stature, just as statesmen and sea captains knew their important counterparts. Stories of the famous and infamous spread throughout the world as quickly as the winds push a brigantine to a far shore or a horse gallops across the countryside.

As you set your sails and cast off your last line for this complicated armchair adventure, my hope is that you sail before fair winds and following seas. If I have stretched or compressed the truth slightly, I beg your indulgence. I was only in possession of the transcript for a very short time. And besides, without a certain degree of journalistic elasticity, my story would simply be a dry expansion of Desmond Robert's testimony.

I leave you with your battle cry:

THE ARMCHAIR PIRATE

The meeker the man, the more pirate he be,
Snug in his armchair, far from the sea.
He has all the fun and none of the woes,
Masters the ladies and scuttles his foes.
His armchair's his ship and reclined his position,
As he cheats the hangman, hellfire and perdition.

Roger L. Johnson
Commander USNR - Retired

PROLOGUE

The Royal Navy Board of Inquiry; called together at the direction of Vice Admiral Cuthbert Collingwood for the purpose of investigating the attack and near-sinking of His Majesty's Ship, the Man-of-War Frigate King James, and the death of its Commanding Officer, Commodore Alexander Stevens; the Ship's Surgeon, Benjamin Cooper; seven of the ship's officers and forty-three crew members, on or about 22 June, in the year of our Lord 1775 near Andros Island in the West Indian Colonies.

Members of this Board of Inquiry are Commodore Henry Stewart, Commander James Reynolds, Commander Abraham Arnold, Lieutenant Christopher James, and myself, Commodore Anton Fairchild as Chairman.

Testifying before this Board of Inquiry is Lieutenant James Andrew Hawkins, R.N., who recently returned to the Royal Navy following a period of imprisonment for eighteen months in the Spanish Territory of Florida.

Following, is the complete transcript of the hearing begun on 3 April 1777 at the Admiralty Offices in London, England. Proceedings recorded by Benjamin Hewett, Yeoman First Class, R.N.

Fairchild: Lieutenant Hawkins, before these hearings begin, I wish to inform you that you have not been charged with any specific crime against the King of England, his subjects, the Royal Navy, nor against any officer or enlisted man of your last assignment, the H.M.S. King James. The purpose of today's questioning is to determine the details leading to the attack upon your ship by the Dutch merchantman Silver Cloud. The survivors of the King James have already told this board what they witnessed that day, but they were unable to testify to several issues, including the identity of the captain of the attacking ship, to what port he sailed after the attack, and finally, the verification of your Executive Officer's claim that certain dispatches received shortly before the attack were false.

Because of the highly sensitive nature of the matters to be discussed at these hearings, the Board is pleased that you have agreed not to be represented by a Public Solicitor. You are, however, cautioned that if the Board deems it necessary to stop the hearings in order to prefer formal charges against you, you are advised to seek legal counsel at that time. Do you still wish to continue this hearing without a Solicitor present?

Hawkins: Yes I do, sir.

Fairchild: Very well. Please approach the bench and surrender your sword. According to the previous testimony of several of your fellow officers, and especially the Executive Officer and Lieutenant Junior Grade Montgomery Mason, you were the only member of the inspection party to meet with and speak to the captain of the Silver Cloud. Therefore, keeping in mind the above previous testimony of your shipmates, I will begin the questioning by asking you to describe in your own words, the exact circumstances surrounding the attack on the *H.M.S. King James* on 22 June 1775.

Hawkins: Well, sir, I'm not certain if that's the right place to begin.

Stewart: You did see the King James attacked, didn't you, Lieutenant Hawkins?

Hawkins: Yes I did, sir. I was in the Silver Cloud's main cabin, standing next to the pirate captain. I saw the whole thing.

Stewart: Then why the uncertainty?

Hawkins: Because there's so much more to it than the attack.

Arnold: So much more?

Hawkins: Well, for one thing, sir, the Silver Cloud was not a Dutch merchantman, as the others have told you.

Stewart: Oh? And just what was she?

Hawkins: She was a disguised twenty-gun Colonial frigate.

Stewart: That can't be. (To the board) According to our records, the first Colonial Navy fighting ships, thirteen of them as I remember, were not built until early last year as a result of their Act of 13 December 1775.

Fairchild: Commodore Stewart is correct, Lieutenant Hawkins. There were no Colonial frigates in existence at the time the King James was attacked.

Hawkins: The Silver Cloud was built in '74 in Charles Town, sir, at the Forrestal Shipping Company. Several last minute modifications suited her to her secret mission.

Fairchild: Secret mission? (to James) Why wasn't I informed of this at yesterday's briefing?

James: I had no idea, sir. The report from Lloyds came in late yesterday evening and there's no record in their registry of a ship by that name.

Fairchild: (to Stewart) Then perhaps we should back our sails for a moment and allow Lieutenant Hawkins to tell his story from the beginning.

Stewart: (to Fairchild) If you wish, sir. (to Hawkins) Go ahead, Mister Hawkins. Tell us about the 'much more' you spoke of a moment ago.

Hawkins: Well, for one thing, there was Captain Silver.

James: (to Fairchild) That's the pirate mentioned at last week's hearing.

Fairchild: (to James) Yes, I remember. (to Hawkins) Didn't he have something to do with a treasure several years back; Flint's Fist, I believe it was called?

Hawkins: No, sir. That's the name the Walrus' men called the treasure map. And yes, John Silver was very involved. When I was twelve years old, helping my Mother run the Admiral Benbow Inn on the coast of Scotland, I came into possession of John Flint's map showing the location of several treasures buried on Grand Turk Island. A good friend of my recently departed father, a Doctor Livesy, led a voyage to recover Flint's treasure. The one-legged pirate, Long John Silver, signed on as ship's cook and fooled us into hiring the rest of his pirates as our crew. None of us suspected anything of course, not until I overheard his mutinous plans as we were nearing Spyglass.

Fairchild: Spyglass?

Hawkins: That's what the pirates called Grand Turk Island, sir.

Fairchild: This treasure; tell us more about it, Mister Hawkins.

Hawkins: The seafaring man I got the treasure map from, a Captain Billy Bones, explained it to me. Flint had been burying treasures on Spyglass for several years before he and his crew buried the 700 pounds. Captain Bones sang a seaman's ballad at the inn every day for several months before he died. I wrote the words down. (Lt. Hawkins hands paper to Commodore Fairchild) None of us realized it at the time, but the second verse of this seaman's ballad tells of a greater portion of the original treasure that Flint had never touched.

Fairchild: Yeoman Hewett, enter this in the record. (to the Board) We'll take a ten-minute recess while the Yeoman finishes.

DEAD MAN'S CHEST

Through winds of treachery a bloody tale's told,
Of Captain Rip Rap and Porto Bello Gold.
How he left Flint an' Silver on Spyglass to wait,
While he took Saint Trinidad's pieces of eight.

Buckets of blood were spilled in the hold,
Flint accused Rip Rap, "The treasure ye've stol'd.
Ye took it to the Island called Dead Man's Chest,
Where ye laid it by fer half a scores rest.

Flint killed Rip Rap an' on Spyglass did hide,
Three fourths million where six men died.
Bones took the map an' to Bristol did run,
An' left Flint's bones to bleach in the sun.

A curse on the jewels, the pearls and the gold,
A curse on the pirates what's honor was sold.
A curse on the Yorkm'n what refuses to tell,
Of the treasure laid by - may he rot in hell.

(Chorus)

Fifteen men on the Dead Man's Chest,
Yo Ho Ho and a bottle of rum.
Drink and the devil had done for the rest,
Yo Ho Ho and a bottle of rum.

Fairchild: So you and this Captain Silver retrieved the entire 700 pounds from Spyglass?

Hawkins: All but the silver bars, sir. And as I found out later, there was also a small chest of jewels hid in the same cave.

Fairchild: Captain Bones' ballad tells quite a story, Mister Hawkins. Can you tell us more about the other portion of the treasure?

Hawkins: Well, sir, as I was saying, Flint buried seven or eight hundred thousand in gold and silver on Grand Turk, and Captain Murray buried the rest, with the help of four friends, on Dead Man's Chest.

Arnold: Dead Man's Chest?

Hawkins: It's actually Buck Island, sir. It's a desolate piece of dirt just off the north coast of Saint Croix, near Christiansted.

Fairchild: This Captain Murry. Would he happen to be the Captain Rip Rap of your ballad?

Hawkins: Yes, sir. Next to Long John Silver, Andrew Murray was perhaps the world's greatest manipulator. And as I found out from Captain Silver and his two mates on the Silver Cloud, Murray and his consort, Colonel O'Donnel hoped to use their part of the treasure to help finance Bonnie Prince Charles'

Arnold: How ironic. If the reports we've received concerning the cannons are true, it would mean the treasure would have been used against the Crown after all, but for an entirely different purpose.

Fairchild: This pirate -- Long John Silver -- what happened to him back in '64, after Grand Turk?

Hawkins: He escaped, sir. The maroon we rescued from Spyglass, Ben Gunn, let him go while the rest of us were off the ship. It wasn't until after the King James was attacked in '75 and I was taken prisoner by Captain Silver that I learned the whole story. Silver was always one who enjoyed talking, and he and the other two spent many evenings aboard the treasure ship discussing their adventures.

Arnold: Who were those 'other two'?

Hawkins: An orphan from Tortuga named Henry Morgan and Billy Bones' young successor, Joshua Smoot. John Silver told me that Smoot was John Flint's illegitimate son.

Arnold: Correct me if I'm wrong, Lieutenant, but is this Board to assume that everything you know about the incident with the King James came from these three pirates?

Hawkins: Most of it, sir, yes. The rest comes from several loyalists in the Colonies who are acquainted with…

Fairchild: (interrupts Hawkins and addresses Arnold) We can discuss those two later, Mister Arnold. (to Hawkins) For the sake of a sequential record of the events leading up to the attack, please get back to this Captain Silver and his escape.

Hawkins: Well, sir, like I was saying, after we loaded what we could of Flint's third of the treasure, Captain Smollet became concerned that the three pirates who had escaped into the jungles of Spyglass might attempt another attack, so we left the silver bars and sailed from that place to the nearest port where John Silver could be tried and executed. Except for Benjamin Gunn, who was left on board to guard John Silver, we all went ashore to purchase provisions and hire a new crew to help us sail the Hispaniola back to England. The officers met the Captain of an English man-of-war and went aboard his ship for several hours to report our recent misfortunes on Spyglass. By the time we got back to the Hispaniola, John Silver was gone. I had a strong notion he'd try something like that, because he kept telling me we'd meet again someday. And I believed him, sir.

Fairchild: You believed him, even though you knew him to be a mutinous cutthroat?

Hawkins: Yes, I did. You see, every time Silver confided something special to me, he would drop the language of the bilges and speak the King's English as straight as you and me. But when he was with the other pirates, his language...

Fairchild: Get back to his escape, Lieutenant Hawkins.

Hawkins: Well sir, according to Long John Silver...

CHAPTER 1

"Damn yer hands, Ben!" cried the old pirate as the water cask crashed into the small boat next to his foot. "That one came close to goin' clean through me planks, ya sun-addled maroon!"

Ben Gunn was as strong as a monkey of equal size, but the years alone on Spyglass without the benefit of cheese and flour had reduced his bulk to less than a hundred pounds.

"Belay!" cried John Silver as he pried at the water cask's lashings. "Slack the damn line, Ben, so's I can set the cursed thing free!" Silver's leathery fingers twisted at the large iron hook. But though its rust was coated with grease, Ben's persistent tension on the halyard kept it set firmly in the knotted hemp.

"Are ya daft, man!" called Silver as he gave up on the hook to see why the old man had refused to slack the line. Thirty feet above the water and twirling in the sky like a marionette caught in a gale, hung Ben Gunn, pulled upwards to within three feet of the block. The water cask outweighed the poor maroon by fifty pounds.

"Pray don't be unhookin' me yet, Cap'n Silver," cried the old man as he clung to the halyard for dear life, "not 'till I can lower meself to the rail!"

"I don't want'a be tellin' you yer business, Ben," chided Silver, "but if it were me, I'd throw a couple turns about that rail fer the next load, that's unless ya don't mind bein' hauled up again and pulled clean through that block next time!"

Cautiously, Ben began to slide down the hoisting line toward the rail. With each of the poor Maroon's spins about the untwisting hemp, Silver laughed louder and louder, until tears were streaming down his sunburned cheeks.

"That's near the best show I've seen in years, Ben Gunn!" cried Silver as he wiped his face dry with a sleeve. "But time's a slippin', an' far more precious to me throat than the good this laughter does me innards."

Silver's wooden sea chest was the next to last load, and contained the bags of gold coin he'd liberated from the ship's lazarette during the night.

"And don't be forgettin' me crutch!" scolded Silver as Ben finally hooked the rail with a foot and pulled himself back to the deck. "It's layin' next to the hatch cover where me victual basket be restin'."

"Aye, Cap'n Silver!" called back Ben as he pushed the old pirate's trusty length of mahogany under the barrel hitch. With a grunt and several kicks, the heavy chest was set free in the air above the waiting pirate. Like the water casks before it, the chest began to spin in the humid air like a winged dove; with the crutch hanging crosswise under the hastily tied hemp.

"Easy there!" pleaded Silver as he watched his trusted crutch begin slipping from its lashings. With each turn, the sharpened metal spur thumped the weathered side of the old Hispaneola until a dozen horizontal lines had been scribed at equal intervals from the deck to just above the water line.

With the skill of a jousting knight, Silver finally caught the twirling stick and eased this most precious load over his boat.

"Steady there, mate, an' give me some slack!" Silver called as the chest dropped into the boat like a fat woman into a church pew in August. "Oof!" Silver complained as he pushed the rectangular chest up next to the mast step amidships, snug against the starboard gunwale. As he waited for his victual basket, he studied the shoreline and the dock at Puerta Plata for any sign of the returning crew.

"If Cap'n Smollet lays 'is 'ands on old Long John," he said to himself, "I'll be swingin' from that same yard what me goods been hoisted from, an' before week's end, I'd wager." It was taking the old maroon far too long to make his knots, so Silver set to urging him with a string of threats.

"An' I lay it wouldn't go too good for you neither, Ben Gunn," he warned, "to be discovered with yer prisoner at the water line, and you bein' on watch o'er him, an' all!" With a kick from the old man, the pirate Captain's victual basket swung out over the water and began it's unsure descent. Silver reached up to stop it from crashing into the ship's side, and then eased it down between the water cask and sea chest.

"Master Silver," the simpleton cried as he loosed the old pirate's hawser and threw it into the small craft. "Would ya be tellin' old Ben once more why I be lettin' ya loose?" His memory was good, but shorter than it used to be. As he waited for Silver's answer, his left hand chased a tick across his chest while his right searched for a louse in his scalp. "When the good Cap'n returns, he'll be askin' me where ye be, on account as he were of a mind to hang ya, says he. Cap'n Smollet won't be takin' kindly to you bein' gone, says I."

"Why, you tell 'im the God's truth, Ben, 'cause that's what it be!" John Silver set his oars into their locks one at a time. "Tell 'im it's to preserve their bloody lives! You tell 'im that, Ben Gunn!" Silver shook his head in wonder at how the old man had been able to survive alone on Spyglass for so many years. "Curse me fer a lubber if I wouldn't be slittin' their throats one by one if I be left onboard fer 'alf a fortnight. Why, in no time at all, there'd be only you, me, and the ship's boy, Jimmy Hawkins, to sail this 'ere ship and them silver bars back to Bristol!"

With a shove of his crutch and a wave to his old friend, Long John Silver spat in his palms and adjusted his oars for their first sweep toward freedom. On the deck above him, the once-again abandoned maroon scratched his throat as he tried to get his story straight for Captain Smollet.

"That be the truth, Ben Gunn!" called John Silver as he drifted toward the Hispaniola's bow. "An' knowin' Cap'n Smollet as I do, he'll be relieved to not have one such as me tangled in his riggin'." Silver lifted his hat high in the evening sky and called out one last time to his mate.

"Farewell, Ben Gunn. Our wakes'll cross again some day, you can lay to that."

After several pulls on the long sweeps, Silver feathered the oars as he twisted about for one last look for his captors. There was no movement on the docks. The light breeze that tickled the dark waters of Puerta Plata bay brought a subtle mixture of smells to the pirate's nostrils; mostly the stench of low tide and the rotting pylons, but it also carried the pungent odors of freshly cooked meals and the perfumes of the ladies, a delight John Silver had been without for much too long.

Satisfied that his escape had gone undetected, Silver turned back to resume his pull Northward. As he set his oars for another bight in the smooth waters, something toward shore caught his eye. A single slate grey fin nearly three times the size of a man's hand sliced through the reflection of the town and dark hills behind it. Silver watched with interest as the shark circled in a wide arc toward the stern of his small craft. At ten feet, it slowed its speed and then stopped next to the larboard oar. "Well, well. Could it be you?" the pirate whispered as he remembered his severed leg being thrown to the sharks nearly forty years before. He reached up and tipped his hat to the predator. Then, as if the creature recognized the human as an equal, it nudged his oar with its snout, much the same as a pet dog during the hunt. With the salute properly returned, the great shark gave a single thrust of its mighty tail and turned about to resume its tireless search for food.

Two hours later and five miles beyond the last gun emplacements of the Spanish town, Silver began to look for a place to beach his small craft for the night. "Five days to Tortuga if I get a Nor'easterly," he said to himself as he came about and pulled toward the mouth of a small stream. A twenty-yard stretch of white sand and low-hanging palms would serve him well for the night.

Daybreak found the old pirate pulling his way northwestward just beyond the surf line and half a mile from where he had made landfall the night before. At 1000 hours, a gentle breeze began to blow from his starboard, so he raised the small lateen sail. The canvas bellied and filled with the pressure of the wind. It was a welcome relief for his blistered hands and sore back to let the wind finally do its work.

By noon and six hours at sea, the soreness in his lower back had turned to resentment. The ever-present ghost pains in his missing left foot acted like a rudder to his thought processes, steering his mind back to that first time at sea.

He was no more than a lad; a powder monkey on the Queen Ann's Revenge under the unpredictable and bloodthirsty Captain Drummond. Old Drummond, or Blackbeard as most of his victims called him, chose young John Silver to stay topside that day during a beam engagement with an Indian pirate named Yamar Booheesh; one of the ablest foes the old scoundrel had ever engaged. Drummond claimed it was for luck that he kept at least one of the powder monkeys topside during battle. The two ships had traded even iron for several minutes when a ball crashed through the starboard rail of the quarterdeck. There was an explosion of splinters and screams, sending the nine year old John Silver spinning through the air like a rag doll without it's oats. When he landed next to the lee rail, his left leg was severed at the knee.

"Good luck, me backside!" Silver mumbled as he was smacked on the right temple by his little sail's boom. He gave the rough piece of wood an angry push.

"Wasn't much luck for Ezra Pew neither!" he called out across the water to Blackbeard's ghost. Ezra Pew was a few years senior to Silver and had earned himself a place at the starboard guns. Moments after Silver's leg had been thrown to the sharks, Pew poked his head out through the gun port to swab his cannon, catching a face full of fire when an unspent pocket of powder ignited. "Blinded the poor wretch, it did," whispered Silver. "But blind as he be, I never seen a man steer a ship straighter nor bring a prize to port quicker than he. Just like a merchant with a bonus ridin' on an early arrival."

Silver turned his craft slightly to windward and trimmed his sail as he reached down and massaged the tender nerves at the end of the mutilated limb. As he did so, his stomach gave out an insubordinate groan, reminding him that it was past his feeding time. He tore a palm-sized piece of hard bread from a moldy loaf that lay in the victual basket and dipped its corner in the sea.

"A cook! That's all they'll allow a cripple like me to be!" he complained as a shadow skipped across the water cask and danced lightly up the sail to meet it's author at the mast head; a brown gull intent on a share of the pirate's meal. John Silver liked animals and the bird seemed to know it, for no sooner had Silver begun to hum his favorite sea shanty than the gull glided to a light-footed landing on his lee gunwale well beyond his reach.

"Welcome aboard, me little lady! Does ye wish a ride west to Tortuga with old Long John?" The gull acknowledged his question with a tilt of its head as it surveyed the contents of the boat. "Be ye hungry, me lass?" He pulled a bird-sized scrap from his lunch and laid it atop the sea chest. The bird studied the morsel for half a glass while she mustered her courage. When she was finally satisfied this human wasn't a threat, she hopped over the water cask and onto the victual basket, dispatching the offered bread in one bite.

"Does ya have it in ya to give yer host a thank you?" Silver asked. "Well, what say ye?" The gull tilted her head slightly at the human for a second time and let go a load of lime on the woven lid of the basket. Before Silver could prevent it, the excrement had run through the wicker and onto the contents within.

"Damn yer feathers!" barked Silver with a backhand at the gull, catching her with a direct hit to her tail as she took wing.

"A curse out o' Egypt on ya, ye ungrateful daughter of a tavern hag!" And then yelling after the scavenger with a raised fist, "You'll be back, I'll lay to that! And when ya touch down next time, it'll be me crutch to yer back, just like the turncoat, John Mary!"

Silver sailed on toward his destination for several hours, brooding over the treasure of the Santissima Trinidad as he went. His fingers tightened on the tiller as he yelled at the sky.

"By all what's holy and unholy, I'll have that treasure some day or I be not Long John Silver!" His thoughts began to wander again, Perhaps I'll sail to New York and strike a bargain directly with the Yorkman. After all, he reasoned, it was me who helped he and them other three escape at Savannah. Maybe he'll scribe me a map fer debts sake. The old pirate slapped himself on the cheek. "Damn yer thoughts, John Silver. Ye're startin' ta sound like Ben Gunn!"

The pickpockets of Bristol reasoned that if a man's neck could be stretched for a farthing, it might as well stretch for a whole purse of gold. Driven to piracy by starvation or the law, most would-be pirates likewise figured they might as well take a whole ship as not. And thus, new names were added to 'the account' every day. And for the pirates of French and English extract, the small island of Tortuga suited this new trade well. Not only were its hills abundant with streams, fruit and game, it was situated at the eastern gate of the most heavily traveled waterway between the Spanish Main and Europe; the Windward Passage.

Warehouses to store the pirate's swag and taverns to fulfill the lusts of their hearts sprang up on Tortuga like weeds. But now, in mid-June 1764, as Long John Silver skirted it's northern coast around Devil's Rock and into what was commonly called Buccaneer's Cove, there remained only the memory of this once-busy port.

"Where to land?" thought Silver as he made a quick survey of the cove. The old wooden pier where Blackbeard's crew would dock their boats was now a broken and scattered skeleton, with its bones sticking up as if trying to crawl from a watery grave. John Silver chose a spot at mid-beach and steered for it, unaware of the battle that was about to unfold upon its white sands.

The rotted hulk of an old ship's boat lay at the high water mark, half filled with sand. Fifteen yards further up the beach lay a pile of dry palm fronds from which a large red and green crab stirred and began to creep forward into the hot afternoon sun. It turned its periscope eyes right and left to scan the beach for its enemies; the three dogs which lived in the burned-out storehouses a hundred yards inland. They must be busy elsewhere, it thought as it crept forward a few more inches, then stopping for a moment to test the winds for scent. Much further and it would be committed to the mad dash for the safety of the water and the spiny coral which provided its room and board.

Nothing stirred. No enemy in sight...except for the two motionless emerald-green eyes of the young pirate, Henry Morgan, peering over the gunwale of the small sand-filled vessel; his windswept orange hair dancing from his scalp like the fires of hell themselves.

Patiently, the nine-year old orphan watched as his nemesis—Captain Claw, as he had named the creature—crept onto the deck of his imaginary ship, the Cobra. Inch by inch, the sea-devil scuttled forward in his characteristic sideways fashion, until he stood next to the boy's mainmast, just three feet from Morgan's hiding place. Suddenly, there was an explosion of curses and long orange hair as the cutlass-wielding buccaneer flew through the air to a perfect landing between the crab and the water's edge.

"Aha!" the lad yelled with raised cutlass. "At last we meet face to face, you bilge-sucking scum!" The surprised crab rose on its legs and spun to meet this unexpected foe, both claws held high in defense.

"Ya thought yer broadside killed me, didn't ya?" cried the lad as he smacked the sand to the crab's left side, blocking it's escape route. "And then ya sneaks aboard the Cobra to steal me treasure? Ha! Ha!" The panic-stricken crab made a dash for the boat, but the end of the boy's cutlass -- a sharpened mandrake root -- once again jabbed into its path.

"Not so fast, Claw!" the lad hissed as he bent low over his armored plaything. "This time, by the gods, yer gonna stand an' fight!"

The crab quickly recognized its fate; that flight was no longer an option. With its large claws waving back and forth to meet each cruel thrust of its tormentor's weapon, the crab had joined the inevitable dance of death. Three pristine gulls stood on a section of the old pier watching the scene with detached interest; their wings twitching now and then in anticipation of a fine meal, should the crab lose to the boy.

"Raise that ugly claw to me once more and it'll be yer last, you barnacle-covered son-of-a-scab! I'll split ya starboard from larboard with me cutlass and send ya to torment yer father, the devil!"

Morgan pinned his enemy to the hot sand with a bare foot as he reached down and grabbed the extended right claw in his hand. With a quick twist, Morgan wrenched it from the socket. Then, holding the claw and his mandrake root high, Morgan threw back his head in triumph. "Ha! Ha! Ha! Morgan triumphs again!"

"Ahoy there," called Silver as his stem began to scrape debris near the water's edge. "I say, lad! Ye wouldn't be of a mind to be helpin' an old seafarin' man ashore, would ya? There be a threepence goes 'long ta sweeten' yer labors!" The boy dropped his arms for a moment as he turned to see from where this strange voice had come.

"Make it a full shillin', Govn'r," answered Morgan, "an' I'll be carryin' yer sea chest all the way to the Inn, I will!" With Morgan's foot off it's back, the crab seized the moment to break into its best sideways gallop toward the bay, its balance thrown off slightly by the missing claw.

"A shilling it be, lad!" called back Silver, loosing his main sheet to luff his sail. The boy ran toward Silver's boat, stopping for just a moment as he passed the escaping crab. With a snap of the wrist, the lad gave the hapless plaything a single crack to its shell with the root, bringing the three gulls diving to the sand to pick clean the newly exposed innards.

At water's edge, Morgan grabbed the old pirate's hawser and tied it to a rusty, half-buried anchor.

"Aye," said the lad as he waded out to Silver's oarlock and studied the old man's belongings with a scavenger's eye, "fer a silver shilling I be a right fine servant, Govn'r! Cap'n Smoot says I'll make one o' the best powder monkeys he's got, he does. Tells me I'll have me own cutlass an' brace o' pistols before I be passin' puberty, he does!" Silver gave the boy one of his squint-eyed looks, wondering if the lad really knew Joshua Smoot.

"So - a pirate ye'd be?" asked Silver, amused by the boy's spunk. "Tell me lad. Have ye the kidney fer cuttin' a man open fer 'is purse?"

"Aye," said the boy as his eyes brightened, "an' I'd wear 'is ears 'bout me neck fer a right fine trophy too, I would."

"And how are ye called, lad?"

"Morgan!" the boy cried, with the mandrake root thrust high in the air. "Henry Morgan's the name, Govn'r! An' it be common knowledge 'ere on Tortuga that I be the great-great-grandson of Sir Henry Morgan, the grandest pirate to ever sink a Spanish galleon or sack a city on the Main!"

As with most orphans on the tiny island, young Henry had assumed the surname of his favorite pirate. There were other orphans named for Henry Avery, William Kidd, Calico Jack Rackham and several other legends of the Caribbean.

"Well, son of Henry Morgan," sang out John Silver, "this old seaman be missin' his larboard leg, so he'll be needin' a strong lad's help from his craft." Silver threw his crutch to the dry sand, sending the three ravenous gulls to the air for a brief moment and giving their dinner one last chance to drag its broken carcass to water's edge.

"Were it a cannon ball what took off yer leg, Govn'r?"

"Aye," answered the old pirate as he gave the stump a rub. "When I were a lad yer size on the Queen Ann's Revenge."

"With Blackbeard?" the lad whispered in reverence.

"The same," said Silver as he slid his backside over the rail and hopped into the shallow water next to the boat. "But tell me, Son-of-Morgan, where might a worn-out sea dog be findin' a soft bunk, a bath and some landlubber's cookin'?"

"There be only one place, Govn'r," answered Morgan as he pointed across the beach, "an' that be the Musket's Muzzle yonder." The two-story brick structure stood alone among a growth of coconut palms. Its roof was shingled with Spanish tiles and the ivy was so thick on its walls that only the windows and doors shone through. The buildings to either side had long since been burned out or salvaged for their building materials. "Innkeeper Smeeks hasn't been servin' much rum these recent weeks, what with the Walrus bein' gone to Europe. But there's sure to be another ship pullin' in any day now, says Keeper Smeeks."

"The Walrus, ye say? That wouldn't be John Flint's old ship, would it?"

"Aye Govn'r, it be the very same ship," said Morgan as he was pulled under the old man's armpit for a crutch. Amongst a chorus of grunts and curses from both Silver and the lad, the old pirate gained the dry sand and retrieved his crutch. Relieved to be free of the smelly man, the boy backed away toward the boat and brushed his long hair from his eyes. "Why, do ya know anybody on the Walrus?" asked the boy as he waded back to the oarlock and began wrestling the heavy sea chest toward the rail. With a string of obscenities that would make any seaman proud, he pulled it over the gunwale and onto his back.

"Let's just say I know a lot of seafarin' men," answered Silver as he watched the lad stomp and weave his way up the beach under the chest's crushing weight. As Silver hopped to the porch, young Morgan turned about and let the chest slip to the weathered planks.

"The Musket's Muzzle, Govn'r," puffed the lad as he rubbed his lower back. "Standin' where she did when me namesake learnt his trade. Has a full history, it does."

"An' can a man book passage to Kings Town in this place?" Silver asked as he hopped forward just far enough to survey the tavern's public room for anyone who might recognize him. As he did so, Morgan turned about toward the beach.

"If ya be leavin' fer Jamaica, what ya be doin' with that boat o' yers, Govn'r?"

"Oh," answered Silver, knowing exactly where the lad was headed, "hadn't thought much about it. Maybe I can find someone to purchase her."

"That piece of jetsam?!" Morgan had a fist full of coins saved up, but hardly enough to buy a fine craft like her. "Only a fool 'd pay good money for such a hulk!"

"Aye," agreed Silver with a quiet chuckle, "she's 'bout ready to sink anyhow. Maybe some lad'll steal her durin' the night and save me the trouble o' hagglin' fer her price."

"Aye," agreed Morgan with a quick glance at the old man. "Hagglin' o'r a ship's boat be nothin' but a waste o'f a fine seafarin' man like you, Govn'r." The boy was thrilled with his good fortune. Captain Claw was finally dead, and with Silver's boat, he was no longer a landlubber.

Soon as this old man's gone to his room, thought the lad, the boat goes 'round the point into Morgan's cove, it does! An' then she gets her new name, he thought as he fingered the chisel that hung like a dirk at his belt, cut with me own hand!

As Silver turned about to take another look inside the tavern, Morgan's admiration for his new vessel turned to curiosity over the unusually heavy sea chest. The lock was of a common type; easily picked by the most dim-witted of the island's orphans. With a quick glance to make sure Silver was occupied else where, Morgan raised the lid and reached for one of the two bags of gold coins. Before he could pull away, Silver's stumped leg pushed down on the lid of the chest, capturing Morgan's left arm at the elbow. As the boy pulled loose his clenched fist, Silver's backhand caught him on the left side of his head, spinning him through the air to the hot sand. Before Morgan could regain his footing, the pirate was off the porch and had grabbed the lad by the long hair at the nape of his neck.

"So! Henry Morgan wants a look-see in me chest, does 'e?" whispered Silver in the boy's ear. Then, with a twist of his wrist, the old man spun the little face about, putting the two nose-to-nose.

It's been said that some people are so mean that they can put a curse on you with just a look. According to one story, John Silver's evil stare had gone beyond curses, actually fracturing a fine lady's china teapot from a distance of six spans. This was one of those looks. And on top of it was the old seaman's foul breath and flecks of saliva that showered the boy's face.

"Aye, ye can look, Henry, but it'll be yer last!" The dull edge of Silver's knife blade was now at Morgan's throat.

"Oh Lordy!" Morgan cried, certain his next words would be spent explaining his sins to Saint Peter himself. "No sir, Govn'r! Henry Morgan 'as no business lookin' in no honest seafarin' man's personal belongin's, he don't!" With that, Silver threw the lad backwards to the sand.

"You've a burden to carry inside," said Silver, pointing to the Inn's door, "if I recollect!"

Thankful for this second chance at living, Morgan hefted the sea chest once again and followed the strange one-legged seaman into the Muzzle and over to the inn-keeper.

"A room overlookin' the bay," Silver said as he scribed his name in the desk ledger. Then, turning back to the waiting lad, "By the powers, boy, I trust ye've learned a lesson this 'ere day, 'bout which business that nose of yer's kin be thrust into."

"Aye, Govn'r, an' I be obliged fer it too," he said as he caught the tossed shilling and backed out of the tavern to the safety of the beach.

A week later, the merchantman Belgium Hawk sailed past an anchored second-rate British Man of War and tied up as the western end of the Kings Town dock. The middle-aged John Silver was the first ashore, and made his way to the door of the Whore's Breath; one of many public houses on the waterfront. If a man wanted to make contacts or gain information, a busy tavern was his best choice. Silver drug his sea chest into the public room by its arm-length lanyard and found him a table near the galley. With a good view of the public room's entrance, he ordered a pint of ale.

"Aye, she's Dutch all right," said a seaman at the next table with apparent author-ity. "And I hear she brings several thousand bolts o' cloth from England." The seaman looked about the tavern to the old pirate and called out. "You, there! You came in on her. Where's she bound?" Silver set his tankard down and wiped the ale from his lip.

"She sails for Cartagena within a fortnight, an' the Master were tellin' me just this mornin' he'll be lookin' to replace a dozen of 'is crew 'afore he ships out." This last piece of information put the group into a lively discussion, leaving the old pirate to his own contemplations and the refreshing drink before him.

As John Silver tilted his head back to drain his third tankard, his eyes focused on the silhouette of a tall, almost military looking man, framed by the doorway. Silver lowered his head and studied the bottom of the ale-stained container as the man walked to the center of the pub and looked about.

"Barkeep!" he called. After a moment, a little man in an apron scuttled from the kitchen like Henry Morgan's crab.

"Here, Mister Noble!" the man said with a twist to his towel.

"Have you seen that son of mine?"

"No sir, Mister Noble," the little man answered nervously. "The lad hasn't been hereabouts fer neigh onto two days now. I'd check up at the boat yards if I were you, sir."

"Ah, yes, the yards!" huffed the man as he studied the men sitting about the tavern. It was the same collection of flotsam and jetsam; nobody he recognized. "If you see him talking to any of the men from that Dutchman out there, you get word to me right away, you hear?"

"As you please, sir," answered the little man with another twist to his towel, "Has the lad run away again?"

"No, he hasn't," answered Mister Noble as his gaze stopped on the older man in the corner. "But I can't be too careful with that Man of War anchored off the point. It never fails. When the Lobsterbacks finally leave, no less than a dozen young boys are missing." As Charles Noble turned to leave, John Silver raised his head slightly and addressed the sailors at the next table, as if to continue a previous conversation.

"Aye mateys!" Silver sang out in a nasal twang. "An' speakin' o' the ridiculous, I once heard of a man bein' named after a galley's stove pipe, I did." The sailors looked confused, but the tall man heard and understood the insult perfectly.

"That'll cost you!" Noble barked, as he drove his thin-bladed knife into the table between Silver's thumb and fore finger.

Without looking up or pulling back his hand, Silver gave a cryptic warning, "I hear tell a man can come up with leprosy from stickin' a man with a gift knife, 'specially when the giver's the one what gets stuck."

"John Silver?!" asked Cahrles in amazement. "Is that you?" Silver raised his head slowly and gave his step-brother one of those sideways looks he had become so well known for.

"Greetings, Charley," said the old pirate with a toothy grin. "Glad to see me?"

"Well you old son-of-a-gun!"

"Son-of-a-gun, is it?" Silver barked back like a bull sea lion backed against a cliff. "An' I suppose you were conceived betwixt the satin sheets o' some fancy palace?"

"Well it wasn't on the gun deck of Brittish frigate like you!" Silver pushed himself up and now stood nose-to-nose with Charles.

"At least I knew who me mum were, bless 'er sweet departed soul," crooned Silver, "which be twice what you know o' yer pedigree."

"I may not know who my parents were, but I'd wager a week's receipts they were better stock than yours!" To the other eight customers of the Whore's Breath, these two middle-aged men sounded as if they would draw weapons at any moment.

"And talking of names," added Noble, "it's pure blasphemy to be named for the thirty pieces of silver old man Taylor purchased you for; it being the same price as they paid for our Lord."

"Blasphemy or not, you can fetch me up daft, Charles, if we weren't cut from the same sail cloth," laughed John Silver, "only usin' a different set o' shears. And just because our adopted father, or should I say owner, taught you the King's English an' I've the tongue of some fouled scupper, it don't make me yer lesser." By now, the other patron's hands were on their weapons.

"Your tongue was your own decision, John Silver," spat Charles, "and has nothing to do with your birthright."

"An' only time'll tell, little brother" said John as he sat back down, "what 'appens to yer birthright."

"My birthright?" asked the younger man as he took the seat across from John.

"And just what's that supposed to mean?"

"Nothing, Charley," laughed John as he signalled for two more tankards of ale. "There be too much water through that scupper to be worth our sweat."

"Tell me," asked Charles as he twisted his knife from the table and pushed it into its sheath. "Did you bring back Flint's treasure, as you said you would?"

"Belay!" Silver whispered as he looked about the tavern and pulled his brother close. "No I didn't, but I came this close," he said, sighting between his fingers.

"Really? That close?" asked Charles with a grin. "What happened this time? I thought nothing could get in the way when Long John Silver put his mind to a thing."

"Charles," Silver continued in a whisper, "sit close so's we can trade wind without bein' overheard. And fer God's sake, stop callin' me by my Christian name in public. I'm a wanted man." He paused for a moment to survey the room again. His evil-eyed stare sent every man back to his own conversation. "As fer the treasure, well, it be a long story."

"A long story! You failed, didn't you?"

Silver's jaw tightened until Charles could hear his older brother's teeth grind.

"And I suppose you'll be wanting your old job back."

"No, Charles, I won't. I've decided I'm not cut out to run a warehouse no more."

"That doesn't leave you many choices, then, especially at your age. How do you intend to fill your belly and keep clothes on your back if you won't work?"

"I've a little money," answered the old cutthroat, "and I've discovered I can run a tavern."

"Money? How much?"

"I still got the 800 pounds screw fer this larboard leg, an'..."

"Screw?"

"You know, Charley. Like what Lloyds pays you when one of your ships is lost."

"I see," answered Charles. "And just when did you learn to run a tavern?"

"I did it fer several months in Bristol while I was waitin' for Billy Bones to show hi'self. Found out I'm right good at it, too."

"Hmmm," said Charles as he sat back and stroked his chin.

"What is it, little brother? Do you know of a tavern for sale?"

"I might," answered Charles.

"Oh?"

"There's a recently widowed woman running the Man-O'-War Tavern down at the west end of the docks...close to my warehouses."

"Nathan Bridger died?"

"You knew him?"

"Aye, and the little woman's quite a looker, too." Silver reached across and grabbed the younger man by the forearm. "Think she'd consider sellin' the place?"

"Wouldn't hurt to ask. I hear she's even looking for a new husband."

"Well, then, what are we waiting for?" asked Silver as he pushed himself up onto his crutch and began hopping toward the door. "Let's go have a talk with the widow Bridger!"

Once outside, John gave his younger brother a backhanded thump to the arm. "Tell me. What have you been up to since I been gone? Still workin' for old man Taylor?"

"No, I'm not," Charles answered with a smile of pride.

"Oh?"

"I'm now the owner of Noble Shipping!"

"So the old man finally rolled belly up?"

"Watch it John! He was good to us!"

"Good to you, ya mean."

"He was better to you than you deserved, John Silver, what with all your running off to sea and stealing his things." Charles realized the conversation was leading nowhere but a fight, so selected a diversion. "But enough of that. Tell me more about you being a wanted man. I thought the King's men were always after you."

"Yeah, but not like this. If they catch me this time, I'll swing fer sure. I be needin' a place to hide out."

"Like the Man-O'-War?" Charles asked. Silver nodded. "Then you're going to need a new identity too, if you're to remain in Kings Town."

"Ya plucked the thought right out'a me brain, little brother."

"And I'd start," added Charles, "by doing something about that missing leg of yours."

"Like what?"

"I've a very talented sawyer in my employ who could fashion you a right smart wooden leg; one that articulates."

"Articulates?"

"That means it bends at the knee. Saw one on a British officer several weeks back, and I think I know how the mechanism works."

"I know what the word means, little brother. I just don't understand how or why you'd want'a put a joint in a peg leg. Hell, the thing'd never hold me up."

"Ha!" laughed Charles. "Then you've never seen one. It's a full leg; looks just like real. But if you'd rather, my man'll carve you a real fancy peg leg and cover it in silver."

"Let me think on it while we walk," said the old pirate with a commanding nod toward the Man-O'-War. "But first I wanta see this widow an' her tavern."

A few minutes later found the two standing under the brightly colored sign of the Man-O'-War Tavern. John leaned his weight against the cold stones next to the front door and turned to his brother.

"I'll take the one that articulates," said Silver as he looked through a pane of colored glass into the busy tavern.

"If that's what you wish."

"Aye, that's me wish. Make me look like a full man again, it will. An' help hide me past from anyone lookin' fer the one-legged pirate named Long John Silver."

CHAPTER 2

In late October 1773, a young Scottish sea captain ran through a rain squall toward a white-washed brick building at the western end of King Street. He ducked into a doorway as the cloudburst increased. He was a short man by the day's standards, with a sharp, wedge-shaped nose and high cheekbones. His jaw line was reminiscent of a Viking, with a strong, deeply cleft chin. And even though he was possibly facing a trial and prison term, his expression was eager and resolute. He wiped the rain from his intelligent brow and gave his head a shake as he looked through the rain for his destination. The sign above the door read; SCARBOROUGH JUSTICE OF THE PEACE: MARCUS CUTTER. He ran across the cobblestones and into the foyer with a crash of the great door, bringing the Justice up from his supper with a start.

"May I help you?" asked the tall man as he walked toward the office, pulling his table linen from his collar.

"Yes you may," said the young man as he threw his cape back, pulled his pistol from his sash and drew his sword. "My name is John Paul, and a short time ago I was forced to kill a man aboard my ship; the merchantman Betsy." The Justice retreated to where his wife stood with a hand to her mouth.

"I've no argument with you, good sir!" said the Justice as he stared at the two weapons. "I know no man aboard the Betsy, and I hold no personal malice against you!"

"But you are Marcus Cutter, the Justice in Scarborough?"

"I am sir, but please..."

"Then I've found the right man after all," the young sea captain said as the Justice reached out for his wife's arm. "There was a mutiny aboard my ship this afternoon, and I was forced to kill the ringleader of the group; a half-breed named Jack Fry. I've come to report the incident and surrender myself."

The tall man's color began to return as he wiped the sweat from his throat and walked forward to his desk, giving his wife a reassuring pat on the hand. "There'll be no need for your arrest, sir, leastwise not until I've investigated the matter."

"And in the meantime?"

"You may return to your ship, with the provision that you'll not leave Scarborough until this matter has been dealt with. There will have to be a hearing."

"Thank you, sir," said Captain Paul as he turned to leave. "When you need me, I'll be aboard my ship, or at my partner's warehouse at Raney's dock."

"Would you be the partner of Archibald Stewart?"

"Yes, I would. Do you know of me?"

"It's a small island, Captain Paul. I know something about every white man on Tobago, and most of the slaves and natives as well."

"Then I'll wait for your call," said the young Scotsman as he backed away from the desk. "I'll either be at the warehouse or aboard the Betsy."

"You may take your weapons, sir. If I can trust you to remain in Scarborough, I'm sure I can trust you to keep your sword and pistol."

The rain had stopped by the time John stepped from the office and onto the wet pavement. He slid the long blade of his sword into its scabbard and set off at a brisk pace toward the bay.

"John Paul!" called a man in a white waistcoat from a nearby porch. "Hold up a minute!" The man kissed a young woman with whom he had been speaking, and then trotted nimbly across the wet cobblestones.

"When did you get back into port, John, and what's your hurry?" It was John's good friend, William Young, the Lieutenant Governor of Tobago. He was the first man to befriend the Scotsman in the West Indian Colonies. John slowed his pace until the other man could catch up and match strides with him.

"Three days ago," answered John as he straightened his sword belt. "The hurry is because I must return to the Betsy as quickly as possible." John stopped and gave William a long look. I must confess, it's good to see a friendly face for a change."

"A friendly face? You talk as if something were amiss." The Lieutenant Governor was a tall man of thirty-five, with premature gray above his ears. And like most of John's friends, William towered over the Scotsman. He motioned toward the bay. "There's some sort of trouble I have to look into down at the docks. We can talk on the way."

"I'm in serious trouble, myself," said John as he attempted to match strides with the taller man.

"Does it have anything to do with that sword?" asked William.

"Yes, it does."

"I figured as much, the way you're never without it. Do you want to talk about it?"

John stopped in the street and faced his friend. If he could tell anybody, it was William.

"There was a mutiny aboard my ship this afternoon, and I had to kill the ship's cook."

"Then it's your ship I was summoned to!"

"You already heard?"

"You said it was the ship's cook?" said William with concern. John nodded. "That wouldn't be the half-breed, Jack Fry, by any unfortunate chance?"

"You know the man?"

"Everybody in Scarborough knows that troublemaker. He's been like a bad case of the gout since he was a pup. I'm surprised he wasn't killed before this."

"Then Magistrate Cutter should find my actions fully justified?"

"Not necessarily," William said with concern. "Fry may have been a chronic problem for the Crown, but among the natives, he's some sort of local hero." William fell silent as they walked. "Why'd you kill him?"

"My first officer signed the bloody troublemaker on for the sail back to Cork not three hours after we docked. First thing he did was to whip the rest of the crew into a flap about their pay."

"Should I assume he attacked you?"

"Of course he did! You don't think I'd kill a man in cold blood, do you?"

"What did Cutter say?"

"He released me to my own keeping, but said I was not to leave port."

"Hmmm," said William as he thought. "He's not thinking of trying you here in Tobago, is he?"

"I assume so," answered John, "if it goes that far. He told me there'd be a hearing." John gave his friend a long look. "Why? What's the matter with that?"

"John, what I'm about to tell you is as your friend and not as an official of Tobago." William took a long breath as he looked up the street toward the Magistrate's house. "You'll have to flee Scarborough. If Fry's relatives don't kill you before the hearing, there's a great probability that you'll be convicted and hanged by a jury made up of his friends. Good Lord, man, why did it have to be Fry?"

"I didn't choose the rotter," cried John. "He chose me!" John strode away several paces and spun about on a heel. "If I'm to flee Scarborough, as you so lightly suggest, just where the hell do I go?"

"Anywhere off the island. Jamaica perhaps. There's revolution in the air, John, and that's drawn nearly every naval officer to the northern blockades. This is rightly an Admiralty case, but I wouldn't put it past Cutter to convene a court of civilians."

"Off the island? That's a wonderful piece of advice!" John searched the branches above him as if an answer to his predicament hid somewhere in the Spanish moss. "I don't have any money with me, William, and what's more, I'm on foot. If what you say is true, I can't even risk returning to the Betsy." John looked at his tall friend for several moments. "So, what am I to do?"

"Well, before we do anything else, let's get you off this public road."

A moment later, William had ushered his young friend back up the street, into his house and through the hallway toward the kitchen. His wife Margaret was helping the maid clear the supper dishes from the table. The two young women gave a start as William stepped into the room.

"William!" she cried, a teacup and saucer crashing to the floor. "What are you doing back so soon?"

"I ran into an old friend."

"But I thought you were needed at the docks...something about a killing."

"Something more important has come up." William pulled John from the hallway. "Margaret, this is...Michael Stevens, a friend to whom I owe a great debt."

"Pleased to make your acquaintance, Mister Stevens," Margaret said as she gave William a questioning look and wiped her hands dry. "Would you like some tea, Mister Stevens?"

"Dear," said William, "I need to speak with Mister Stevens alone. Do you mind?"

"Of course not," she agreed, as she set a pot of water on the stove and woofed up the fire. "This stove will need more wood anyway," she added with an embarrassed smile. "I'll just be a moment." Margaret gave the maid a gentle push toward the back door.

"You have a lovely wife," said John in admiration as the two young women stepped out the door and walked to the woodpile. "I hope I can find a woman that nice someday."

"Thank you, but let's keep our voices down. I don't want her to know what's going on here."

"Is that why you lied about my name?"

"I don't believe she would tell intentionally," answered William as he pulled a duffle bag from a closet, "but the less she knows about you, the less she can tell her father, should the subject come up."

"Her father?"

"Her maiden name is Cutter."

"The Magistrate's daughter?" William nodded.

"John," began the older man after a long moment, "you must take my horse and ride to the west side of the island. There should be a British postal packet arriving in a day or two at Courland Bay. It will take you as far as Jamaica. As I said, that's your only chance of living through this affair. There should be enough naval officers there to convene a proper hearing." John sat at the table in a daze as William left the kitchen. After several minutes, he returned with the gray duffle bag filled.

"Everything you'll need—several changes of under garments, toiletries—is in this bag," William said as he set the bag on the table and opened a small metal box. "I'm loaning you L50. When you arrive at Plymouth, leave my mare with the innkeeper at the Milk n' Honey tavern. He'll get her back to me." William hesitated. "Do you have a weapon?"

"I have my sword and..." John searched his belt for the pistol. It was gone. "I left my pistol at the Magistrate's house!"

"I know you're handy with that blade, John, but I'm afraid it won't be enough," said William as he turned and left the kitchen once more. A moment later, he was back with a polished cherry wood box. "You can have this fowling pistol."

"But..."

"Don't worry," William said as he placed the fifty pounds inside the box and pushed it into the bag. "I've three others just like it. Seems every time I'm re-elected, somebody gives me another one."

"My partners have all my money. When this gets straightened out, I'll pay you back, double."

"Don't bother yourself, John. Consider all this as an opportunity to stretch my soul a bit." As William escorted John to the stables, Margaret and the maid passed them with their basket of firewood. Margaret looked at the duffle bag suspiciously.

"Is something the mater, William?" she asked.

"No, dear. I'm loaning Mister Stevens one of the horses. He needs to ride to Plymouth."

She gave William a long look and then walked into the house with the maid at her heels. Once inside, she stood at the window watching as William saddled a horse and then sent John on his way. "Emily, I'm going to my parents home for a few minutes."

John couldn't believe what had occurred. In a little over two hours from the time his sword had pierced Jack Fry's heart, he was on horseback; fleeing for his very life. He arrived in the small seaport of Plymouth just before dawn on the 25th of October 1773. Because of the early hour, John left William's mare in the Milk n' Honey stable with a note attached to the saddle. The twenty-five ton topsail schooner, Falmouth Packet had just finished taking on its cargo when John reached the dock.

"Ahoy there! Captain of the Falmouth Packet!" called John, as he stepped to the dock's edge. "Ahoy! Have you room for a passenger?"

"Not for a paying passenger, we don't!" came a gruff voice from within the bowels of the small craft. "But if you're willing to work," continued the booming voice as the Master climbed from the companionway and looked to the dock, "you can go with us as far as you'd like."

"Aye!" said John excitedly.

"But so you know where that is before you commit yourself, young man, we'll be stopping at George Town on Barbados, Saint Vincent, Saint John and then on to Kings Town."

"Kings Town will be just fine!" answered John, happy to hear that William was correct. "May I come aboard?" With a wave of the master's hand, John picked up his newly acquired duffle bag and stepped across the gangway.

The Falmouth Packet was a typical inter-island schooner of the sharp design with a single mast and square topsail aloft. A cutlass-like bowsprit nearly as long as her hull enabled the agile craft to carry an enormous jib and fore staysail, giving her an edge over the brigantine and most of the larger schooners favored by the pirates. A single swivel gun, which could be moved to several stations along her rail, was all the protection she carried. With the signing of his clearance papers, the master ordered the sails unfurled and the lines singled up. In moments, the spry craft was loose from the dock and into Courland Bay.

"My name is James Jones," the master said as he pushed the tiller to windward to steer the small vessel to open water. "And how shall we hail you, young man?"

"My name's John Paul, and I'm a Captain out of Cork, England. My ship, the..." John stammered for a moment as he realized he'd already said too much. "My ship is laying up for repairs at Scarborough for a few weeks," he lied, "so I fancied a leave to the other islands." It would do no good to tell the truth, especially to a British master carrying the King's mail. "Do you have an estimate to Jamaica?"

"If all goes well," answered the master, "we should tie up at the place early in the second week of November." With the packet's speed, John figured he would reach Kings Town far ahead of any warrant for his arrest. And then, with any luck, he could obtain passage to the Colonies in America within a week of arrival. An Admiralty court far removed from the incident was always the best choice.

"Why no cannons, sir? Aren't you afraid of pirates?"

"Oh, I'm afraid of them, Mister Paul, but as long as we have winds, we can outrun nearly anything afloat, that is, anything up to twice our waterline. But you're correct to be concerned. These are lean times for the few pirates still working these waters. They might think we're carrying more than mail." He called out for the men to trim the topsail. "There's one other group I'm very wary of, however, even though they seldom come this far south."

"And who would that be?"

"American privateers. There are hundreds of them prowling the trading routes of the Atlantic and down as far as Cuba and Hispaniola, looking for anything with a British flag on it. There's a chance that we could run up against one as we near Jamaica. If it comes to that, John, I could use your help on that swivel gun."

"I'll consider it my special assignment."

"Grady!" barked the Master at one of the hands. "Report aft!" The Master turned back to his new crewmember. "Seaman Grady will show you where you can stow your gear. We're short on bunks, but we've some extra blankets you can use for a mattress." As John followed the seaman forward, he glanced back toward shore. Two soldiers on horseback now stood on the dock. One of them was pointing at the small ship while the other was waving his arms above his head. As John wondered after the two, there was a of smoke from the hand of the one pointing. John grabbed James and pulled him down to the deck just as a ball whistled overhead and punched a clean hole through the mainsail just beyond their heads, followed by the pistols report from shore.

"What the...!?" demanded James as he stood and looked aft.

"They're shooting at us!" answered John as he joined James. The two soldiers were still waving their arms for the ship to return to the dock.

"They've done that before…fired a weapon to hail me back to the dock. But this is the first time they've tried to hit me!"

"They were shooting at you?" asked John, with a note of confusion in his voice. James gave him a questioning look.

"How Did you know they would shot at us?" James demanded. "That ball was meant for you, wasn't it?" John didn't answer. "Level with me, Captain Paul, or I'll turn about and deliver you into their hands." John gritted his teeth as he looked aft at the two soldiers.

"My ship is the merchantman Betsy. I was forced to kill a mutineer yesterday in Scarsborough. I have to get to King's Town where I can be heard before a proper Admiralty Court of Inquiry."

"This man you killed," asked James, "might he be someone I might know?"

"He was my new cook…a half-breed…some sort of local hero," answered John. "Not Jack Fry!?"

"You knew him also?"

"Everybody in the Antillies knows Jack Fry!" James gave the two soldiers another look and turned back to John. "Good Lord, man! You'd have done better shooting Magistrate Cutter!"

"What now?" asked John.

"If they fire again, you have my permission to use the swivel gun."

John smiled at the older man.

"You know, of course," added James, "that you are now in my debt."

"And glad to be there, sir."

It took the small craft two days to reach Bridge Town. After the routine of off-loading cargo, taking on the outgoing mail and some new supplies, the Falmouth Packet was at sea again, westward bound toward St. Vincent; a five day journey.

Just before 1000 hours of the third day out from Bridge Town, seaman Kirkland approached the Scotsman as he trimmed the mainsail.

"Mister Paul?" the young seaman began. "Excuse me, sir, but Master Jones hasn't come from his cabin yet. I'm worried."

"Is his fever worse?"

"Don't know," answered the seaman. "He didn't show for his mid watch last night an' he never touched his supper, neither. The other men an' me be obliged if you'd be lookin' in on 'im for us."

"Of course I will. Fetch me a pitcher of fresh water and some towels." The young Scotsman made his way aft and down the short ladder to the cabin door. He listened for a moment but could hear nothing.

"James?" he called, but there was no answer. He tapped three times. "James, are you awake?" There was no answer, but only the quiet hiss of the sea as it slipped along the weathered hull and the creaking of hemp against the spars aloft.

"Is he about, sir?" asked Kirkland, holding the water and towels the Scotsman had requested.

Without answering the young seaman, John Paul pushed open the narrow cabin door. The distinct odor of malaria filled his nostrils, causing him to recoil a step.

"Kirkland, is there any quinine in the medical chest?"

"I believe so, sir, but flog me if I could tell ya which bottle it's in. Master Jones be the only man aboard what's able to read."

"Bring the chest, and quickly." As the seaman rushed to do the Scotsman's bidding, John entered the dark cabin with the pitcher and towels. Lighted only by the hatchway behind him, John could barely make out the tormented figure of the master. He lay twisted in his sweat-soaked blankets; the stench of his illness almost more than John could bear.

"James?" John called quietly. The Master jerked awake with a cry. "I'm bringing some medications for your fever. Do you think you can sit up in your chair while I change your blankets and swab you clean?"

"John? Is...is that you?" James asked weakly as he looked about the cabin, confused. "Are we still at sea?" His breath was strong with the smell of his sickness, and the voice which ventured from his parched throat was no more than a harsh whisper.

"Don't talk," John said as he poured a large glass of cool water and squeezed two limes into it. From his waistcoat pocket, he pulled half a dozen red cherries he had picked on Barbados and laid them on the small table. He helped his shivering friend to the chair and offered the drink.

"Drink this, James. And when you're able, I want you to eat all of these berries. They prevent scurvy, and I suspect they'll help with your fever also."

"Thank you, John," the master said as he sipped the limewater. "That taste's good." As he nursed the cool liquid, John stripped the bunk and threw the foul bedding to the waiting seaman. Turning back to James, he began to swab his friend's wet skin.

"My sister lives on Saint Vincent with her husband," whispered James between sips. "We have to make port there anyway, so I'll stay with them until I get well."

"But what about the ship and the crew?" asked John, worried that a warrant might be close in their wake. "You could be laid up for five or six weeks."

"I know," he said as he turned to face the Scotsman. "There's mail aboard which must reach Kings Town as quickly as possible, and the next postal packet won't be by for two weeks." He reached out and took John's arm. "I know it's a lot to ask of you, but would you be willing to take the Falmouth to Kings Town?"

"The Postal Service would allow that?"

"The mail is their only concern, not who delivers it."

It was perfect; exactly what John needed. A ship of his own that would take him to the Colonies. He feigned uncertainty. "But how..?" he began, knowing James would give him not only permission to take the Falmouth to Jamaica, but the encouragement also.

"It would be simple, John. All you'd have to do is sign as I do; J. Jones on the entrance and clearance papers at the stops between St. Vincent and Kings Town. Once there, you could leave my ship with the port authority until I'm well enough to come for her."

"I'll consider it," answered John.

It was the late fall of 1773, nine and a half years since Long John Silver had returned a fugitive to his birthplace, Jamaica. Within three months of that return, John had proposed and married Betty Bridger, the owner of the Man O' War Tavern. Taking the name of Jack Bridger, John Silver changed the name of the tavern to Silver Jack's. As promised, his brother Charles had commissioned one of his carpenters to fashion an articulated leg for the old pirate, giving him the look of a full man.

John Silver stood looking south toward the open sea as the Falmouth Packet rounded Port Royal for her starboard reach to Kings Town.

"Captain Paul!" called Sanders, the first mate, as he secured a sheet to a pinrail to windward. "What town was that, and why's it in such a state?"

"This must be your first time to Jamaica," said John.

"It is, sir," affirmed the seaman as he shaded his eyes.

"That's Port Royal," the young Scotsman answered as he studied the sun-bleached remains of the wasted town for several moments. A dozen hermits in tattered rags scuttled about the shadows of the littered streets and broken buildings with their pull carts, picking up anything that might bring the price of a loaf of bread and a tankard of ale.

"Is that where Sir Henry Morgan ruled when he was still a pirate?" asked the sailor. Captain Jones nodded. "Was it a long battle?"

"Wasn't a battle at all."

"Then what happened to the place?"

"Some may disagree with me, Sanders, but I believe it was the Lord's Judgment for her sins, while others say it was just an ordinary earthquake that brought her down." John gave the young seaman a quick look.

"The Lord did that?" said the seaman with a long whistle of respect. "How long ago?"

"I believe it was the early summer of '92. They say it shook so hard, the sea swallowed up Fort James and landward as far back as two streets. By best count, two thousand souls perished that day, besides the town."

"Why would anybody build a town on a sand spit in the first place?" asked Sanders.

"Pirates don't always think of such things. They must have figured it served their needs better than a town further up the bay, like where they finally built Kings Town. Needed a port where they could unload their swag quickly and make a run for open water if a man-o'-war showed on the horizon."

"They should have read the Good Book, sir," said the young seaman slowly, "before they built their town on sand."

"Aye!" agreed Captain Paul. "That they should."

After a long moment, Sanders changed the subject.

"What do you expect will happen to the Falmouth until Captain Jones comes for her?"

"She'll be docked at the mail house, unless a new master is assigned," John answered. "I may get a new crew and return her to Captain Jones myself," he lied.

"Then you don't mind if we sign onto another ship?"

"Don't worry about me," answered John. "I know Kings Town well."

"Where will you go next?"

"Haven't decided yet," answered John as he ran his hand along the rail. "I have some business with the..."

"I hear tell the Americans are putting together a navy."

"Hmmm," thought John as he considered Sander's suggestion. Although John Paul had called at Kings Town several times in the past, this was the first time he had tied up so far toward the west end of the waterfront. He was tired and hungry and wanted to get away from the ship. After turning over the mail and packages to the postal authorities and paying the crew their wages, John closed up the Falmouth Packet and walked along the dock toward the setting sun. The Kings Town dock was strewn with small shops selling fish and chandlery, and interspersed among these were the taverns where a seaman could quench his thirst and satisfy his animal needs. Their names reflected the exploits and demise of heroes and pirates, such as Morgan's Revenge, Blackbeard's Liver and Captain Jacob's Gallows. There were also the usual names...the ones so common along the harbors of England and the new world; The Bucket of Blood, The Ivory Bosom and The King's Ransom.

John looked west along the dock to where an old man in an apron and carrying a garbage bucket was holding open the door to Silver Jack's Tavern, the last tavern and only one made in the shape of a ship. The old man hesitated for a moment and looked at John, and then disappeared into the tavern.

"Silver Jack's," John mused as he checked the rigging of the miniature bowsprit that adorned the cleverly decorated sign. As accurate as a real bowsprit, he mused. A moment later, John stepped into the public room; a perfect replica of the gun deck of a frigate. The room was empty of patrons, except for one young man sitting near the galley. Assorted charts and a Nautical Almanac lay on the table in front of him.

"Good afternoon, sir," said the Scotsman as he approached. The lad looked up from his studies. "Do you mind if I join you?" The young man stood and extended a hand and a broad smile.

"My name is David Noble. That was quite a landing you made."

"Pardon?"

"We watched as you docked your postal packet. You've done that many times."

"I'm John Paul...Jones," said John as he took David's hand of greeting.

"Pleased to meet you, John Paul...Jones," mimicked David. John didn't like this young pup making fun of him, but pretended he hadn't noticed the barb. David released John's hand and swept his hands over the table.

"As you can see, I'm in the midst of my studies, and I could certainly benefit from the advice and instruction of an experienced Sea Captain." David was just seventeen years old, but tall and muscular. His hair was coal black and cut neatly about the ears. He had intelligent features, with a fine Roman nose and an almost lyrical tone when he spoke.

John looked about the table. There was a Seaman's Almanac, a book on basic navigation and assorted pencils and charts. "Navigation can be a difficult subject without the proper instruction."

"Exactly!" agreed David. "I'll pay for as much ale as you want if you'll give me some help with this."

As John pulled back the chair to sit down, Long John Silver approached their table with two fresh tankards of cool ale. The old cutthroat hadn't reached his height of six feet two inches until after he had returned from England in '25. It was then that the title 'Long' was added to his name.

"Welcome to Silver Jack's!" the retired pirate sang out as he set the tankards between the two young men. "I be Jack Bridger, the 'umble proprietor of this 'ere tavern." He looked out the window at John's ship. "That be a winsome little lass ye be master of, good sir. "Will ya be takin' 'er north or back to the Antilies?"

"I haven't decided," lied John.

"Well, until ya makes that decision, might ya be gracin' me humble inn with at least one night o' yer presence?" John Silver had taken to this landlubber's life and it rode well on his planking. His gaunt and leathery lines from years in the 'Brotherhood of The Coast', as the pirates called their evil organization, had changed remarkably with the addition of thirty pounds to his frame. In the nine years he had owned the tavern, his full head of dark brown hair had turned snowy white and he had acquired a grandfather's mannerisms: including a cherub-like twinkle to his eye. "An' what might be yer name, young sir?"

"I'm John Paul Jones," answered the Scot as he stood to shake Silver's large hand. "And regarding my staying here; if your price is right, I'll take one of your rooms for two or three nights."

"I'm a shillin' below the rest, Cap'n Jones," said Silver with a wink. "An' if ya don't believe old Jack Bridger, just you ask about."

"I'll take your word on it," said John. "And I'd like a bath later, if you can oblige."

"Aye," said the old man as he walked toward the galley. He stopped and turned back. "An' at no extra cost, neither."

"David," asked John as he watched the old man disappear into the galley, "what's that clicking sound when the old man walks?"

"It's my uncle's wooden leg. My father's sawyer made it for him almost a decade ago. As I understand the thing, it uses a catch and a length of sword blade as a spring. It's the catch you're hearing."

"Your uncle?"

"Aye," answered David. "He and my father were both orphans and kept their surnames when they were purchased as children."

"Interesting," said John as he downed his ale and set his tankard on a corner of David's chart. "So, back to your studies. What kind of assistance were you looking for?"

"Well," David began with a scratch to his chin, "except for deep water navigation, I'm nearly ready to take a position on one of my father's ships." David brightened. "You may have heard of my father! Charles Noble, of Noble Shipping?" His British accent had a touch of the French, which gave David that familiar Jamaican accent.

"I've heard the name, but I've never met your father." John turned one of the charts about so he could see David's calculations. As he studied the young man's notes, John Silver came back with two more drinks.

"Here be some fresh spirits, good sirs!" said Silver as he slid the two tankards onto the table. "An' just call out when them two be empty!" As he turned to leave, Silver gave David a stern look and a tilt of the head toward the Scotsman. David gave his uncle a perturbed stare and slight nod.

"I've crewed aboard many of my father's ships between the islands," said David, as his uncle walked away to the kitchen, "and I've even been up to the American Colonies on two occasions." David pushed the Almanac across the table to John. "My question, sir, is, how do you know where you are east and west in the open sea, without reference to land?"

"Well," began John as he took a sip of his fresh ale, "I won't try to convince you that it's a simple matter, because it's not." John paused as he remembered something. "But before I go any further, I should get something from my ship."

John rose and left the tavern. As soon as he was out of the door, John Silver hurried to David's table.

"Find out anything yet, Davey?"

"Find out anything?" asked David.

"Damn yer memory!" yelled the old pirate with a worried look toward the docks. "What the hell 'ave I been lookin' fer these past nine years!?"

"Oh, that!"

"Yes, that!" Silver glared at the lad. "Well? Who is he and what's he doin' in Kings Town?"

"I don't know yet," answered David, "but I'll find out what I can when he returns."

"You do that," hissed the old man with a quick glance toward the tavern doors, "and quickly!"

John returned ten minutes later and set a polished cherry wood case in front of David.

"Have you ever used one of these?" He unlatched the hook and opened case, revealing a Hadley's quadrant. John lifted the finely crafted instrument from its green felt indentations.

"Yes, sir," answered the lad as he studied the polished brass scales and hinged mirrors. "My father has a special one that he keeps it in a glass case above the mantle. Claims it belonged to Sir Henry Morgan when he was a pirate. He's promised to give it to me some day."

"By knowing the day of the year and the actual angle of the sun above the horizon at noon, you have your latitude north or south of the equator," said John.

"Like I told you, John, I've done it often." John gave David a sideways look and continued.

"Longitude is a little more difficult, and this is where I use an old seaman's trick." John unrolled a large map of the Atlantic and held its corners in place with their empty tankards.

"Longitude would be much easier to find if we had better time pieces. All we would need to know is the time at Greenwich, England and compare it to the time on board when the sun's at it's highest angle."

David looked up from the map. "Well, since we don't have good time pieces, what's the trick? How do you make a proper landfall?"

"The trick is to first depart on the general course toward your destination; say the Bristol Channel. Then, when your quadrant says you've reached 51 degrees north, you alter your course to due east. Continue on that latitude until you raise land and then follow the coastline until you reach the port you want."

"Well, that's no trick!" cried the lad with a slap to the table. "Everyone I ask keeps telling me some rot about the sea birds and the water temperature. They were guessing too!"

John smiled. "Aye, navigation's a lot of guesswork." At this, John Silver returned to their table.

"Excuse the intrusion, Captain Jones, but might I be interestin' you in a plate o' me little wife's lamb an' cabbage? She's a Scot like yerself, an' still cooks like the old people."

"Lamb and cabbage! I'd love some!"

"An' I've a score bottles of Madeira wine on me shelf what would wash yer throat clean as a maiden's soul, it would."

"I'm sure your wine's the finest in the colonies, Mister Bridger, but there's another I'd fancy if you have it, good sir."

"Aye!" sang the old pirate with a twinkle in his eye and a finger to his nose. "I knew ye were a man of distinction, I did! What be yer poison?"

"Single blend Scotch Whiskey," whispered John as if he were saying the secret name of God Himself. "You wouldn't have any about, would you?"

"If I do, good sir, ye could have the whole bottle. But the only whisker I be havin' is diluted three times now, once by the merchant what sold it to me and twice by me. But I'll look about me larder."

"Then it'll be two plates of lamb and cabbage," John sang out as he picked up his tankard. "And unless you find that Whiskey, I'll stick with the ale." John reached across and put a hand on David's forearm. "Since you're buying the ale, I'll buy the supper, David. Just payment for the good fellowship you've given me so far this evening."

Dinner was a treat. The lamb was freshly killed, lightly seasoned with garlic and laid up beside a quarter slab of steamed cabbage. After dinner, John and David shared their backgrounds and experiences until nearly 2200 hours. John hadn't intended to tell anybody about his recent troubles in Tobago, but regret it as he might, he, and the spirits that shared his brain, couldn't take the words back. The late hour finally took its toll on John, so he excused himself to his room and the feathered bed that beckoned.

Captain Jones shadow had no more disappeared up the stairway when John Silver seated himself across the board from his nephew.

"So tell me, Davey," began the retired pirate as he gripped the lad's right forearm, "what did you learn? Might our little Scottish Captain be the one?" John Silver's heavy accent and salty vernacular had mysteriously vanished.

"His real name is John Paul," answered David with a wince. "Jones is an assumed name to prevent the authorities from catching him. He's a fugitive from Tobago where he killed the ringleader of a mutiny. As soon as he can get supplies and a crew together, he sails for Fredericksburg, Virginia where his older brother lives. I don't know how serious he is, but he mentioned that he wants to get an officer's commission with the Continental Navy and fight the British."

Silver's grip remained firm as he let his eyes drop slowly to the chart of the Atlantic Ocean. With his right index finger, he traced several invisible lines across the chart.

"Go to your father and tell him I must meet with him at his home in half a glass. That'll give me time to close the tavern and do a little more thinking." Silver released David's arm and pulled a large gold watch from his pocket. The protective lid sprung open with a loud click. Silver snapped the lid shut and looked up at the lad. "Go now, boy, and do as I say!"

The ship's clock over the fireplace struck seven bells as Long John neared the courtyard door of the Noble estate. Charles Noble stood at the mantle stuffing a clay pipe with white burley tobacco. He stood an inch taller than David and had the same Roman features as his son, except that his hair had begun to gray at the temples.

"So," asked Charles as he lit the pipe from a sliver of kindling, "what is it about this Scotsman that has your uncle so excited?"

"He thinks this might be the one," answered David as he rubbed his right forearm.

"Hmmm," said Charles as a familiar sound in the courtyard drew his attention. It was the courtyard door opening and closing on its rusty hinges, followed by the familiar double click of John Silver's mechanical leg echoing down the hallway. "The man is obsessed."

"Fetch aft the brandy, Charles Noble," called the old cutthroat, "an' a towel what ta wipe off me transom." The old pirate stopped in the library doorway as he made a quick survey of the familiar room. The thick layer of dust on the poetry books and a single yellowed doily gave mute testimony that a woman's hand hadn't touched the place in more than a decade. A knife the old pirate had stuck in the desktop several weeks before stood undisturbed. Silver walked across the room and removed the dirk as his brother poured him a glass of the thick liquor.

"Fell on your butt, I see," chuckled Charles as he threw the older man a tea towel. "How long have I been telling you that mechanism needed work?"

"There's nothin' wrong with the mechanism," Silver barked as he took a step to demonstrate. As he swung the leg forward for the next step, he gave it a stronger than usual kick, just to make sure it would lock this time. "See?"

"Well, then," demanded Charles impatiently, "if that's none of my business, get to what is! Why this important meeting?" Silver threw the towel back to his brother while he downed the brandy and pulled a whet stone from his pocket.

"If ye'll shiver yer timbers fer a span, I will." Silver spat on the stone and began stroking the blade. "Nine years ago, when Flint's treasure slipped through these fingers, I swore I'd have the other part of it some day; the part Murray's nephew buried on Dead Man's Chest." Silver hesitated to sight down the blade, looking for irregularities along its edge. "I've kept tellin' myself that there be a man out there somewhere who'll bring it to me if I be patient." He leaned forward and gave the two a hard stare as his cockney twang was replaced with the finest King's English either had ever heard the old man speak.

"Gentlemen, unless I'm a poor judge of character, David's new friend--this fugitive captain named John Paul Jones--is that man."

"So that is it!" said Charles with disgust. "David told me he thought you had another one."

"Another one?" spat the old pirate. "What's that supposed to mean?"

"Well," answered Charles with a note of sarcasm, "by my count, he'll be the tenth—or does he make the eleventh?"

"It's different this time!"

"That's what you said about the last three. Just what makes...?"

"I've changed the plan, and this man's better suited to the task than any of the rest." Silver slowed his speech for emphasis. "And this time, Charles, I'll have it."

"But even if you could finally get it, you don't need it," argued Charles, "nor do you need all the grief it'll bring you."

"And why, pray tell, don't I need it?"

"Because you have a fine wife, a prosperous tavern, and all the money a man of your age needs!"

Silver considered his brother's words for a moment as he set his empty glass on an end table and sat down in his favorite chair.

"You're correct, Charles. I do have everything a man my age needs." He hesitated while he searched his soul for the words. "But that treasure's...maybe it's to fulfill a dream or remove a curse, I don't know. Or maybe it's so that the world will know that Long John Silver made it happen." Silver took a deep breath as he touched his chest with an open hand. "The treasure of Dead Man's Chest has become a legend and I'm part of it. I was there through the whole thing. I was John Flint's quartermaster. I'm the only one left. Yes, Charles, I don't need any more money, but I do need the treasure of Dead Man's Chest."

Charles began to protest, but was stopped by the old pirate's upheld hand.

"Call it the soul of a pirate, if you must, but I know I'm not going to live much longer and I'd like to go out with the knowledge that I was the one..." said Silver with his hand still at his heart. "It's this hunger deep inside me—deep as my marrow--that'll eat me up if I don't get it."

"You're really serious this time, aren't you?"

"More serious than you know," answered Silver, his eyes ablaze with excitement.

"And you think this new plan will work, when all the rest have failed?"

"Yes, I do," answered the old man slowly. "And it started several months ago when you traded away the Hesperus to John Flint's bastard son."

"Joshua Smoot?" Charles considered for a moment and continued. "You figure this trouble up in the America Colonies might work to your advantage, don't you?"

"It was tailor-made for me, Charles." Silver pulled a piece of folded paper from his vest pocket and read down the list aloud. When he had finished, he leaned back and waited for his brother's reaction.

"All of that sounds grand, but I still don't understand why you need Captain Jones. We have the bait, and we know the man in New York. What's more, I believe I've done ... no, I'm sure of it!"

"Sure of what?" asked Silver.

"I've done business with this Yorkman you talk about."

"Go on," said Silver, fully aware of where Charles was headed.

"Well," continued Charles, "since I already have an established link with the man, why not strike a deal direct, without Captain Jones?"

"Because I've already tried."

"You did?" asked David.

"You never told us," added Charles.

"I didn't want to involve you, in case anything went wrong. Nobody knew except the two men I hired." Silver stared across the room as if the far wall had vanished. "And I wish the whole thing had never happened."

"Why, Uncle Silver?"

"It's a long story, lad, but suffice it to say that things didn't work out exactly the way I had planned. My two agents got greedy and exceeded their authority; a risk you take when you send others to do your bidding." Silver poured himself a second drink.

"Does this Mister Ormerod know you sent them?" asked David.

"I must assume not, Davey, since he never came after me."

"Why would he need to come after you?" asked Charles. "What happened?"

"It's not important now," answered the old man as he lapsed into his memories for a long moment.

"Then he won't be apt to draw a map for us, will he?" affirmed Charles.

"No, he won't," said Silver as he shook his head slowly from side to side. "I know the man well. The only way he'll ever do it is if I can appeal to something he considers a..." He searched for the words. "A higher purpose."

"A higher purpose?" asked David.

"Yes, Davey, and that's where Captain Jones, and the cannons fit into my plan." Silver took back the note and skimmed over it quickly. "But timing is everything, Davey. If we use them at the wrong moment, the whole plan will go up in smoke."

"How we use them?" asked David slowly.

"Aye, and that's where you come in, Davey."

"Sir?"

"It's important that Captain Jones doesn't suspect there's a connection between the Noble's and the innkeeper, Jack Bridger."

"I don't follow you," said Charles as he puffed at the pipe. "What difference should that make?"

"None, as long as he never tells the Yorkman about me."

"I still don't follow," said Charles.

"Think about it, Charles. The Yorkman and I spent several months together on the Walrus with John Flint and his crew. He knows me, and he knows I want that treasure. He could have learned it was me who sent those two men for his map. And he's certain to ask Captain Jones if there's a one-legged old man involved in all this. If this articulated leg didn't fool him tonight, he and the Yorkman might put the pieces together." John Silver turned to David. "Back to what I was saying, lad."

"Yes?"

"If he asks, you're to tell him you've only been in Silver Jack's one other time and you consider me..." John Silver thought for a moment. "You tell him I'm just a demented old tavern keeper. The name and image of the limping Jack Bridger must fade from our little Captain's memory."

"It's too late," said David with a worried look to his uncle."

"Too late?" spat the old pirate.

"He heard your leg clicking and asked about it. I let it slip that you were my uncle."

"Damn you!" cried John Silver as he threw the knife past David at the far wall. It stuck deeply into the wood paneling.

"I'm sorry," cried David, craning his neck for a look at the still-quivering blade. "It was before I...before you reminded me..."

"It's done, John!" shouted Charles. "Leave the boy alone!"

"And there's something else," added David meekly.

"Something else?" asked Silver as he glared back at the youth.

"I'm not so sure he wants to be a Colonial naval officer after all; or at least not as much as you're hoping he does."

"What are you saying?" asked Silver as he stood and advanced upon the lad.

"Well..." David looked to his father for support as he stepped toward the fireplace. "It's just that your whole plan depends on Captain Jones, and he could change his mind once he reaches Virginia."

"Change his mind?" hissed the old pirate as he took another step toward the lad. "Go on!"

"After he came back from his ship last night, he talked about the naval commission, but..."

"But what?" demanded Silver.

"He told me his brother owns a very prosperous tailor shop with a highly-placed clientele, and if things went well for him, he'd like to get himself a wife and a plantation where he could, retire in calm contemplation and poetic ease."

"He used those words?" asked Charles.

"Those were his very words, sir." David turned back to his uncle. "I'm just saying it might not work out the way you've said." The old pirate returned to his chair and fell into deep thought as his brother and nephew waited for his change of plans.

"I'm getting too old to wait for 'The Seasons'," he said slowly, as if reading his own obituary. "If Captain Jones chooses to purchase a plantation and retire, then my dream probably goes with him."

"The seasons?" asked Charles.

"It's a line from the poem," answered Silver as if Charles should be familiar with the words. "Seems our little captain is a man of letters."

Charles walked away to his desk and stopped. "This whole thing is a waste of your time, and David's also!"

"How's it a waste our time?"

"Face it. You're getting along in years, and the strain of this thing could kill you. And besides, I'll have no more of my son sitting in your tavern every afternoon drinking ale!"

"As far as the killing of me is concerned, it's the treasure's that's kept me going this long. And your son doesn't drink ale all afternoon!"

Charles turned to David for confirmation.

"Uncle Silver's right, father. He fills my tankards with water."

Charles gritted his teeth while he loaded his second barrel. "But your plan hasn't a prayer of working anyway," demanded Charles, "even if Captain Jones wants that commission!"

"Oh?" asked Silver. "Why not?"

"Well..." Charles hesitated while he thought of an illustration his older brother might accept. "Here!" David and his uncle watched as Charles reached in his pocket and withdrew a handful of coins. Selecting six, he laid them in a straight row on the table and then placed his pocket watch several inches beyond the last coin. "This'll convince you."

"Farthings?" laughed Silver.

"Aye," answered Charles. "Your plan is too much like Farthings."

"That's a child's game! We're talking about a real treasure here!"

"But the principle of it demonstrates my point," insisted Charles as he leaned forward. "There are too many ways for this fantastic plan of yours to go wrong between today in Kings Town and some day on Dead Man's Chest."

"Would one of you explain what you're talking about?" asked David. "What's Farthings?"

"It's a game I taught your father when he was just a pup," answered Silver as he stood and walked across the room. With a twist, he pulled his knife from the wall.

"The watch," said Charles as he gave his brother a sideways look, "represents your Uncle's treasure."

"And the coins?" asked David.

"The coins are all the people and elements in his plan, with this last coin, the one nearest the watch, representing the Yorkman." Charles looked to his brother for confirmation. The retired pirate nodded in agreement.

"What am I supposed to do?" asked David. "How does the game work?"

"Very simple. Put your finger on the coin nearest you, and push at the row so the one at the far end moves across the table and touches my watch."

"That's easy enough," said David as he gave the line of coins a confident shove. But just as John and Charles knew they would, the coins slid askew, like so many boats without rudders, with the last coin never moving from its original position.

"That game has nothing to do with my plan," spat John, "and you know it!"

"Oh?" Charles picked up the last two coins, the ones nearest the watch, and held them up to his older brother. "Unless you can guide the Yorkman and your Little Captain, as you call him, in just the right direction, and at just the right time, you'll never see that treasure. And as you so aptly pointed out, if they ever suspect they're being manipulated by Long John Silver, the whole thing will fail." He replaced the coins in front of his son.

"Exactly!" said Silver as he stood and walked to the table. "But if I could somehow control this one," he said as he rested the tip of the blade on the third coin from the watch, "then I could reach the watch every time, regardless of how many other coins there were in the line." Silver gave the blade a flick, driving the last coin against the pocket watch with a metallic clink. "Right?"

"And how do you propose to accomplish that?" asked Charles. "You'd have to put a mouse in Captain Jones' pocket, or at the least have somebody..." Charles fell silent as he watched the older man circle around behind David and rest his hand on the lad's shoulder.

"David," Charles said coldly. "Go to the kitchen until I call you. Your Uncle and I need to speak in private." Obediently, David was up and out of the room.

"If your plan calls for my son..." began Charles as he picked up the coin and took a step toward John.

"There's no other way, Charles. Davey has to go."

"Absolutely not!"

"Good Lord, Charles! Davey's a grown man! You were already married and I had a price on my head by his age. You've got to let him go sooner or later."

"But he's all I have left!"

"Charles, Charles, Charles," Silver said as he stepped around to his chair and refilled his drink. "You make me so tired when you get on that subject."

"What subject?" demanded the younger man. "My family?"

"Aye! Your widow, bless her soul, and that son you're afraid to let grow up!"

"How will he grow up if he's hanged as a spy or traitor against the Crown?" Charles walked across to the fireplace and turned about. "If you're so determined to get that treasure, then go along with Captain Jones yourself. I'll not agree to letting my son..." Charles fell silent as he and Silver noticed the kitchen door open an inch and then pull shut.

"There, Charles!" sang out the old pirate as he stepped across the room and pulled the door open to reveal the eavesdropping lad. "Davey's a spy after all, whether you like it or not."

"A spy?" asked David as he stepped into the room.

"It has nothing to do with you," lied Charles.

"Wrong!" insisted Silver as he put an arm about the lad's shoulder and led him to the couch. "It has everything to do with you."

"You want me to go to America with Captain Jones, don't you?"

"No he doesn't!" insisted Charles. "Captain Jones can go alone. Once your uncle explains the plan to him..."

"That won't work, father."

"You can't know that!" Charles was fast reaching the point of rage.

"But don't you see? Captain Jones can't know he's part of Uncle Silver's plan. I have to go with him to America as your eyes and ears. And when the time's right..."

"Your uncle already tried, so hold your breath."

"Captain Jones was right," said David coldly.

"Right about what, Davey?" asked Silver, thrilled to see the animosity growing between David and his over-protective father.

"You don't want me to ever go to sea, do you, Father?" There was a long moment of silence.

"Let the lad grow up, Charles. We all need this."

Charles picked up a small painting of his widow and held it near his chest. After several minutes, he set the picture down and turned back to his brother.

"If I agree, I'll want several assurances."

"Anything, little brother!" sang out Silver. "Anything you want!"

"He's only to be a messenger. I don't want him going to Dead Man's Chest," demanded Charles, as Silver gave the lad a wink.

"Done!" chirped the old man as he put an arm about the lad's shoulder and squeezed. "The lad'll never go near the place, will ya, Davey?"

"No, sir," said David with a wince of pain.

"Then it's back to business!" cried Silver with a clap of his large hands. "For starters, Captain Jones will need provisions and a crew to help him sail to Virginia," said the old man as he turned his attention to the younger Noble. "He's sure to ask for your help, Davey. When he does, be sure to take him to your father's main warehouse to make the arrangements. And mind you," added Silver, "it's essential that you've already got him to agree to let you go along, before you meet with your father." Silver turned to Charles.

"Can you arrange..?"

"Since David is going along, I'll take care of the provisions."

"And a crew?" asked Silver.

"There'll be no problem getting three or four men willing to take working passage," said Charles as he turned to David. "You can tell Captain Jones that."

"And you, Charles, will need to play the part of a reluctant father."

"That'll be the easiest job I have," said Charles with a huff. "But tell me something. How'd you know that verse was from 'The Seasons'?"

"Oxford, or don't you remember?" Charles gave a puzzled look as John realized his mistake. "No...you wouldn't know, would you? You were only born in '20, and I went to England the same year they hanged Jack Rackham and his crew. That would be, what, three years before old man Taylor bought you."

Charles folded his arms and leaned back against the fireplace mantle, braced for the yarn.

"I was a restless lad," said Silver as he sat down and sheathed his knife. "My left leg had only been cut off for a couple years when I caught that ship. Met a kind-hearted professor on board who took me under his wing. Figured it would be quite a feather in his cap if he could take a poor, one-legged lad what can't 'ardly speak a lick, an' make a genteelm'n o' 'im." Silver winked at David as his speech returned to that of an educated man. "Four years of free tutoring he gave me, in exchange for all my pirate stories, most of which I had to make up. By the time I returned to Kings Town in '25, I could read and write like a master. Read all of Defoe's works and half of Shakespeare's." Silver took another sip of his brandy.

"John Silver! Do you honestly think David and I believe such a tall tale? You at Oxford University?"

"Check the record, little brother! I sat behind Sir Berrymore--that was my professor's name--when he debated the authorship of the Shakespearean plays in '24." Silver leaned forward and whispered. "It was the Seventeenth Earl of Oxford, Edward de Vere, who really wrote those plays. Used his father-in-law, Lord Burghley, for the character Polonius in Hamlet."

"But why put on the salt around your tavern?" asked David.

"Ah!" he sang out. "Long John Silver's nobody's fool." He resumed his thickest cockney twang for effect. "Why, me clientele would be slippin' their hawsers an' spillin' their gold at the Bucket o' Blood or the Maiden's Breath if I be drivin' 'em off wi' the words o' some bleedin' professor, Har! Har! Har!"

A second bottle of fine brandy was emptied before the meeting ended. At Charles' insistence, the old pirate allowed a few squirts of oil to be applied to the mechanism of his wooden leg before he left for the tavern.

"Might keep you from falling in another mud puddle," said Charles as he pushed his foster brother out the courtyard door toward the wharf.

Just before first light, Captain Jones was awakened by two gulls fighting over a fish carcass on the roof outside his room. After a quick shave, he dressed, set the octant in it's case and walked down to the tavern. The public room was empty, with the chairs still stacked atop the tables. A woman was humming an Irish tune to the cadence of rattling pans.

"Hello!" he called out toward the galley. "Are you there, Mister Bridger?"

"He's outside dumping the garbage, Captain Jones," answered Mrs. Bridger from the kitchen. She walked to the public room and pointed with a large spoon. She was a short woman at five foot four inches, and a little overweight. Her hair was turning gray across the forelocks.

"Thank you, Ma'am," said John as he gave her a curt salute and walked through the front doors.

Jack Bridger, as Captain Jones knew him, was standing alone at the edge of the dock. He held a two-gallon cask beneath his left arm, and dug at its contents with his free hand. A dozen gray and white gulls circled overhead in the sultry dawn air, hoping to take part in this oft-acted ritual.

"Come to Silver, me little orphans, an' get yer mornin' vittles!" A handful of kitchen cuttings flew into the sky amongst the scavengers, sending them into a mad dive toward the water. "And you too, Sadie!" he called to one of the birds as she took flight from the chains of a nearby bowsprit, "unless yer gettin' too fat to fly." A second handful flew skyward in her direction. "Catch it girl!" he called as the overweight gull folded her wings for a half-second in an unsuccessful interception of one of the larger pieces of waste.

Without turning about, John Silver recognized the distinctive, almost military gait of the young Sea Captain approaching from the tavern. "Top o' the mornin' to ya, Captain Jones!"

"Good morning, Mister Bridger!" the young man called back as he walked to Silver's side. "Have you seen your nephew yet this fine morning?" Without answering, Silver turned and shot the rancid-smelling right hand toward the young captain. John stepped back two paces and transferred the octant to his right hand; Silver's intended target.

"Haven't seen the lad since you an' he was tradin' wind last night in me tavern." Silver stepped toward John and pointed eastward with his dirty hand. "My guess is he's down lookin' at yer ship." Silver looked right and left as if someone might overhear him and took yet another step toward John. "Between you an' me," he said with a tap to John's waistcoat, "the lad wants to go to sea with ya."

"Ahhh!" John cried as he looked down at the spot of filth on the blue wool.

"Now I done it!" apologized Silver. "Just when we was gettin' to know each other on a first name basis, we was, an' I hav'ta go an' soil yer fine waistcoat." Silver snickered to himself as he offered his dirty waist towel.

"No thank you!" insisted John as he backed away from the old pirate. "I can clean it off when I get aboard my ship." He turned and walked quickly along the dock toward his ship. As he approached, the sun burst from behind a cloud, silhouetting the topsail yard with its neatly furled sail, forming a distorted crucifix in the bright morning sky. A light morning breeze brought with it the sweat-like smell of the warm seawater, and the ever-present odor of rotting fish carcasses from under the dock.

The changing tide had upset the gangway, so John gave it a kick as he stepped aboard. As he passed the binnacle, he stowed the octant in its drawer, and then dropped through the companionway and aft to his cabin. He took up the ship's logbook and made his daily entry; "Thursday, 11 November 1773: Laid up at Kings Town for provisions and a fresh crew. Mail delivered to the Postal House. J. Jones; Master." As he signed the entry, his attention was drawn to footsteps on the deck above the cabin.

"Hello!" It was the voice of David Noble. "Are you aboard, Captain Jones?"

"Down here! Come down and I'll show you about."

The young man stepped down the short ladder and stood at the small cabin's doorway. He made a quick survey of the cramped space. John closed the logbook and looked up at his new friend.

"Good morning!" said John as he stood and offered his hand. "Welcome aboard the Falmouth Packet."

"And good morning to you, Captain Jones! Did you sleep well?"

"I never sleep well the first night ashore," answered John. "One gets used to the roll of a ship, so the steady deck ashore can be quite unnerving." The two young men stood looking at each other for an awkward moment. "So…how about a look around the ship?"

"I was just going to ask," said David. John led the way topside and forward toward the bow, stopping beside the main hold. "The ship is empty now, but I'm hoping I can contract to take a cargo north to Virginia."

"Then you're serious about sailing north?"

"I am," answered John, noticing the younger man's interest. "I'll be needing a crew. If you'd agree to working passage, I'd enjoy having you along."

"But what about provisions and the rest of your crew? You'd need at least four others to man this ship properly."

"Last night," began John, "you mentioned that your father is a merchant." John crossed to the larboard rail and looked across the water at the line of anchored ships. "You don't suppose he'd need a cargo taken to Virginia?"

"I believe my father's at his main warehouse right now. If we're quick, we might be able to catch him before his first appointment."

"I appreciate this, David."

"My pleasure. I believe my father would enjoy meeting you."

"Well, then," asked John as he stepped to the gangplank, "what are we waiting for?"

The walk westward along Harbor Street and inland to the Noble warehouses took just ten minutes, giving David the time he needed to obey John Silver's instructions. The narrow cobblestone road was lined on either side by ornate homes, with the ever-present ivy clinging tenaciously to the white-washed walls. The Spanish moss added a carnival-like atmosphere to the trees, which formed a thick canopy over the road. Two dogs pulling at an empty sugar sack retreated at the two men's approach.

"Last evening," said David inquisitively as they strode across Buccaneer's Park, "you were saying something about a commission in the Continental Navy."

"That's true."

"I've been hearing quite a few rumors," David fished, "that the Americans are on the verge of a revolt against the Crown."

"I've heard those same rumors," answered John. "But whether or not I could get such a commission doesn't change the fact that I must get to America as quickly as possible. There's another postal packet due from Trinidad within a fortnight, and I'm certain that arrest warrant I told you about will be among her papers."

"John," began David as he remembered his Uncle's admonition from the night before, "I'm serious about going with you, but I've never been away from my father." The two young men stopped. David stood looking into the older man's eyes like a schoolboy awaiting his grades. The corners of John's mouth curled up ever so slightly as he put a hand on the younger man's shoulder.

"I can't give you any guarantees," said John. "We could become naval officers or we could end up as common seamen on a garbage scow. This could be the adventure of our lives, or we could die at sea. But yes, I do want you to come with me." John offered his right hand. "To the Colonies then, at whatever the price?"

"At whatever the price!" David echoed as he took John's hand and shook it vigorously. "And if we find my father in a good mood, we'll have both provisions and a crew!" David turned and broke into a run toward his father's warehouse with John close behind. As John Silver had planned it, Charles Noble was waiting in his office.

"Excuse me, Father," said David, as he pushed the door open, "are you busy?" Mister Noble had his back to the two as he worked at his large desk. He removed his reading glasses and turned.

"No, not yet." He laid his quill aside and rubbed his eyes. "Just a few figures to put together before I meet with Mister Ericksen. I'm rather reluctant to do business with the old thief. Cheated me out of 500 pounds last year." He looked at Captain Jones. "This must be the young man you told me about last evening."

"Father, I'd like you to meet Captain John Paul Jones. John, this is my father, Charles Noble."

"I'm honored to meet one the King's Postal Captains," said Charles as he shook John's hand. You and your little fleet of ships are a merchant's lifeblood." The older man turned to his stove as John flashed a questioning look at David. David shook his head. "Could I offer you a cup of tea, Captain Jones?"

"That would be nice, sir," said John as he looked to David once again and mouthed the words, "Are you going to ask?"

The merchant poured three steaming cups, and set John's on the ledge of the warehouse window.

"My son was telling me that you're on your way to Virginia?"

"That's true, sir. I was hoping that you might be able to help me."

"Help you with what?" asked Charles as he added a half spoon of sugar to his tea.

"I'm…" began John as he looked through the window down onto the warehouse floor. There, lined up like dead soldiers were the thousand new cannons Charles and David had found in the belly of Joshua Smoot's prize ship.

"He's out of money, father, and needs provisions and a crew for the passage."

"Out of money?" asked Charles. "But doesn't the Postal Service provide what you need?" John was quickly counting the cannons and multiplying by the number of rows. Charles smiled at David. "Captain Jones?"

"Sir?" answered John, turning back to the merchant.

"Did you hear anything I said?"

"I'm sorry, sir. I was counting your cannons." John turned back to the warehouse. "I've never seen so many new cannons in one place. How did you get them?"

"That's none of your business, Captain Jones," said Charles as he took a sip of tea and walked to his desk. "But my son tells me you need provisions and a crew to sail to Virginia. Is that true?"

"I have some money, sir, but I'm afraid it wouldn't be enough."

"Manpower's never a problem in Kings Town, Captain Jones, but provisions are another matter. How much money do you have?"

"I have 40 sovereigns of my own and another 32 in the ship's till. Will seventy-two..?"

"For the trip you describe, your 72 sovereigns would purchase provisions for only three; maybe four men at most. If you could get together another, let's say..." the merchant scratched some figures on the paper, "...50 pounds, I think I could outfit a crew of six." He paused as he looked over his glasses at the young man. "But there is another possibility."

John had turned and was looking at the cannons again.

"Mister Jones?"

"I'm sorry, sir," John said as he looked back at his host. "What were you saying?"

"I was going to say that there might be another way for you to finance your trip to Virginia, provided my business deal goes well this morning. But if it doesn't work out, you'd need at least fifty pounds more."

"Fifty pounds? But I only..."

"John," interrupted David. "I can provide the extra money you need."

"What are you saying, son?" asked the merchant. "Captain Jones may not even make it all the way to the Colonies, much less be able to repay you."

"I'm going with him, father."

"You're what?" bellowed Charles.

"They're looking for men to become officers in the Continental Navy." David gave John a quick look. "He's already agreed to take me along." John was on his feet and once again looking at the cannons, only half aware of the argument going on next to him.

"I forbid it!" thundered the older man as he gave his son a wink. "I have plans for you, and they don't include you running off to fight against your own King!"

"I'm eighteen years old, father, and I'm going, with or without your permission! It would be better for both of us if it was with your approval." The two looked around at John, hoping he was enjoying their theatrics, but he was looking down at the cannons again. Charles stepped to the window and pulled the sash cord, closing the curtain.

"Those are Carronades from Scotland!" said John. "I was born and raised not a furlong from the Carron Iron Foundry."

"Captain Jones!" barked Charles.

"Sir?" John flinched as he snapped about.

"I was under the impression that you desired my assistance in acquiring a crew and provisions for your trip to Virginia! Is that true or not?"

"It's true, Sir!"

"Then you'll attend to the conversation at hand and have a word with my son!"

"Your son?"

"He seems to have it in his mind to go with you. If you want my assistance, Captain Jones, then you'll join me in convincing him of the folly of this decision."

"Your son is old enough to make his own decisions, Mister Noble. He's welcomed to come with me to Virginia, but I'll not intervene for either of you. It's not my place to get involved."

"Since it seems that you and he have already agreed to his going along, you are very involved. Do you intend that my son take up arms against his King?"

"My intentions are to get to Virginia as quickly as possible. If it's his or my fate to fight in America's revolt, then none of us can stop that." John looked to David. "It's up to you and your father, David." David looked at his father.

"I'm still going with him, Father."

"Damn!" the older man hissed as he turned away from his son. "I've neither the time, nor the patience to discuss this matter further this morning. I can only pray that within the next few days you'll change your mind. I would appreciate being left alone now."

CHAPTER 3

A week later, Charles Noble stood in his office with his arms crossed and jaw set, scanning the dormant arsenal which lay below in his warehouse. None of the brass and iron monsters had ever tasted gunpowder, nor had their bellies yet been filled with the hideous pieces of iron which would someday rob good men of their lives and limbs. Yet, he could somehow hear the faint roll of battle drums and the bugler's call to arms; signals which would quicken this silent, metallic army into battle. It was a good exchange, albeit somewhat felonious, that he'd made with Joshua Smoot; the Dutch merchantman with the thousand cannons secreted away in her bilge, for the 40-gun clipper ship Hesperus. While he had gained an arsenal with tremendous political leverage, the pirate had acquired a ship without equal in the Caribbean.

"But no matter!" the merchant thought to himself. "After all, business is business. Let the Lord sort the victor from the victim." There was a knock at the door. "Come!"

"You asked to see me, sir?"

"Yes, John, have a seat."

"I'd rather stand, sir," said John nervously as he looked at the clock. "David told me this was urgent, sir."

"My son sometimes exaggerates things." Mister Noble pulled three rolled parchments from a map holder beside his desk and offered them to John.

"I already have a full compliment of charts, sir. Was there something else?"

"Have my fitters completed the work as you requested?"

"Yes, sir," answered John as he glanced toward the bay and his waiting ship. "The cannons are set just as I ordered."

"And do you have the right assortment and quantity of ammunition?"

"Sir!" said John impatiently, bringing Mister Noble from his contemplations. "The provisions are fine, the cannons are adequate, and David tells me the last of my four crewmen will be aboard before we sail. There's nothing left but for me to get underway."

"You sound upset, young man."

"I don't mean to appear insubordinate, sir, but you didn't ask me back this morning just to discuss my provisions and crew. There's something else, isn't there?"

Charles moved across to his desk where the stack of coins stood from the previous evening. He tipped them on their side and ran his finger along their edges as if to take a count.

"Yes there is," the older man said as he walked past his observation window to a shelf set with various nautical instruments, including the glass case which held the octant David had been hoping to use someday. Next to the octant stood a painting of a young woman.

"Pardon me, sir, but I'm in rather a hurry. I must reach the ruins at Port Royal before the tide turns." John could see that the older man would have his say, so offered a sympathetic word. "I know this is difficult for you."

"Difficult!" Charles yelled as he spun on his heel. "You don't know anything, Captain Jones!" The older man ground his teeth. "It's clear the lad never told you about his mother."

"No sir, except that she died when he was young."

"He's my only son and the only heir to my estate. You'll be taking him to a strange land and possibly into a war against his own people." Tears began to well in Charles' eyes as the pain of his memories returned. "I don't think I could bear it if David were killed also."

"Also?" asked John. "David said his mother died of natural causes."

"He was only five at the time; hardly knew his mother." Charles picked up the painting. "Oh Alexandria..." He turned back to John, the tears now flowing freely over his cheeks. "I killed her, John. I killed my beloved Alexandria."

"I don't understand, sir."

"She was already sick with the flu; weak beyond measure. It must have been the tainted meat I brought her, because she fell into convulsions within an hour after she ate it. I called a physician, but nothing could be done."

"If it was food poisoning, then it was an accident. You didn't kill her."

"But don't you see? I was the one who brought it to her." He set her picture down on the desk. "If I were to lose David..."

"I don't mean to be blunt, sir, but you're going to have to face the fact that David's a grown man and will do what he wants. He told me about your fear of him being abducted by pirates or one of the King's men-of-war. Isn't it better that he go to America with me?"

"It's no longer my decision." The older man ran his fingers through his thick, graying hair as he thought. "Moments before she died, she asked me to promise to never let David go to sea. I didn't want to agree to such a thing and I may have waited too long to answer. I'm afraid she died before she heard my promise."

"If she didn't hear it, then I'd say you aren't bound..."

"Whether she heard my promise or not, I still made it to her." Charles wiped a tear from his cheek. "I'd like to make a bargain with you, Captain Jones."

"A bargain?" John's eyes narrowed with suspicion.

"No," Charles corrected himself. "Let's call it an agreement between friends. My part of the agreement concerns those four cannons and the provisions for your ship."

"Sir," John protested, "I've already paid you the forty five pounds for the provisions, and you said those cannons were throw-aways!" John reached into his waistcoat for his purse. "You've left me with only twenty two pounds until I reach Virginia. Surely you don't intend to take..?"

"Put your money away," said the merchant with an upheld hand. "What I'm proposing is that you take back the money you've already paid me in exchange for..."

"But we had an agreement. Your concern for your son's safety is justified, but I'm a man of my word."

"And that's exactly what I'm hoping to purchase from you Captain Jones; your word."

"Sir?" John was confused.

"David's young and sometimes acts in a foolhardy manner. I can't begin to tell you how many times I've had to rescue the lad from the local constable or an irate father protecting his daughter's virtue. I want your word that you'll watch after him."

"Go on."

"In exchange for your promise, you may have the provisions, the cannons, the extra powder you asked for, and the forty five pounds you've already paid me." Captain Jones began to speak, but Mister Noble stopped him. "We'll call it my investment in David's and your future in the Continental Navy, if they ever get around to putting one together."

"I need no bribe to stand by a friend, be he your son or another's. I'll be just as dependent upon his protection as he'll be on mine. That's what friendship is about!"

"You'll not give me a lesson in friendship, young man."

"No?" John grabbed the small stack of coins and held them in Mister Noble's face. "Then why do you insist it carries a price?"

"Forgive me, sir," said Mister Noble as he picked up the painting of his wife once again and stared at her likeness. "I underestimated you. I only wanted..."

"What any father wants," interrupted John, recognizing the older man's repentance. "I understand."

"Then you'll accept my ...uh, gift?"

"I will, sir, but only as a gift," answered John as he took the coins.

"Then a gift it is!" said Mister Noble with relief.

"This will certainly help," said John as he replaced the money in his purse and offered his benefactor his right hand. "With any luck, I'll send your son back as not only a man, but as a naval officer."

"It's not luck that'll bring my son back to me, but rather the Good Lord. May He go with both of you, John Jones."

"Thank you, sir," said John as he picked up his hat and moved toward the door. "If there's nothing else, sir, I'll..."

"There is one more thing."

"Sir?"

"Please don't say anything to David about my fear of his going to sea with pirates. I'd rather he go believing it's to get the commission and to establish contacts for my shipping company that I let him go. Will you do that for me?"

"I will, sir," said John as he opened the office door, "if that's your desire."

"Thank you, young man, and have a safe journey."

The narrow streets were still wet from the rain squall which had passed across the island just before sunrise. A Negro child chased one of the many stray cats into a tree with her stick. Fearing the well-dressed white man who approached from the Noble warehouses, she ran into a stone house and peered from the door. John gave her a curt salute, and in exchange the girl stuck out her tongue.

"Be gettin' underway this fine mornin' I see!" called the keeper of Silver Jack's as the young Scot rounded the corner onto Harbor Street. "May the winds be friendly to yer riggin'."

"Thank you, Mister Bridger," called back John. "And thank you for your hospitality. I'll carry fond memories of Kings Town for many a year because of you."

"The least I could do fer a seafarin' man o' yer fine caliber," said the old pirate as he remembered something. "An' regardin' that bottle o' scotch I promised ya, I'll make good on it some day, by the powers." John gave the old man a smile and hurried away.

As John skipped across the gangway onto his small craft, two men were lowering a turtle into the hold. The deck was stacked neatly with flour barrels, grain bags, and salted beef in new wooden boxes.

"Do any of you men know where Mister Noble has got off to?" John asked as he surveyed the provisions.

"He's below, sir," answered the younger of the three, "with Albert." The young seaman pointed at the mid ship hatch.

"David!" called John as he left the three to their duties. "Are we ready to sail?"

"Aye, Captain Jones!" answered the youth, with a four pound cannon ball in each hand. "Matter of fact, if you hadn't come pretty soon, I was sending Barragan after you."

A well-tanned Irishman in his late thirties poked his head out of the hold. He was a skinny man with the look of a Gecko lizard. The deep lines about his squinted eyes testified to many an hour spent peering across the sea.

"You must be the new man," said John as he watched the Irishman lower the live green turtle into the hold.

"Aye, sir, that I am. Mister Noble been tellin' me an' the rest o' the crew 'bout ya sir, an' we be lookin' f'ward to this 'ere trip o' yers," he said as a second thought flashed across his little mind. "An' it were my idea ta take these turtles along fer fresh meat, seein' as how..."

"We can talk about that later," interrupted John, "once we clear Port Royal." John turned his attention to David. "Stow those cannon balls, David. We need to get underway."

A broad smile flashed across the youth's face as he tossed the rusty iron spheres to Barragan. With the agility of a cat, David leaped up the ladder and into the bright sun.

"Clark! Carini!" David called out. "Unfurl the mainsa'l! Etinger and Barragan, stand by to cast off all lines!"

There was a flurry of running about the deck and slacking of sheets as David barked out his well-rehearsed commands. As the east wind caught the backside of the staysail to pull the little ship's bow from the dock, the last line was cast off, freeing the craft for its long voyage to America. The flying jib and square topsail soon joined their larger canvas sibling, opening like the wings of a butterfly to grab their share of the breeze coming over the green hills of Jamaica.

As John Silver stood in the doorway of his tavern, watching his investment shrink away toward the ruins of Port Royal, a second figure stepped from the shadows of the public room and stood next to the old pirate.

"Well, Charles," said Silver as he placed a hand on his brother's shoulder, "from what I read in this dispatch I intercepted, our plan is working out better than I expected."

"What does it say?" asked Charles vacantly as he watched his son disappear.

"The British are going to prohibit the importing of all large weapons and gun powder to the Colonies. Something's about to happen, little brother, and my plan will be right in the middle of it." He waited for the younger man to answer, but there was none. "You aren't having any regrets, are you?"

"I wouldn't call it a regret, exactly."

"Then what would you call it?"

"Doesn't it matter to you that my cannons might change the outcome of the revolution?"

"Why should it?" asked Silver.

"Because we're both British subjects, that's why."

"Speak for yourself, Charles. I may be British by birth, but my soul is pirate, through and through. My breed profits regardless of who sits on a throne far across the sea. If America's destined to be free from the Crown, those few cannons won't make the difference."

"I guess you're right," answered Charles as the muscles about his jaw tightened. "I just don't like using my son and his friend this way."

"Cheer up, little Brother! You'll see the good in it when they bring us that treasure." John Silver brightened. "And maybe they'll even write a fifth verse to Dead Man's Chest in my honor!"

The Falmouth Packet responded like a yearling colt as she was steered around Port Royal and into the deeper waters of the Caribbean. The winds had freshened and shifted to the southeast by mid-morning, putting the three day reach for Hispaniola and the Windward Passage well within the craft's lay line. Captain Jones leaned against the windward rail as David eased the tiller to lee.

"Your father had a very difficult time letting you go."

"I know." David cast a long gaze across the isthmus toward the row of shops and taverns of Kings Town. His father and John Silver were gone.

John pulled the small leather bag from his inner pocket. "He wouldn't take my money."

"I figured he'd do something like that." David pulled a similar bag from his own pocket. "He gave me a hundred pounds to help us when we reached Virginia. Said it was part of my inheritance." David scanned the rigging and barked an order at one of the crewmen. "He tries so hard to come across like a taskmaster, but under that thin coat, he's as soft as cream pudding."

"He told me about your mother," said John. "About the tainted meat he brought her."

"Hmmm," said David. "He's told very few people about that. Every year at her birthday, and then again on their wedding anniversary, he takes her painting into his room and locks the door. I've listened to him cry for her every year for as long as I can remember." He fell silent as his own voice began to tremble and a cold tear spilled from his eye.

"He's quite a man. You're fortunate to have him."

"I know," answered David thoughtfully. "And I know how deeply this hurts him."

As they spoke, the topsail rotated on it's rigging and caught the wind on its front side. The little ship heeled over to lee and came to a near stop. A harsh order from David brought the crew alive to correct the problem. Within seconds, the loose brace was captured and the topsail, as they called the single square sail high atop the main mast, was secured and trimmed.

"Your father didn't see you off. Did you and he have words?"

Before David could answer, seaman Barragan approached from amidships.

"By yer leave, Mister Noble," said the Irishman, "but this here be my watch. You an' the Cap'n can go 'bout yer affairs, if it pleases ya."

"Thank you, Albert," said David as he turned the helm over to the Irishman.

"Hold her near shore until we pass Morant Point, and then steer for the center of the Windward Passage."

"Aye, aye, sir," answered the seaman with a knuckle to his forelock; man-o-war style.

The days and nights were long as Jamaica shrank in the West. When the natives of Hispaniola were finally distinguishable on the western beaches of their island, Captain Jones ordered a course change for Punta Maisa on the eastern tip of Cuba.

On the 15th of December, as the Falmouth Packet began her run along Cuba's North coast, David stepped up to John. He had been around his new friend long enough to know John wanted to talk about something. After several minutes, David finally spoke.

"Something's bothering you, isn't it, John?"

"How could you tell?" John leaned forward against the stern rail and looked across the waves as Cuba shrank to the South.

"You've been especially quiet for the last two days. What's the matter?"

John turned about and faced the young Jamaican. "Is your father using me?"

"Using you?"

"You heard me. That first day you introduced us; it was as if he was waiting for me. As if you two were reading lines from a carefully written play."

David didn't answer.

"You haven't told me everything, have you?" John waited for the younger man's answer. When it didn't come, he continued. "This whole matter of getting my ship provisioned and you coming to the Colonies with me; there's something going on that I don't know about, isn't there?""

"I don't know what you're talking about," lied David as a hot tingle creep up from his mid-back, upwards toward his neck. He looked into the rigging as if to study the trim of the sails.

"I'll be blunt, David. Has your father turned me into a smuggler?"

"A smuggler!?" cried David, relieved that John's suspicions were so far from the truth. "That's ridiculous! Why would you think such a thing?"

"Because nothing else fits." John studied David's expression for any hint that his guess was right. "Maybe it's my suspicious nature, but it seems to me that your father agreed much too quickly to your going along."

"And that makes you think we're carrying something illegal in our hold?"

"I've thought of everything, and smuggling is the only thing that fits."

"Well, it's not smuggling!"

"Then there is something!" John snapped back.

"What?"

"The way you answered my question. It implies there is something else; besides smuggling. What is it?"

"There's nothing, John, except..."

"Aha! cried John, proud that he had broken the younger man's resolve so quickly.

"He's afraid that I was about to go to sea with one of the pirates. I've heard he and my uncle argue about it many times."

"Your father mentioned that to me, but it still doesn't quite fit."

"If you don't want my father's help, then turn about and take me and all of this charity back to Kings Town!"

"I guess you're right," answered John as he considered his options. "It's just that I've never seen a man so generous with his property or so caring for his son. I can't help it, David. It suggested..." John extended his hand to the young Jamaican.

"Can you forgive my suspicions?"

"Apology accepted," said David as he shook the older man's hand. "I'm sure I'd have reacted the same way in your place."

The winter of '73 was mild in comparison to several in the past. The small postal packet had run into two insignificant storms between Kings Town and the north coast of Florida, a rarity during December and January. Their luck with the weather was matched by their seeming immunity to other ships they had passed along the way. Three different colonial privateers had come close, but had broken off when it was clear the Falmouth was only a postal packet.

Passing three leagues seaward of Point Royal Sound, the sky turned dark, and a cold southeasterly began to whip at the rigging. The gentle swells which had lifted and pushed the small craft forward for so many days now became angry at the wind's touch, with whitecaps leaping from the dark waves like rabbits running before a wildfire.

"Etinger," called David, "go below and get Captain Jones!" The young Dutchman ran to the aft hatch and dropped out of sight. The wiry seaman knocked urgently at the door.

"Yes?" answered the Scotsman.

"It's Etinger, sir! Mister Noble wants you topside. We've another storm pressing from the sou'west, and it looks to be a bad one this time!"

"Tell Mister Noble to begin reefing the sails, Charles. I'll be topside in a few minutes."

"But, Mister Noble said..."

"I'll only be a moment."

"Aye, aye, Captain!"

By the time John had donned his foul weather gear and made his way topside, the raging wind had already begun to tear at the tiny maiden of a ship with the ferocity of an angry lion. David had waited too long to take action and had lacked the experience to give his frightened and confused crew the orders necessary to fight off this sudden attacker. It was no more than a third-rate storm, but to this green crew, it was a monster. It had no compassion, only claws and teeth, and an insatiable hunger to destroy. Captain Jones surveyed the situation quickly and barked out a series of orders.

"David, I'll take the helm. I want you to get all hands on that topsa'l! If we don't lower the yard and furl the sail quickly, we're likely to lose it, along with the top mast!" John took the tiller under his right arm and braced himself in a wide-legged stance. The following sea was throwing the small vessel sideways with such force that the tiller nearly lifted John from the deck.

"David!" John shouted. "Break out the sea anchor and rig it forward. Once we've those sails down we'll put her nose to the sea and ride this thing out." David dropped through the forward hatch as the others went about their assigned tasks. Coordinating their efforts, the two teams lowered the mainsail and lashed it securely to its boom. The two jibs offered no immediate problem, so all hands went to work on the topsail. Without the buntlines found on most square sails, the first step was to lower the yard and pivot it to spill its wind. At Barragan's signal, both the lift lines were slacked, but the left side wouldn't lower.

"What's the matter, Barragan?" John yelled.

"It's the larboard lift, sir! It's fouled at the mast head." The Irishman pointed at the slacked line where it was twisted about the block. "Should I go up an' loose it, Captain?"

"Not in this gale!" The winds had reached thirty knots and were increasing several knots every minute. "We'll have to release the sheets and let it fly free and hope for the best!"

"Secure the starboard lift and stand by the braces!" ordered Captain Jones. But it was too late. Before the sheets could be untied, the topmast broke just above its housing, releasing not only the flying jib, but allowing the topsail to hang upside-down against the main mast.

"Damn it!" John cried against the wind. Then, deciding on the only course of action left to him, he barked new orders to the crew.

"Stand by to come about!" By this time, David had pulled the sea anchor from its bag and had it's line secured to the cat's head. "David," John called forward, "when I give the word, deploy the sea anchor to windward!"

Captain Jones watched the swells rushing upon their craft from astern, watching for just the right moment to turn. Blue water had already begun breaking over the bow and into the bilges, leaving no time to waste.

Before he could give the command to deploy the canvas anchor, a large swell crashed against the stern, pushing the rudder flat against the transom. The force of the tiller swinging sideways lifted John off the deck and threw him headlong against the starboard rail.

As the wave devoured the quarterdeck and ripped along the planking forward, the little ship turned sideways in the trough, washing several of the crew, and two of the hatch covers about the deck making the Falmouth Packet's deck resembled the trash-filled streets of Jamaica during a monsoon.

There was a flurry of confusion and frantic gesturing at the main mast. The fouled topsail had caught the wind and billowed like a spinnaker, pulling sideways on the main mast and heeling the ship over on her side. As the sea began to spill across the deck, Captain Jones made a quick decision. Since there was no way to spill the wind from the uncontrolled sail, his only option was to run with the wind.

"David!" he yelled. "Hold that sea anchor and come aft to help me on the tiller!"

"Aye, but we can't run with the sea!" David bellowed back as he leaped across the deck. "We're taking water over the bow and the hold's beginning to fill!"

"We have no choice!" John cried against the wind.

"Can't we at least run on a quarter, so our bow doesn't dig into the swells so badly?"

"I tried that already," John shouted, "and it's worse." David struggled against the wind to John at the helm, and together they managed to turn the little ship northward again to run with the swells.

"Barragan!" John called out. "Put two men on the pump!"

The storm's full force was now upon the tiny ship. With each push from astern, the bowsprit cut deep into the swell ahead. John felt it first; that unmistakable heavy wallowing which meant the hold was filling. Barragan had put Clark and Carini on the bilge pump, but water was coming over the bow and into the missing hatch covers faster than the pump could push it back. The Irishman came aft to report.

"I know, Barragan. If we don't figure a way to lighten the bow, we'll continue to ship water till we swamp." John looked about him for some glimmer of hope. "I'm open to suggestions."

Barragan pondered the situation for a moment and then brightened.

"The anchor chain, sir!" he yelled over the wind. "If Mister Noble can find something to cover the hatches, Etinger and I could move the chain aft!"

"Move it aft?"

"Aye," the Irishman called back. "We gotta shift the load, not just lighten it. An' the anchor chain's the only thing heavy enough!"

"How heavy do you figure?"

"Sixty, maybe sixty-five stone, sir," the Irishman answered, "if we be lucky."

"Leave Clark on the pump and the rest of you get to it. It may be our only chance."

As Barragan, Etinger and Carini went about their unorthodox task, the sea continued to flow over the bow with each swell. The water in the hold was now deep enough that the three turtles which had not yet been slaughtered had righted themselves, thrilled with the prospect of escape. As John struggled with the tiller, the rusty chain began to snake out of the forward hatch and aft across the deck.

"Albert!" called Captain Jones. "Where's that thing going?"

"Into your cabin, sir. It's the only place to put it if we want to raise the bow." The Irishman disappeared down the hatch for a moment and then reappeared. "But don't worry, Cap'n. We're putting it to starboard, away from your desk and bunk."

Slowly, almost imperceptibly at first, the bow began to ride higher and higher as the heavy links moved aft. By the time the chain locker was empty, the man on the pump saw the water stop rising and then begin to drop. With the chain moved, the three men turned their efforts toward the last uncovered hatch. Within minutes, a spare piece of canvas had been lashed over the hole, stopping most of the water that rushed across the deck and filled the bilges.

"We're going to make it!" called John, more to himself than to the crew. He was bruised and battered from the thrashing the tiller had given him, with blood running down his side under his right arm. It was painful to take a breath, but with any luck, none of his ribs would be broken.

"Thank you, Lord," he whispered involuntarily through his agnosticism. "Thank you."

By dusk, the storm had moved beyond the Falmouth Packet to the Northeast, leaving the sea as it had been before its attack. The sea anchor was deployed and all hands spent a well-deserved night in their hammocks. The upper main mast was broken and the topsail was badly torn, but the six-man crew had survived.

Captain Jones slept a painful twenty hours. The tiller had left its grizzly signature on his body from head to toe, with at least two cracked ribs and a score of bruises. It would be a month before he was fully himself, and it would be necessary for the small vessel to lie fallow until repairs could be made.

Most of the tangled lines and broken yards had been cleared by the time the afternoon sunlight began to play across John's face through the open port hole. There was a heavy odor in his nostrils as he heaved into painful consciousness.

"Aaaahh!" he cried out as he turned onto the injured ribs and caught the first whiff of the rusting iron. Am I still bleeding? he thought as he surveyed the front surfaces of his legs and torso. The dressings are all in place, yet I smell fresh blood. He turned his hands in the bright sunlight, looking at his skin color. Normal, but that smell?

On the starboard side of his small cabin, piled high against the ships planking, was the large hump of rusty anchor chain they had moved aft during the storm.

"That's what I'm smelling," he said as he struggled from his bunk. Without washing, he climbed the short ladder to the main deck.

"Welcome back from the dead!" called David from aloft. The lad sat in a rope sling high above the deck where he was working to repair the masthead. "What finally woke you?"

"The sun through the port hole and the smell of that rusty chain." John shaded his eyes to get a good look at his young friend. "Hope you know what you're doing up there. Tie the wrong hitches and we'll have that yard down around our ears again with the first wind."

"Don't worry about my knots!" David gave two firm tugs on the fresh manila line and drove a marlin spike through its strands to hold it in place. "It's that torn tops'l we've to worry about. None of us has ever mended a sail before." John's eyes were now becoming used to the bright afternoon sun, but he still had to peer between his hands at the men on the deck. Clark, Barragan and Carini had the large topsail spread across the deck and were stitching closed the single rip it had sustained the previous afternoon. Barragan looked up at his Captain.

"If we can just make 'er strong enough to get us into Charles Town," the Irishman said as he sucked at one of the three fresh needle wounds in his left hand, "we should be able to find us a real sail-maker, sir."

"Do the best you can, Albert." John walked forward. At the bow, he looked again to David high atop the damaged mast and called out. "How long before we can be underway?"

David pulled one of the lifting lines up and passed it through a double sheave block as he considered the question. "It'll be a couple of days," he called back. "Maybe as many as three. There's a lot more damage than I thought."

"No faster?"

"What's your hurry?" called David with a jerk on one of the lifts. "Wouldn't it be better to put the ship back together the right way and get to Charles Town in one piece than risk a sinking?" David cut a piece of the old rigging away and threw it to the deck near John. "And besides, you've some bad injuries that could use the time to mend."

"I guess you're right," agreed John as he rubbed his ribs. "Take whatever time you need."

As the current pulled the Falmouth Packet Northward toward Savannah, the list of broken items became shorter and shorter. The topgallant mast was fished together with pieces of oars and wedged lashings, and the square topsail was lashed to the yard as best the crew could manage. The rip was closed, but each of the three crewmen used his own brand of stitch, making the large sail look as though it had been mended during an argument.

True to David's prediction, the ship was ready to get underway just before noon the fourth day after the storm. John was in no condition to stand his watch, so the others agreed to fill in. But hurt as he was, he remained topside throughout most of the remaining repairs. As he paced about the deck, he remembered one additional task.

"David, before we pull in the sea anchor and get underway, I have a request.

"What is it, John?"

"Would you and the others move that chain from my cabin? Three nights with that smell is enough for any man."

"I've three of the men working on the pump packing. As soon as they're done, we'll jump to it."

"Thank you. I guess if I had to, I could..." Captain Jones was interrupted by seaman Etinger's cry.

"Sail on the horizon, sir! Starboard quarter!"

"David, go to the binnacle and fetch my spyglass." A moment later, John was peering at the distant sail in hopes it would be another merchantman or a fisher. "If we're lucky, she'll pass us by like the rest."

"I don't like the looks of her, John. She's too big for a fisherman and her course is wrong for a merchantman. Can you make out her colors yet?"

"I'm afraid so. It's a skull and crossed cutlasses." John handed the glass to his young friend. "They're pirates, and by their course, I'd say they're after us."

"Crossed cutlasses?" David steadied himself against the main mast. "That's Jack Rackham's flag."

"But Rackham's dead, isn't he?" asked John.

"Hung for piracy in Kings Town back in '21."

"Any idea who this might be?"

"Fortunately for us, I know that ship well," answered David with a smile.

"She must be fast," said John as he watched the approaching ship leap the waves.

"That's the fastest ship in the Atlantic. My father designed her himself, and with several important modifications."

"Modifications?"

"Her hull speed for starters," began David. She's longer than a man-o'-war, with the lines of a French racing sloop. And with the 40 cannons, you have the perfect pirate—superior speed and the fire power of a frigate."

"Who is she?"

"When my father owned her, she was the Hesperus, the crown jewel of his fleet. Now she's called the Walrus. She carries a crew of between one hundred and fifty and two hundred of the most bloodthirsty pirates these waters have tasted since Blackbeard was killed in '18."

"The Walrus? Wasn't that John Flint's..?"

"It was, but Flint's been dead for years."

"Then who's at her helm now?"

"The flag belongs to Joshua Smoot," answered David. "Some say Smoot's the illegitimate spawn of John Flint, and that he was slitting sailor's throats in back alleys before he was thirteen. But from what I've seen of him lately, he's mellowed considerably."

"Hmmm," said John as he studied the Walrus from under a shading hand. "What are the chances your Captain Smoot will allow us to pass once he finds out we have nothing worth his effort?"

"Very good," answered David with the glass still to his eye, "especially when he recognizes..." Something caught David's attention. "Oh, my God!"

"What's the matter?" demanded John. "What do you see?"

"They're dropping Smoot's flag," answered the youth as he watched through the spyglass, "and replacing it with another. It isn't going to matter now whether we have any cargo or even that I'm on speaking terms with Smoot."

"I don't understand. Why would he..?"

"Because Alacan the Turk, the second Captain of the Walrus, is in charge of this attack, and he never grants quarter, not even to Charles Noble's son."

"What?" John grabbed the spyglass and watched as the red 'no quarter' flag was hoisted aloft. He lowered the glass as a moment of panic gripped his spine. He spun about to study the coastline and the only option remaining to the little crew and their crippled ship.

"Cut the sea anchor and spread all the canvas she'll carry! We've a race to run with death!"

John Flint had been dead from rum for many years; his bones picked clean long ago by the crabs which infested the brackish waters of Savannah Harbor. His ship, the Walrus, was in disrepair, taking on seawater at an alarming rate and requiring that two men be kept on the bilge pumps through every watch. The despised teredo worms, those mollusks which infested the warm tropical waters of the Caribbean, had done their work well.

She was an old ship, easily twenty years beyond her glory; weather-beaten and tired. All of her topside timbers were parched and worn, the grain open and mean; rewarding any carelessly placed hand or shoulder with a bouquet of deeply imbedded splinters and at least two weeks of the fever which the infection carried with it. Pirates were never known for taking pride in their ships, and likewise, they seldom put up with discomfort when a more pleasurable life presented itself. Such was the case during the summer of '73 when Flint's apprentice, Joshua Smoot, traded a captured Dutch cargo ship for the Hesperus, a three-masted, square-rigged clipper ship carrying forty cannons and six swivel guns. She was of an intimidating size; nearly 200 feet at the water line and 350 tons displacement. Painted black and red with gold trim, she was more than a match for the average British man-of-war.

The pirates scuttled the old Walrus and renamed their new prize by the same name--Flint would have been pleased. For the most part, the crew had varied in size from seventy to 150 men, reaching its peak at 185 men in '72. It had shrunk back to eighty-six men on the day it's watch spotted the small British postal packet drifting on her sea anchor off the coast of South Carolina.

There were several clearly distinguishable factions among the crew of the Walrus, the largest and most powerful being led by Joshua Smoot, one of John Flint's 'students of the art', as Flint called them. The next most powerful faction was headed by a very large and boisterous beast who called himself Alacan the Turk. Nobody really knew where he got the name 'Turk', or whether he was even of that breed. He claimed to have signed articles on Madagascar, but most believed he was simply a large Irishman with tar-black hair and a put-on accent. His leadership of the thirty-seven men who followed him was based neither upon intelligence nor common sense, but rather upon his massive size and unique ability to intimidate men of lesser stature and mind.

"Smoot!" roared Alacan. "She be me prize this time, or by the powers, I'll have yer cowardly heart fer me supper!" Smoot lowered his spyglass and turned to rest his backside against the rail.

"Why waste yer time on her, Alacan? She's only a postal packet," retorted the older and wiser Captain in his calmest voice. Given the right circumstances, he and his men could easily overcome the Turk, but this wasn't the time or the place for such an undertaking. "The most you can expect from her is shippin' schedules an' news from England an' the Carib'. Surely ye'd rather wait yer turn fer somethin' with a larger prize in 'er hold, wouldn't ya?"

Alacan's tiny brain grappled with the concept, but the immediacy of a possible double-share of a prize, even a small one, overpowered any shred of common sense that might have tried to poke itself into his reasoning powers.

"Aye, she's a small ship," answered the Turk with an eye to the spyglass. "But if there be any gold aboard, it be my turn fer that double-share ye been gettin' fer so long."

It'd be like spittin' t' windward to try reasonin' with the Turk any further, reasoned Smoot to himself. And besides, I'll still be obtainin' all the information from the dispatch bags, regardless o' who leads the attack.

"If I agree," asked Smoot, "to help ya man the ship an' all, it don't mean we'll be gettin' yer neck outta no noose."

"Noose?!" Alacan threw back his head and laughed at the rigging. "Why, it'll be easier takin' that little Brit than takin' a maiden's favors in springtime. Ha! Ha!" He threw an arm about Smoot's shoulder and pointed at the prey. "Look at her, Joshua! She's lyin' dead in the sea -- just waitin' ta be plucked like the sweet fruit she be."

"Very well," answered Smoot, like a permissive parent giving in to a disobedient son. "But don't underestimate her. She might have a cannon or two aboard. She could hurt the Walrus bad with just a couple well-placed pieces o' iron."

"A couple pieces o' iron, ye say?" Alacan grabbed Smoot's spyglass and gave the little sloop a closer look. "She's a swivel gun on 'er poop, an' nothin' more! Them postal packets got sail, not cannons."

"Just the same, Turk, watch yerself." A half naked seaman with a large scar across his throat from ear to collar bone approached the two captains.

"Turk!" cried the seaman from just outside cutlass range. "Are we runnin' the ship again?" The Turk's lips peeled back from his yellow-stained teeth in an evil smile of expectation as he surveyed his prey.

"Aye, matey. Strike Smoot's flag an' have me red one hoisted in her place."

As the scarlet flag of Alacan the Turk climbed its halyard, his men gave a demonic cheer. The sound of their revelry traveled across the waves, bringing a stop to all work on the Falmouth Packet.

"We've precious little time before she's within range," called Captain Jones to his frantic crew, "so let's step lively. I'll man the helm while the rest of you set all the sail she can hold."

The men scattered themselves about the deck in what appeared at first to be mass confusion. Halyards were hauled and belaying pins were pulled. While several sheets to lee were released, their counterparts to weather were hauled; all of this while Barragan yelled orders only a seaman could understand. From the midst of the confusion emerged a well-planned and executed set of tasks which had the main and foresail set wing-and-wing for the run downwind. There was no time to hank the flying jib to the newly repaired topgallant mast, so it was secured where it lay, along with the newly stitched topsail.

"Carini!" barked Captain Jones. "Break out the medical supplies and put all the irons on the fire. Even if we survive this, there's sure to be casualties."

"The irons?"

"You've cauterized a wound before, haven't you, Mario?"

"No sir, not me!"

"Oh, Lord!" said John under his breath. "I'm probably the only one who knows anything about medicine or battle surgery!" After some hasty instructions, the Italian set to his task.

"Clark!" called David. "I want all the small arms loaded and stacked at the rails, with plenty of ammunition. And we'll need two axes at each rail to cut grappling hooks." As the second seaman went about his tasks, David's attention was drawn to the distinctive sound of a luffing sail. "Etinger, take up on the stays'l sheet and ease the main!"

"Aye, aye, sir!"

Within minutes, the wounded bird had spread her wings and was fluttering toward the safety of the shore, three leagues to the west. On her tail and closing quickly, followed the cruel and bloodthirsty Walrus, intent on her first kill in three days.

"What do you think, John?" asked David as he pointed at the shore directly past the bowsprit. "Can we make that inlet with this canvas, or would we stand a better chance by reaching for that other one, just outboard of the cat head?"

"Our only hope is on a direct run, wing and wing. The Walrus' aft sails will block her fore sails and perhaps give us the edge we need." John laid a hip to the tiller and looked aft once more at their pursuer. She was now less than three thousand yards aft. "I'd sure like to know what's inside that inlet."

"My father provided several detailed charts of this coastline. Why don't I take the helm while you go below. You need a break anyway." The Scotsman was grateful he had such an observant second-in-command, and relinquished the tiller without objections. As he stepped away from the long boom, he stumbled slightly from fatigue. Catching himself, he turned back to his friend and took a long, slow breath.

"Thank you, David."

"You'd do it for me," answered the lad. "Now, get below and find us a safe haven."

A moment later, John slumped into the chair before his table and let his tortured body rest. "Just a moment, that's all I need," he said to himself as he pulled a chart labeled S. CARO. from the tall box to his left. With four books, he anchored its corners while he searched for his landmark. "That's it!" he said. "Saint Helena Sound. That's where we'll put in. If we can just make it into the Edisto River and then into one of the small tributaries. It should be narrow enough that the pirates can only bring their swivel guns to bear. That'll give us a near equal advantage while we outdistance them. And with our shallow draft...we could...oh Lord, I'm so tired. I'll just put my head down for a moment..."

The table shuddered as if broken in half as the large dagger plunged through the Scotsman's hand, pinning it to the oak planks. Looking up through the blur of searing pain, John Paul looked into the bloodshot eyes of none other than Joshua Smoot.

"Me blade were gettin' thirsty fer the taste o' Scottish blood, Captain Paul. An' now, whilst I has yer undivided attention an' yer fightin' hand pinioned to this 'ere table, what say ye shows me the spot on this 'ere chart where yer gold might be hid?" John wanted to scream, but his vocal chords were numb with pain and fear.

My sword! Where is it?" he thought. His heart was racing, the sound of it becoming louder and louder until its pounding had become a deafening roar against his temples. "The pounding...stop the pounding!" he yelled.

"John! Are you there?" David was now pounding as hard as he could at the locked cabin door. "John, are you all right?"

Smoot was suddenly gone, and the dagger no longer stood in the flesh of his hand. John stared down at the chart. "Charles Town...Savannah...I've got to get to shore," he whispered. "That pounding...what on earth...?" The door suddenly burst open in a shower of splinters.

"John!" The door swung back and struck the bunk next to the Scotsman, startling him out of his nightmare. "The stays'ls aren't enough! They'll be on us in a few minutes! What's taking so long?"

"I must've drifted off." He turned back to the map and set a point of his dividers to a small river stretching inland from Saint Helena Sound. "The Edisto River - that's where we'll make our stand." He hesitated as David's words finally reached his still-confused brain. "Did you say they'd be on us in a few minutes?"

"John, we need you topside, now!"

As the two reached the deck, a cannon ball splashed a hundred yards off the larboard bow, followed a moment later by the cannon's report from a half mile aft.

"Damn, we're within range!" swore John as he and David looked to their two gun crews crouched near their pieces.

"Barragan, Etinger," called Captain Jones, "are your cannons loaded and ready?"

"Aye, Cap'n," came back Barragan in an excited voice. "Both fore guns is loaded wi' grape shot an' the aft two be carryin' barstock, just as ye ordered, sir." The Irishman was proud of his preparations for battle and welcomed the chance to trade iron with such a famous pirate as Joshua Smoot. "Our powder be dry an' the linstocks is burnin' bright, Cap'n Jones, jest like ye showed us!"

"And those muskets, are they loaded also?"

"That they be, Cap'n! An' every jack man o' us be totin' a brace o' pistols, fer close-in fightin'!" Barragan and the other two pulled open their shirts to expose the weapons hidden in their belts.

"And we got our cutlasses an' daggers besides!" called Carini as he pulled and brandished the long blade over his head.

"I hope it doesn't come to that, Mario," said John as they watched the Walrus gain on them. Within ten minutes, the greater ship was upon them, maneuvering for their attack.

"David," shouted John, "go relieve Clark at the tiller so he can man his gun with Barragan. I'll be staying forward with the cannons as long as possible."

"Are you sure you're strong enough for that?" asked David. The Scotsman was in no mood for arguing and barked back at the younger man.

"We've no choice, David! I need Clark forward...now!"

No sooner had Clark joined Barragan at the larboard cannons than the Walrus made another course change. Like every student of blue water warfare, John recognized the tactic.

"Watch her!" cried John. "It's an old ploy to make us think she's going to overshoot!" He turned to David at the helm. "When I drop my hand, I want you to throw the tiller to larboard as far as it'll go, no matter what's happening at the time!" He looked at his first officer for a moment and added, "Is that clear?"

"Clear!" the Jamaican answered.

"Once she's in position," John continued, "she'll spill her timbers and back down just enough so our gunwales meet, at which time we can expect their grappling hooks." The Walrus was now nearly parallel to the little packet, gaining three to four spans a minute.

Suddenly, there was an explosion from one of the Walrus' forward guns, followed a moment later by a sickening shudder along the entire length of little packet's frame.

"How could they be so stupid?" John yelled as he ran aft to survey the damage. Leaning over the starboard rail, he could see two jagged rows of splinters raised, pivot-like on the ship's ribs, where the ball had pierced the oak planking. It was one of the worst hits a ship could take, for it was below the water line. Looking up at the Walrus in defiance, John saw the first sheet released to shiver the timbers for her expected backing-down maneuver. John called to the starboard gun crew as he ran forward.

"Ready on both cannons!" he shouted as leaped between the two seamen, watching for the exact moment. "Fire!"

Both cannons kicked aft as their deadly loads ripped at the Walrus' great stern. The barstock took a large chunk off the upper edge of the rudder while the second cannon's grapeshot peppered the Master's cabin, breaking out most of the windows.

"Now, David!" cried John as he raised and lowered his arm in a cutting motion. "Tiller hard to larboard!" Turning about, John leaped across the deck to his second gun crew.

"Barragan, Clark, stand ready!" Both seamen crouched next to their pieces, linstocks held at the ready. As John crouched between his men, the little packet was well into its starboard turn behind the Walrus' stern, avoiding the rest of the larger vessel's broadside. As they watched with gritted teeth, the Falmouth's bowsprit clipped the great lanthorn hanging from the Walrus' taffrail, sending it twisting as it fell end over end into the dark blue waters of the Bahamas; the same waters that had been flowing into the little ship's belly several days before.

Startled at this unexpected change in their plans, Alacan and Smoot ran aft and peered down at the little ship passing under their stern. Alacan pulled a pistol from his sash, and mistaking Noble for the captain, leveled his barrel on the lad.

"Run an' twist, me little harem girl! Alacan'll have you fer his prize, or send you to Davey Jones' locker!" As he sighted down his barrel at the young Jamaican, the Scotsman's hand rested on Barragan's shoulder, waiting for the exact moment.

"Fire!"

Barragan's linstock dropped an inch and ignited the powder in the cannon's base ring. There was the momentary huff of the primer, followed an instant later by the six-pounder belching forth it's deadly load of grapeshot at the great ship. The crew of the Falmouth Packet would never know how effective that third shot had been, for it stopped the Walrus' attack completely. Inside the cloud of white smoke, the spreading pellets ripped upward through the larger ship's taffrail and into her lower rigging. Alacan, and three feet of polished rail were now raining over the Walrus' foredeck and sails in a grisly shower of blood, shattered bones, and mahogany splinters.

Not having the time, nor the manpower to trim the sails for their starboard reach, the Falmouth lost much, if not all of her headway. Before the acrid cloud of their first larboard shot had cleared, the Walrus' great rudder began to pass the second cannon. As with Barragan, Captain Jones held Clark by the shoulder, waiting for just the right moment. And then, with a whispered, "Now!", the second cannon barked forth it's destructive barstock.

For several moments, the smoke from both cannons hung between the two ships, obscuring not only the setting sun, but the entire stern of the ominous foe which stood over the Falmouth. Then, as if a blacksmith's hut had been caught up in a tornado, oak splinters and enormous pieces of flat iron and bolts began to rain onto the Falmouth's deck. John ran to the larboard rail for an unobstructed look at his foe. Whatever they had done, it was working, because the great ship had lost all headway, but for a slow turn to larboard.

"Larboard cannons, reload with barstock! Starboard cannons, haul in the starboard sheets!" Captain Jones shouted. "David, I want a starboard beam reach! We've a hole below the water line aft, and we'll sink if we don't keep her heeled over to larboard!" John and the four seamen set about their tasks as David watched the wind to select the optimum course. "That's good!" John called aft as he looked to the Walrus again. She was still floundering. "Hold that heading until we can assess damage and get a wet patch on that hole!" David pushed the tiller back to midships and then noticed something.

"Look, John!" David cried as he pointed at the Walrus. "Her rudder! It's gone! We beat the Walrus at her own game!"

"Aye, we beat her, but we've no time to glory in our small victory until we can get out of range and patch that hole." With their cannons reloaded, Barragan and Clark joined the others hauling the mainsail sheet to bring the great boom directly over the helm.

"Barragan," cried John, "you said you've some carpentry experience. Is that true?"

"Aye, Cap'n! I were a planker an' caulker...!"

"Not now!" cried John to shut the Irishman's mouth. "Can you make up a canvas patch and get it in place as soon as we put some distance between us and the Walrus?" Before Barragan could answer, a ball from one of the Walrus' forward swivel guns whistled overhead, followed a half second later by the cannon's report.

"I never done it 'afore, Cap'n," said Barragan as he ducked, "but I seen it once on that man-o'-war I were tellin' ya 'bout. Cap'n Jenkins told me he'd..."

"Do your best, man," said John, cutting the Irishman off again. "We've no more than an hour before we sink." John turned back to David. "I'm going below to see where that ball went. If we're lucky, it stopped somewhere inside the ship. If not, then we'll have two holes to repair."

As John descended the short ladder which led to his cabin, his fears were confirmed. Water was still flowing at a steady, but greatly reduced rate, from his open cabin door and forward, into the main hold, much to the pleasure of the one remaining green turtle. Once inside the cabin, it was immediately clear what had stopped the ball. In the center of the small cabin, where it had been pushed by the impact, lay the anchor chain. And inside its coils was the single six-inch ball, stopped dead in its linear path of destruction. As John made a quick assessment of the damage to the hull, he heard the ever-familiar crack of a second ball passing over his little ship. "Damn, we're still in range!" he cursed as the small ship lurched upright and water began flowing into the cabin once again.

"Don't mind him!" cried David at one of the hands as John stepped onto the deck. "Man the main sheet with Barragan till we're underway!"

As his eyes once again adjusted to the bright sunlight, John was met with screams and running men. The mainsail sheet trailed across the deck and over the rail into the sea. But worse, the great mainsail had swung out to larboard and the ship had lost her heel.

"What happened?" called John as he searched the rigging.

"Carini's been hit!" answered David as he pointed forward. Propped against the mainmast with his head resting in Clark's hands lay the young Italian, his left arm torn away at the shoulder.

"John!" called David from the tiller, "I need someone on that main sheet with Barragan!"

"Clark," ordered Captain Jones, "get back to your duties! We're still in range and we're taking on water!" The kneeling seaman looked up from his dying mate.

"Get back to 'em yerself, Mister Jones!" Clark hissed through tears and clenched teeth. "I'll not let Mario lay here to die fer any mains'l."

There's no time to argue about it now, thought John. The man could be disciplined later. He knew the Walrus wouldn't stop firing and Carini needed more than the mere hand-holding Clark was giving him.

"Etinger, man that mains'l sheet with Barragan!" John barked as he ran forward to the galley. He hoped, for Carini's sake, that the young Italian had put enough irons on the fire to cauterize his shoulder. "Good," he whispered as he pulled the three glowing instruments from deep within the coals. Their tips burned bright orange, appearing almost transparent from the heat. Returning to the injured seaman's side, John gave Clark an angry stare.

"Is he still alive?" Clark wouldn't look up. "Damn your sympathetic soul!" John gave him a rough kick to the knee. "You claim he's your friend, but if you don't help me, he'll bleed out in your arms!" Clark gave a jump and a cry of pain as he looked up.

"Turn him so I can see that shoulder!" ordered the captain as he knelt in the fresh blood.

"His arm - it's clean off, Cap'n!" cried Clark. "The ball hit him in the elbow an' tore his whole arm off!" Tears streamed down both of Clark's cheeks as he choked the words out. "Help him, sir! Please help him!"

"Turn him, Edgar! I have to see!" Just as Clark had said, the limb was gone, torn away at the shoulder. As the first of the three irons was applied to an open artery, Carini's body stiffened.

"Good!" said John. "He's still alive."

A sickening stream of blue smoke climbed quickly into the air, swirled about the mast and trailed over the lee rail. As the second iron was pressed against the wound, Carini's body relaxed. A moment later, the bleeding stopped. Clark looked up at his captain with a smile of gratitude.

"Ya did it, sir! Ya stopped the bleeding, just like a surgeon, ya did."

"It wasn't me that did it," said John as he stood and dropped the last iron to the deck. It gave out a cryptic hiss as it settled in the pool of blood. "The bleeding stopped because his heart isn't beating anymore. He's dead, Edgar. There was just too much damage." Clark eased his friend's limp body back to the deck and looked up. "There's nothing we can do for him, but there's a lot we'd best do for ourselves. We've a ship to sail and a hole to patch before we all join Carini."

The grieving seaman rose slowly to his feet and stood over his friend's torn and lifeless body.

"Has he any family?" asked Captain Jones.

"Yes," answered Barragan. "His parents live in Alexandria."

"We can't have him aboard that long. We'll have to bury him at sea. Can you tell his people what happened and give them his belongings?"

"I'll tell them, sir," answered Barragan as he moved to Clark's side.

"Come on, Edgar," said the older man as he put an arm over his mate's shoulder. "Cap'n Jones'll take care o' Mario. We got work to do."

At approximately 1500 yards from the floundering Walrus, the Falmouth's mainsail boom was finally pulled far to windward, flat against the wind, bring the small ship to a crawl. By adjusting the jib and mainsail, the wind was held on the starboard beam, keeping the little ship heeled over far enough to put the canvas patch in place while raising the hole above the waterline. Clark and Etinger, being the better swimmers, volunteered to pull the two larboard ropes under the keel to hold the lower two corners of the patch in place. Within an hour, the Falmouth Packet was once again underway, but no longer headed for Virginia.

"David, since we're damaged," said John, "I want to put in at Saint Helena Sound and anchor in the shallows for the night. If something happens to that patch, I don't want to be caught in deep water. I've checked in our hold and we don't have any planking to repair the hull."

"Think it'll hold through the night?" asked David.

"Oh, I'm sure of that, but we'll need to keep a man on the pump from now on, or at least until we make Charles Town. If I remember right, there are several large shipyards where we can get the wood and tools Barragan will need to fix her properly."

"The crew'll be glad to make port for a few days. And your ribs could use the time to begin knitting properly."

John walked to the larboard rail and peered at the thickly wooded coastline. "You wouldn't know there was anything wrong in America by looking at the place, would you?" He turned and leaned his backside against the rail. "When we make Charles Town, let's poke around a little. Maybe we can find out about the Navy."

On the 10th of January 1774, Captain Jones and his crew of five sailed past Sullivan's Lighthouse and into Charles Town Harbor. Barragan, being the oldest, was given the money for patching materials and set in charge over the two younger men.

"Albert," said John as he stepped across to Tipton's dock, "Mister Noble and I will be going into town on some business. Do what you can until dark and then let the men go on liberty. I believe it would be safe to use that stretch of beach just upstream to haul the packet down." John fished through the inside pocket of his waistcoat and produced four silver coins.

"Aye, aye, Cap'n!"

"And give each man one of these for dinner and entertainment." The Irishman knuckled his forehead in gratitude as he accepted the money.

"You and Mister Noble watch yerselves, now," admonished Barragan. "I been here 'afore an' there's some rough characters in some o' them taverns." The two assured the seaman they would be all right and then strode off along the dock.

As with Kings Town, Charles Town had it's long row of taverns strewn along the docks, catering to the animal needs of the men who had just come up from the sea. It was neither by tradition, nor design that these public houses served as the collection point for word from the four points of the compass. There was no better place for learning the latest news than the Patriot's Rest.

John and David took a small table at the back of the public room, near several well-dressed businessmen. The older of the four was very angry, so it wasn't difficult to overhear his conversation. As the two sat down, they caught the older man in mid-sentence.

"...taken about all they can, James. If the damned Brits don't back off soon, they're going to be up to here in..." He broke off as the younger man on his left put a hand of caution on the older man's arm. With a quick look about the tavern for spies, the older man continued in a quieter voice. "Word's come from the Committees of Correspondence in Virginia of some trouble at Griffin's Wharf in Boston Harbor in protest of this bloody tea tax. I read the letter myself and recognized the signatures of both Henry and Jefferson. Seems some 'Indians' dumped a whole shipload of 'monopoly tea' into the harbor the 16th of last month. Word has it that the Indian Chief's name was Sam Adams." The other three roared with laughter.

"Then that explains why the customs men locked up all the East India Company tea the other day in the government warehouses," said the man in the beaver hat. "They must be afraid a group of Charles Town Indians'll dump their tea in the harbor."

"Or maybe a Negro tea party?" the older man suggested, nearly choking in laughter. Catching his breath, he continued. "But there's more, gentlemen. That same letter spoke of a new Quartering Act, which is expected to take effect any day." The others stopped laughing and leaned slightly forward. "As you know, the present law allows British troops to take quarters in taverns and unoccupied buildings. This new law expands that older one to include private homes."

"I'll be damned before any Brit's going to sleep in my house uninvited!" yelled the man with the mustache. The others tried to calm him down.

"Well, hell!" he continued against their cautions. "Mother England's sitting on her brain again, and this time she's gonna get bit! She's got a treasure chest in these American Colonies. Yet, to pacify a few whimpering British merchants who don't have the mettle to compete with us, or lack the foresight to adjust to this new source of commerce, she's going to tax us until we revolt! I tell you gentlemen, this pressure can't be contained much longer."

"You don't know how prophetic your last words are, Christopher." It was the older gentleman speaking, once again just above a whisper. "There's strong evidence that most of the members of the Marine Committee have been chosen, and that Esek Hopkins will be selected as Commander in Chief of the Continental Navy."

"But why not you, Mister Forrestal?" asked one of the others.

"I've the name, but not the military background for it, William. No, Hopkins would be the best choice. Besides, I'm too old and broken in body for the strain."

"How soon do you think they'll be outfitting ships and selecting the men to man them, Alex?"

The older man leaned forward to answer. "I'll be laying the keels for two large Dutch brigs at my yard this summer, William. I expect them to be ready to float by the following spring at the latest. Depending on the decisions made between now and then, they can become merchantmen or frigates."

John and David had heard enough. A Continental Navy was more than a rumor, and possibly within a year! They paid for their drinks and left the tavern to look for the provisions they would need to continue their trip.

CHAPTER 4

Charles Town is situated on a point of land between the Ashley and Cooper rivers, and six miles from the open Atlantic Ocean. Most of the adjacent countryside consists of low farm and pasture lands, little elevated above tide water, making the city liable to occasional inundation from ocean swells. It was early morning of the third day when the Falmouth Packet's repairs were finally completed. The crew stood at attention while John made his inspection.

"You do fine work, Barragan," said Captain Jones from under the hull. "I've no doubt whatsoever that she'll be seaworthy."

"Thank you, sir!" said Barragan with a quick look to Etinger and Clark.

"David," said John as he walked past the rudder, "I've some business with the harbor master. Would you oversee her launching and the loading of our new provisions?"

"Don't worry, John. We'll be ready to sail when you return."

By 1000 hours, Captain Jones had signed clearance papers for departure. As he walked past the Patriot's Rest, he could just make out the Falmouth being pushed away from the beach for the short haul back to Tipton's dock. By 1100 hours, the newly repaired vessel was once again underway. Upon David's orders, she spread her sails in the morning breeze and took up a starboard reach toward the partially built Fort Sullivan. Three days before, when the crippled craft had entered Charles Town harbor, a large merchantman lay aground on the sandbar which blocked most of the entrance to the bay. Passing close by the fort, Noble ordered the ship slightly to windward to follow the seaward side of Sullivan's Island, and then into the open waters. By noon on the thirtieth of January, the Falmouth Packet was once again en route to the north coast of Virginia.

As the crew finished their noon meal of fresh fruit, biscuits and salt pork, Captain Jones stepped up on deck from his cabin. He held a leather bag. After a quick survey of the rigging, he stepped near the main mast.

"Assemble for Captain's Mast!" David and the remaining three crewmen looked at the young Scotsman with puzzlement.

"Captain's Mast!?" asked David. "What on earth..?"

"Seaman Clark, front and center!" demanded John.

"You have to be jokin', Captain Jones!" answered Clark as he stood and stepped toward John. "What did I do now?"

"It's what you did when Carini was killed. Not only were you insubordinate, but you disobeyed a direct order to man the mains'l during battle."

"And you're gonna punish me now, nearly two weeks after it happened!?"

"I could have you hung for what you did, but considering your worth to the crew, you'll receive only six lashes," answered John as he pulled the cat-of-nine-tails from its bag.

David and the others stood looking at John for several moments.

"Etinger and Barragan, tie Clark to the main!" demanded John as he held the cat out to David. The two seamen did not move.

"Not me, Captain!" David said with a snarl.

"Is this simply disobedience, or are you inciting a mutiny, Mister Noble?"

"It's not a mutiny, so it must be simple disobedience! I'll not be the instrument of your anger."

John suddenly realized the stupidity of his actions, but the cat was out of the bag and by tradition, had to be laid against someone's back before it was returned. The standoff continued for another two minutes when Clark finally stepped forward to the mast and wrapped his arms about it in surrender. The others backed away slightly as John positioned himself to apply the punishment. The wind seemed to die and the sun lost part of its brightness during those six lashes. When the cat was once again in it's bag, the others helped Clark below to his rack and attended to his wounds with an application of salve.

The twelve day trip from Charles Town was uneventful, except for two separate colonial merchantmen they had observed being detained by British men-of-war near the Cape Hatteras Inlet. Although there was not yet a formal blockade to colonial shipping, the 'pressure', mentioned by the elderly gentleman at the Patriot's Rest, was certainly apparent.

On the tenth of February, just before change of watch, Captain Jones came from his cabin with a chart of the North Virginia coastline. "David, when I take the helm at eight bells, I want to speak to the men. I've decided where we'll dock the Falmouth."

"I'll pass the word, John," answered David.

"You'll address me as Captain while we're under sail, Mister Noble."

"Sorry...Captain," the lad answered sarcastically. He, like the rest of the crew, had taken a dislike to their young master ever since his flogging of seaman Clark.

When Captain Jones took the helm at 1600 hours, David and the three seaman stood just aft of the main mast as ordered. The chart John had been studying lay tacked to the deck before him.

"I don't know whether Mister Noble has told you yet, but we should reach the Potomac River tomorrow." He pointed to the large body of water with the tip of his sword. "As you can see, there are several small towns on the east bank of the river where we can dock. Mister Noble and I will be going to Fredericksburg, so we'll be landing as close to that place as possible." He looked at each of the men. "The map shows a small town named Dalgren, about twenty-four miles from Fredericksburg where we should be able to turn the Falmouth over to another master." He waited for the men to answer. "Since there are no objections, Dalgren it is."

By now, the two younger seamen looked to Barragan for leadership, and let him be their spokesman when it came to matters with the captain.

"Dalgren'll be just fine, Cap'n," answered the Irishman nervously. "Clark an' me, we got family in Hanover township, an' Etinger'll be goin' along with us fer a job. Dalgren's 'bout as close as any place else, Cap'n."

"Good," said John as he took up the chart and stowed it in the binnacle.

"David," said John as he closed the binnacle and turned the latch, "something's been eating at me."

"That you waited so long to flog Clark?"

"If that's an attempt at insubordination, Mister Noble, then go on! Until we dock in Virginia and I give up command of the Falmouth, I'm in command and you will be subject to me!"

"Sorry, Captain," said David with a slight blush. "I was out of line. What was it you wished to ask me?"

"Do you have any idea why the Walrus would attack us?"

"I've been thinking about that also, and all I can figure is that it's the cannons."

"The cannons?

"My father got them from Joshua Smoot."

"I don't understand. If Smoot wanted the cannons..." John broke off to consider. "The cannons are in King's Town."

"It's complicated, Captain."

"Then uncomplicate it for me. We nearly got killed, for God's sake!"

"There was a Dutch merchantman on its way from Scotland to the Colonies. Smoot figured she'd be a good prize so he took her, only to find out all she was carrying were hundreds of bolts of cloth."

"What's that have to do with your father's cannons?"

"I'm getting to that."

"Sorry. Go on."

"Smoot figured the cloth wasn't worth that much so decided to bargain with my father for a fast French Corvette. My father knew a market for the cloth so agreed to trade ship for ship, straight across and Smoot went his way with the new Walrus."

"The one that attacked us off Cuba." David nods.

"It was a week before my father discovered the cannons. They were in the bilge...used for ballast. When word got back to Smoot, he was furious."

"He wanted his cannons back," asked John.

"Right."

"And when your father refused?"

"Pirates like to take important people for ransom," said David. "He must have known somehow I was aboard the Falmouth."

"You for the cannons. That makes sense."

Before Dawn on 15 February, while John and David lay asleep in their cabin, Barragan steered the small sloop from the Potomac River into Machotick Creek, a small tributary several miles short of their intended landfall. Between the cannons lay three duffle bags. At Barragan's signal, Clark and Etinger moved quietly to the bow with pike poles to help ease the ship onto a mud bank. Only Captain Jones stirred as the slow moving craft came to a quiet rest.

"David?" said John as he raised himself on an elbow and looked about. The younger man groaned and threw an arm across his eyes to block out the light. "Did you feel something?"

"What is it, Captain?" David groaned. "My watch already?"

"No, it's not your watch. I felt something." John sat up and pulled on his boots. "I think we've gone aground." Within a minute John was back, dragging his companion up from his makeshift bed of sailcloth.

"Get up!" John demanded. "I was right, and those three seamen your father gave us have jumped ship!"

"Aground? Jumped ship?" Confused, David followed John to the deck where they quickly scanned their surroundings. The men were indeed gone, swallowed up by the thick trees and dense fog hanging over the creek. Their deep footprints in the mud were the only testimony that they had been aboard.

"Do you have any idea where we are?"

"No," answered John as he looked up and down the narrow waterway. "This is obviously not the Potomac, and there's no telling how far we've come since I came down from watch last night."

"What about Dalgren? Are we going back to the Potomac?"

"No," answered John as he walked aft toward their cabin. "We'll take what valuables we can carry and leave the ship here."

"But..." David began to protest as he followed John down the short ladder.

"I suppose we can tell somebody about her when we reach the first settlement. Otherwise, she's the property of the first to find her."

"But won't we be in trouble with Lloyds or somebody?"

"Not at all," said John angrily as he began throwing his things into his duffle bag. "The log still shows James Jones as her master, and I plan to resume using my real name from now on. Get your things together. I don't want to stay aboard any longer than we must."

Within a half hour, the two young travelers were walking across the frozen mud, through the same trees their crew had so recently used for their escape. By John's estimate from the ships compass and his memory of the area, they would reach a roadway within a day or two, which would then take them northward into Fredericksburg.

The following article appeared in Purdie & Dixon's Virginia Gazette, published at Williamsburg on 17 March 1774:

Virginia Gazette

Purdie & Dixon
Williamsburg, Virginia   17 March 1774

Some time last month a sloop of about 100 hogsheads burthen stood in for Machotick Creek, on the Potomac, and ran aground on a mud bank a little way up the creek. Soon after, a decent well looking man and his young companion of slightly lesser years, both dressed in black, with gold laced hats, came on shore from the sloop, and calling at a gentlewoman's house in the neighborhood, told her they were bound for Alexandria, to purchase a load of wheat, but that their hands had left them, and they wanted the loan of two horses to carry them to Leeds Town, to engage others. Being disappointed in getting the horses, they went to a planter's house a few miles distant, where they lodged all night, went off in the morning, and were never heard of since. On their way they stopped at a petty ordinary, where they left three ruffled shirts, a neat fouling piece in a cherry wood case, and a great coat; but the older man carried with him a pair of saddle bags, which the landlord concluded, from their weight, contained a considerable sum of money. After the vessel had continued near a fortnight in the creek, with her sails standing, some of the gentlemen in the neighborhood went on board; and upon search- ing her, found neither provisions nor water, chests, papers, or any other ef- fects, than one feather bed, a gold laced hat, a sailor's jacket, a pair of trou- sers, some cooking utensils, and two sea compasses made in Salem and four small ship's cannons. She is a long sharp-built vessel, with only a cabin, containing five berths, and hold. On her stern is painted, in white letters, Falmouth Packet; and the same words, in white Letters made of cloth, are on her pendant.

A two-day-old snow had turned to a muddy slush, making the last three miles to Fredericksburg both cold and difficult for the two weary travelers. As John and David approached the modest home of William Paul, a young boy with red cheeks and a runny nose hurried by with a quarter cord of firewood on a pull sled. Al- though it was not unusual for strangers to be seen coming and going from the Paul residence, the lad gave the two a suspicious glance as he quickened his pace.

"We must look a sight," said John as he attempted to brush some mud from his stockings.

"You certainly do." said David as he straightened his hair with his hands. "How much further to your brother's home?"

"Unless he's moved in the last couple years, that should be his house just ahead."

The Paul residence was a modest affair, typical for a prosperous merchant or shopkeeper. It was two-storied, of grey stone, with two chimneys; one standing above the parlor and the other from the kitchen at the back of the house. A double row of rose bushes covered with tight buds lined the short walkway leading to the single large front door. A few of last autumn's orange colored leaves scuttled past the travelers feet in the icy wind as they walked the short pathway and gained the modest protection of the enclosed porch. John paused before lifting the iron knocker to announce their arrival.

"You'll like my brother," said John dryly, "he's nothing at all like me." David wasn't sure how to take the remark, so he simply smiled as he sniffed and wiped his runny nose.

"When did you see him last?"

"Hmmm, I reckon it was late '68 or early '69," answered John as he lifted the knocker and let it fall against the heavy oak door. "Six years or ten, if we don't get out of this cold, William won't be able to recognize me for the body parts I'll lose shortly to the frostbite."

A very attractive young woman opened the door several inches and held it against the cold. "May I help you?" she asked.

"Uh..." John stammered. "Who are you?"

"I'm Dorothea Dandridge," she answered as she closed the door slightly. "Who are you?"

"I'm..." John began. "We've come from Kings Town to see William Paul. Has he moved away?"

"He still lives here, but he's with his doctor and can't receive any guests."

"His doctor? Is he ill?" asked John, concerned.

"If you're not going to give me your names or your business with Mister Paul, I'm afraid you'll have to go, sirs."

"I'm his younger brother, John, and this is my traveling companion, David Noble."

"Why didn't you say something sooner?" she asked as she opened the door and ushered them into the hallway. "Wait here and I'll see if the doctor is finished." As the two weary travelers unwrapped their coats and scarfs, Dorothea walked up the hallway to the parlor door. A temporary bed had been placed near the fire place for the sick man.

"Excuse me, sirs," Dorothea began, "but there are two gentlemen from Kings Town to see William." She stepped into the parlor and continued. "One of them claims to be your younger brother, John."

The two men sat close to the warming fire, William in a large wingback chair and Doctor Read on a stool at his right side. The flickering light from the large fireplace cast a dancing patchwork of amber shadows across the parlor.

William was thirty-five, a full nine years older than John and the oldest son of John and Jean Paul of Kirkcudbright, Scotland. He stood three inches taller than his younger brother, but his chronic illness had reduced his former bulk of a hundred and sixty pounds to what resembled a stack of yard under rain-soaked sailcloth. Dr. Read, at least ten years William's senior, rose and stepped into the hall where John and David waited.

"I'm pleased to make your acquaintance," said the doctor as he took the younger man's outstretched hand. "Your brother has told me many stories about your exploits."

"Thank you, sir. I hope they were accurate."

"They were!" cried William as he pushed himself up from the wingback and turned to greet John. But before he could take a step toward the hallway, he was convulsed into a fit of deep rasping coughs, bringing both John and Dorothea to his side.

"Good Lord, man," cried John as they helped him back to his chair, "what's gotten hold of you?" William tried to answer, but could only choke out two or three unintelligible syllables. John gave the young woman an inquiring look, wondering who she was and what had happened to his brother. She met his stare with a sympathetic scowl.

"It's just a cold," whispered William through his kerchief as he settled back into the warm chair and struggled to pull the lap blanket across his knees. "I picked it up a few weeks ago, and these two insist on treating me like an old lady."

As the young girl helped William with the blanket, David stepped close to the fire.

"Who's this?" asked William as he accepted his cup of hot tea and laudanum.

"This is my good friend and traveling companion, David Noble," John said as David stepped to William. "David, this is my older brother, William."

"Well, well," sang William as he pumped David's hand. "This is a special treat. John's never had a close friend before."

"He has one now, sir," said David as he handed his raincoat to Dorothea and turned his backside to the fire. There was an uneasy moment as Dorothea gave William a scolding look.

"Forgive me, dear," whispered William through his kerchief, "but with all this attention you and the doctor have given me, I've forgotten my manners." William struggled to his feet. "Gentlemen, this fair lass isn't my housekeeper, as I've mistakenly allowed you to believe. Other than my tormentor, Dr. Read, she's one of the few friends I have left in this world. She's Dorothea Dandridge, one of Virginia's finest young ladies, and a most capable nurse, I must add."

She was now at William's side, facing the two cold travelers. William touched her hand. "Why, without her constant help these past three weeks, I would surely have succumbed to this dreadful cough." Dorothea gave the ailing Mister Paul a motherly pat on the shoulder.

"I'm very pleased to meet you, John. William's told me so much about you," she said, holding their rain-soaked outer garments firmly to her. "And welcome to Virginia, Mister Noble. Please excuse me while I put these wet things on the back porch." She hurried off and was back in a few minutes with two large mugs of hot apple cider.

"So, tell me," began William, "what brings you and David to Virginia?" John took a sip of his warm drink as he considered how to answer. Before he could form his words, David was already speaking.

"It's the Continental Navy!" he blurted. "John and I have come to seek commissions so we can go fight the British."

"Is that true, John?" asked William, turning to his younger brother.

"Well..."

"You were never one to get involved in politics, much less fight somebody else's battle. You're a Scotsman like me, and this war that's brewing between these Americans and their King has nothing to do with us." A thick silence hung over the room while the four waited for John's side of the story.

"My young friend tends to exaggerate sometimes." He paused to take another sip of his cider and give David a stern look. "What I really want is to purchase a small plantation of my own where I can live someday in leisure."

"That's the John Paul I remember!" shouted William, throwing himself into another fit of painful coughing. Dorothea crossed to the sideboard where she fetched a fresh kerchief to replace the blood-stained one William had been using.

"I'm a little low on funds right now," whispered William as he wiped his mouth, "but you're free to stay here while you raise the money you'll need." He thought for a moment and brightened. "I might even know of one or two small farms nearby that you could have for next to nothing." As William choked out the words, John couldn't help but notice the high sign Dorothea was giving him.

"William," she interrupted, "why don't you and the good doctor talk to David about their sea voyage for a few minutes while I get your brother to help me with the goose?" She looked to John. "You do know how to carve a roast goose, don't you?"

"Just lead the way, Miss Dandridge." He pulled his sword halfway from its sheath and winked at his older brother. "I've been known to carve a few geese in my day." Turning, he followed the young woman to the hallway and toward the kitchen.

"Miss Dandridge?" he asked as they reached the kitchen. "I got the impression that you wanted to speak with me alone."

"Your impression is correct, Mister Paul," she answered. Tears had begun to well in her eyes as she lowered herself into one of the two kitchen chairs. "I...I don't really know where to begin."

"Are you and my brother..." began John as he seated himself across the table, but fell silent when he realized such a question might not be appropriate. He pulled a wadded, not so clean kerchief from his back pocket and offered it to dry her tears. She thanked him but declined.

"There's nothing going on between your brother and me, Mister Paul. I live a half-day's journey to the west, in Hanover County. I've been a very close friend of your brother and his wife, Helen, for several years." She paused to wipe a tear from her cheek. Would you be offended if I spoke candidly, Mister Paul?"

"Not at all," John said. "And please call me John."

"Your brother is a very selfish man."

"I know that."

"Then it won't surprise you that his selfishness has driven his wife away." She searched her soul for strength. "You can't imagine how painful it's been watching William..." She stopped to choke back a sob. "I've stood by him during these last several months since she left him, watching the toll the affair has taken on him, both mentally and physically."

"His illness?" John glanced back toward the parlor as his brother began to cough once more. "How long has he been this way?"

"More than four months. And before it's finished, I fear he'll lose more than just his wife." She lowered her head and began to sob quietly.

"Are you saying he may die?"

"It isn't just a cough, as William claims. Dr. Read says it's consumption, and he told me this very evening that he doesn't expect William to make it through the spring." John rose to his feet and walked to the door, looking back toward the parlor. The coughing had stopped for the moment.

"But there must be something..." He turned back to meet the teary stare of the young women. "Surely a change of climate?" She shook her head.

"It's too late for that. I suggested it to the Doctor, but he said any trip would only weaken him further."

"Then why not a medication or a poultice? There must be something," he said as he walked back to the small table. She could feel his pain and frustration, for it had been her own for several months.

"I know it would be presumptuous of me to say I love William as much as you do, but he's been like my older brother, also." She reached forward and took John's hand in an attempt to comfort his troubled spirit. He didn't pull back. His eyes ran over her peach-smooth face like a child across a spring meadow, fascinated at the way the blond ringlets caressed her delicate throat and how her light blue eyes reminded him of raindrops on alabaster. Remembering why she had brought him to the kitchen, he dropped her hand.

"Does he know?" asked John quietly. "Has he been told how bad his condition is?" She shook her head no. "Surely he must suspect something, what with no improvement in so many months."

"No, neither Dr. Read or I have had the courage to tell him. But I'm sure you're correct; that he suspects the worst." She paused for a moment and continued. "I've already told my father that I'll be staying with William as long as he needs me, and he's consented. But now that you and your friend David are here, I..."

"Please don't leave, Miss Dandridge," John pleaded. "William needs you. And besides, David and I wouldn't know how to care for him properly." She considered for a moment.

"If you're sure I wouldn't be in the way..."

"In the way! My brother needs a nurse more than he needs two extra mouths to feed."

"Very well. I'll stay." She dried her face on her apron and looked back toward the parlor. "I think we'd best be getting back to your brother and the others. It's early yet to carve the goose, and besides, William will be anxious to hear of your recent adventures--of which I'm certain there must be many."

As they entered the parlor, David was in the middle of the cannon battle between the Walrus and the Falmouth Packet.

"You'd have loved it," cried David with his arms flung wide. "Alacan the Turk had just been parcelled and blown to the four winds when Captain Paul lowered his slow match to the touch hole of the second cannon!" William noticed John and Dorothea first.

"And where have you two been for so long?" He winked at John. "Goose all carved?"

"Not yet," answered John. "Miss Dandridge checked the bird and decided it needed a little more time."

"Your friend is quite the storyteller," said Dr. Read. "I'm anxious to hear your version of the adventure and why you left your shipping company in Tobago to come to America."

"How much did David tell you?"

"Just that you had to kill one of your crewmen in Tobago," answered William with an accusing tone. "Is that true?"

"It was a mutiny," John said as he watched Dorothea return to the kitchen. "I had no choice."

"But why wouldn't you remain for a trial?" asked William. "Surely you were provoked."

"True," agreed John, "I had to run the man through. He was attacking me. But even though Tobago's a British Colony, there's an informal political system amongst the natives I could never have survived."

"Now that I find difficult to believe," interjected William with a muffled cough.

"That's because you don't know the natives as I do, William, and neither do you know who recommended I flee. It was none other than the Lieutenant Governor."

"And that's how you ended up in Kings Town?" asked Dr. Read.

"My intention was to turn myself in at the nearest Admiralty, but…"

"And?" asked William, with his familiar accusing tone.

"When the master of the Falmouth Packet took ill with malaria and asked that I take his ship on to Jamaica, I decided I could report my affair as easily in that place as anywhere else."

"Did you?" asked William.

"Did I what?

"Did you report it?

"I didn't get a chance, what with all…"

"I figured as much," said William with a wry smile. "And what's this that David tells us about you taking on the surname of Jones? Sounds to me like you'd decided long before Jamaica that you were headed for America."

"Well, yes and no," said John nervously. He gave David another angry stare. "I took on the surname so I could sign the port clearance papers as we made our rounds of the islands. It was only after I got to Jamaica and found out that David and I could continue to America that I decided to retain it."

"David also tells us you left your ship on a mud bank on the Machotick," said Dr. Read. "What do you intend to do with it?"

"It belongs to a Michael McClure of Cork," answered John. "I was hoping to find a new master for her when we passed through Leeds Town; someone who might sail her back to England."

"And?" asked the doctor.

"There were no takers."

"I have a friend," began the doctor, "an Irishman named Allan Cosgrove who is looking for a ship to sail back to Ireland. Shall I ask him to speak with you?"

"By all means," answered John, "provided my brother can keep from telling the King's men about me." He gave William a hard look.

"Would I do that?" asked William with a look of childlike innocence. "I don't want you to get the idea I'm forcing you into anything, but I've a proposition for you, little brother."

"A proposition?"

"I had to close my tailor shop just over a month ago. If you were inclined to open and run it for me until I'm back on my feet, say in exchange for..."

"Your silence?" John hissed through narrow eyes.

"Now, there you go!" William looked to the good Doctor and the lad from Jamaica, and then back to John. "Do you think I'd...?"

"Of course you would!" answered John as he considered the offer. "Assuming I'd agree to your...uh, proposition, how are we to split the profits?"

"In twain, naturally. I'd have it no other way."

"And what about David? He'll be needing an income as well." He leaned forward and pointed a finger at the older man. "Split the profit three ways, with each getting equal shares, and we'll do it." William wanted such an arrangement from the start and chuckled to himself.

"Agreed!"

"William," John whispered as he leaned close, "promise me you'll keep all this about the trouble in Tobago and my temporary surname from Miss Dandridge."

"Why, of course, John," he answered with a wry smile. "Anything for my new business partner."

"Keep what from me, William?" Miss Dandridge stood at the parlor door with a mixing spoon in her hand.

"Nothing important," William lied. "Just... man talk."

"Man talk, eh?" she said with a huff and a wave of the spoon. "Here's a little woman talk for you. Supper will be on the table in five minutes. If you don't wash up now, you'll go without." As she turned to leave, William stood and imitated her scolding manner to the others.

"Watch it, William," she scolded. "You're not too old or too ill to be spanked."

"Oops!" said William sheepishly.

"Do you need help to the back porch?" asked John as he took his brother's arm.

"No," William answered as he pushed himself up from the wingback, "I'll be fine. You two go first. I'd rather wait here with the good doctor till the food's actually on the table."

The two young travelers walked down the hallway past the kitchen and stopped at the door to the back porch.

"John," said David as he pushed the door open, "your brother doesn't look at all well."

"He has consumption."

"Is it bad?"

"As bad as it can be."

"Then he'll..." David handed the lye soap to John and shook his head slowly in sympathy. "Why is it that we always lose the people we love the most?"

"I don't know, David. I don't know."

Supper was a symphony of flavors. The young goose was spiced and baked to perfection, with plates of fresh string beans, pickled peaches and honeyed yams on the side. The delicious aromas and provocative flavors were the best the two seafaring men had experienced in months; far better than the constant diet of turtle soup and salt pork they had eaten en route to Virginia. The hot cornbread and molasses was a special treat for David, for it was exactly as his mother had made for him when he was a child. William ate very little, but made up for it with conversation.

Midway through dinner, an icy wind blew up the hallway, through the dining room and out past the kitchen, followed by the front door closing solidly. All eyes were riveted on the hallway as a man's footsteps approached.

"Well, I'll be parcelled and thrown to the tax collectors!" cried William Paul as he twisted in his chair to see his unexpected guest. "If it isn't Patrick Henry himself!"

While the statesman laid his saddlebags and coat in the corner, Dorothea brought a sixth chair from the wall and pushed it up next to the doctor.

"Good evening, Dorothea," Patrick said as he kissed her on the cheek. "You're looking beautiful as usual." Dorothea blushed as John sent a questioning look to this elderly intruder. He had heard of Patrick Henry, but only as a rebel to the King.

"And how's our patient tonight?" Patrick asked as he placed a cautious hand on the sick man's arm.

"Oh, much better," answered William with a cough. Everyone knew it to be a lie except William, and even he suspected Dorothea and Dr. Read were hiding the truth from him.

"And who might these two seafaring gentlemen be?" asked Patrick, as he took a well-used kerchief from his waistcoat and blew the chill from his nose. John and David looked down at their clothing, amazed he could tell their profession by their dress.

"It's the smell of the sea which betrays you, good sirs. You'll not be rid of it until you've had a thorough bathing and William sews you a new set of clothes. Besides, William's talked of his younger brother the seaman, and you match the description to a tee."

"Forgive me, sirs," begged William, "but for the second time in one evening I've failed as a proper host." The tailor began to stand, but sank back into his chair at Patrick's protest.

"As you've correctly guessed," began William, "this is my little brother, John. And the young man at his side is his friend and traveling companion, David Noble. They've just arrived from Kings Town this night, and they've had some grand adventures en route." William gave David a quick glance, and looked back to Patrick.

"David was just telling us about an encounter they had with pirates off the coast of South Carolina," added Dr. Read.

"Pirates, you say?" asked Patrick with a raise of the brow. "Finally a topic William and I can discuss without the clash of writer's quill and tailor's needle."

"And I suppose the clothes-making business is too boring for you?" spat William. He and the lawyer had a long running argument over which profession was the most valuable or noble.

"Do I detect a wounded spirit?" Patrick was thrilled that he finally got back at the tailor for all the jabs against the legal profession and those who called it ignoble. "I don't know that I'd call it boring, but I've never heard of a person getting their blood up over a pair of knickers."

"And what would you wear before a judge if it weren't for the fine clothes I've fashioned for you!?"

"I didn't intend it as an attack, William, but since it was so well executed, I'll just let it stand." Dorothea set a glass of brandy beside Patrick's plate as she gave William a mother's look of anger.

"Ah!" said Patrick as he grabbed Dorothea around the waist and gave her a tickle. "Thank you, my dear. My mouth's been waiting for this for the past three or four hours."

"Is that all your mouth's been waiting for?" she asked with an edge.

"And the sweet lips of my fiancé," he said as he pulled her close and kissed her long and hard. She pulled away, embarrassed.

John was irritated by the display of affection, and it showed on his face.

"You seem concerned about something, John," said Patrick. "Didn't William tell you about me?" Patrick gave William a nudge in the ribs. William was still in a bristle from the last jab and jerked away from the friendly poke.

"We didn't have time, Patrick," answered William. "John and his friend have only been here for a little over an hour, and we've done nothing but talk about their voyage." William took a sip of his brandy and wiped his mouth on his shirtsleeve. Patrick became impatient.

"Well if you're not going to tell them about me, I'll have to," said Patrick. John and David looked at the newcomer. "I've been a close friend of your brother for the better part of five years. It is he who has graciously supplied me with most of my clothing, and at no cost, I must gratefully add. His kindness has indirectly provided a substantial part of the tuition to become a lawyer. And but for his kindness this cold evening, I'd probably spend it in a stable."

"And I'm not so sure you don't deserve that bed of straw either, the way you barged in tonight without an invitation," said William as he took a sip of his drink and pushed the conversation in a new direction. "But enough of that. What new treason have you and your little band of renegades hatched since we last spoke?"

"Why do you insist on provoking me, William? The things I'm involved in will affect you as surely as any other man in the Colonies, be he loyal to the King or not."

"Oooh..." snickered William. "Who's getting testy now?"

"Gentlemen!" interrupted Dr. Read. "Can we keep this civil?"

Both men sat upright in their chairs as if scolded by a stern schoolmaster.

"I'm sorry, Patrick," said William with a quick look to Dr. Read. "Watching you get worked up about this trouble with the King is about the only stimulation I've gotten since I caught this damned cold."

"Apology accepted," said Patrick, "and I'm equally to blame. Sometimes I get so caught up with all of this that I lose my sense of humor."

"But what of the war?" asked David.

"What business is that of yours?" asked Patrick as he stood and walked to the fireplace mantle where three clay pipes lay in a neat row. He selected the longest one, broke off a half inch of used stem and began filling it with tobacco. "You're a Jamaican. What do you two know of the troubles in the Colonies?"

"Plenty!" cried David before John could speak. "We know about Sam Adams dumping all that monopoly tea up in Boston Harbor last month, and the Quartering Act that includes private residences."

"Interesting," said Patrick. "Anything else?"

"Yes, sir," answered David proudly. "We also know that Esek Hopkins will be appointed as Commander in Chief of the new navy."

"You know quite a bit," said Patrick as he lit the pipe and puffed it alive. "And you think you qualify as officers?"

"Tell him, John," said David as he gave his friend a nudge. "Tell him that's why we came to Virginia."

"Well, John?" asked Patrick as he blew a smoke ring. "Does your young friend speak for you also?"

"Not exactly."

"But you told my father..." cried David.

"No, David. You told your father I was coming to America to join their navy."

"Then why..?"

"Not now," said John.

A long and uncomfortable silence hung over the dining room until William finally spoke.

"Patrick?" asked William. "I'm assuming you'll avail yourself of my hospitality and stay the night in my stable."

"Ah," sang out Patrick. "Your grace abounds, Mister Paul." Patrick took up his saddlebags and coat and waited for a sign from his host.

"I was only joking, Patrick! You can stay in your regular room and these other two will take the guest room in the North wing. Dr. Read already has his place with me." William gave the doctor a poke with his fork.

"Ouch!"

"He's almost like a pet," said William as he threw a scrap of bread onto the doctor's plate, "the way I've been keeping him by my side these last three days."

The Paul Tailor Shop was located a hundred yards from William Paul's home, on Allenby Street, in a row of several other small shops. The large hall upstairs was used by the sail maker next door, and served as a meeting place every Friday night for the Masons. Provided with a list of William's previous employees, John and David made a personal visit to each, with an offer to return to their old jobs. Then, using the shop's last three years of receipts, the two new proprietors circulated printed handouts to as many of William's regular customers as they could locate. Within a week, three of the four previous tailors were once again at work, and nearly all of the past clientele had returned.

"Dorothea," called William from his place near the fireplace, "it's after five. Won't John and David be returning from the shop in a few minutes?"

"Oh my!" she said as she set William's tray of picked-at food on the hearth and began to walk quickly from the room.

"You're in love with my brother, aren't you?" Dorothea stopped at the door and turned, placing her hands on her hips with her head tilted like a schoolgirl.

"It isn't love," she giggled. Her bubbly laughter rivaled the sound of sleigh bells. "I just enjoy watching John and David come home. That's all."

"Of course!" agreed William with a toothy grin. The young woman gave a huff and spun away. A moment later, she sat in the window seat of her second story bedroom, watching for her young man to turn the corner onto their street.

Just as they had done for a month, John and David appeared from behind the large birch tree at the corner of Allenby and Meadowbrook Lane, throwing a ball of tailor's twine back and forth across the street. With the last throw, they broke into a foot race to the front door. As usual, David reached the door first, and received a special treat from the pantry.

William's condition worsened in mid-March, confining him to his bed. Dr. Read had done all that he could and had left laudanum and the necessary instructions for the dying man's care. It was a trying time for the three to stand by helplessly as William lost more weight, along with his desire to live. It was especially difficult for Dorothea in the last weeks, having to care for the poor soul in his decimated condition. On the 28th of July, almost exactly when the doctor had predicted, William Paul died of advanced tuberculosis. As agreed, Dorothea returned to her father's plantation in Hanover County, some fifteen miles to the Southwest.

Throughout the summer and fall of '74, John and David were regular guests at the Dandridge estate, spending the entire second weekend of each month. Captain Dandridge and John had become the best of friends and Dorothea had fallen deeply in love with John.

Unbeknown to John, David had maintained a regular correspondence with his father in Kings Town. On the 20th of January 1775, a letter arrived at the counting house of Charles Noble.

> Dear Father,
>
> I am writing to you with great concern and frustration. I now agree fully with your first estimation of Uncle Silver's plan, and not without reason. It was, as you predicted, only a pipe dream. Do you remember me telling you about the tailor shop John inherited from his brother? Well, it's doing much better than John and I expected. So well, in fact, that Captain Jones is on the verge of asking Dorothea for her hand in marriage and purchasing a farm in the countryside. I've lost all hope that he still intends to seek that naval commission.
>
> The only impediment to the Captain's matrimonial plans lie with her father, Nathaniel West Dandridge. It is no secret that he intends that his daughter marries Patrick Henry, but Captain Jones doesn't seem at all put off by this paternal insistence.
>
> I'm certain Uncle Silver has erred, Father, and I believe my continued presence in Virginia is without purpose. I would like to come home as soon as possible. Please advise.
>
> Your son,
> David Noble

A thick course of raucous laughter erupted from the public room as Charles Noble stepped through the arched doorway of Silver Jack's tavern. He held David's folded letter in his left hand as he scanned the dimly lit room for his older brother.

"Charles!" came the excited cry of John Silver from his left. "So, ye've decided to take me up on me bet after all!"

Charles strode to the table where John had just set out a half dozen tankards of warm ale and had begun collecting the empties.

"I'm not here for your stupid bet!"

"Now it's a stupid bet?"

"Morbid is more like it," scolded Charles.

"The scurvy swabs'll die whether we lay a wager on their heads or not, little brother, so I don't see the harm in it."

"Aye!" cried one of the intoxicated seamen at the table as he wiped the warm foam from his beard. "An' if'n the King's Men don't sink 'em, then the toredo worms will!"

"You'd bet on anything, wouldn't you?"

"Life be one bet after 'nother, little brother," laughed Silver as he winked at one of the drunk seamen. "It be the spice what makes the livin' palatable, as me more sophisticated clientele would say."

"Well, big brother," answered Charles as he raised the letter, "this is one meal that might have lost it's flavor altogether."

"Aaaah.," said Silver as he gave the seamen an apologetic shrug. "You good sirs'll hafta 'scuze me fer a glass while I have a word with Charley, here," the old pirate said as he set the empty tankards on a nearby table. Snatching the letter from Charles' hand, he marched toward his private office with his familiar clicking leg.

"It's from David," said Charles as he followed at a pace. "I'm afraid it's not good news."

"What?" asked Silver as he pushed through the office door and rapidly scanned his nephew's words. "Since when is it bad news that a man has fallen in love with a maiden?"

"That's not what I refer to, John," answered Charles. "Read on." A moment later, Silver found it.

"The hell he has!" cried the old pirate as he crumpled the letter in his fist and threw it across the room. "What's the matter with that good-for-nothing son of yours?"

"There's nothing the matter with David! What's wrong is your plan!"

"My plan was perfect. All your son had to do was to keep Captain Jones on the right course. Evidently he's not capable of even the simplest instructions!"

"David's done exactly what you've demanded of him!"

"That," bellowed Silver as he pointed to the crumpled letter, "says he hasn't!"

"But all you required was that he keep us informed of his progress, and to tell Captain Jones about the treasure when it was most appropriate." Charles picked up the letter and spread it flat. "He had no control over Captain Jones giving up his desire for the naval commission and purchasing a farm. Even if you were there in person, you couldn't have done any better."

"No, little brother," said Silver as he pulled a King's Warrant from a stack of papers, "you're wrong. There's something I can still do."

"What?"

"It's time once again to intervene in our little Captain's affairs; to apply a little leverage, if you will."

"But how?"

"With this," answered John Silver as he held forth the parchment.

"Jenny!" shouted the retired British Captain from his second floor study. "See who's banging at our front door!" The housekeeper rushed through the hall to where the impatient caller was still knocking.

"Yes?" the housekeeper said from behind the half-opened door. "Oh, it's you, sir?" She liked Captain Paul, but had been given specific instructions if he should call for Miss Dandridge.

"What's the matter, Jenny?" John asked. "Aren't you going to let me in?"

"I would sir, but..." Jenny looked nervously behind her.

"But what?" John demanded as he pushed the door against her.

"Please, sir," she added in a whisper as she resisted. She looked once more up the hallway towards the stairs. "I'm not supposed to let you in, sir. He'll sell me to another master. Please, sir."

"You're not supposed to...what insanity is..." John yelled. "Where's Miss Dandridge?"

"She's in her room, but Captain Dandridge told me just minutes ago..." Before she could finish, Dorothea pulled the door open and gave the housekeeper a stern look.

"What's going on!" John asked as he stepped back onto the porch.

"Outside, John," she answered with a gesture of caution. Dorothea stepped outside next to him and looked up to her father's window. "We can talk under the oak tree."

"Dorothea!" he demanded, trying to match her rapid pace across the lawn. "What's the matter with Jenny, and why wouldn't she let me in the house?"

She walked quickly to the bench on the far side of the enormous tree trunk and sat down. John followed at several paces and took the seat next to her.

"I didn't want my father to hear us."

"Why not!" John asked with a look back at the house. "What difference would it make if he did?"

"Something's happened, John."

"What are you talking about? What could have happened?"

"My father's taken a dislike to you."

"A dislike? But why? What have I done?"

"I'm as baffled as you. This morning, just after that man arrived, Father told Jenny and me that you're no longer welcomed in our home. I asked him why, but he refused to explain."

"That man?"

"A tall man with an accent. He carried a satchel with the seal of the Magistrate of Tobago."

John stared at the flower garden without answering her. It's finally caught up with me, he thought.

"What is it, John? What's happening?"

"We'll have to meet somewhere else," he said as he turned back to her. "Perhaps at Dr. Read's home."

"Do you think he would help us?"

"Yes, provided I can convince him to keep it a secret from your father."

"Will you be speaking to the doctor soon?"

"I've been invited for dinner tonight." John rubbed his chin in thought. "Is there somewhere nearby where we might meet tomorrow, after I speak with him?"

She considered for a moment. "There's that small park just this side of the bridge."

"I know the place," answered John as he looked along the road toward Fredericksburg. "Will you meet me there at noon?"

"Of course I will," answered Dorothea, "and I'll pack us a lunch."

"Good. If he agrees, I'll arrange to stay with him a second night. We can ride there together after the park."

Dorothea put her arms around John's chest and pressed her cheek against his. "Father's been talking more lately about my marrying Mister Henry."

"That must be it!" said John, not wanting her to know about the warrant. "He doesn't think I'm good enough for you, does he?"

"Please keep your voice down," she whispered as she put her hand to his lips. "I don't know that for certain, but it's no secret that Patrick's been courting me since at least a year before you and David arrived in Fredericksburg."

"If that's all it is," said John, "then there's no problem. I'll stand toe to toe with Mister Henry any day." John looked toward the setting sun and realized the hour. "It's late. I'll have to leave now. I'll see you at the park tomorrow?"

"I'll be there, John." He gave her a light kiss on the cheek as he held here hands tightly. Within a minute, he was once again on his horse and riding away toward the southwest. Dorothea watched him until he vanished beyond the bend in the road, and then returned to the house.

The housekeeper was busy in the kitchen, putting together the last touches for dinner.

"Jenny," Dorothea said as she tasted one of the cooked onions, "Captain Paul told me he sent a letter shortly after his last visit. It should have arrived by now. Have you seen it?"

"No, Miss Dotty. I'm sure none have come." The housekeeper wouldn't look up at her mistress.

"If I find out you had anything to do with this, you can be sure the remaining four years of your bond contract with us will be sold to somebody awful." Turning indignantly, she walked to the base of the stairs and stopped. "I'll be in my room. Call me for dinner." She started up the stairs and then stopped a second time as she remembered about her picnic with John.

"There is one thing. I'll be needing a basket lunch for two people tomorrow morning. Have it ready by 11:30."

"Yes, Ma'am." As soon as Dorothea had gone, Jenny walked to the hallway and up the stairs past Dorothea's room to the Master's study.

Dorothea's father was a large, powerful man in his mid-forties; his full head of coal-black hair just beginning to show grey at the temples. His long career onboard His Majesty's men-of-war had given him that weathered and adventurous look that women say they find so attractive. The room was stark; much like the master's cabin on a British ship of the line. There were two prudently stuffed chairs, a small table between them, and a large desk and chair, nothing more. Captain Dandridge sat at the desk reading the warrant while his tall visitor sat in one of the two chairs sipping at his brandy.

"Ahem!" said the visitor as Dandridge re-read the warrant.

"I'm sorry," said Dandridge, looking about at his visitor. "You were saying?"

"I said, sometimes it's the smallest things that count the most."

"Sir?"

"Take our mutual friend, John Paul," continued the visitor. "If it weren't for my wife's brother being a bachelor, the King's men would be arresting him in Fredericksburg, rather than me coming to ask your assistance to insure his safety."

"I don't follow you, Mister Young."

"Please, call me William."

"And you can call me Nathaniel. How could your brother-in-law's marital status have anything to do with your visit or John Paul's safety?"

"Samuel is the Postmaster of Scarborough and has never been married. The only home-cooked meals he gets are when he brings my mail, which is always at suppertime. He wasn't looking for that specific letter, but the King's men were. So you see, Nathaniel, that Samuel's marital status did make a difference."

"But you said you told John he should never write you."

"That's true, but he was ready to burst at the seams to tell me how well he was doing at his brother's tailor shop, and about you and his love for your daughter. It's only a matter of time before the King's men discover he has a brother in Virginia."

"I suppose you're correct," said Nathaniel.

"So you can see why I had to come in person, before he wrote again?"

"But why not go to him in Fredericksburg?"

"That was my intention until I discovered I was being followed."

"Followed?" asked Nathaniel. "How do you know?"

"First, the King's men have a certain smell," said the visitor as he touched his nose. "We weren't aboard the Bristol Twins more than an hour before this little man began to circle me like a fly. The moment he found out I was headed for Virginia, he told me this was his destination also." There was a soft knock on the door.

"Come!" called out Mister Dandridge.

"Master Dandridge," the housekeeper called through the half-opened door. "May I have a word with you, sir?"

"What is it, Jenny?" he demanded as he made a gesture of silence to his guest.

"He's gone, sir." She stepped into the room and looked across to the man seated near the window. "You asked that I tell you. Will there be anything else?"

"Yes, Jenny, there is one other thing," said Mister Dandridge as he unlocked and opened the center drawer of his desk. "I'm finished with Captain Paul's letter. See that it's included with tomorrow's mail."

"Sir?" she asked as she took the resealed letter.

"Was there something else?"

"Please don't require this of me again," she said as she held up the letter. "It's not right, and Miss Dotty said that if she finds out it was me, she'll sell my contract to someone dreadful. I agree that Miss Dotty should marry Mister Henry, but it grieves my soul to deceive her like this."

"Jenny," he said as he closed and locked the drawer, "if there's anything which might be considered questionable, I'll take full responsibility. You've only done that which I've required of you. And unless you feel compelled to tell her, my daughter will never know you had anything to do with this matter." He took up his glass of brandy. "And concerning your contract, you needn't worry about those remaining four years. I'm your master, not Dorothea. Was there anything else?"

"Just one more thing, sir," she said with a nervous look at the tall visitor. "Miss Dotty has asked that I prepare a basket lunch for two. I believe she's meeting Captain Paul somewhere at noon tomorrow."

"Thank you for that information, Jenny. Call me when dinner's ready."

"Yes, sir," she answered as she stepped into the hallway and pulled the door closed.

"Did I hear right?" asked the visitor. "Did your housekeeper say that John Paul was just here?"

"Yes he was, but he's gone now."

"Damn! I could have told him all of this, rather than relay it through you! Did you know he was coming?"

"Of course I did."

"His letter..." said the visitor with a look to the door and back to his host. "What did you tell them...your housekeeper and Dorothea about Captain Paul?"

"Only that he was no longer welcome in my home," answered Mister Dandridge. "Wasn't that your purpose in showing me this warrant?"

"Well...yes and no."

"Which is it? Dorothea's my daughter, and Captain Paul is a fugitive, isn't he?"

"True, but..."

"You're not making any sense, Mister Young," said Captain Dandridge. "If it's so important that you talk to him face-to-face, then you can still catch him if you leave now."

"Not out in public; at least not while that little man is still sniffing around. Besides, I've already shown you the warrant, and John would eventually find out it was me. I don't want him to think me a traitor. You can see that, can't you?"

"I suppose so," answered Nathaniel. "But you didn't come all this way just to show me this warrant. You want me to do something else for you."

"John's in immediate danger, Nathaniel, and must leave Virginia as quickly as possible. You're the only person, besides your daughter, who cares for him enough to do this for me."

"Leave Virginia...hmmm," thought Nathaniel as he stroked his chin. "There might be a way." He picked up the parchment. "Tell me about this warrant, William. What really happened in Tobago?"

"Well, according to Captain Paul, he was attacked aboard ship by one of his men. The man—Jack Fry was his name—was fomenting a mutiny over the crew's pay."

"And you believed John without question?"

"Not fully," answered the tall man, sensing Nathaniel's skepticism, "until he told me who it was he had to kill. Fry was a good-for-nothing half-breed who had been in trouble from birth. I was surprised he hadn't been killed sooner."

"Just before my housekeeper interrupted us, you were saying that you'd be willing to testify on Captain Paul's behalf."

"That's true," answered the taller man.

"Then why don't I simply inform the authorities that..?"

"Your word, Mister Dandridge! You gave me your word that if I confided in you, that you'd maintain what I told you in the strictest confidence."

"Calm down, William. I was only suggesting that acquittal would be preferable to flight."

"But he wouldn't be acquitted," answered the tall man, "given the heightened level of animosity between the Americans and The Crown, and the fact that John has fled Tobago."

"Then what do you propose?"

"He mentioned in his letter that up until he fell in love with your daughter and the tailor business was doing so well, that he was considering a commission in the Continental Navy. I was counting on you and your connections; that you might know someone who could write him a letter of recommendation. If not, his only hope is to disappear until he can see what comes of this unrest with Mother England. Then, perhaps..."

"Disappear..." said Nathanial, half to himself. "Yes. I do know some people."

As Mister Dandridge pondered the challenge, the taller man stood and walked across the room to refill his glass with brandy. There was a double clicking sound each time the left leg straightened for its next step.

After four hours of riding through the chilly morning countryside, John Paul reigned his horse to a stop. He was early, but Dorothea was usually early also. After a quick survey of the park, he dismounted and tied his horse to a tree. Two couples sat on their blankets watching their children near water's edge. John walked toward them, but stopped when he heard his name called from windward.

"Captain Jones!"

John spun about to meet the cold stare of Nathaniel Dandridge. He held a single piece of parchment in his left hand. At his left side, and partially hidden under his long coat, hung a British naval officer's sword. Only the tip of the scabbard was visible next to his boot.

"So it is true! You have been using an alias! What is it today, Paul or Jones?" John's hand went instinctively to where his sword normally hung. It wasn't there.

"Mister Dandridge!" he said defensively. "What are you doing here?"

"You expected my daughter, didn't you?" Mister Dandridge stood a full four inches above John, and outweighed him by at least fifty pounds. The older man walked slowly forward.

"I've very little time, so I'll make this short. I know you're fond of Dorothea, and may even have secret plans for marriage someday." His countenance darkened. "Forget my daughter! I would never give her hand in marriage to a fugitive and a murderer." He raised the document so John could see his circled name. It was the arrest warrant for the killing of Jack Fry, with the seal of the Admiralty at Kings Town at it's top. "Is that clear, Mister Paul?"

"Yes, perfectly clear, sir." John stiffened each time the older man hissed his name. He was neither prepared, nor able to fight Mister Dandridge for his daughter. "But shouldn't we consult Dorothea about her future?"

"It isn't a matter of what Dorothea wants. I'm telling you to never see her again. If it wasn't for her feelings toward you, I'd have brought the constable with me today. But I'm assuming you're a reasonable man, Mister Paul. I'll not report you in exchange for your word to never see my daughter again. Do I have it?"

John stared into the older man's eyes for half a minute, but refused to speak the words he demanded.

"You seem to have difficulty with the concept, Mister Paul, so I'll put it in the clearest terms I can." Captain Dandridge took a long breath while he considered. "If you ever meet with my daughter again, or even write to her, then I'll inform the King's men of your whereabouts that very day. Is that clear enough?"

"Yes," said John reluctantly. "Does that include my meeting with her today?"

"It does," answered Dandridge coldly. "I've seen to it that my daughter is delayed somewhat, giving us plenty of time to complete our business and to see you on your way back toward Fredericksburg."

"But..."

"But nothing!" Dandridge pressed his finger firmly against John's chest, pushing the smaller man back a step. "If you persist; not only will the King's men come for you, but I'll show Dorothea this warrant."

John wanted to argue with the older man, but there was no point.

"I'll take your silence as an agreement to my demands, Mister Paul. Don't show your face in Hanover County again, or you'll find yourself hanging from a gibbet."

Without a word of protest, John turned and walked to his horse. Within a minute, he was across the footbridge and swallowed up by the trees to the east.

CHAPTER 5

On Wednesday, the twenty second of March 1775, just before lunch time, an elderly man of slight frame and feeble countenance stood in the cutting room of the Paul Tailor Shop. He carried a canvas satchel on his left arm and his brown felt hat in the other. Mister Peters, the first tailor to be hired back when the shop reopened the previous year, motioned for his friend to set his things next to the bench seat and wait.

"Master Paul hasn't been himself these past two weeks," Peters whispered. "Comes in before the rest of us and stays to lock up every night. Very unlike his normal self."

"Do you think this is a bad time to solicit him for a job?" the old man asked as he set his hat carefully atop his satchel.

"Not at all," answered Mister Peters. "I've recommended you highly, and he's expecting you."

With that, Mister Peters knocked lightly upon the frame of John's office door.

"Yes?" came John's reply.

"The tailor I told you about, Mister McCreedy, is here to see you, sir. Shall I show him in?"

"By all means," answered John as he looked at his pocket watch. "Come in, good sir. I didn't realize how quickly the time had passed." John set a chair in the middle of the room and motioned for the man to sit down.

"Jason tells me you've been a tailor in New York Town for eighteen years, and there's none quicker or better at cutting and fitting."

"My friend flatters me, Mister Paul."

"Well, I've never known Jason to lie, so I'll take him at his word." As John spoke, he couldn't help but notice the old man was having trouble with his left shoe. "Pick up a stone?"

"No, sir," the man answered as he crossed his left leg over his right and untied the lace. "The laces are old and keep loosening. If I don't keep it tight, I'm sure to wear myself a blister." At that, he gave the strings a firm tug. "Damn!" the old tailor whispered as the right string broke off an inch from the eyelet. He looked up at John with an embarrassed look.

"Don't worry about it," said John with a snicker. "Happens to me all the time. We have plenty of twine in the shop. I'll have Jason get..."

"No need, sir," answered the old man as his nimble fingers spun a slipping noose in the end of the broken lace. And then, with a quick snap, he captured the short piece of string a quarter inch above the eyelet. John was curious.

"Do that again," said John as he handed two short lengths of rope to the man. "I've never seen a knot like that before."

"It's nothing new, Mister Paul, but I'm surprised at how few there are who know how it works. Besides shoe laces and thread, it makes a wonderful parlor trick," the man said as he handed one of the ropes back to John. "It works best if you tie one rope to a rafter just beyond your guest's reach and then challenge them to jump up and tie their rope to the one hanging from the ceiling." John moved his chair to the center of the room, climbed up on it and dangled his rope while the old man formed his special knot as before. "If the loop in your noose is large enough, it takes only a small amount of dexterity to capture the hanging rope."

With a slight jump and a snap of the ends of the noose, the two ropes were joined.

"Why, that's a sheet bend!" exclaimed John as he inspected the knot. "Where'd you learn that?"

"It's an old tailor's trick, sir," said the old man with a proud smile. "We call it a short end bend. Nothing new at all."

"Well, it's new to me and I'm very impressed."

"Impressed enough to offer me a job?"

John gave the old man a broad smile. "When can you start?"

"This afternoon, if that's all right with you, sir"

John began to answer, but noticed a wagon parked in front of the shop. "Did you come to Fredericksburg alone?"

"No, sir," he answered with a look to the street. "I have the missus with me."

"Have you found a place to stay yet?"

"I wanted to be sure I had the job first."

"I've...reconsidered, Mister McCreedy," said John. "You can't start today after all." John turned and pulled a metal box from his desk drawer.

"But, sir," said the old man in disappointment. "You said..."

"First," said John as he held out three gold crowns, "you'll find a home for your wife. Once you're settled, then you can start work." The old man was shocked. "And so that I can properly address you, what's your first name, Mister McCreedy?"

"It's Angus, sir," the old man said with a crack to his voice, "and may the Lord bless you for your kindness." He took the shiny coins and pressed them to his lips for a moment as his eyes filled with tears. As he began to thank his new employer again, John held up a hand.

"Enough, Angus. Go now, and see to your wife. Jason will show you the ropes tomorrow." With that, the older tailor excused himself, leaving John to the two pieces of rope on his desk.

Shortly after lunch while John was occupied with his new rope trick, a tall visitor entered the Paul Tailor Shop. One of the tailors brightened as he recognized an old customer.

"Mister Henry!" Albert cried as he dropped his scissors and took up his tape. In a moment, he had circled the statesman and taken several preliminary measurements. "It's a little worn, sir, but still quite a respectable riding coat." He continued to circle the tall man. "We've just received the latest patterns from England and could have you a new one in two days."

"I'd love a new set of clothes, Albert, but not today."

"Then how may we help you?" asked the tailor, a little crestfallen.

"I'm here to speak with one of your proprietors. Is Mister Paul in?"

"You'll find him in the back, sir," answered Albert as he pointed toward a door. "He'll be glad for a visitor." Albert walked toward the office and stopped. "Shall I announce you, sir?"

"It won't be necessary," answered Patrick as he pushed the door open. John was seated at his desk with his back to the door.

"John?" At the sound of his name, John whirled about and leaped to his feet.

"You!" said John as he took a step toward his sword.

"Did I come at a bad time?" asked Patrick with a note of caution.

"Yes, considering!" said John as he grasped his sword and pulled it half from its sheath.

"Considering what?" asked Patrick.

"Did Mister Dandridge send you here to threaten me also?"

"To threaten you?" cried Patrick as he retreated a step. "My God, man, I've come to offer you and David something few men..." he hesitated to give John a moment to cool down. "Do you remember that first evening we met -- I believe it was in late February of last year?"

"Of course I do!" answered John, still holding the sword.

"Then you also remember what David told me in the parlor, why you had come to the Colonies?" John remembered nearly every word from that most interesting evening, but gave Patrick an inquisitive look.

"Correct me if I'm wrong, but I understood that you and David came to Virginia to seek commissions in the Continental Navy, if and when it began to form."

"You're wrong, Patrick," answered John slowly. "I talked about it the night David and I met in Kings Town, but only in passing. I'm afraid it was David's wishful thinking you heard last year, and I was only going along to patronize him. But go on. What have you come here to offer us?"

"Evidently, you have a friend; a James Smith of Kirkcudbright, Scotland whose brother is the partner of a Mister Joseph Hewes of Edenton, North Carolina."

"Hmmm..." said John as he let the sword slip back into the sheath.. "That would be Robert Smith. Yes. James and I were lodge brothers in Scotland. He did mention that he had a brother in America."

"Joseph Hewes and Robert Smith own the largest shipping company in North Carolina. Both of these gentlemen were present with myself and several other influential patriots at a meeting of the Committee of Correspondence three nights ago at Harrisonburg. Several very important decisions were made at that meeting."

"Was there any talk of the Navy?"

"Yes, there was. But what I wanted to tell you is that Mister Hewes has been appointed as the Chairman of the Marine Commission." John's heart flew to his throat.

"Did Smith tell Hewes that he knew me?"

"I mentioned your name to Robert and he remembered that you were his brother's friend, but that was all."

"You had the chance to recommend me and didn't?"

"Calm down, John. It would have been highly presumptuous of me to suggest that he recommend you and David to Mister Hewes, at this time."

"But..."

"I'm prepared to write you and your young friend a letter of introduction to Joseph Hewes today, provided you can leave for Edenton tomorrow morning. Mister Hewes told me that he'll be sailing to Edenton where he has several meetings planned before sailing back up to Boston the middle of next month."

"Of course I can go!" John pulled a piece of writing paper from the desk drawer, along with a bar of red sealing wax.

"When you introduce me, would you use the surname of Jones? It seems the King's men are still looking for John Paul."

"If you desire," agreed Patrick as he wrote out several sentences. After signing his well-known signature, he handed the letter to John for his approval. "You'll notice I refrained from making any direct recommendations. Mister Hewes' partner will know of you, and besides, it would be best if you were selected for your qualifications, rather than your connections."

"But..." John looked up from the letter. "Couldn't you say something more? This only says..."

"I'm sorry, John. Console yourself that I've recommended no other men for commissions as yet."

"Be honest with me, Patrick. Do we have a chance?"

"I'd consider your chances very good, unless there's something I'm not privy to."

"Well," said John as he read the letter once more, "it's better than most of the others will have, I suppose. Seal it, sir, and I'll begin packing." A large drop of red wax was dripped onto the folded letter and impressed with the signet ring on the statesman's right forefinger. As Patrick turned to leave, John remembered something.

"Before you go," said John as he pulled a second piece of paper from his desk, "could I prevail upon you to deliver a letter for me?"

"Of course. Who's it to?"

"Dorothea. She'll wonder where I've gone, and I won't have time to make the side trip to her home."

"I'll be passing through there within the week and I'd be glad to deliver it for you." A moment later, John had scribed two short paragraphs and sealed the letter with the same wax Patrick had used.

"Here," said John as he handed over the letter. "And I'd ask that you hand deliver this."

"As you wish," said Patrick as he opened his coat and put the letter into his inside pocket.

"And don't worry, sir. If I get a naval commission, I won't disappoint you or the Colonies."

"If I had any doubts about that, I wouldn't have given you the introduction to Mister Hewes. I'm not worried, John. You and David will do just fine."

John followed him to the street, where Mister Henry stopped.

"Considering that we're rivals for Dorothea's hand, are you sure you can trust me with this?" As Patrick pulled the letter from his coat, a small scrap of brown paper fluttered to the ground next to John's foot.

"What's this?" asked John as he picked up and read the three sentences. "These are powerful words."

"They're not mine," said Patrick in a somber tone.

"Oh?"

"I'm scheduled to speak tomorrow night at the Henrico Parish Church in Richmond before the House of Burgesses. Because of what inspired that note, I've rewritten the speech I was to give."

"I'm sorry I'll miss it," said John as he handed the note back to Patrick. "It certainly must be important."

"It is," answered Patrick. "And since you'll likely be in the center of the war that these words may help create, you should know more about what inspired them." Patrick looked about for eavesdroppers and then suggested they return to his office. Once inside, John offered the statesman a cup of tea.

"So, whose words are they?"

"On my way back from that meeting the other day in Harrisonburg, I stopped for the night at Culpeper," said Patrick as he pointed toward the northwest. "That's a small hamlet about twenty miles from here."

"I know of the place."

"I arrived just in time to witness a man in his mid-sixties being led in chains to the whipping post at the town center. Now that I've had time to consider the affair in retrospect, I find it incredible the constable even consented to give the brittle old man the opportunity to speak his peace." Patrick ground his teeth. "Poked him in the side with a sharp stick when he asked that he be tried by his neighbors, rather than the authorities. Torn and bleeding, the old man choked out these words; 'Neighbors and friends. You all know me. I've baptized your children and comforted you when sickness was upon your homes. I've joined you in marriage and spoken the last words over the graves of your loved ones. You're about to behold how Mother England treats a minister of the Gospel when he does that which his Lord demands; preaching Jesus Christ without the King's permission. I told yonder constable that I will never submit to taking their license... that I am controlled by the Holy Spirit and authorized by God Almighty, not the King. I'll not allow them to control me by a license, no matter what they may do to me! Watch carefully my friends. Watch, and learn a lesson in liberty, and what happens to you when your loving King doesn't get his way.'

Patrick crumpled the piece of paper in his fist. "You should have seen it, John! That peevish little bureaucrat was so infuriated by those words that he took the cat and whipped the man himself, but not before he threw the preacher headlong against the post and then chained him up so hard that his unshod toes barely reached the ground!"

"What's happening to England?" asked John. "Why would she set herself up against Almighty God like that?"

"It's her soul, my friend."

"Her soul?"

"Aye," answered Patrick, "and this incident in Culpeper proves it. She's dying, and if we're not careful, she'll drag these thirteen fledgling colonies down into her grave and pull the dirt in upon them before they can take their first breath of freedom." Patrick unfolded the note and read it again in silence. "This is what it's all about! These last few words of a preacher, just before they took his life! Listen to the words once more, my young friend, but this time, visualize that little man of God in chains, and a fat and sweating British constable taking his personal revenge." He spoke the words from memory this time, putting them in paraphrase.

"Is life so dear, or peace so sweet, as to be purchased at the price of chains and slavery? Forbid it, Almighty God! I know not what course others may take; but as for me, give me liberty or give me death!"

"Aye," whispered John as he nodded slowly.

"I stood helpless with the rest of the townsfolk and watched as the flesh was torn, piece by piece from his back. When the constable finally tired of his play, the preacher hung unconscious in his chains, with no less than seven ribs exposed to the elements. I'd never seen anything so heinous nor so cruel. As I rode out of Culpeper early yesterday morning, I saw them dropping his lifeless body into an unmarked grave by the roadside."

"Do you think the constable meant for him to die?"

"I watched the whole thing from not more than twenty feet away," answered Patrick as he nodded slowly. "He wanted the preacher to die, first as an example to the other eleven preachers, and second to the townsfolk. The sadistic little bastard enjoyed every stripe of the cat." Patrick Henry was a strong man, a man willing to stand against any foe. But as he seated himself next to John, a single tear broke forth from his eye and fell over his cheek.

"You see it, don't you, John?"

"Yes," answered the younger man thoughtfully, "I believe I do. The real issue between the King and these American Colonies is liberty, isn't it?"

"Exactly!" cried Patrick triumphantly. "It's the battle for man's God-given right to live his life without a saddle on his back, and without the spurs of some tyrant digging into his sides." Patrick took a long breath. "Liberty will never come to these shores until we are guaranteed the mutual protection of our neighbors. That, my friend, will never exist until we and our peers are allowed to judge one another in an open and public court."

"Judge one another?"

"By the Bill of Rights of England," answered Patrick, "a subject has a right to a trial by his peers. What is meant by his peers? Those who reside near him, his neighbors, and those who are well acquainted with his character and situation in life." As John pondered this new concept, Patrick continued. "Every time we accept the King's license, we let him turn a right into a privilege. He wants to control us, John, and I'm one of many who simply won't abide it."

"Slow down, Patrick," said John, somewhat confused.

"We're on the brink of a revolution, John, and if we prevail, we'll have just one chance to form a new kind of government; one that's forever limited in it's power over free men. God help us to do it right!"

Both men sat with their emotions for several minutes before Patrick finally stood to leave.

"We both have important missions," said Patrick at the door of the tailor shop. "Compromise your convictions for no man." Patrick took John's hand and squeezed it firmly. "May God go with you and your friend."

"And you, Patrick." A moment later, as the statesman rode south along the main street of Fredericksburg, David entered the shop and laid his satchel across the cutting table.

"John, you wouldn't believe who I just saw riding through town."

"Throw a crown on the table and you'll have yourself a wager," said John with a twinkle in his eye.

"He was here, wasn't he?"

"Yes he was, and I have some tremendous news! He's arranged for us to meet with Mister Joseph Hewes, the newly appointed Chairman of the Marine Commission. Hewes will be selecting the first naval officers!"

"You're jesting!" cried David, hardly able to believe the good news. "When do we leave?"

"I'm not jesting," said John as he held forth the letter. "Pack your things, because we depart for Edenton at first light."

"What about the shop?" asked David. "Who..?"

"Mister Peters is fully capable to run things while we're gone."

As the two went about their preparations for the trip, Patrick Henry rode to a tavern at the Southern edge of town, entering the public room of the Blue Grass Tavern. A tall man in his mid-forties beckoned from the shadows of a corner table.

"Did he accept the letter?"

"They'll be leaving at dawn tomorrow, just as you expected they would." He paused. "But tell me something, Nathaniel. Why did you ask me to approach John when you had made all the arrangements? Does this have anything to do with Dorothea?"

"That's my concern, not yours. I have a very good reason for everything I'm doing. You'll see it in the end; that it'll work to both our benefits." He could see that Patrick wasn't convinced. "If you really consider, wouldn't a letter of introduction from Patrick Henry, the new Statesman, carry more weight than one from a retired sailor?"

"Maybe. I just hope those two aren't disappointed."

"Does it really matter?"

Patrick studied Nathaniel carefully. "I thought I understood your intentions, sir, but now..."

"Didn't you tell me you wanted to ask for my daughter's hand?"

"Yes I did," answered Patrick, "just as soon as I get back from my trip."

"Well?"

"I don't need John out of Virginia for that."

"I agree," answered Nathaniel, "but it can't hurt. And besides, they might actually get their commissions."

"I presume this satisfies my debt."

"Debt? What debt?"

"The money you loaned me for law school," said Patrick. "William Paul helped me somewhat, but yours was the bulk of the money I needed."

"You disappoint me, Patrick. To satisfy that debt--and I never intended to call it due--you'd have to pay back the entire sum, or do something..."

"Dishonorable?"

"That's a dangerous word, my good friend."

"Nathaniel," said Patrick in a whisper, "you know as well as I, that those two will never..."

"Very well," said the older man with a raised hand, "your debt to me is satisfied."

"Thank you. And now, if there's nothing else you require of me, I've a long ride to make."

"Oh?"

"I'm giving a speech tomorrow night in Richmond." As he spoke, he put his hand to the pocket where the three-paged speech rested, and felt the letter he had promised to deliver for John. "And since you'll be riding back to your home tonight, would you deliver this letter to your daughter?"

"I'd be glad to. She'll be pleased to hear from you."

"It's not from me."

"Then who is it from?"

"It's from Captain Paul."

"She'll have it before she retires tonight," Nathaniel lied.

The moment the statesman was out of the tavern, Mister Dandridge broke the wax seal and read the short note:

22 March 1775

My darling Dorothea,
Time did not allow me to tell you this in person, but

as you read this note, David and I will be well on our way toward Richmond and then to Edenton, North Carolina. We are going there to request Naval Commissions from Mister Joseph Hewes and may not return to Virginia for several weeks.

I apologize for not meeting you at the park last week, but your father met me and forbid that we meet again, or even write. This hand delivered letter is the only way I could tell you I was leaving.

Dorothea, I know it's premature at this time to promise it, but if I obtain my commission, I'll return to your home at the earliest moment to ask your father for your hand in marriage. Please wait for me.

Eternally yours,
John Paul

Nathaniel Dandridge smiled to himself as he refolded the note and placed it in his pocket. "It's too late, Captain Paul."

By the time the sun had begun to rise from behind the rolling hills of Fredericksburg to paint the chilly March morning a dark pink, John and David's surrey had carried them across the covered bridge at the Mattaponi River and into the low farmlands surrounding the town of Spotsylvania. The new housekeeper had packed them a basket of fried chicken, honeyed cornbread and dried fruit, enough for the first two days of their journey. Their chestnut mare trotted along the muddy roadway at an easy pace, with little clouds of moist breath blowing from her swollen nostrils.

"He must have told you something encouraging," said David as he brushed the cornbread crumbs from the seat between them.

"The most I could get was that Mister Hewes will be at his shipping company in Edenton from the twenty seventh of March through the second of April, and that our names were brought up at a planning meeting in Harrisonburg a few days ago. This letter of introduction from Mister Henry is all we have."

"Only an introduction?" asked David. "Surely he could have..."

"No," answered John. "That's the one thing he wouldn't do. He said that it will be up to us to convince Mister Hewes of our integrity and qualifications."

"Well, at least we've an open door, and that's better than nothing."

John only huffed.

The trip South went without incident as they passed through mile after mile of beautiful countryside and quaint townships. On the twenty-sixth of March, the two weary travelers stopped at a medium-sized roadhouse in Richmond. John pulled a crown piece from his pocket and flipped it high into the air.

"Queen's head!" called David just before the silver coin struck the cobblestone apron in front of the Inn.

"Ah! Sorry, David. You get to stall and feed the horse again, while I see to our room."

"Let me see that coin!" the younger man demanded as he jumped from the surrey.

"Well, David Noble!" John threw back sarcastically. "Do I detect a spark of mistrust in your voice? You wouldn't be suggesting that I'd use a trick coin just to get out of doing your work, would you?"

"For one thing, it's only my work if I lose the toss. And yes, I'd suggest exactly that!" David inspecting the coin carefully.

"Satisfied?"

"Yes, but somehow you've managed to get the easy job every night since we left Fredericksburg!"

Grabbing his duffle, John hopped from the carriage and walked past his young companion to the tavern door.

"When you're finished with your chores," John said tauntingly, "you can meet me inside for dinner and a drink."

"My chores? Ha!" David pocketed the coin as he led their horse to the back of the building. By the time he had finished, John was involved in a lively discussion with two Virginia militiamen.

"David! Over here!" called John to his young friend. "Take a seat and wash the Virginia road from your throat!" He pushed a large tankard of ale across the table.

"David Noble," began John, "this is Gunnar Andersen and his traveling companion, Thomas Matthews. They're both in the Virginia Volunteers!"

"Pleased to meet you, David," said Gunnar, offering his hand. "John was telling us you're from Kings Town."

"That's right. Born and raised there. And if it weren't for..."

"Gunnar was just telling me about an incident here in Richmond," interrupted John, "very similar to what Mister Henry described last week."

"That wouldn't be Patrick Henry, would it?" asked Thomas.

"Of course it's Patrick Henry." John was proud to be able to claim the acquaintance of so great a man. "He lives only two miles from us, and we have him over for dinner often." The militiaman studied the two travelers carefully. "If you don't believe me, look at this." John pulled Patrick's letter from his pocket and showed them the wax seal with the statesman's signet ring impression.

"So, tell me," asked David, "what's this incident you were telling John about?"

"Our preacher is sitting in the Richmond jailhouse as we speak," said Gunnar. "As I was telling your friend, he was arrested for tearing in half his license to preach the gospel.

"License to preach? Since when..?" asked David.

"For a little over two weeks."

"And he went to jail for that?"

"Aye," answered Thomas. "He wouldn't be there, except he did it in front of his congregation."

"One of his flock reported him?" asked David.

"No," answered Gunnar. "The constable was sitting in the back of the church, but we didn't know it until he left and returned a few minutes later with two of his soldiers. Took Pastor Allen off to jail right after prayer, they did!"

"Damn those British!" John yelled as his fist slammed down on the table. A hush fell over the tavern. Then, one at a time, each of the other fifteen or so men seated about them joined in the curse of their oppressors across the sea. "Can't his solicitor do something for him?"

"Solicitor?" laughed Thomas. "His wife's tried to retain one, but nobody'll have the case." He pulled his own letter from his pocket. "That's why we're riding to Fredericksburg. We carry a letter signed by every faithful member of Pastor Allen's church asking your Mister Henry to come and defend him." He looked to Gunnar and back to John. "Perhaps you would do us a favor and put an endorsement at the bottom of the letter? Tell him how desperately we need his help?"

"I'd be honored," answered John. Getting a quill and ink from the Innkeeper, John penned a short note of introduction below all the other signatures and handed the letter back to Thomas.

"You have to understand that Mister Henry's a busy man, what with all his meetings and speeches. He may not be able to help you right away."

"Thank you, Mister Jones. I'm sure he'll help when he sees your name on our letter." Thomas refolded the petition and put it away. After a quick sip of ale he continued.

"John, just before we invited you to sit down, we were discussing artillery pieces and the desperate situation in the Colonies."

"Desperate situation?" asked John.

"I told you they'd be concerned, Gunnar!" The younger man was anxious to tell his story and moved his chair a little closer to John. "There are only a handful of foundries in all of America; six at the most. And the few weapons they produce are truly dangerous to the men who have to use them; nothing like what they make over in Europe. Yet, even with the inferior workmanship and performance, a pair of locally produced naval cannons can cost as much as 3,000 pounds!"

"The colonies can't manufacture any good cannons?" asked David.

"Not yet," answered Thomas. "There are two new foundries being built in Massachusetts and Pennsylvania that will, but they won't go into production until September, at the earliest. Couple that with the recent embargo on the importation of both cannons and gun powder, and you have the desperate situation."

As Thomas spoke, there was a commotion at the far end of the public room. Thomas leaned a little closer and continued at just above a whisper. "Most privateers go to sea with only two cannons, one at each gunwale. The rest of their ports are either kept closed or filled with Quakers."

"Quakers?" asked David. "What's a Quaker?"

"Not so loud, David," cautioned Thomas as he made a gesture toward the two soldiers. "It's a cannon made from wood and painted black. Half a privateer's success depends upon bluff, and if a merchantman thinks they're heavily armed, he'll often strike his colors without a fight. Then, one at a time, the privateer captain will replace his Quakers with real cannons. It's slow and risky, but I'm afraid it's the only way the Colonies can arm their ships."

"It's strange that I hadn't heard of this before tonight." said John.

"I'm not making this up, Mister Jones, if that's what you're suggesting," said Thomas. "My father owns one of those six foundries."

"I'm not saying you are," answered John, "it's just so difficult to believe."

"I find it difficult to believe that Mister Henry hasn't told you all of this, being such a close friend," said Gunnar as he gave John a curious look.

"Mister Henry and I are close, but he doesn't..." Before John could finish, a middle-aged man in buckskins bolted from a nearby table with a curse and ran out the side door into the night. It took the four only a moment to figure out what had caused the incident. There, standing in the open front doorway was a small man in a dark suit and beaver skin hat, surveying the occupants. After a moment, the little man swore and walked back out the way he had come in, leaving the soldiers standing alone. The room was as quiet as a morgue.

"Listen up!" said one of the men in uniform. "There was a tall man in buckskins here a few minutes ago, and we've a writ for his arrest!" The soldier looked slowly about the room until he found a stranger; someone he might intimidate.

"You there! Sea Captain! Did you see him leave?" John figured the fugitive had put enough distance between his pursuers and himself by now, so cooperated.

"Aye, we all saw him leave."

"Well?" barked the soldier as he started toward John's table. "Are you gonna tell me where he's got off to, or do I take you in his place?"

"He was out the side door as you came in the front." With the grace of a wounded bull, the soldier pushed his way past three tables and through the door into the night, with his partner close behind.

"Why'd you tell them?" demanded Gunnar.

"You must not have seen what the soldier next to the door was doing," offered David. "He had his pistol drawn and cocked, and was ready to fire into the crowd. I've seen that mood before."

"I'm sorry," apologized Gunnar. "You're correct. I didn't notice."

"Nice town you have here," said David as he righted an upset chair. "Any idea what that man's wanted for?"

"There's been several of his cut picked up in the last several days," answered Thomas. "Seems a soldier was roughed up last week by a mountain man after the soldier made a lewd remark about his wife. He had it coming, if you ask me."

After another round of drinks, John and David excused themselves and climbed the stairs to their room. It was small, but clean. As David unpacked his night clothes, John stood by the window looking out on the night.

"I've seen that look before, John," said David. "What's bothering you?"

"It's your father's cannons. If they were in the bilge of a merchantman, they were being smuggled into the Colonies. I can't help wondering who they belonged to."

"Does it really matter? My father owns them now and Smoot will never get his hands on them again."

On the thirty-first of March, John and David arrived at the offices of Hewes and Smith Ships, in the port town of Edenton, North Carolina; a small but vital link between the Colonies and the outside world. An unbroken chain of wagons snaked through the wide gate at the entrance to the yards, their cargos of tobacco and cotton spilled over their sides as they plowed through the mud toward the loading docks beyond. To their larboard, not more than a stone's throw away, rolled the departing wagons with finished goods from England.

"What if Mister Hewes refuses our application?"

"I've already considered that," answered John as he reigned the mare off the main road and into a spot next to the counting house.

"If we can't get the commissions, then we'll return to Fredericksburg as quickly as we can; maybe on one of Mister Hewes' merchantmen." He pulled Patrick Henry's letter from his coat and stepped from the surrey. "Amusing, isn't it..." John stopped a few feet short of the door and faced his young friend. "Now that we're so close, the object of this trip seems even further away than when we first discussed it in Kings Town."

"Chin up, old man," said David with a fist to John's shoulder. "Things'll work out. You'll see."

The counting house stood just beyond the last warehouse overlooking the Edenton River and the clutter of ships waiting to get to the docks. The company sign over the door indicated that this was where they should find Joseph Hewes. A young clerk sat at a neat but crowded desk just inside the doorway with his back to the window. He turned and studied John and David for a moment.

"May I help you?"

"Yes you may," answered John. "We would like to speak with your master, Mister Hewes."

"Do you have an appointment?"

"No, but we carry a letter of introduction from Patrick Henry." At the statesman's name the clerk's demeanor changed from detachment to urgency.

"If you'll give me your letter, I'll announce you and your friend." In less than a minute, the clerk had returned, followed by a short man in his late sixties. The older man wore a heavy hunting jacket, which carried the strong odor of pipe tobacco.

"Mister Jones, Mister Noble?" he said with an extended hand. "I'm Joseph Hewes. Won't you come in?" The two rose to accept the offered handshake and followed the man into his office.

"Isn't that one of the men we saw in Charles Town?" whispered David.

"I believe you're right, David. He was the one who joked about the Negro party."

"You'll have to excuse the mess, gentlemen," apologized the elderly man, "but as you can see, you've caught me at loading time."

While John and David looked about, the clerk brought two oak chairs and placed them before his master's desk. The cluttered office was large and richly decorated. A dozen certificates, attesting to the man's importance, hung on the dark oak wood paneling behind the massive mahogany desk. Models of ships and various other nautical implements of navigation competed for the meager shelf space near the ceiling. A small potbelly stove burned hotly in the corner, removing the morning's chill from the room.

"Please be seated, gentlemen," began Joseph as he sat Patrick's letter on the desk, "and tell me how I may be of service?"

"Sir," said John, "we have just arrived from Fredericksburg. As you can see from that letter, my companion and I are here to apply for commissions in the Continental Navy."

There followed a very long and uncomfortable silence as Mister Hewes looked at the two young travelers and then read the letter of introduction a second time. As he scanned the words, he pulled at his lower lip, causing it to deform in a most unseemly manner.

"Ah yes!" he finally said. "Now I recall where I heard your names." The man lowered the letter and peered at the two through his spectacles. "It was Nathaniel Dandridge--a meeting last month up in Virginia. Of course!"

"Dandridge?" asked John.

"He said something about you two coming to see me." He paused to collect his thoughts.

"Don't you mean Patrick Henry?" asked John. The old man continued with his dialogue, ignoring John's question.

"It's true that we'll be forming a navy soon, and you've been told correctly that I'll be heading the committee to select the first officers." He exhaled loudly through his nose with a distinct whistling sound, and then picked at the nostril. "But the selection process is a little more complicated than my merely saying yes."

"More complicated?" asked David with a sideways glance at John.

"Exactly." The old man studied the two young men again for several moments. "Have either of you been told what kind of men we're looking for?"

"No, sir," answered John. "But we assumed that you would want men with experience as ship's captains and a knowledge of how the British fight. Is there anything else?"

Without answering, Mister Hewes took a piece of paper from his top desk drawer and walked to the window.

"Is there something the matter, sir?" asked David.

"There most assuredly is, young man," answered Mister Hewes as he held up the piece of paper. "These are the requirements the Marine Commission has decided upon." He adjusted his wire-rimmed glasses and began to read. "First and foremost, he must be able to prove he was born in the American Colonies." Hewes gave the two an inquiring look over the tops of his spectacles. They made no move, so he continued.

"Second, he must be a privateer captain who has distinguished himself in combat against British or Spanish shipping." He gave the two another quick look. "And finally, he must present a personal letter of recommendation from the Governor of his Colony." He laid the paper on the desk and removed his glasses. "Do either of you possess these three prerequisites?"

John and David sat silent in their chairs while Mister Hewes pulled a tall stack of letters from his desk.

"I already have far too many qualified men to choose from, Mister Jones, and I've only been authorized to appoint sixty officers; twelve of whom will be chosen as ships captains."

"Sir," began John after a long and uncomfortable pause, "my friend and I have already taken too much of your time." He took a long breath while he thought. "We'll not trouble you any longer, except to ask one small favor."

"And what might that be, young man?"

"Is it possible that you have a couple of openings in your shipping company? We would make fine officers on one of your merchant vessels."

"I respect your enthusiasm and I truly sympathize with your difficult situation, but there's something you can't possibly know." He beckoned John to the window. "You undoubtedly observed the confusion at my docks when you arrived. Normally, such activity would indicate a surplus of jobs, but the opposite is true." He took a long breath and continued. "You see, Mister Jones, I lost three ships to pirates last month and all but a handful of the crewmen have returned, all of them expecting to be re-employed. Until I can replace those ships and put those three crews back at work, I simply can't hire any new seamen, much less two new officers. And before things get any better, I expect them to get worse."

"Then we'll trouble you no longer, sir," said John as he stood. "But I have one question before we leave. Why did you say that it was Mister Dandridge who told you about us?"

"Young man, your letter of introduction may have been signed by Patrick Henry, but it wasn't he who sent you to Edenton."

David was on his feet and moving toward the door, hoping to disengage he and John from this fruitless and uncomfortable situation. Mister Hewes could feel David's discomfort, so he offered a scrap.

"Gentlemen, if you're still in Edenton tomorrow morning, come back to see me. I may be able to find you some temporary work; possibly working passage back to Fredericksburg."

"We're not lacking for money, sir," said John as he and David excused themselves from the office, "but thank you for the gesture. We came to Edenton for naval commissions, not employment as common seamen."

At the surrey, John stopped and looked down at the ground for several moments in despair. "David," he began, "I want to apologize..."

"You needn't say a thing, John. You were acting on the best information available at the time, and nobody could ask for more." David put a comforting hand on John's shoulder. "Let's go back to our room and talk."

Their Inn lay two leagues to the Northwest; a small, out-of-the-way place on the banks of the Chowan River. As they passed the last farmhouse and into the open countryside, David broke the silence.

"What was that about Mister Dandridge? You told me it was Patrick Henry who recommended we come to Edenton."

"I thought he did," said John, shaking his head slowly. "You heard what Hewes said. It was Henry who came to the shop, but it was Dandridge who was behind the whole thing." He fell silent for a moment, pondering whether to tell David the rest.

"Hmmm," said David. "I had no idea Dorothea's father cared for us that much. But why send Patrick instead of coming to us himself? He was at the meeting in Harrisonburg, and surely he had the time to stop by the shop on his way home." David considered, and continued. "And another thing; a letter of introduction from Captain Dandridge would have been just as good as Mister Henry's, if not better."

"David, there's something I didn't tell you."

"Oh?"

"Mister Dandridge knew from the beginning that we could never qualify for those commissions."

"What?" David couldn't believe his ears. "Why would he do such a thing? I thought he liked us."

"It wasn't a matter of liking us or not. It was to get me out of Fredericksburg." John tightened his grip on the reigns. "It all makes sense now."

"What are you talking about? What makes sense?"

"Mister Dandridge knows Dorothea and I are in love, and he's sent us on this fool's journey to get me out of her life. And if he had his way, I'd never come back!"

"But, I thought..."

"Two weeks before Patrick wrote us the letter, Mister Dandridge confronted me at a park near his home. He had a copy of the King's Warrant for my arrest. That's why I've been..."

"Hiding in the shop?" asked David.

"Exactly."

"Then he knew about the warrant all along!" said David slowly. "But how?"

"He must still maintain correspondence with some of his Royal Navy friends. There's no other explanation."

"Well," said David thoughtfully, "that explains Captain Dandridge's motive, but why would Patrick be a party to such a cruel stunt? He seemed to be a man of integrity."

"I don't believe Mister Henry knew about the warrant. He was probably under the impression that he was doing a favor for both Dandridge and me. No, this was all Dandridge's doing."

"Will Dorothea wait for you?"

"Yes, unless..."

"Unless what?"

"Unless her father intercepted the letter I sent her the morning we left."

"And if he did?"

"One condition that he wouldn't inform the King of my presence in Virginia was that I not see or write his daughter again. If he intercepted that letter, then there's a good chance the authorities in Fredericksburg are looking for me as we speak." John turned and looked at David. "And he said he'd tell Dorothea also."

"If that's true," said David, "then what do we do now?"

"I don't know, David. You could always return to Jamaica, and I suppose I could sail back to Europe." John took a long breath. "I don't know."

It was dinnertime when they reached their Inn, but John wasn't hungry. Instead, he purchased a bottle of Scotch Whiskey.

"David," said John as he followed the younger man down the short hallway to their room. "I'd like to be left alone for a while, if you don't mind."

"Are you all right?"

"I'm as right as I can be, considering what we've been through today," said John vacantly as he pulled the stopper and raised the bottle to his lips."

"Before you suck the monkey, I've something very important to tell you."

"Suck the...?" John began with a cough as the fumes from the strong drink choked him for a moment. "Oh, you mean the rum."

"Aye, and you're not going to help things a bit by drowning yourself in spirits."

"You're neither my Holy Spirit, nor my Father Confessor," said John as he pushed the door open with his foot and raised the bottle toward his lips a second time. He paused just long enough to give his friend a stern look. "Please go away."

"Not until you hear me out."

John gave a long sigh as he lowered the bottle and sat down on the edge of the bed. "What is it?"

"We don't need Mister Hewes."

"What?"

"You heard me," said David. "We have something better."

"The only thing I want right now is to be left along with this bottle."

"I'm serious, John. We really do have something more valuable than Mister Hewes and his commissions, something so valuable that you could purchase a commission, or that plantation you want."

"Don't mock me, David. You heard Mister Hewes. We'd be lucky to get working passage on one of his ships, much less a paying job."

"John," began David slowly, "have you ever heard of the Treasure of Dead Man's Chest?"

"The Treasure of...? I've heard it many times. My crew sang the ballad often enough."

"I don't mean the song, John. I mean the actual Treasure of Dead Man's Chest."

"Go on."

"Dead Man's Chest is a small island off the North coast of Saint Croix. That's not its real name, of course, but the one given to it by pirates."

"Okay, so there's an island called Dead Man's Chest. Are you telling me there's actually a treasure?" David was pleased that John still had a spark of interest in him. He pulled a chair close and straddled it.

"In July of 1754, one of the last Spanish treasure galleons to put out from Porto Bello lost its treasure of L2,200,000 to pirates. A third of that treasure, roughly 700,000 pounds, was buried on an island in the Southern Bahamas and retrieved in '64 by an expedition out of Bristol. I know for a fact that the remaining two-thirds of the galleon's treasure was buried on Dead Man's Chest the same year."

"A million and a half pounds? Why, that's as much as Henry Morgan took when he sacked Panama!" John sat the bottle on the floor and gave David a piercing look. "How can you be so sure it's still there?"

"Because the man who buried it never drew a map."

"I miss your point, David." John was out of his depression, but his despair was turning to frustration and anger. "If there's no map, then how in God's name are we supposed to find a treasure that was buried twenty or thirty years ago?"

"Twenty years," said David.

"Twenty or five hundred years...it doesn't much matter if nobody knows where it's buried, does it!?"

The moment John Silver had planned and hoped for had finally arrived. David leaned back in his chair to savor it.

"I know who buried it!"

"You know who buried over a million pounds in Spanish treasure and waited till now to tell me?" David just sat with a smile on his face as John yelled. "Good God, man! Why didn't you say something about this in Kings Town? We wouldn't have had to go through all of this! Who is he?"

"He's a merchant in New York Town, but there's a problem."

"Large or small," asked John.

"Well..." David pretended to wrestle with the facts for a moment. "For some reason that nobody quite knows, the man has no intention of ever going back to Dead Man's Chest. Several men have tried to convince him to scribe a map, but to no avail. I'm afraid that without a very convincing argument, we would meet with the same disappointment."

"And where in God's name are we going to come up with that?"

"That's the problem, John. I don't know."

"But you know who this Yorkman is, right?"

"My father's done business with him for years."

John was up and pacing about the room in a frenzy. After several laps, he came to a sudden stop and spun to face David.

"A million and a half pounds, you say?"

"That was it's value twenty years ago. Why?"

"What are your father's cannons worth?"

"My father's cannons?" David feigned confusion. "I suppose on the right market they'd go for fifteen hundred pounds each, but..."

"Do you remember our conversation with those two volunteers at that Richmond tavern last week?" David pursed his lips and tilted his head as if he was having difficulty recollecting the place. John didn't wait for his answer.

"They were telling us about the critical shortage of cannons and artillery pieces in the Colonies!"

"Was that the place where I got caught stealing the..."

"I wrote a note to Patrick Henry on their letter!"

"Oh yes, now I remember! Thomas Matthews and that Dane; Gunnar Andersen!" David's heart was beating with anticipation as he continued to play his part, amazed at how accurately John Silver had predicted his friend's thought processes.

"Don't you see it yet?" John began counting on his fingers. "The Colonies are sure to be at war soon with England, right?"

"It certainly looks that way."

"And they lack good naval and artillery cannons, right?" David nodded. "Your father has eight or nine hundred high quality European cannons sitting in his ware-house, right!"

"There's a thousand of them, John, give or take a few, along with all the..."

"Right!" John continued quickly. "And if we could somehow convince this Yorkman to help us get that treasure, with the understanding that it's to be used to purchase your father's cannons to fight the British, Mister Hewes would certainly grant us two of his sixty naval commissions."

"As a reward for our service to the American Colonies!" added David. "But why do we need the commissions if we have the treasure?"

"Because I want Dorothea's hand in marriage, and her father considers me a commoner. He won't even talk to me unless I can achieve true respectability, and a naval commission will give me that."

"Then...you think Mister Hewes and the Yorkman..?" began David, seeming to have difficulty in grasping the several elements of the plan. He screwed his face this way and that for understanding. Then, as if struck by lightening, he leaped to his feet and began dancing around the room like a schoolboy dismissed for summer vacation.

"Calm down, David!" cried John as he grabbed him by the shoulders.

"But it'll work!" cried David as he continued jumping about the room. "I know it will!"

"There's too many unknown factors remaining to begin celebrating just yet, but we've all afternoon to figure the thing out," said John as David's thoughts returned to that night in Kings Town when his father showed him the game of farthings. "Let's get to it!"

During the remainder of the day, the two discussed every piece of the plan at least a dozen times. David was careful to let John think that all the important ideas were his, with David only suggesting possible solutions to a couple of minor problems.

The next morning, their surrey carried them back over the rough country road to the Hewes and Smith Shipping Company.

"Sir, the two gentlemen you spoke to yesterday morning are back. They say you asked them to return?"

"Thank you, Jenkins. Yes, I did ask them back." It had been a long and tiresome night for the elderly ship owner. He removed his spectacles and massaged his eyes for a long moment.

"Shall I show them in?"

"Yes, but pray give me a few minutes to freshen up first." As the bookkeeper returned to the outer office, Joseph Hewes washed and dried his face at the side-board.

"Why," he muttered to himself, "would Dandridge send these two on such a long and costly trip when he knew I had no positions open? It just isn't like him, espe-cially after I made it so clear what had happened to my ships, unless..." His thoughts drifted back to the meeting in Harrisonburgh where Dandridge made the joke about his daughter's two suitors and that one would have to go away.

"Mister Hewes?" asked John through the half-opened door. "May we come in?"

"By all means, Mister Jones. I've some fresh tea if you're inclined." The elderly man finished wiping his hands dry and then bent painfully backwards at the waist to stretch his cramped and complaining muscles. "I've sugar, but I'm fast out of lemon."

"Thank you, sir!" said John as he reached out and grabbed Mister Hewes' moist hand and shook it long and hard. "I'll take a dash of salt unmixed, to commemorate Sam Adams' tea party."

"You two are acting very strangely," said the old man as he retrieved his hand. "What happened yesterday after you left?"

"We spent the whole day at our inn, sir," said David, giving John a wink.

"Then you didn't look for work?"

"Before I try to explain," began John, "did you find us the openings you were hoping for?"

"No, and your cheerful attitude doesn't make it any easier to tell you, either."

"So there's nothing available?" asked David. "Nothing at all?"

"The jobs I spoke of were with Captain Steele; one of my former merchant masters. He's going to sea tomorrow in a new sloop, just as soon as word comes back from Lloyds that the ship is properly insured. He had two openings, and if you had been hired, it might have been yours and David's first step toward eventual naval commissions." The older man began shaking his head from side to side as he continued. "Gentlemen..."

"Before you say anything else, sir," interrupted John, "perhaps I had best explain what we discovered yesterday evening." John nudged David.

"You tell him, John. It's your plan."

"David and I may be able to earn those commissions."

"Earn them? I thought I made myself clear. Captain Steele already filled the only two positions."

"Oh, you did, sir," interjected David. "You were perfectly clear. It's just that..."

"Then why do you insist on putting me, and yourselves, through any more discomfort? You can't earn or qualify for those naval commissions, and unless you're willing to work as shipwrights, I have nothing for you." Mister Hewes was doing his best at containing himself, but the veins at his temple were already beginning to swell.

"Sir, what John has to say is well worth the hearing," said David, trying to mediate between the two. "His plan might be just the..."

"I'll tell him, David."

"One of you had better tell me quickly while I retain a small portion of my patience!"

"Is it true," began John, "that there is a critical shortage of quality naval and artillery weapons in the Colonies?" He already knew the answer, but it was essential that Mister Hewes be taken one step at a time through their plan.

"No...that's absurd!" the older man blurted instinctively. "We have all the foundries we need, and they're turning out high quality weapons every day; especially the two up in Pennsylvania and Massachusetts."

"We know about the new foundries, sir, and that they won't begin production for at least six months," affirmed David.

"What's your source for this ridiculous information?"

"A week ago, David and I spoke with a Virginia militiaman in Richmond who's father runs one of the colony's only operating foundries."

"Well, I'm a curious fellow," Hewes said as he regained his composure and leaned back in his chair. "Let's say, just for the sake of this conversation, that your information is reliable; and mind you it isn't. What could it possibly have to do with you two and those commissions you don't qualify for?"

"In the first place, sir, I am correct about the shortage of cannons, and you know that to be true," said John with arrogance. "And what I'm about to propose may just change the future of this country you love so much." John waited for a reaction.

"Go on," the elderly man answered calmly.

"Since Mister Adams' so-called tea party in Boston Harbor, not a single cannon or artillery piece has been allowed into the Colonies. It's no secret the British want our weapons limited to small arms and swords." John stopped for a sip of tea and a glance at his companion as he set his cup on the sideboard and continued slowly.

"If David and I could lead an expedition that would provide the Colonies with nearly a thousand of the latest naval and artillery cannons, weapons made at the foundries at Carron, Scotland, and at very little cost to the Colonies, would you grant David and myself two of your naval commissions in exchange?"

Hewes was stunned. One of the major subjects of concern at the meeting in Harrisonburg two weeks before was this very lack of heavy weaponry.

"Mister Jones, if you could accomplish what you are suggesting, I would not only see to it that you are commissioned, but that you'd both have your own commands within six months of putting on the uniform." He leaned forward and stared intently at the two. "Can you do what you're claiming, Mister Jones?"

"I believe we can, sir. But before we reveal how we'll do it, I need to know whether you have the authority to deliver on your part of the bargain."

"I have that authority. Now tell me, how do you two expect to accomplish such a miraculous feat?"

"There's a king's ransom in gold buried on one of the small islands in the Virgin group. The value, when it was put there in 1754, was estimated at around 1,500,000 pounds sterling. The thousand weapons lay in a warehouse in Kings Town, and David's father owns that warehouse. If we can overcome just one obstacle, David and I can purchase those weapons for the Colonies with that treasure."

"How can you be sure the treasure is still there?"

"We know the man who buried it," interjected David.

"And you think he'll be willing to help you retrieve it, after leaving it there for so long?" asked Mister Hewes as both young men nodded he would. "And just how can you be sure he's sympathetic to our cause?"

"We don't know his loyalties yet, sir, but David tells me the man's father was killed by British soldiers back in '70 during that massacre in Boston. If that doesn't make him hate the English, nothing else could."

"And you don't think he's already struck a bargain with someone else?"

"No," said David, a bit too confidently.

"You seem quite sure of that, young man."

"I am, sir. Not much happens in the Caribbean, especially if it involves treasure, that doesn't reach the waterfront of Kings Town. If the treasure had been found, everyone in the West Indies would have known."

The ship owner pushed himself up from his desk and walked stiffly to the window. A large merchant vessel was taking on a cargo of tobacco.

"Gentlemen," began Hewes as he pulled out his pocket watch and flipped open the cover, "before we can go further with this fantastic plan, I'll have to confer with several men I'm meeting for breakfast. I like your plan, but I can't guarantee my associates will share my enthusiasm."

"That's understandable," said John.

"I'm almost certain they'll go along with my recommendation, but I can't go to them without one vital piece of information; something you may not be willing to provide at this time."

"Sir?" asked John.

"They will want to know the name of the man who buried the treasure."

"But, sir?" said David nervously. "If we tell you the man's name, before you get a commitment, what's..."

"Let's hear him out, David." John turned back to the older man. "Why do you need his name? Isn't it enough that we..?"

"The men I'll be meeting with are as honest as they are powerful, Captain Jones. If they agree to give your plan a try, they'll need your man's name so they can write the required letters of introduction. This wouldn't be necessary, but for the unfortunate fact that one of them must leave for Richmond by noon."

"And you'll want us to return this afternoon for their answer?" affirmed John as he wrote the name of Robert Ormerod on a sheet of paper.

"I think it would be better if you came to my home for supper at...say, 1800 hours?" He wrote his address on another sheet of paper and traded it with John. "And you'll have no need for your room at that inn, my friends, because you'll be my guests for the remainder of your stay in Edenton." He stood and led John and David to the door. "And now, sirs, I have much to do before we meet this evening."

"Thank you, Mister Hewes," said John as he gave the ship owner a curt salute.

Once out of the office and beyond earshot, David broke into his loudest war cry.

"Yahoo! We're on our way!"

As the two travelers approached the front gate of the Hewes estate, the last glow of the setting sun left a pink hue in the western sky. The quiet crunch of wet sand and mud under the wheels of their carriage fell silent as their way turned to the green carpet of well-swept grass which led to the front of the two-story home. A Negro servant met them at the front steps.

"You must be Masters Noble and Jones," the black man said with a small bow. "Mister Hewes is expecting you." He took their bags and led them up the steps and across the wide porch to the front door. A maid stepped forward to receive them.

"We're a little early," said John to the girl. "Mister Hewes asked us to..."

"You're exactly ten minutes early, Captain Jones," called Mister Hewes from behind her, "but that's perfectly all right! I've been telling my other guests a little of your plan and they're anxious to meet you." With this, the older man turned to lead the way to the meeting in progress.

"Mister Hewes?" asked John as he caught his host by the sleeve. "Before we meet with these other men, who are they, and how much have you told them?"

Joseph stopped in the hallway. "Relax, young man. These are the very people we need to make your plan work. I can assure you that your information is safe with them."

"But..."

"Be patient, Captain Jones. You'll understand when I introduce you." He gave John a fatherly squeeze on the arm. "Shall we go in now?"

A moment later, John and David stood in the wide entrance to the sitting room.

"Look, John!" said David in a whisper.

"Good Lord," answered John slowly. "It's the other men from Charles Town."

"Gentlemen," said Mister Hewes with a flourish, "may I introduce Captain John Paul Jones and his companion, Master David Noble of Kings Town. John, David, please meet my distinguished guests and our partners in possibly the most important single venture in the fight for American independence."

The glow of the fireplace cast an amber hue over the three men. John and David only recognized one. His picture hung on the wall at the Paul residence in Fredericksburg.

"John," whispered David. "Isn't that Thomas Jefferson?"

"I believe so," John whispered back slowly. The two young mariners stood in amazement at the men and the room before them.

The library was a sacred place, a massive wood and velvet cathedral dedicated to the worship of the hunt and of man's battles against himself. The walls were lined with the instruments of this high religious order; firearms and sharp-edged weapons of various sizes from two previous centuries and countless crusades. Between these, hung at regular intervals, were the martyrs; the stuffed heads of beasts and the uniforms of several foreign soldiers taken from the mission fields. An officer's sword, far more elegant than John's, hung over the fireplace, framed on either side by models of famous British ships of the line. And serving as pews, four massive chairs upholstered with roughly tanned leather sat about the fireplace at perfect intervals. Finally, standing alone in a small alcove, stood the Patron Saint of this worship of the masculine; a small bronze cannon which had been inscribed with gratitude and presented to Joseph Hewes by the Royal Navy.

Women were not allowed in this hallowed hall, except to tidy up after the royal priests had conducted their rites. It must have been the housekeeper who had set the holy water of this male ritual; a yet-unopened bottle of brandy and six glasses on the doilies.

"John and David," said Mister Hewes as he stuffed the doilies into a pocket and flashed a disapproving glance at the butler, "this is Assemblyman Jefferson, the most enthusiastic supporter of our plan."

"Very pleased to make your acquaintance, Mister Jefferson," said John as he shook the older man's hand.

"Likewise, Captain Jones," the statesman answered. Before David could properly greet the older man, Mister Hewes had pulled John and him across the room to a man in his early 50's.

"And this is Esek Hopkins, the favored nominee for the position of Commander in Chief of our Navy."

"This is a special privilege, sir," said John.

"And for me, also, Captain Jones. Joseph has told us the main points of your plan, but I'm very anxious to hear it from you."

The third man was the oldest, a man with white hair and a limp.

"Our last distinguished colleague is Alexander Forrestal, the owner of perhaps the largest shipyard in South Carolina."

As the six men exchanged handshakes and introductory information, Mister Hewes became aware of the maid standing in the doorway.

"Gentlemen," Mister Hewes interrupted, "I believe supper is served. If you'll follow me to the dining room, we can continue our discussion over some of the finest cooking this side of the Atlantic Ocean."

The enthusiasm for treasure quickly changed to a manly drive to satisfy a hearty appetite as the men took their places about the massive cherry wood table. So as to allow for their continued discussion, all six men were seated toward one end, Mister Jefferson on one side with John and David, and the other three across from them.

"Well, Captain Jones," said Mister Jefferson, "Joseph has had us here since early morning. He tells me there's more than enough treasure to purchase 500 of the new carronades and an equal number of long range artillery pieces."

"That's true, sir," answered John, "but..."

"And I must assume that all the necessary support equipment will be included in the purchase?"

"Yes, sir, it is," answered John. "But I must correct one thing you said. I didn't tell Mister Hewes that there were an equal number of shipboard and artillery weapons. It's nearly an even mix, but David can give you the exact number because they belong to his father." The older men gave David a questioning look.

"And just how did your father come by so many of these wonderful weapons?" asked Jefferson. "I'm sure you're aware they've only been making carronades for a little under two years."

"I know that, sir," answered David. "As I understand it, the Dutch ship's log only spoke of seven hundred and fifty-five bolts of linen from the mills in England. Obviously, someone was smuggling the weapons into the Colonies. But before the ship could reach South Carolina, it was captured by a pirate of my father's acquaintance. This pirate...his name is Joshua Smoot...had no idea the cannons were in the bilge. He traded the ship and cargo for a fast French Corvette my father owned. It was a week later that we discovered the cannons. When Smoot heard about what he'd overlooked, he came demanding that we return his cannons."

"Your father deals with pirates?" asked Hopkins, the most religious of the four.

"My father's a businessman, sir, and makes deals with whomever he must."

"It doesn't matter, Esek," said Mister Jefferson with a hand to the older man's shoulder. "Can you tell us more about the cannons, David?"

"Aye. There are 540 naval carronades, varying in bore from eight to twelve inches, and 645 of the long range cannons that can serve equally well aboard ship or in the field. If you and my father agree to this exchange, he'll provide a detailed list of not only their bore sizes, but the dimensions of their mounting points."

"Good," answered Mister Hewes. "That will expedite their deployment throughout the Colonies."

"I have an important question," said Mister Jefferson, "and I trust it won't offend you."

"Sir?" asked David.

"Why hasn't your father already begun selling them, a few at a time?"

"As I said, sir, he's a business man. The value of a certain piece of merchandise is dictated by how badly it's needed at any given moment. He knows of the trouble between the Colonies and England, and he's simply been waiting for the right time to accept an offer."

"Will he agree to sell his weapons for the million and-a-half pounds, should you be successful on Dead Man's Chest?"

"He'd be thrilled to get that much, Mister Jefferson. And to set your minds at ease, I also know that he favors America over England, even though he's a British subject."

"Oh?" asked Jefferson. "And why is that?"

"Because he knows America will be a vast treasure of commerce, sir, and he desires to be a part of it. It's as simple as that." David took a sip of wine and continued. "I know how my father thinks. He'll sell his weapons to the Colonies."

"David," interjected Mister Hewes, "would you tell us how the treasure got on Dead Man's Chest? I tried to tell your story, but I'm afraid I left out most of the finer details."

"It's a rather complex set of circumstances, gentlemen," began David, "but as best as I remember, it came from a Spanish treasure galleon called the Santissima Trinidad. She was one of the last to transport gold and silver from Porto Bello to Spain. An especially large treasure."

"And this New York merchant's great uncle was the one who took it from the Spaniards?" asked Mister Hopkins.

"Yes he was, sir," answered David. "His name was Andrew Murray. He and John Flint were partners and commanded two ships -- the Royal James and the Walrus. Murray talked Flint into laying up at Grand Turk to construct a fort while he attacked the galleon."

"I've heard tales of John Flint," said Forrestal, "and I find it difficult to believe he'd sit on an island while another pirate captured a Spanish Galleon carrying over two million in treasure."

"That's how Robert Ormerod got involved," continued David. "Flint agreed to keep his unruly crew on Grand Turk only if he was provided with a worthwhile hostage."

"Captain Murray would risk hiding two-thirds of the treasure on Dead Man's Chest with his grandnephew held hostage?"

"Aye, Mister Hopkins. Even though Flint agreed to one part of a three-way split, Murray knew he'd kill for the other two. It was a desperate act that ended up costing Murray his life anyway, but the treasure is still there, right where Robert Ormerod buried it."

"I don't understand," added Hopkins. "If Ormerod was held hostage, how could he also bury the treasure?"

"Murray's intention was to provide Robert as a hostage, but the Santissima Trinidad presented itself before Murray had to deliver Robert."

"Why hasn't Ormerod gone back to Dead Man's Chest himself?" asked Forrestal. "Surely he has the money to hire a crew. And considering the size of the treasure...well, it just doesn't make any sense."

"It's not that simple, sir," interrupted John. "As David explained to me last night, there are at least two very good reasons why he hasn't. In the first place, Dead Man's Chest lies no more than two miles off the north coast of Saint Croix, fully visible from Christiansted. Ormerod knows, as well as the pirates who sail those waters, that the moment a ship departs from Dead Man's Chest, it'll be boarded and searched by the first pirates who can reach it. The other reason has to do with a promise he made to his bride at the alter."

"Then how," asked Jefferson, "supposing that we can elude these pirates, do you expect to persuade Ormerod to donate his treasure to our cause?"

"I've thought of that," answered John. "This morning, Mister Hewes mentioned some letters of introduction. If you'll send David and me to New York Town with those letters stating why the Colonies need the cannons, I believe he'll change his mind. He must be feeling the King's grip by now, like every other merchant along the Eastern Seaboard. And after all, he's a native American, isn't he?"

"You've a point there, Captain Jones," said Hewes as he looked to the others for confirmation. "But before we go any further, might I suggest we move this discussion back to the library where we started it? I've some very old and friendly brandy I'd like you all to try."

As promised by their host, the brandy was spectacular. After a sea story from Mister Hewes, Captain Jones moved toward Mister Jefferson.

"Sir? Concerning these letters...you said something about me going to New York, but you didn't mention David. Will he be going with me?"

"You heard correctly, Captain Jones. No, he won't," answered Jefferson. "At the same time you depart for New York with your letters, David will be sent with a similar packet to his father in Kings Town. By the time you each return to Mister Forrestal's yards at Charles Town, you with the map and David with his father's agreement, the twin frigates should be ready to sail."

"Twin frigates?" asked John.

"Yes, Captain Jones," answered Forrestal, stepping up to the two. "It has to do with the exchange at sea. Joseph will explain later."

"It'll be up to you, David," said Jefferson, "whether you want to go with Captain Jones to Dead Man's Chest or return to Kings Town on the second ship."

"I'll go with John."

"We expected you would."

"Mister Jefferson?" asked John. "How soon will David and I leave with our letters?"

"You can leave on the morning tide. But there's one more matter we must settle."

"Sir?"

"It has to do with the King's Warrant for the arrest of a certain Scottish Captain named John Paul." The statesman pulled a folded piece of paper from his waist pocket and handed it to John.

John read the familiar warrant. Before he had finished, the statesman was speaking again.

"Yes, Captain Paul," added Mister Jefferson, "we know all about the man you killed at Tobago, and of your subsequent flight to Kings Town and then Virginia."

"But how?"

"You've a room above your tailor shop," said Mister Jefferson. "Do you know how it's used?"

"It's a storage room."

"What else is it used for?"

"I rent it out to the Masons. They meet there once a month."

"General Washington belongs to those Masons."

"How long has he been watching me?"

"Since last year when you and your friend arrived from Jamaica," answered Jefferson. "He learned you were a ship's master from Captain Dandridge, and thought you might be valuable to our cause."

"Was it Captain Dandridge who told the General about the warrant?"

"We have many friends in the government, Captain Paul," added Mister Jefferson. "As far as I know, Dandridge knows nothing of your fugitive status."

"Yes he does," said John with a note of shame in his voice.

"Oh?" asked Joseph. "What makes you think so?"

"That's the reason David and I are here. He threatened to turn me in to the King's Men if I had any further contact with his daughter, and then Mister Henry gave us his letter of introduction to you, sir."

"So your coming here..." began Mister Jefferson.

"I thought that if I could get a naval commission, it might make a difference with Captain Dandridge." John thought for a moment and then continued. "Does this warrant change things?"

"What do you mean," asked Hewes, "does it change things?"

"Can you still trust me to lead this secret mission for you?"

"It makes you perfect for the mission," answered Jefferson.

"But..." began John.

"You're a desperate man, Captain Paul," interrupted Forrestal, "and that means you'll go the extra league to make sure your mission is completed."

"I've just had a thought," said Jefferson as he leaned against the fireplace and looked at John. "This warrant may work to our advantage, but only with your permission and careful cooperation."

"Sir?"

"I'd like to make it appear that you're hiding somewhere in the North."

"For what reason?" asked John.

"Now that the King's Warrant is about, it's necessary that the British be looking for the fugitive John Paul up North, while the treasure hunter John Jones is in the West Indies."

"How would you accomplish that?" asked John.

"By having you carry on a weekly correspondence from New York Town."

"But..." protested John.

"I already have someone in mind who'd write and receive letters in your name."

"Isn't that a bit dangerous?" asked John.

"Not if you provide me with enough information about those who might write to you." John considered for a long moment. "This isn't up to you, Captain Jones."

"Very well, sir," said John obediently. "Perhaps while your man is at it, he can write to my partners in Tobago. They owe me some money."

"Perhaps," Jefferson agreed. "There is one other thing we'll need, and it's quite personal."

"Sir?"

"We'll need to know everything about your relationship with Miss Dandridge."

"But she has nothing to do with..."

"She has everything to do with it," protested Jefferson. "What better way to send the King's Men searching in the opposite direction than by an angry father. That's why you'll have to provide me with those personal facts about yourself and this girl, and especially what you told her about this trip to Edenton."

"But my partners on Tobago could provide the King's men with that information," John protested. "I owe the Lieutenant Governor some money. They could deliver it to the Magistrate and I'm certain..."

"Of course that would work if we had the time for a postal packet to sail down and back, but we don't. It'll have to be Captain Dandridge who turns you in."

"Very well," said John reluctantly. "But whoever writes for me must follow my instructions to the letter, otherwise..."

"Don't worry, Captain Jones," said Jefferson. "Everything will be done exactly as it should, and with the utmost discretion."

"I hope I can trust you, sir, because I won't tolerate my relationship with Miss Dandridge being jeopardized further."

"Thomas," interrupted Joseph, "I think our two young friends should retire now.

They have to be at my docks early and Captain Paul has a lot of notes to write."

Mister Jefferson looked at his pocket watch and then at the two young men.

"Joseph is right, gentlemen. If all goes as planned, we'll meet again in a few months to celebrate the success of this mission."

"Sirs," said John as David followed the servant to the hallway, "I speak for both of us when I say thank you for placing this special trust in us. We'll do everything within our power to accomplish this mission for you and the Colonies."

"I'm sure you will, Captain Paul," answered Mister Jefferson as he raised his glass in a salute to the two young seamen. "May God give you fair winds and following seas..." He hesitated at the look on John's face. "Is there something else, Captain?

"Yes, there is, sir. What are David and I to be during this voyage?"

"I don't follow you, John."

"Are we to be merchants, privateers, or pirates?"

"Does it matter?" asked David.

"Not unless we get caught," answered John as he gave Mister Jefferson a questioning look.

"I see what you mean," said the statesman.

"Are you saying," asked David of his companion, "that we could be hanged?"

"Yes," answered John, "unless we have a Letter of Marque from one of the Colonial Governors."

"I'm not sure that would be enough," offered Mister Jefferson. "Our plan was that you and your men would pose as a Dutch crew trading with the islands. I suppose..."

"Sir?" asked John.

"Give the others and me some time to consider the problem. Hopefully, we'll have an answer before you depart in the morning."

"Good enough, sir," answered John with a nudge at David's ribs. As John and David climbed the stairs to the second floor, Hewes put a hand on Jefferson's shoulder.

"Well, Thomas, was I right?"

"About our cannons, or these two young men?"

"Both," answered Hewes.

"Well, it's no longer a mystery where our cannons went. What's important is that we get them back." Jefferson took a sip of his drink and continued. "If these two prove to be what they appear, I'd say we've made a very worthwhile investment. And even if they turn out to be crooks or complete incompetents, what have we lost?"

"Two very expensive ships!" interjected the old ship builder with obvious concern.

"Alex," Jefferson assured, "you can trust us for the ships."

"And when the Continental Navy is formed," added Joseph, "I'm certain congress will authorize the reimbursement of the moneys we've taken from our pockets."

"And my Dutch investors?" added Forrestal. "What shall I tell them?"

"Tell them the British commandeered the ships and you'll build them two more," answered Hewes, "exactly like the first."

"I suppose you're correct," answered Forrestal after a moment of deep thought.

"I am, Alex," said Hewes as he took quills, paper and an inkwell from his desk. "We've some letters to write, gentlemen, and several important matters to agree upon."

"Oh!" said Jefferson to his host. "There's one thing you must tell Captain Jones before he sails."

"And that is?" asked Hewes.

"He must not go anywhere other than New York and then back to Charles Town. To do otherwise could hurt not only himself, but jeopardize the security of this mission.

"I'll tell him in the morning."

"Gentlemen!" said Esek Hopkins. "May I offer a short prayer?"

The other three men set their glasses on the table and lowered their heads.

"Our heavenly and most Gracious Father, please extend Your Mighty Hand of protection an extra span this day, so that the efforts of Captain Paul and David Noble may succeed. And grant our fervent prayer for the release from the grasp of England every man, woman and child of these thirteen American Colonies which You have given into our stewardship. It is in the name of our sovereign Lord and Savior, Jesus Christ that we ask it, Amen."

"And here's to liberty!" said Jefferson as he opened his eyes and raised his glass high in the air. "May she reign forever!"

CHAPTER 6

Two hours before dawn, three silent figures stood at the upper end of the Hewes and Smith Shipping Company's dock, which extended into the Chowan River's frigid waters. Their knit caps were pulled sailor-fashion over their ears, with their collars overlapping the lower edges, leaving only the minimum of skin exposed to the nip of the chilling breeze. Tied up at either side of the dock were two nearly identical Virginia privateers, the most beautiful vessels John and David had ever seen. Each carried fourteen cannons and combined the best features of both the sloop and the brigantine, with masts raked aft nearly ten degrees for the greatest advantage in stiff winds. As they watched in silence, a dozen men aboard each craft were making their final preparations for getting under way, their bodies silhouetted against the light of the lanterns hanging from their taffrails. The complaints of the rigging against the timbers, and the smells of fresh varnish and bare wood made John's pulse quicken. Mister Hewes thrust a small leather packet toward the young Captain.

"These are the letters you'll present to Mister Ormerod. I must insist that once he reads them, they be destroyed. This mission is much too important to be compromised by them falling into the wrong hands." John took the leather case, but it fell to the dock with a deep thud.

"Oops!" said John as he reached for the packet. "Why's it so heavy?" asked John, turning it over in his hands.

"I've had a pound of lead sewn into the bottom so it'll sink. If boarded by a British scout ship, throw the packet into the sea." He handed David an identical leather pouch, weighted as the first. "David, you'll carry similar letters to your father in Kings Town, but I doubt you'll have as much difficulty convincing your father to sell his weapons as Captain Paul will have convincing Mister Ormerod to reveal the location of the treasure."

"How do the letters refer to me?" asked John.

"Pardon?"

"I'm assuming the surname of Jones for this mission, aren't I?"

"You're quite right," answered the old man as he began walking down the ramp toward the waiting ships. The river's current dragged at the pilings, bringing a gurgling sound from beneath the dock.

"John, you'll sail onboard the Eagle with Captain Henry Steele. He'll see to your every need. And if you desire it, he'll even accompany you to Mister Ormerod's home. The Swan will take David to Kings Town. I would enjoy speaking with both of you longer, but you must set sail now or you may not clear the sound before the tide changes."

"Thank you for trusting us with so much, Sir," said John. After a long handshake with the elderly man, John gave David a manly hug and a fist to the shoulder. "Give your father my best."

"I will, John. And be extra careful in New York Town. I hear the women up there are hungry for husbands."

"Ha!" answered John with a wink. "And I suppose those Jamaican women aren't?" Several of the seamen joined the two in a knowing chuckle.

"Oh!" added Mister Hewes. "I knew there was something else!"

"Sir?" asked John.

"It took us a while, but Mister Jefferson and I finally arrived at an answer to your question."

"My question?"

"You asked about your status while on your mission."

"Then we're to be privateers, aren't we?" asked David.

"Better still," answered the elderly man, "you're to be commissioned officers in the Continental Navy."

"But there is no Continental Navy," protested John, as Joseph pulled two rolled parchments from his waistcoat pocket.

"These are only temporary," said Joseph as he handed each man his appointment, "but they'll serve the purpose much better than privateer commissions. If you're arrested by the King, we'll insure that the necessary documents are prepared in order to convince him that our Navy was formed prior to your departure."

John and David studied their commissions and then looked at each other's.

After taking solemn oaths to serve and protect the Colonies, the young adventurers stowed their precious packets in their duffle bags and leaped aboard their ships. Moments later, the bow lines of both craft were released as they piked away from the dock far enough to allow the four long sweeps to be set for the pull into mid-river.

"Captain Jones!" called Mister Hewes as he remembered Jefferson's warning. "Go nowhere but New York and back!"

"And you as well, sir!" called back Captain Jones, unable to hear the old man's feeble voice above the clatter of the ship.

The strong current of the Chowan River carried the two craft eastward to the Currituck Sound by six bells, about the time the winds began to pick up. Until they were well past the anchored ships and into the easy current, the Swan and the Eagle held close formation, the Eagle leading the way. The only sounds reaching back to the elderly ship owner were the faint calls of the watches and the orders of the first officers. As planned, both ships glided out through Oregon Inlet and into the open sea just after nine in the morning. As the Eagle dipped it's colors in a salute to the Swan, John and David exchanged their final farewells. It would be at least a month before their paths would cross again at Charles Town.

The Eagle was extremely fast, taking only three days to reach the Northern Colonies and round Sandy Hook for the predawn glide into New York Harbor. A thick and tiresome ground fog surrounded them from water line to mid-mast. It began at Gibbet Island and carried on far into the East River, obscuring the town completely as they pulled their way against the gentle current. If one looked straight up at the dark sky, most of the stars were still visible, with faint streaks of sunlight trailing in over the eastern sky.

"Gibbet Island, three points off the larboard bow!" called the watch from his perch atop the mainmast.

"At the tiller!" commanded Captain Steele. "Come starboard half a point!"

As the tiller was brought over, the only sounds breaking the death-like silence were the rhythmical dip of the long sweeps and the dripping water from their tips as they swung forward for their next stroke, mixed with the ever-present whisper of the icy water sliding past the oak planks of the Eagle's hull. As the sun sent more of its illuminating rays across the harbor, the watch aloft could just begin to make out the tops of the higher structures along the town's approaching skyline.

"Battery and Crager's Wharf 400 yards off the larboard bow!" cried the top watch. "There's two of them, Captain Steele!"

"Bosun!" called Captain Steele through his graying and droplet-covered beard. "Go below an' get Jones! Tell him to get his things together. Tell him we'll be at Peck's Dock within a glass."

Captain Steele had taken a quick dislike to the Pup Captain, as he called John. In only three short days, the younger man had managed to disrupt Steele's chain of command with his continual meddling and criticism of the older man's control over his men. Steele would be glad to be rid of the man for a day or two. A few minutes later, John joined Steele on the quarterdeck.

"What's this about Peck's Dock?" asked John with a look to larboard. "You told me Pearl Street was next to the Battery. Why not land at Crager's, nearer to Mister Ormerod's home?"

"Because two British men-o'-war are tied up there, Mister Jones. That's why!" said Steele angrily as he walked forward a few paces. "Mister Peck's a good friend of mine, and there should be less chance of questions being asked at his dock." The forty year-old Captain turned back to John with a wry smile. "And besides, you'll enjoy the walk through the streets." Steele relished the thought of John suffering through the two and a half mile gauntlet of hucksters and beggars. "Jones could use the humbling," he mused to himself.

John moved to the larboard rail to get a glimpse of the town and the two British warships just becoming visible through the fog. Eight ruddy ducks were startled by the dip and feather of the Eagle's four great sweeps. They scurried across the water toward the shore. As they settled back into the cold brine, several scolded the Eagle while the rest resumed their feeding. Another quarter mile up river, the Eagle emerged from the low fog, exposing the moisture-covered rigging to the new sun; the droplets sparkling like diamonds about a countess's throat.

"We must be near a shipyard," said John, half to himself.

"Brilliant observation!" said Steele sarcastically as he squirted a stream of tobacco juice over the rail at a scrap of freshly cut oak.

"You're still angry with me, aren't you, Henry?"

"It's Captain Steele to you, and yes, I'm very angry."

"Your problem is that you just can't take constructive criticism."

"Wrong!" barked Henry. "You questioned my authority in front of my crew, and you never apologized!"

"But I was right! You had no cause..."

"Enough!" growled Captain Steele as he glanced forward at his crew. They had stopped their work to listen to this latest dispute. "I'll not speak to you of these matters in front of my crew again!" The two captains stared at each other for several moments before Captain Steele spoke. "I've something to do below. Do you think you can get the Eagle to Peck's dock without losing discipline?"

John turned to look where Steele was pointing. "Aye," John answered coldly.

"Then be about it, Mister Jones."

New York Town wasn't but twice the size of Kings Town, albeit more elegant and at least as busy for this early hour. As the sleek privateer came within a hundred yards of the slip, Captain Jones brought the tiller to starboard. "Stand by forward with the lines!" ordered John as they closed on an anchored Dutch merchantman that was taking on fresh cut oak planking and dark barrels.

"Ship your sweeps!" cried John as the Eagle eased forward toward the single open slip. As the bow eased between the two docks, the two crewmen leaped across and threw turns about the bollards to stop the Eagle's forward motion.

"Ahoy there!" called the taller of two British soldiers from the dock as they walked forward amongst the flying hawsers and busy crewmen. "State your business and present your papers!" John strode across the deck toward the two, and then turned back to see if Captain Steele had come topside yet. To his astonishment, a British Naval Lieutenant stood next to the tiller with the Royal Navy's Ensign hanging behind him at the half-staff.

"'Tis the H.M.S. Eagle, on the King's business!" returned Steele with a perfect British accent. He looked the two young men up and down for a moment. "By the looks of your uniforms, I'd say you've spent the night asleep yonder on that pile of fishing nets!" Steele jumped to the dock with his false papers in hand. "Who's in charge of you two sorry excuses for soldiers?"

"General Gage, sir, but he's up in Boston." The taller of the two men was completely intimidated and gave the papers only a cursory inspection before returning them to the imposing officer.

"And it's a good thing for you he is!" Steele barked. "If I had my way, you'd be before him within an hour explaining your slovenly appearance! Now, be about your duties!" he ordered firmly. "But first, see to those filthy uniforms."

"Yes, sir!" the taller soldier shouted back obediently and then marched smartly to where his bewildered compatriot stood.

"You did that well, Captain," whispered John.

"I used to be one of 'em," answered Steele. "But now to your mission, Mister Jones. According to my employer's instructions, I'm to send two armed men to accompany you on your way."

"Mister Jefferson's orders?

"No, Mister Hewes'," answered Steele coldly.

"I expect to be gone at least until nightfall," said John. "I'll be sending your two men back once I reach Mister Ormerod's home. Whatever the outcome of my meeting, I would expect my host will provide me a carriage for the ride back to the Eagle." John began to walk away, but stopped and looked back at the disguised British Captain.

"Was there something else?" asked Steele.

"Just a thought," John said as he took a step back toward Captain Steele.

"Well, let's hear it man!" Steele barked. "Ya never held yer tongue since North Carolina whenever ya thought to correct my command of the Eagle, so why hold it now?"

"I know you don't like me, Henry, so I'll make this easy for both of us. Since David Noble won't return to Charles Town for at least a month, I may want to return by land."

"And when will you know for sure?"

"I'll let you know when I return."

"You do that!" Steele hissed, pleased at the thought of having nothing more to do with the impudent fellow.

With the packet of letters under his arm and his sword hanging from his belt, John and his two escorts marched off the dock and onto the wet cobblestones of Water Street. A rainsquall passing earlier had left a silver sheen on the cold stones and across the slate roofs of the closely huddled shops. The many peddlers driving their carts from the docks into town were silhouetted in the bright reflections. An equal number of vendors and runners from the various brothels along Queen Street jostled past the three men, racing to be first at the sea-weary crewmen.

As the three neared the south end of Water Street, they passed several dank smelling sail lofts and chandler's shops, which huddled under the tangle of ship's bowsprits. Finally, they broke from the crowded narrows and into the little open courtyard at the head of Crager's Wharf. A knot of British sailors standing at the foot of one of the great Men-of-war's gangplanks took only slight notice of the three as they passed over to Great Dock Street, across Parade Street, almost to Hanover Square and the edge of the shore battery. Here finally, was Pearl Street, containing only six large homes. The second on the right was number 86-90, the home of Robert and Moira Ormerod.

Robert Ormerod was a third generation New Yorker, and was considered to be one of the three wealthiest merchants in the town. He had become so by inheriting his father's well-established business in '70. His home reflected his affluence; being a two-storied structure of red bricks laid in the rarely used Flemish Cross Bond pattern. The checkerboard of small windows covering its face was an artist's gallery of French lace curtains, attesting to the presence of a woman of taste and quality. It was Mrs. Ormerod who answered the heavy knock on the double oak doors.

"Good morning, sir," she said as she opened the door, "may I help you?" Mrs. Omerod was an exceptionally fine woman, hardly the sort John would expect to help bury a treasure on some God-forsaken island in the Caribbean. Although she was clearly in her early forties, John was taken by her youthful beauty. Her light Irish brogue and dark brown eyes reminded him of the girl he hoped was waiting for him in Virginia.

"Yes you may, Ma'am," John answered with a curt salute. "I've come about Mister Ormerod." Moira was confused for a moment. Robert had never met with business associates at their home, especially not with an armed escort.

"My husband left for the docks a half hour ago. I expect him to return at any moment." She paused as she reconsidered the three men, her hand coming to her lips as she went pale. "Has something happened to my husband?"

"No, Ma'am, at least not to our knowledge." John could sense her uneasiness and wished to cause her no further distress.

"I'm Captain Jones from Edenton, North Carolina. I carry several very important dispatches for your husband." He touched the leather pouch hnaging at his side. "Would you mind if we waited here on the porch?" As she considered, a highly polished black carriage turned into the drive and stopped adjacent to John and his two escorts.

"Oh, there he is now," exclaimed Mrs. Omerod. "Robert," called Moira to the occupant of the carriage, "these gentlemen are here to see you! They've some dispatches from North Carolina!" John walked to Mister Ormerod's carriage with an extended hand.

"I'm Captain John Paul Jones, sir. I carry letters from several men, including Thomas Jefferson, George Washington and Esek Hopkins."

"Well, in that case, won't you and your friends join us for morning tea?" Robert stepped from the carriage and turned to his wife. "That's if we have enough."

"Don't be silly, Robert! We have enough tea for an army!"

"It would only be me, as my escorts will be returning to our ship."

"Very well, Captain Jones. Won't you come inside?" said Robert as John turned to his two escorts.

"You may return to the ship." With a salute, the two were gone.

"Must be rather important letters to have a ship's Captain hand carry them all this way," said Robert as he led John inside and into his library.

"They are, sir. Very important." John broke the wax seal from the single buckle and laid back the flap it protected. Inside the pouch were the five letters Joseph Hewes said would be there. Mister Ormerod took the first and most general of the five--the one from the General of the Virginia Militia--and walked to the desk by the front window. As with the leather packet, each letter was sealed with wax; a different color and signet on each.

> *To Mister Robert Ormerod:*
>
> *The purpose of this letter is twofold; first to introduce Captain John Paul Jones, and second, to request your assistance in a most important and strategic mission for these thirteen American Colonies.*
>
> *As I'm certain you already know, the relationship between the Colonies and King George III has deteriorated to an intolerable level; a level most certain to foment a revolution in the near future. The Colonies are ill-prepared at this time for such a conflict. We are dealing as best we can with most of the deficiencies, but I fear that in our present state, we have little chance of holding the British back, much less of defeating them either on land or at sea. The four other letters Captain Jones carries will explain in detail how you may serve your fellow Americans.*
>
> *Mister Ormerod, your country needs your help ,and I beseech you to assist Captain Jones with his mission. May God give you the wisdom to make the right decision in this most urgent matter.*
>
> *G. Washington,*
> *General, Virginia Militia*

"Interesting," said Ormerod as he looked up at the younger man. "I was expecting you two weeks ago."

"Two weeks ago?" asked John in amazement as Ormerod crossed to his desk. "But we hadn't even..." As John searched for the words, Robert held out a letter.

"Here, read this." John took the letter and read quickly.

"Who sent this?"

"Someone who didn't want his identity known," answered the Yorkman. "But his intent was clear. He was preparing me for your coming."

"I'm not the agent this letter introduces, Mister Ormerod," said John as he turned the letter over. "And there's nothing here about the cannons or the treasure."

"The treasure?"

"Yes," answered John, "the Treasure of Dead Man's Chest."

"Hmmm," said Robert as he gave John a curious look and opened the second letter.

"Where did this letter come from, Mister Ormerod?" asked John. "It has no return address."

"Look at the wax seal," answered Robert without looking up from his reading. It was the same imprint as was on the leather pouch. "Someone in the Committees of Correspondence wanted to soften me up before your arrival; perhaps one of these men," said Robert as he waved the five letters in the air.

"No," said John. "It couldn't be one of them."

"Oh? And why not?"

"Because I only approached them a week ago with my plan."

"Then there's obviously another explanation," said Robert as he took up the third letter. For the next quarter hour, the merchant sat at his desk reading and re-reading the lengthy letters. As he read, he made several notes and underlined sections he found questionable. Finally he turned to the young captain.

"How did they find out about my daughter, Captain Jones?"

"Your daughter?"

"Who told you about the fire?"

"David Noble told us, sir. He spoke as if it was common knowledge in Kings Town."

"David Noble?"

"Aye. He's the son of the Kings Town merchant, Charles Noble."

"Hmmm," said Robert as he thought. "You know of course, that they want me to accompany you to Dead Man's Chest?"

"Oh?" John was surprised. "My understanding was that you were only being asked to provide me with a map. May I read that letter?"

"No, you may not."

"But?"

"But nothing, Captain Jones" the Yorkman said as he dropped the letters one by one into the fire. "And regarding the map, your friends are correct. I'd go with you before I'd ever consent to draw another."

"You would?"

"In an instant, but for a promise I made on my wedding day."

"Sir?"

"Captain Jones," began Robert slowly, "there's so much you don't know."

"Can you tell me?"

"Moira was a passenger on that treasure ship we attacked twenty years ago. During the three months we were in league with my great uncle, and then prisoners of John Flint, she and I witnessed more than 150 men lose their lives because of the treasure you and your supporters want so badly. She saw my great uncle killed by pirates, and she was standing next to her own father when the concussion of a cannon ball felled him. Every farthing of that treasure was paid for by the blood of good and bad men. On our wedding day, Moira asked me to promise her that no matter what happened, I would never go back to Dead Man's Chest, or aid another in retrieving that treasure. As much as I want to go with you, Captain Jones, I can't break my vow to Moira, any more than I could divorce her without cause or bring my little girl back from the grave." Robert gave John a long look. "I know how badly the Colonies need a thousand cannons, but I can't break my vow. I'm sorry you had to travel so far for nothing, Captain Jones."

"Is there no way I can change...?" John broke off his question as Mrs. Ormerod backed through the partially opened door with a tray.

"Excuse the intrusion, Captain Jones, but if my husband is to be back to his office at a decent hour, he needs to eat breakfast." She set the tray on the sideboard and served up two bowls of oatmeal with raw sugar and butter. "I would assume you haven't eaten either, Captain Jones."

"No, I haven't," said John with a smile as he picked up the bowl. "Thank you."

Moira leaned close to her husband and whispered. "Robert, may I speak to you alone for a moment?"

"Certainly, Dear." He looked at John. "Has it anything to do with Captain Jones?"

"It's something..." She hesitated while she gave Captain Jones a long look. "It's something you both should hear." She handed Robert his cereal and then took a seat opposite the fireplace.

"First," she began, "I must apologize for eavesdropping on your conversation a moment ago."

"How much did you hear?" asked Robert.

"Enough," she answered as she looked to the sea captain and then back to her husband. "Robert, I know I made you swear never to go back to that evil place. But there's now a greater need than my fear of further bloodshed. The colonies need those cannons and gun powder, and you owe it to your father and the families of those other four people killed with him in Boston." Moira stood and walked to her husband. "I want you to go with him, Robert."

"Then you release me from my oath?" he asked as he took his wife by the shoulders and looked deeply into her brown Irish eyes.

"Yes, I do, Robert. And I know the good Lord would have it that way also."

"Thank you, Moira." He took his wife's left hand and kissed the open palm gently, just where he had been forced to cut the cross twenty years before at Savannah. The scar had never disappeared completely, leaving a small white "X" over her heart line. It was a constant reminder of that fateful night on the Walrus when he had cut Billy Bones, and John Silver helped the young couple escape. The experience had been bloody and almost more than either of them could endure. But during the idle moments, when his thoughts were allowed to wander, they always went back to the deck of the Royal James and the excitement of his short career as a pirate.

"Captain Jones," asked Robert as he released his wife, "do you have transportation back to Charles Town?"

"Yes, I do. The privateer Eagle is waiting for me at Peck's Dock. But I was hoping to make other arrangements."

"Other arrangements?"

"I told the Captain I may go back to Charles Town by land. I'm to send him word as soon as I know your decision."

"Why would you go by land?" asked Robert. "It would be so much quicker by ship, provided the weather remains good."

"Well..." John hesitated, searching for the best way to put it. "There's a girl living near Fredericksburg I wish to see."

"But you could see her much quicker if we went by sea, and you were dropped off in the Rappahannock. You could reach Fredericksburg in a day from there by horseback."

"I suppose you're right." John didn't want to see Captain Steele again, but neither did he want the New Yorker to know of the trouble between them. "You're right. We'll go back on the Eagle."

"Captain Jones," continued Robert as he dipped his spoon in his cereal, "when you learned of the treasure, were you told of any other part of it; any part not on Dead Man's Chest?"

"No. David only mentioned the million and a half." John cocked his head slightly. "Is there more?"

"Yes." Robert paced across the room and returned to the hearth as he thought. "I have in my employ an elderly gentleman by the name of Benjamin Gunn. He was my Great Uncle's personal steward on the Royal James. The man's a little odd, but he has a heart of pure gold."

"Odd?"

"Yes, a natural half-wit. My uncle chose him because he's totally incapable of the most benign treachery. He operates my Boston warehouse, but he's as close to this treasure as anyone."

"But how..?"

"After we buried our two shares of the treasure on Dead Man's Chest," continued Robert, ignoring John's question, "we took the other third to John Flint on Spyglass. No sooner did we have it ashore than there was a great battle that ended with my uncle killed and Moira and me taken captive aboard the Walrus. As fate, or the good Lord, would have it, one of the pirates -- a fellow named Long John Silver -- helped us escape several weeks later in Savannah Harbor, along with three others. One of those others was Ben Gunn."

"And this is your employee in Boston?"

"The same. I offered him a job that night in Savannah, but being the strange fellow he is, he declined it for the first passage that would take him back to sea. There was a Barbados packet leaving Savannah the next day, so he stayed behind as we made our way north. I cautioned him to keep quiet about Flint's treasure, but as he tells it, he couldn't resist the temptation to brag to the small crew. He and his new mates searched Spyglass for nearly a fortnight before they finally marooned the poor soul for treachery. He was rescued a few years later by a group of men out of Bristol who had somehow come into possession of Flint's map. As you might guess, many of the pirates from the Walrus managed to get aboard that ship as crewmen, and once on the island, turned on their employers. Ben tells me the pirate's leader was that same man who freed us in Savannah."

"Long John Silver?"

"Yes," answered the Yorkman. "What I'm getting at is this," continued Robert. "There were, according to Mister Gunn, several hundred bars of silver left in his secret cave. If I can convince him to go back with us, he can lead us there." Robert paused for a spoon-full of oatmeal. "Oh, he also mentioned a small chest of jewels, but I haven't been able to get any details from him. Would there be anything to prevent us from stopping at Grand Turk, just long enough to find and load the extra treasure?"

"I'll be the master of the treasure ship. If I choose to stop at Spyglass, we'll stop. And as long as there's enough treasure to pay for the cannons, what should Mister Jefferson and the others care about splitting the extra swag with the crew?"

The two smiled at each other like two schoolboys preparing to steal apples.

"When can we contact this Mister Gunn?" asked John.

"He's on his way from Boston at this moment with some Dutch contracts. Would it pose a problem to wait a few days until he arrives?"

"I don't see why," said John, thinking of how it would anger Captain Steele.

"Then you can stay here with us in the Pirate Room, Captain Jones," said Moira, anxious for the opportunity to have a visitor and the stimulating conversations he might provide.

"The Pirate Room?"

Moira laughed. "The family who sold us this house told us that Captain William Kidd once lived here, and that the room you'll be using was his. It's quite manly. You'll like it."

"Then it's settled," affirmed Robert with a clap of his hands. "As soon as Ben arrives, we'll be off to Dead Man's Chest!"

CHAPTER 7

Long John Silver sat at his desk, quickly sorting through a stack of mail. A very wet and nervous man in the uniform of the Royal Navy stood next to him, looking through a peephole in the alleyway door.

"Will you quit yer fidgetin', Jeffrey?" scolded Silver. "Nobody followed you!"

"Sorry, Mister Bridger," begged the man. "I just don't want to be caught..."

"Is this all for the King James?" Silver interrupted.

"Yes, sir," answered the sailor. "That's the only bag."

"Then this shouldn't take long." The old pirate shuffled through a few more letters, coming upon one he recognized. Taking a sharp penknife, Silver carefully scraped the wax seal from the parchment. "Perfect," he whispered.

"Anything there, sir?" asked the nervous soldier with another look at the alleyway.

"The lad's been promoted again," Silver crooned as he took up a quill and wrote his initials in the artwork atop the document. "There. Now we'll see if he's as clever as he used to be."

"Somebody I might know, Mister Bridger?"

"Not unless ye've been aboard the King James."

There was a soft knock at the hallway door. Both men jumped.

"John?" called a woman's voice softly.

"Yes, dear?" answered the white-haired man as he gestured to the courier that there was no danger.

"That ship's boat you asked me to watch for has just docked, and your nephew was onboard."

"Thank you, darling!" answered John, as he turned back to the man with the mailbags.

"I've seen enough, Jeffrey." Silver held three of the opened letters in his hand and reached for his journal.

"Those three? Something you can use this time, Mister Bridger?" asked the soldier, hoping to increase his reward by a shilling or two.

"Very useful!" Silver said as he made a note in his journal. "You can bag those other letters while I take care of these."

While the courier went about his task, John Silver selected the appropriate seal from a tray and dripped a fresh puddle of hot wax on the first of the two military dispatches. As he pressed the counterfeit tool into the red wax, he gave a slight twist, making the deception impossible to detect, even to the most careful eye.

"That should do it," he said as he dropped the dispatches and the love letter into the bag with the rest. He then reached into his pocket and pulled out a gold sovereign.

"Why, thank you, sir!" said the surprised courier. He had never received so generous a reward from the old man.

"You're welcome, Jeffrey."

"Will you have anything to be sending out, sir?"

"Yes I will, but not today. The timing must be perfect."

After a careful check of the alleyway, the courier was out of the little office and on his way to the postal house on the other side of Kings Town.

"Dear," said John as he emerged from the office and threw on his coat. "I'll be going to see my brother."

"How long will you be gone, John?"

"No more than an hour or so." He stepped to the kitchen door, and hesitated. He crossed back to his gentle wife and took her face in his hands. "If I ever get myself another ship, it'll be your likeness beneath her bowsprit. And I'll name her after you too; the Bride O' Kings Town, she'll be." A kiss on her nose and a pinch to her backside brought a maiden's blush to the elderly woman's cheeks.

"You're still a pirate, John Silver" she giggled, "but I love you anyway. Be careful on that clicking leg, you hear?"

"You worry too much about me, woman," he said as he grabbed at her breast and then ducked under her slap.

A moment later, John Silver had taken to the cobblestones of the side streets and was en route to his brother's home as quickly as his uncertain gait would carry him. As David and his two escorts neared the front gate, the old pirate stepped behind a nearby wall.

"It's this next gate," said David. "Albert, you and Samuel can go back to the Swan now. When you get there, tell Captain Johnson that I'll be spending the night with my father. You can call for me at noon tomorrow."

"By yer leave, sir, but..." Albert stammered, "Uh,...Cap'n Johnson told us not to leave ya 'till ya was inside, safe an' sound."

"Oh, very well," David complained as he walked across the small courtyard and pushed open the front door of his father's home.

"Orders, sir!" called Albert from the gate.

"I'm in the door," the young man called, "so you can be on your way now!"

"Is that you, David?" called Mister Noble as he hurried to the hallway. "Well, I'll be flogged! It is you! Come in, boy, and tell me all about the Colonies and your trip!" As the excited father ushered his son inside, the two seamen retreated to the street.

"Noon on the 'morrow," said Albert to his mate, "an' not to be late."

John Silver pressed himself flat against the whitewashed wall as the two seamen turned about for their walk back to the docks. As they approached his hiding place, he moved several feet sideways to take advantage of the shadows until they passed, then he crossed the narrow street and into his brother's garden door just in time to see Charles pull the five letters from David's satchel.

"Ah, John!" Charles called as he pulled his older brother's favorite chair forward. "Take a seat and listen up." The old sea dog growled as he dropped into the chair, his wooden leg standing out before him like a bowsprit. He reached down and depressed a catch on the outside of the knee to release the lock, but the lower half of the leg dropped only an inch. With an oath, he gave the thing a kick, driving it to the floor.

"Damned thing started making noises again, right at the worst possible time!" Silver complained. "I had to lie. Claimed it was a childhood accident."

"I told you it was overdue for attention before you went," said Charles, "and you know it. If you'll leave it with for me a couple of days, my carpenter will service the mechanism."

"Forget my leg!" scolded Silver as he gestured at the letters. "What'd the Americans say?"

"It's good, brother, very good. Everything's gone exactly as you said it would."

"With only a couple of exceptions," added David."

"Exceptions?" asked Silver through squinted eyes. "What exceptions?"

"Listen to this!" interrupted Charles, looking up from the first letter. "Captain Jones is in New York Town with Robert Ormerod, and the chairman of the Colony's Marine Commission, a Mister Joseph Hewes, has offered me a million and a half pounds for my cannons!"

"The treasure!" cried the old pirate, his hands massaging the air. He and Charles looked to David for confirmation.

"Aye," answered David. "When I return to Charles Town, I'll know whether or not Mister Ormerod has agreed to lead us to Dead Man's Chest."

"Lead you?" asked Silver. "What about the map?"

"There won't be a map," said Charles as he held up the second letter.

"That's one of the exceptions I mentioned," said David. "Mister Jefferson says that Ormerod will be asked to accompany Captain Jones to Dead Man's Chest."

"What went wrong, Davey?" demanded Silver as he reached out and grabbed the lad by the upper arm.

"It was Jefferson's idea!" David said quickly with a wince. "He and the others must have figured that if there's a map...ouch!...it'd be too easy for somebody to take it from Captain Jones and then go get the treasure for themselves; and that includes Jones and me!" The old pirate released his grip and looked to his brother.

"Then we're going to have to deliver the cannons after all."

"Of course we will!" said Charles. "What else did you have in mind?"

"We could still overpower Jones and his crew when they tie up at your dock."

"Now I see what you're planning, John Silver," said Charles, "but it won't work!"

"Won't work?!" barked Silver. "You're not going honest on me, are you?"

"It won't work because they're sending twin ships," said Charles as he waved the second letter at his older brother, "one to be filled with the cannons and the other to retrieve the treasure."

"Twin ships? Why would they...?"

"I can answer that," interrupted David, rubbing his bruised arm. "They know it would take at least two weeks to load the cannons here in Kings Town, and too many things could happen, this being a British port and all."

"So how's the exchange to take place, if they don't trust us?" By now, Silver's nervousness had him stroking his knife on his whetstone. "And how, in God's name, can so many cannons be..." He stopped stroking the blade as Jefferson's plan finally dawned on him. "They want us to exchange ships at sea."

"Exactly," answered Charles, holding up the letters.

"Well, that's not how I planned it, but if it gets me the gold, I guess I can agree to it."

"We can agree to it," corrected Charles.

"Don't worry," Silver said, sensing his brother's mistrust. "You'll be more than compensated for both your trouble and the cannons."

"You can be sure of that, John," echoed Charles. "I'll be well compensated, or else." There was an uncomfortable moment while the two stared at each other. Finally, the older man spoke.

"Why don't you get us some of your fine brandy while Davey tells us what prompted our Little Captain to finally apply for his naval commission?"

"Yes, David," agreed Charles as he poured three drinks, "we were very upset when you wrote that he just wanted to get married and be a farmer."

"I was upset too!" agreed the lad. "He's so in love with this Miss Dandridge that I think he'd have promised her anything for her hand."

"Even promising to never go back to sea?" asked Charles.

"Exactly!" David shook his head from side to side. "I was so convinced the plan was dead that I nearly...well, you both read my letter."

"And why didn't you come home, Davey?"

"It was the strangest thing. John was making regular visits to the Dandridge estate and the girl's father seemed to really like him." David took a sip of brandy. "Then he stopped talking about her all together and hid himself away in the tailor shop. Next thing I knew, Patrick Henry gave us a letter of introduction to Joseph Hewes."

Silver held up Hewes' letter.

"Yes, that Joseph Hewes," said David. "In a matter of hours, we were on our way to Edenton."

"You have no idea, then," asked Charles, "why Captain Jones changed his mind about the commission or why Mister Henry gave you the letter?"

"No," answered David. "And I didn't want to ask him for fear it might ruin the plan."

"Sounds to me like you lost control of the situation," growled Silver as he put the tip of his knife within inches of the lad's nose.

"Don't do it, John," warned Charles, "or you'll have me to reckon with."

"I was only playing with the lad," said Silver with a chuckle as he messed up David's hair. "I wouldn't have hurt him."

"Would one of you tell me what you're talking about?" David asked, by now thoroughly confused.

"I will," answered his father. "When you wrote us about this girl he had fallen in love with, John Silver provided Nathaniel Dandridge with a copy of the King's warrant. And just to make sure Captain Dandridge would choose the right option, your Uncle went to Virginia in person." David's mouth opened for several moments before he spoke.

"So that's how..!" cried David. "John told me that Mister Dandridge had a copy of his warrant, and Mister Hewes told us that it was Dandridge, not Patrick Henry, who told him about John and me at their meeting in Harrisburgh." He paused to consider further. "John must have figured the King's men were already looking for him in Virginia, when in reality that warrant may not have reached America at all! Ha!"

"That'll teach you to underestimate an old pirate's powers, Davey," chuckled Silver.

"So, David," asked Charles, "what's next? How will we know whether Ormerod has agreed to lead Captain Jones to the treasure?"

"As I understand it, you won't until one of the twin frigates arrives here in Kings Town."

"Frigates!?" Silver coughed half a mouthful of brandy onto his trousers. "What about the British? My God, man, these Americans are either very brave or very daft!"

"It's here in Forrestal's letter," said David as he searched for the right one. "When they're finished with certain modifications, the British will think they're Dutch merchantmen, even to the point of putting a Dutch crew aboard."

"And cannons?" asked Charles. "They'll both carry cannons, won't they?"

"Only the one headed for Dead Man's Chest," answered David. "They want you to fill your ship's gun positions with a standard mix of long cannons and carronades from the inventory, and store the rest in the bilges, instead of ballast.

"And tell us, Davey. How many ships is this Mister Forrestal sending along to Dead Man's Chest?"

"Sending along?"

"Escorts!" cried Silver. "These statesmen must know there are pirates in the Caribbean, for God's sake!"

"Well, I don't know," answered David as he thought back to the night at Edenton. "Mister Jefferson did say something about sending the privateer Eagle along."

"A privateer, huh?" Silver groaned as he pulled his blade across the whetstone and then cut a one-inch square of hair from his left forearm to test its edge. "It won't be enough."

The Swan had been at sea for just under two weeks when the forward watch spotted the lonely Charles Town lighthouse in the predawn light; standing like a naked man marooned on a finger of sand. "Charles Town light, two points to larboard!"

"Edwards!" the First Officer barked at one of the seamen. "Go aft an' get the Captain." The young seaman knuckled his forelock and ran barefoot across the deck to the Master's ladder. "And tell him we'll be makin' the Forrestal yards by noon!"

"Aye, aye, sir!" Edwards shouted back and then dropped into the darkness. A moment later he was at the door.

"Captain Johnson!" the lad shouted, following the customary three knocks his Captain preferred. "Charles Town light on the larboard bow, sir! Mister Peters says we be makin' Forrestal's yards by noon!"

"Thank you, Edwards!" called the somewhat portly man from his bunk. He turned to the young man sharing his cabin. "That's good news, David! This has been too long a voyage, what with no prizes to take and passing some of the best ports o' call in the world." He swung his legs out from under his stack of blankets and pushed himself carefully to the sitting position.

"I'm truly sorry, sir," said David with a groan, "but just like you, I've been sworn to secrecy. All I can tell you is that you've done your part well. Very well." David liked Captain Johnson, but the man had complained about the strictness of his orders every day en route to Kings Town and every day since.

As the Swan passed the lighthouse and neared the large sand bar which stretched across the mouth of Charles Town harbor, David somehow felt at home. It was here that he and John had put in for three days of repairs on the Falmouth Packet more than a year before.

By noon, just as the First Officer had predicted, the Swan pulled up to the leeward side of the outfitter's dock where two beautiful Dutch merchantmen the size of frigates were undergoing their final work. They were stately creatures, with lines much like the Swan, but nearly twice her size. The presence of certain decorations and the total absence of gun ports left no doubt that these were indeed merchantmen. A slow-moving wagon carrying several tons of anchor chain pulled onto the dock between the waiting ships as a crew of fitters secured the hardware to a yard.

"I see our arrival hasn't gone unnoticed." The Captain gestured with his bushy blond eyebrows toward an approaching carriage. "If I'm not mistaken, that's Mister Forrestal's personal carriage. Whatever you and Captain Jones are up to, it has to be something very important."

"It is!" answered David proudly.

Alex Forrestal's carriage was equally as impressive as the two great ships, with a Duke's ransom in rich enamel paint and gold leaf decorating it's edges. The coachman reigned the matching coal-black stallions in a lazy arc to the left and stopped at the end of the Swan's gangway. A footman riding on the rear step jumped to the ground and was already at the carriage door before the wheels had come to a complete stop.

"Farewell, Captain Johnson," said David as he shook the shipmaster's hand. "I've learned much from you these past weeks."

"It was my pleasure, lad. Now be off with ya before I receive a reprimand from our employer."

"Welcome to Charles Town, Mister Noble!" came the voice of the single occupant of the carriage. "Won't you join Mrs. Forrestal and me for dinner?" David threw his duffle up to the coachman and climbed inside, next to his distinguished host.

"I'd love to, sir!"

"So, what of the cannons? Has your father agreed to the terms and conditions of our offer?"

"He has, sir, just as I told you he would." David loved to be in the midst of such momentous goings-on. "By the way, where are the two frigates we're to use?"

"Ha! Ha! Ha!" The ship builder was amused. "Why, they stand right next to us, young man!" He pointed across the dock to right and left at the two Dutch traders David had been studying a moment before.

"But I thought..."

"You thought you'd be able to see the gun ports, didn't you; especially at such close range?" David leaned across his host and peered carefully at the solid planking where the gun ports should have been. There wasn't the slightest evidence, not even a single vertical crack to give the frigate's secret away.

"That's amazing!"

"Aye!" chirped the old man. "The first time I've taken on a project like this. You might consider these two ships true hybrids."

"Just like the Walrus."

"Like a walrus?" asked Mister Forrestal with a hand cupped to his ear. "I don't follow you, Mister Noble."

"It was nothing, sir," lied David. "Just thinking out loud." The old man gave his guest a queer look and continued.

"After dinner, I'll bring you back to the dock for a closer look. We Americans can be quite clever when we put our minds to it." Forrestal pulled a sash cord next to him and the driver laid his whip to the backs of the stallions, sweeping the carriage off the dock and through the yards to the town named for a previous King of England.

The Forrestal estate was by far the grandest home David had ever seen. Two masonry stallions stood guard at either side of the entrance to the estate. The black iron gates which hung from the whitewashed stone walls provided the only opening between the Forrestal grounds and the outside world. As the carriage slowed and passed at a walk, the gates were pushed closed behind them by the footman.

The long drive was bordered on each side by red brick walls two feet high. Cypress trees as tall and as straight as ships masts stood soldier-like in two neat rows from the gate to the great parking circle before the porch steps. At the center of the circle stood a fountain of snow white alabaster marble with three dolphins of black stone, leaping skyward like startled birds. Around the fountain was a belt of well-manicured grass.

The great Forrestal mansion was pure white and seemed to stretch from horizon to horizon. Its roof was flat, yet the outside height was nearly thirty feet from the rose beds about its base to the rain gutters at its majestic head. A narrow row of basement windows skirted the massive porch to either side, with twelve steps leading up to the extended porch. And at the top of the twelve marble steps, and just inboard of the six Corinthian pillars, stood two Negro servants dressed in red waistcoats and white gloves.

As the carriage came to a stop, the servants trotted down the steps and moved to their well-rehearsed positions to receive their master's guest in the proper southern fashion.

"Will you be needing help from the carriage, Master Forrestal?" asked one of the Negroes.

"Not this time, Abraham. My hip's much better today." The old man let out a muffled groan as he lowered himself to the ground. "Please take Mister Noble's bag to the guest room and inform Lady Forrestal that we'll be having a guest for dinner."

"Very well, sir," said the servant as he rushed off to comply.

"You'll like Mrs. Forrestal," said the elderly man. "She's a...well, let's just say she's quite a woman." He led the young Jamaican up the long steps, refusing David's offer of assistance until the pain finally forced him to take the lad's arm at the last three steps. The pain was as bad as ever, but he had determined not to complain in front of the young seafarer.

The foyer of the mansion was like another world to David, equally impressive as it's exterior. The closest thing David had ever seen to it's grandeur was the Governor's mansion at Kings Town; the very one Sir Henry Morgan had originally commissioned to be built as his private residence following the sack of Panama in 1666. Except for the fresco ceiling depicting the founding of the Colonies and their thirteen crests, the interior of the Forrestal mansion was made entirely of hand carved mahogany and cedar. As David stood in awe, he failed to notice the stately woman in her early seventies approach from a room behind him.

"Alex," she asked, "did you let in another mockingbird?"

"No, dear," said the elderly man with a nervous chuckle. "Our guest is just admiring the art work on our ceiling." David turned to look at the elderly lady.

"Well, in that case," she said with a prankish grin, "perhaps you should introduce your embarrassed young friend."

Mrs. Forrestal stood to nearly David's height of five foot ten inches, with strong, almost manly features framed in a close arc of silver curls. She wore a high-necked gown of light blue brocade and carried a small book of poetry before her in cupped hands. As her gaze fixed on David, her face paled slightly, as if an arctic wind had touched her fair skin. The book of poems fell to the floor with a slap as she brought her right hand to her mouth to cover her astonishment.

"Dear, what is it?" Mister Forrestal called as David rushed to her side.

"David," the old man begged as he took her other arm, "help me get my wife to the couch!" With a man on each arm, Mrs. Forrestal was assisted to the parlor where a servant girl was cleaning.

"Maggie," called Mister Forrestal, "get your mistress a moist cloth and smelling salts! Quickly now!"

As the servant rushed from the room, Alex tried to communicate with his wife, but her eyes were fixed on David as if she had seen death himself.

"What is it, Dear? What's the matter?" She turned her head slowly to gaze into her husband's eyes and began to blink.

"Who is he? Where did you find the lad?"

"This is David Noble, the young man I've been telling you about for days. He's the one who'll be going with Captain Jones to bring the cannons from Kings Town." As Alex patted her hand, the indentured servant returned and handed her mistress the cool cloth. "Dear, are you all right?"

"Yes, I think so," Mrs. Forrestal answered as she looked once again into the young visitor's eyes and shuddered slightly. Some of the color had now returned to her cheeks. "When I first looked at you, I mistook you for someone I knew as a young girl. It must have been the light; the way it was cast across your eyes and nose."

"I was in Charles Town last year, but I don't believe we met, Mrs. Forrestal," said David as he stroked her hand. "I'm told I have a strong resemblance to my father. Perhaps you met him."

"David," she said, confused, "you will stay for dinner with Alex and me, won't you?"

"Yes, Ma'am," answered David with a concerned look at Alex. "I'd welcome a real meal for a change." The old man gave him an assuring pat on the arm. "I'd be a fool to turn down such a kind invitation, Ma'am."

"One of our servants has already begun to lay your things out in your room, David," said Alex. "We've a few minutes before we eat, and I'm sure you'd like to freshen up before we sit down." As he spoke, one of the male servants stood patiently in the doorway.

"Thomas," said Alex, "would you show David to his room and the bath? He'll be staying with us for several days." Then turning back to David, "We'll dine in twenty minutes."

"Thank you again, Mister and Misses Forrestal." David followed the servant to the second floor where he attended to his needs.

Lunch was a simple but tasty affair; open-faced sandwiches of roast beef and chicken with candied peaches and tea. As David helped himself to a second serving of peaches, Misses Forrestal cleared her throat.

"Alex has told me all about this fantastic quest you and Captain Jones are about to embark upon. I must assume everything went well in Kings Town?"

"There isn't that much to tell, Ma'am," said David as he wiped his mouth with a fine linen napkin. "He read the letters and was pleased. He'll begin loading the cannons just as soon as the ship arrives."

"What about the rendezvous at sea?" asked Alex. "Did he have any difficulty with that aspect of the agreement?"

"Yes, until he read Mister Hopkin's letter. His first reaction was that you didn't trust him, but now he agrees that the transfer at Kings Town would present an enormous security problem."

"David," asked Mrs. Forrestal, "what do you know about your father's background?"

"Nothing much…just that he was an orphan, Ma'am. One of hundreds of orphans in the West Indies. He was purchased and raised by a wealthy merchant who left the business to my father when he died."

"So you don't know where he was born, or to whom?"

"No," answered David. "We don't even know his real name."

"Does it really matter who his father was," asked Alex, "as long as he delivers those weapons?" Suddenly she was embarrassed again.

"Of course it doesn't matter," she answered with a nervous laugh. "I was just making conversation." Grasping the opportunity, she made an excuse to go to the kitchen. David used the break to change the subject to a topic he knew Mister Forrestal would enjoy.

"Sir, will there still be time to tour our ships this afternoon?"

"Of course there will!" said Alex as he wiped his mouth and pushed himself up from his chair with a groan. "Give me a minute to tell the Missus we're leaving, and then I'll be right with you."

In the kitchen, he found his wife moistening her face with a cloth. He put a comforting arm around her shoulders. "Dear, are you sure you're all right? You were getting pale again just before you left the table."

"I don't know what it is," she lied. "Maybe I just need a little rest."

"Why don't you lie down while I take David down to the fitter's dock?"

"That would be good. Yes, a short nap would help." Her mind was preoccupied with the young man from Jamaica as she kissed her husband and retired to the sitting room. Alex waited at the door while she stood next to the couch. Sensing he was still there, she turned.

"Don't fret yourself, Alex," she said with a smile. "I'm better than you think."

By the time the Forrestal carriage had arrived back at the dock, the fitters had hoisted most the enormous yard and were securing it to the lower crosstrees of the foremast. A flock of local children scrambled about the remaining stack of hewn timbers waiting their turn at the hoist. Alex and David stepped from the carriage, amidst the teams of sawyers and fitting gangs moving to and from the massive ships.

"Come here, David," the old man said as he limped toward the stern of the closest ship. "I want you to see a true artisan at work." High on the stern, like monkeys perched on the side of an Indian mosque, hung two half-naked carpenters. With each strike of mallet against chisel, walnut-sized chips flew from the expensive wood. David stood for a moment marveling at the workmen's craft.

"You, there, with the red hair," called David over the pounding. "Where'd you learn your craft?"

"You talkin' to me, Govn'r?" answered the carpenter with a flash of his green eyes.

"Yes, you! I was admiring your work!"

"Learnt it on Tortuga, I did! Innkeeper o' the Musket's Muzzle; 'e be the one what learned me the trade, Govn'r!" There was something familiar about the lad.

"Your name wouldn't be Henry Morgan, would it?"

"Now there was a true word as ever was heard spoke!" sang out Morgan. "Aye, an' I be the great, great, great Grandson o' Sir 'enry Morgan; the same what sacked Panama in '66 an' took the King's blade on 'is shoulder fer it!" The lad took another careful slice of mahogany from the side of a partially carved windmill. "Say, 'ow it be ya knows me name, Govn'r? I don't 'member speakin' to yer likes 'afore."

"I heard stories about you in Kings Town," answered David. "I especially liked the one about you killing the notorious Captain Claw with one swing of a mangrove root." The orange-haired lad smacked his fellow carver on the toe with his mallet.

"Tolt ya I were famous!" Then, calling down to David, "You tell 'im, Govn'r! He'll believe ya!" Morgan tilted his head as he thought. "Captain Claw? With a mangrove root? That were a long time ago, Govn'r!"

"Quite the craftsman, that Morgan," bragged Forrestal. "I've hired only the best to prepare these two ships; only the best." While they continued to admire the ornate carvings, a large man with bushy blond eyebrows and an unkempt mustache thundered down the gangway and across the dock towards them. Over his bald crown lay a powdered wig, which looked like last year's robin's nest blown to his head in a gale. His nose and cheeks were covered with a spider web of purple veins; mute testimony to the thousand hogsheads of brew he'd consumed over the years.

"Ahoy, Alex!" bellowed the approaching hulk. "You come to see how Van Mourik hide der cannons, ya?"

"This is going to be an experience you'll not soon forget, David," the ship builder whispered to his young guest as he turned to greet the approaching Woodshoe. "Ah, Captain Van Mourik!"

"Don't tell me," whispered David. "This is our Dutch captain."

"Right," whispered Forrestal as the Dutchman's ham hock of a right hand was already extended for the painful greeting. "Don't ever underestimate the man for his blubber. I've seen him break an oak belaying pin with his bare hands." David's eyes began to flicker in anticipation.

"Jack Van Mourik," said Alex, "this is David Noble. You two will be spending a lot of time together in the next few months." Like so many hefty people, the large Dutchman was loud and tended to get too close when he spoke. There was an intermittent shower of saliva as he pumped the lad's hand.

"I been waiting long time to meet der man mit' der cannons an' der treasure!" He paused for a labored breath. "You call me Dutch, ya?"

"Damn it, Jack," hissed Forrestal in the fat man's ear. "I told you to keep quiet about that! Do you want every pirate in the Atlantic on our heels?"

"Oh, you forgive me please, Mister Forrestal?" the big man begged as he let go of David's hand. "I be more careful, you see."

"If you can keep your mouth shut, you can show Mister Noble what you've been up to on the gun deck."

"Ah goot!" yelled Dutch, sure that his forgiveness had been granted. "You follow mit me to de gun deck, an watch yer steps, ya?" They followed his stumbling gate up to the gangway, holding back so their combined weight wouldn't break the straining planks.

The main deck was cluttered with workmen, each with his set of tools and specific job. Van Mourik led the two men aft to the companionway and down to the second deck where several large bales of cotton obscured two of the gun stations. Next to the bales were several large chains laid in parallel rows.

"Morgan an' me been tryin' fer days mit der cannons, Mister Forrestal, an' we tink we got her done goot dis time."

"Morgan?" asked Forrestal.

"Aye. He had some goot ideas on how we gonna hide dem."

"Well, since Morgan knows already, why don't we call him in while you explain your plan to us, Dutch?"

"Goot idea," the Dutchman answered, followed by a bellow to stern. "Morgan!"

"So, Dutch," asked David with a wide sweep of his arms, "just what are we supposed to be looking at?"

"Them bales, Govn'r!" came the cry of Henry Morgan from astern. The red-headed lad ran forward along the gun deck, ducking under the low overhead as he came. "They ain't real!"

Dutch joined Morgan and together they pulled the bale of cotton up and away from the gun port. The whole thing was no more than three inches thick and hanging from hinges in the overhead. When they were pushed all the way up and secured to an eye in an overhead deck beam, the gun way was exposed, leaving more than enough room for cannons.

"That's inspired!" David said with a clap of his hands. "Who's idea was that?"

"Mostly young Morgan's," answered Dutch.

"Ah, Dutch," said Henry, "ya ain't doin' yerself 'alf fair."

"Well, I don't care who's more responsible," said Forrestal as he pulled two shiny gold coins from his watch pocket and handed them to the pair. "Go have yourselves a nice dinner on me. You both deserve it." The Dutchman put the coin between his oversized teeth to test it's metal, but noticed Mister Forrestal's disapproving stare.

"Just a habit, sir," said Morgan as he apologized for the large man. "We know yer money's good."

"I know you do," said Mister Forrestal with a grin. "But if you'll excuse us, I've several more things to show my friend before tea time."

"It were a pleasure meetin' ya, Govn'r," said the redheaded youth, with the gold coin stuck in his right eye like a gentleman's monocle.

"And you, Henry!" laughed David as he started up the ladder behind Mister Forrestal. A moment later, the shipbuilder and the Jamaican stood on the gangway studying the planking.

"Your men did an incredible job, Mister Forrestal. We're no more than ten feet away and I still can't see the gun ports."

"One of my other sawyers did it. He cut the planks extra thin and butted the ends together, but with different lengths so you wouldn't see a hard vertical line. And just like those bales of cotton, the sections hinge upward to expose the ports. A thick coat of paint'll finish the job."

"I've dreamed," said David as he reached out and touched the heavy wood, "of going to sea in a ship like this."

"Not this one. It won't be carrying any guns until they're loaded by your father at Kings Town." He pointed to the second Silver Cloud, across the dock. "There's your ship. An exact duplicate of this one, but she's going fully armed."

"How many cannons?"

"Twenty in all. We've collected them from every source available and have come up with an excellent mix of short and long range pieces, plus a half dozen swivel guns for the rails."

"Are they from our foundries or from Europe?"

"They're all from Europe. Some from Scotland, a few from England, and the rest from Spanish and French ships my privateers have taken. She's as big as a frigate, but since she's only a conversion, her design only allowed for twenty cannons. Captain Jones should be pleased."

"I have a question, sir," said David as he looked back at the special planking.

"Yes?"

"If our mission and these disguised frigates are supposed to be a secret, then what about all these carpenters and fitters? Won't they figure it out when they bring the cannons aboard?"

"When these men are paid and dismissed, another set of men -- your crew for the voyage -- will come up from Mister Hewes' shipping company in Edenton."

"Mister Hewes told us about all the men who were out of work because of his lost ships."

"Well, it's those very men who'll install the cannons and other special provisions. As I said, other than the Dutchman and that redheaded lad, these workmen and your crew will never meet."

"It'll be good having Morgan along," said David. "My uncle tells me it's good luck to have at least one man aboard with red hair."

The two continued their tour of the ships for another hour and then returned to the mansion for tea, as they had promised Mrs. Forrestal they would. By 1800 hours, the spring sun had fallen so low toward the western hills that further work in the yards was impossible. The sawyers and painters, and other ship fitters left the dock in small groups. Two of the last to depart were Henry Morgan and the Dutch captain, Jack Van Mourik.

"Me belly be cryin' fer a noggin o' grog, Dutch. What say we stop at the Patriot fer a drink?" Morgan flipped his sovereign high into the evening sky and caught it behind his back. Dutch, admiring the lad's trick, tried to imitate the feat, but failed. He scrambled around on the ground searching for his lost treasure. After a lengthy and unsuccessful search in the grass, Dutch looked up at the lad.

"Ya!" the fat man puffed. "Sounds goot to me. And maybe we get some grub too, ya?" By now the Captain's knees were wet with mud.

"Why looky 'ere!" cried the lad as he lifted his foot. "There's yer bleedin' sovereign, right there under me foot!" Morgan was pleased with his joke on the Dutchman, but the cruelty was wasted on the good-natured Woodshoe.

The Patriot's Rest was noisier than Forrestal's dock, what with all the sailors and tavern wenches calling obscenities at each other from across the public room, and fighting for the silver which flowed so fast and free. The two men grabbed a small table as one of the women-of-the-night lured a rum-soaked sailor away to her nest. Morgan ordered a bottle of the Patriot's best, the stuff that hadn't been diluted yet, along with two cups. Within a half hour, Dutch had consumed most of the bottle himself, and set to bragging.

"Related to the pirate, are ya?" shouted Van Mourik as he struggled for a full breath. "Well back in der olt country, I were a constable fer six years, ya?"

"Go on!" slurred Morgan as he pushed at Van Mourik's shoulder and pretended he was equally intoxicated. "You? A bleedin' constable?"

"I was! An' a right goot one too!" The large man spilled half his glass on the table and burst into hysterical laughter as he mopped the caustic liquid up with his wig. "Comes in handy, dis here vig, ya?" He weaved back and forth in his chair as he twisted the hairpiece between his large hands, squeezed what he could back into his cup. Satisfied with the effort, he attempted to replace the tangled mess squarely on his bald head.

"If you can keep a secret, Dutch," Morgan whispered as he leaned against the big man, "I'll tell ya 'bout a treasure what I know of on Tortuga."

"A treasure, you say?" Dutch looked about the tavern suspiciously as he pulled a fat finger across his lips in a salute of silence and then surged forward and turned an ear to the lad. "My lips are sealed, Henry?"

"I helped Joshua Smoot bury nearly a thousand pieces of eight behind the Musket's Muzzle four years ago." It was a lie, but it would serve Morgan's purpose just as well as a truth.

"Dat's not'ing!" Dutch grabbed his young friend by the collar and pulled him nose-to-nose, forcing Morgan to turn his head away from the fowl breath. "The Cloud with the cannons is sailin' fer Dead Man's Chest in a fortnight ta dig up a million an' a half in golt! An' Henry, we're part of dat crew!" Dutch toppled backward into the upright position and wiped his itchy nose. When he finally opened his eyes, he made the proudest look he could. "How's dat?"

"I've heard tell of that treasure, Dutch, but word is nobody's alive what knows where it's buried."

"Don't be so sure o' dat, my little friend!" said Dutch as his beady blue eyes flashed with pride. He looked about the tavern once again and tried to lower his voice. "I hear one of dem who buried it'll be goin' wid us soon as we got her ready fer sailin'." As Dutch finished, his attention was seized by the prominent bosoms of the well-endowed bar maid standing next to his shoulder.

"You two done with them cups, or what?" she cried in a nasal twang that could curdle milk.

"Come here an' give Dutch a little kiss!" the fat man bellowed as he pulled the girl down into his lap. She let out a giggle and slipped her hand into his pocket as they traded kisses.

It was just the diversion Morgan needed to slip from the tavern and disappear into the night.

After waiting two days for Ben Gunn's arrival from Boston, the Ormerod carriage rolled onto Peck's Dock. A short distance away, the Staten Island Ferry was getting underway for its morning run across the East River. Captain Steele sat with William Peck in the tiny dock house engrossed by a game of cribbage when a crewman from the Eagle knocked at the door.

"Cap'n Steele, sir?" the seaman called through the small porthole of a window.

"Are they finally back, Martin?" asked the Captain as he pulled the door open and looked about toward the town.

"That they are, sir, an' there's three of 'em."

"Three, you say?" He threw his cards on the table, took up his winnings, and stepped onto the dock with his hat and coat in hand. "Did Jones tell you who the others were?"

"I didn't talk to him, sir," Martin apologized. "Came straight to you when I seen 'em comin'."

"Don't worry about it," Steele said as he pushed past the seaman. "I'll find out soon enough. I was hoping he had decided to go back by land."

As the angry Captain marched toward the Eagle, the large Ormerod carriage finished discharging its passengers at the gangway. As quickly as it had come, it thundered away over the weathered planking and onto the street beyond.

"Ah, here he comes now," said John to his companions. "Just as I described him, right?" Ormerod and Gunn agreed quietly. They could sense the approaching man was in a bad mood.

"Captain Steele!" John called out in a forced tone of friendship. "I've two passengers returning with us to Charles Town."

Steele strode up to the three and stopped abruptly. "I'd love to have a friendly chat, gentlemen, but we've just enough time to get into the open sea before dark."

"Of course, Henry," said John as he gave the other two an apologetic look. "We'll get to know one another once we're under way."

Captain Steele barked orders at his men, bringing the small ship alive. Within minutes, the lines were thrown from the dock and the Eagle had piked clear and into the current of the East River. An offshore breeze added several knots to their down-river reach to the sea. By dusk they had cleared the Narrows and were once again into the icy waters of the Atlantic.

After a quick dinner, the Yorkman went aft to introduce himself properly to the ship's Master. Captain Steele was the first to speak.

"So you're the object of this voyage!" said Captain Steele as he pressed his hip against the tiller and studied the rigging.

"Yes I am, sir." Robert leaned against the railing several yards from the Captain and sipped his cup of coffee. "I'm sorry it took so long, but I needed to wait for Mister Gunn's arrival from Boston."

Steele gave Robert a cold stare. "Mister Jones could have had the decency to inform me of the delay!"

"You didn't know he might be delayed?"

"No, Mister Ormerod, and he probably forgot to tell you my crew wasn't allowed to make liberty in New York."

"He didn't mention it," answered Robert. "How long has it been?"

"We spent three days en route from Edenton, and they've had to sit for three more days watching the crowds come and go along the docks. That's no way to treat men."

"Well, that doesn't make any sense," said Robert, "unless your crew had been told why they've come to New York."

"Mister Ormerod, I don't even know the nature of your mission, much less my men. And that's what makes me so angry. Mister Hewes was adamant that except for Mister Jones, none of us were to go ashore for any reason. If we weren't privy to why, then what possible harm could there have been?"

"Hmmm," said Robert as he looked forward to where he had left John. "Did Mister Hewes give you any special instructions concerning the voyage back to Charles Town?"

"Only that I'm to get you and Mister Jones back to Charles Town as quickly as possible."

"I wish I could tell you what it is we're up to, Captain Steele, but..."

"Never mind, sir. It's probably best that I don't know."

For the next day and a half, the Eagle beat southwesterly along the rugged New England coast. John didn't talk as much about Dorothea on this return trip as he had on their trip to New York, not until the forward watch sighted Cape Charles, at the mouth of the Chesapeake Bay.

"Henry," said John with his usual arrogance. "I want you to take me to Fredericksburg."

"Is this something Mister Hewes has ordered you to do?" asked Steele stiffly.

"Does it matter?"

"You're damned right it matters!" barked Steele as he turned on the smaller man. "If Hewes has given you some additional mission, and it's in writing -- because this is the first I've heard of it -- then I'll take you. Otherwise, we're sailing straight through to Charles Town!"

"It's a personal matter," said John.

"Of course it's a personal matter!" cried Steele as he realized what John was after. "You want to go see Miss Dandridge, don't you?"

"What difference does it make to you if I do? You're supposed to take me wherever I say."

"That's a damned lie, and you know it! My orders were to take you to New York Town and then back to Charles Town! He didn't authorize any side trips, especially not to Virginia!" Captain Steele watched as John began to turn red.

"Especially not Virginia?" echoed John. "If that's true, why didn't he tell me?"

"He did," answered Captain Steele, "as we were pulling away from the dock at Edenton!"

"Well, I didn't hear it!"

"I expected that! You only hear what you want to hear!"

"That's not true!"

"And even if Mister Hewes had not forbid my taking you to Virginia, I would still refuse."

"You hate me that much?"

"Oh, it's not for hatred's sake I refuse, Mister Jones. It's because my men were confined to this ship for three days in New York while you were ashore. I'll not put in at Virginia and subject them to any more of that!"

"Confined to the ship?" yelled John. "What in God's name for?"

"Because Mister Hewes ordered it, that's why!"

"And you assumed I knew?"

"You should have!" Steele hissed back. "Just like you should know that your mission has to be kept a secret!"

"Are you implying that I'd let it slip to Miss Dandridge?"

"It doesn't matter what I'm implying, because I'm not taking you anywhere close to Virginia!"

"Steele, you dried up old man!" yelled John. "You've forgotten what it's like to love a woman!"

"The hell you say!"

"You went to sea with a sick wife at home and let her die, and you haven't been with a woman since!"

Six seamen who were coiling ropes nearby began moving to the rail behind Captain Jones, anticipating the argument's inevitable escalation. Ben Gunn came topside to see what all the yelling was about.

"You bastard!" Steele hissed through clenched teeth. "You insolent, self-serving, egotistical bastard! I told you about my wife in confidence, only because you were so depressed about that girl in Virginia. And now, just because you want to go see her, you'd throw my dead wife in my face?" Steele's hand went for a belaying pin as John began to draw his sword. "Damn your selfish soul to hell, John Jones! And before you pull that blade, consider where this crew's loyalties lie!"

Just as John had reacted when the half-breed attacked him at Scarborough a year earlier, his sword flashed through the cold air with a demon's howl. The two weapons met just inches above Captain Steele's forehead, the sword's razor edge cutting a third of the way into the belaying pin. As Captain Steele wrenched his weapon free for a second swing at John's head, the six crewmen grabbed and threw John to the deck and twisted his sword from his hand.

"I'll take that!" said Henry as he grabbed the weapon and walked to the rail. "If you were anybody else," said Henry as he drew back to throw the sword into the cold Atlantic waters, "I'd hang you for that!"

"Wait!" cried John as he watched his sword.

"For what?" asked Henry as he hesitated, the sword poised over his head.

"Don't throw it away! Please!"

"Are you suggesting I should give it back so you can use it on me a second time?" Henry raised his arm slightly to throw.

"It was given to me by my father just before I left home!" cried John. "I love...it has sentimental value!"

"So you're capable of love after all." John nodded. "Well, I love this ship and it's crew. It's my world—my private little kingdom, if you will—and as you've noticed by the twelve hands holding you down, my men love it too. I may be rough, and my speech might offend a landlubber now and then, but I'm a God-fearing man who's learned to recognize and respect authority when I see it! You, on the other hand, lack that maturity." Henry paused to take a breath. As he did so, he touched John's exposed abdomen with the tip of the sword. "You like to quote Pat Henry, don't you?"

John nodded.

"I know he's important to the Colonies, but with all due respect for your friend, I find myself unimpressed with his character. He evidently speaks volumes on liberty, but very little of loyalty. Take a lesson from real life, Mister Jones. There's no question as to whom my men obey. At my command, they'd kill you where you lie!"

John said nothing, but only watched the tip of his sword as it hovered above his stomach.

"Very well," said Captain Steele as he stepped back from his antagonist. "I'll not throw your sword away this time, but it goes into the armory under lock and key until you're off my ship! Now, get out of my sight!" With a nod to his men, John was released.

"John," whispered Robert as he helped the Scotsman to his feet, "go to the bow!" The infuriated youth hesitated longer than Robert felt he should. "Now, John, while you still can!"

Captain Jones backed slowly from the quarterdeck, and then after a long moment, turned away as ordered.

"Keep him away from me, Robert!" hissed Captain Steele as he let Robert take the belaying pin and return it to its place. "One more confrontation like that and one of us is going to die!"

"Don't worry. I'll see to it that the two of you are not left alone again." Robert watched John until he had reached the bowsprit, and then turned back to Captain Steele. "I think it might be best if you reconsider his request."

"That was no request, Mister Ormerod. He ordered me to take him to Virginia. I'll be damned if I..."

"Calm down, Henry, and think about it," said Robert. "It'll give Captain Jones and yourself time to cool down. And besides, you and your men can take a day of liberty at Dalgren once he's gone."

"You can authorize that?"

"Of course I can," the Yorkman said with an air of impunity. "I can do most anything I want until I provide the information Mister Jefferson needs."

Henry paced from one rail to the other for several minutes as he considered the Yorkman's suggestion.

"Very well," said Henry as he stopped pacing. "I'll put him ashore, Robert, but not alone." Steele turned and strode to the fife rail where he placed his hand on the belaying pin so recently cut by John's blade. "He may be a bastard, but my employer says he's a valuable bastard."

"Well, I'll agree with you that he's valuable, Captain, but your differences are strictly your own. And if you don't have anybody in mind to go with him, I'd welcome the visit to Fredericksburg. I've been meaning to go there for several years now anyway."

"Absolutely not!" Henry objected. "If that man needs a companion, I'll send anybody before I send you. Mister Jefferson and the others haven't gone to all this trouble to have you and Mister Jones lost on the highway together, not that I'd miss him at all."

"Then what if my assistant, Mister Gunn, accompanies him?"

"That's fine by me, as long as Mister Gunn's life isn't essential to this mission." Henry considered for a moment. "Since our employer didn't expect your Mister Gunn to be coming along, the old man can't matter that much anyway; to the mission, that is."

"Shall we tell Captain Jones?" asked Robert.

"I'll leave that to you!" spat Henry as he looked forward at John. "I want nothing more to do with him."

"You're not going to forgive John for what he said about your wife, are you?"

"He cut me deep," answered the elderly Captain. "The Good Book says I have to forgive a man if he repents, but it'll be a cold day in hell before Jones asks for forgiveness."

"Can I have your word you'll try to avoid any further confrontations?"

"You get him to promise that first, and then ask me again."

Robert strode forward to John's side and the two had a lengthy discussion. Finally, Robert returned to the quarterdeck.

"Well?" asked Henry.

"He's agreed to take a carriage all the way to Charles Town if you'll take him to Fredericksburg. Oh...and he wants his sword back."

"Then we have a deal, Mister Ormerod! He'll get the sword as he leaves my ship, and good riddance to Mister Jones!"

CHAPTER 8

Twelve hours later, the Eagle made port at Dahlgren, the intended landing of the Falmouth Packet the year before. With his sword returned to his side, Captain Jones rented a small carriage from the town's blacksmith, and by 1000 hours, he and the ex-pirate, Ben Gunn, were out of the small riverfront town and into the wooded countryside on their way toward Fredericksburg.

"Tell me, Mister Gunn," began John, "how'd you get associated with John Flint and that treasure on Spyglass?"

"Ah, John Flint," answered the old man, thrilled that somebody actually asked him to tell his story. He crossed his fingers as he continued. "We was like this, we were," began Ben, holding up his hand. "Met on the merchant ship Elizabeth, takin' indentured servants from England to the West Indies."

"You and he were Crewmen on the Elizabeth?"

"No!" cried the old man. "We was indentured to Cuba!"

"You indentured yourselves?"

"Aye, sir, for seven years, me an' Flint did. And that bein' my first time at sea, I must 'a spent half the trip hangin' over the lee rail feedin' the fish. Ha!" Ben didn't mean to laugh quite so loudly, but a quick look to the Captain assured him that he wasn't in trouble. "When we got to the dock in Havana, they stood me an' Flint on the block together. They must 'a thought we were a matched pair. Leastwise, they sent us to the same plantation."

"Was it your own idea to indenture yourself?"

"Had no choice," said Ben vacantly. "The whole family was put off the land when they brought in the sheep, so we followed everybody else to London."

"For work?" asked John.

"Aye. But there weren't no jobs to be had."

"How did you and your family live?"

"While my father and I looked for work, my sisters and Mum sold off our belongings for food." Ben fell silent. After a long moment, John continued.

"Ben?"

"It was a very bad time, Captain Jones. I watched my father work his teeth loose and pull them out'a his mouth one by one with worry. So we wouldn't be a burden on them anymore, us children indentured ourselves at the docks. That's where I met John Flint."

"How old were you?"

"I was eleven," he answered as he scratched his cheek, "and I think Flint was twelve or thirteen."

"So you spent seven years on a plantation?"

"Oh no, sir. Wouldn't have survived, an' that's for certain. Had to run off after six months."

"But you signed on for seven years. I don't understand."

"That's 'cause you weren't there, sir. They treat their blackbirds better 'n any indentured." John gave Ben a questioning look. "They pay good money fer them blackbirds, so they want 'em to last! Flint figured it out before me, an' we ran away the first chance we got."

"You must have bitter feelings for the Africans."

"Oh, not at all, sir," answered Ben. "Them Africans had no choice 'bout being slaves, no more than the white slaves before them. We were the only ones with a choice."

"White slaves?" asked John. "What white slaves?"

"You don't know?" asked Ben as he gave the Scotsman a questioning look. "Fifty or sixty years before there was any blackbirds in the West Indies, the Spanish slavers were tradin' in whites. At first it was the criminals and the prisoners o' war of course, but when them ran out, the slavers began kidnappin' anybody they could find. Nowadays, a full third of the respectable white folk up in New York and Boston can trace their lines back to the plantations in Jamaica and Cuba."

"I know something about the black slave trade," said John, not wanting to admit he had been a slaver several years before.

"But did ya know that the amount of slavin' the Brits an' Scots done was only a speck to what the Spaniards were doin'? Figure the thing out, sir. Who owns most all the land in the new world? Not the Brits or Scots. Why, every time one of our privateers comes on a slaver, they free the blacks."

"So you and Flint ran off because you were treated badly?" asked John, hoping to change the subject.

"That's puttin' it mild." Ben scratched his right thigh and chased the itch up to his rib cage and around to his upper back. "There were no beds, the food weren't fit fer pigs, an' the water was so bad you'd drink it through yer beard to get the bugs and other floating stuff out; that's if you were old enough to have a beard." The itch became worse. "Me an' Flint were just lads, so we used each other's hair. It was Flint's idea to run off, all right. Took him five lashings an' watchin' half a dozen o' the other indentureds dyin' of their infections before he struck upon the truth of it."

"Where'd you go?"

"Into the hills at first, until our empty bellies finally drove us down to Havana. We jumped the first ship leavin' port. Then Flint got to thinkin' that we'd be worse off back in England--that's where the ship was headed--so when we were passin' Hispaniola close abeam, we peed in the ship's water."

"You did what?"

"Peed in their water!" Gunn winked as he snickered. "You never done that?"

"Can't say I've had the pleasure."

"Had to get 'em to stop somehow before they left the Caribee."

"And?" asked John with a smirk.

"Worked like a charm, it did! Next thing we knew, everybody's yellin' an' cursin' and then we're droppin' anchor on the North coast of Hispaniola. Me an' Flint slipped over the side an' were ashore without them knowin' we was ever aboard."

"What did you do on Hispaniola?"

"Joined the Buccaneers, we did!"

"Buccaneers, eh?" mused Jones. "I've always wondered what kind of life that was."

"Hard, sir, damned hard!" Gunn fell silent for a moment, and then brightened. "But at least you're free."

"That's worth more than most of us realize," said John, remembering Patrick Henry's account of the preacher in Culpeper.

"Aye," agreed Gunn passively. "Six months me an' Flint spent as cutters an' smokers before they let us start huntin' with 'em. Had to earn yer musket, ya did."

"How'd you and Flint become pirates?"

"It were them Spaniards what done it to us." John noticed that as Ben told his story, the old man's English began sounding more and more like a pirate. "Once a year, regular as the seasons, they'd make a sweep o' the island lookin' fer us. Didn't want us shootin' their beef they said, yet it was their ships what bought most of the meat we smoked!" Ben scratched himself under the arm and then behind the right ear. The lice had been gone for over ten years, but the memory was there, and old habits die hard.

"So you joined a pirate crew after that?"

"Not directly," said Gunn as he continued to scratch nervously. "We was chased to the coast where some of the others had a boat. It was their idea to go to Tortuga, an' we were sorta swept along, as they say."

"Tortuga's where most of the French pirates held up, wasn't it?"

"Aye, an' it was there we signed articles with Charles Vane, not two months before he was voted out in favor of John Rackham."

"Rackham? Calico Jack Rackham?"

"The same."

"But Rackham's crew was caught in their sleep and all hung in Jamaica."

"Not me an' Flint!"

"How'd you escape, if the whole crew was captured?"

"Weren't a matter of escapin', 'cause me an' Flint was marooned before they was caught."

"Then you were marooned twice?" John asked as the old man smiled proudly. "But why? I heard Calico Jack was one of the easiest Captains to pirate with."

"Flint an' Rackham got into a scrap when we found out he was hiding these two females out on the ship, disguised as men. Flint was a superstitious sort, twice what I was." Ben rubbed his nose till it was raw. "Mind ya, when things get rough I'll plant my blade in the mainmast with the best of 'em, but the thing worked on Flint somethin' fierce. He told Rackham the crew was double cursed, there bein' two o' them females aboard an' all. One of 'em - no more than a child herself - got pregnant an' Rackham put her off at Havana in '20 to have the pup. That's how we found out, and that's when we was marooned--while Jack was ashore at Cuba."

"They marooned you on Cuba?"

"A real botch of a job, 'cause we were signin' articles within two weeks aboard the Walrus." Gunn squirmed sideways in the seat to scratch his underside. "Wasn't but two or three months an' we heard a Brit man-o'-war took the whole crew an' hung 'em at Jamaica."

"Did the women hang also?"

"Not them two."

"Because they were women?"

"Not strictly speakin'," said Ben. "You see, when judgement was spoke on the whole bunch, them two seamen done a strange thing."

"The two seamen? You mean the two women, don't you?"

"Seamen! The court didn't know they was females till they stood up and said, 'We plead our bellies!'"

"They were both pregnant?"

"Both of 'em, sir!" answered Ben. "Both by John Rackham, hisself, and just after this younger of the two returned from Cuba. The judge wouldn't hang them two 'cause of the law about not killing the innocent unborn child, regardless of the mother's crime."

"I know the law, Ben," said John in a louder voice as they clattered across a small bridge. "So, what did the court do with them?"

"Put 'em in prison, sir, right there in Kings Town. But Mary Read took sick an' died 'afore she had hers."

"And the other girl?"

"Ann Bonny's father sent the money from the Colonies an' ransomed her."

"What about her child?"

"Died during birth. Never had a fightin' chance."

"Who told you all of this?"

"Why, Long John Silver, of course!" answered Ben, as if the story was common knowledge.

"And how does this Long John Silver know so much about her?" asked John as he reigned the horse into the open field to avoid a fallen tree.

"Why, he went along with Mister Taylor when they paid her ransom."

"Taylor?"

"You wouldn't know him neither," apologized Ben as his scalp began to itch again. "Mister Taylor bought John Silver as a lad; sorta like an adopted son."

"Hmmm. Mister Ormerod mentioned John Silver that first evening in New York. He told me Silver was on Spyglass with the group out of Bristol back in '64, and that you released him the night they anchored at Puerta Plata."

"Aye," said Ben proudly, "an' if it weren' for me, Silver would have been hung fer sure!" Ben fell silent as he thought back to Spyglass. "I owed John Silver. If he hadn't come fer the treasure when he did, I would 'ave died there fer sure."

"How'd you meet Silver?"

"He signed articles with Captain Rip Rap in '40, an' then Flint traded me to Rip Rap fer Silver a couple weeks later, right after he marooned those fifteen mutineers on Dead Man's Chest with only a cask o' rum. Ya can't live on rum very long without water."

"I know," agreed John.

"Captain Rip Rap saw that I was special, so he made me his personal steward right off. First time Flint an' me were apart since we was indentured, but lookin' back, it was best fer both us."

"Slow down, Ben. Who's Captain Rip Rap?"

"Master Robert didn't tell you?" John shook his head. "My socks! Robert's great uncle was destined to be one of the most famous pirates in the Atlantic, if he hadn't been killed at Spyglass. His real name was Andrew Murray, and he's the one what took the treasure off the Santissima Trinidad."

"The same treasure we're going after!"

"Aye. Murray an' Flint worked as a team; Murray on the Royal James an' Flint on the Walrus. Master Murray was the brains an' Flint were the muscle, ya might say. Worked great till Murray pulled his double cross an' buried most of the treasure on Dead Man's Chest."

"Let's get back to John Silver. You say he went with James Taylor when they ransomed Ann Bonny?"

"Aye," answered Ben. John Silver was an orphan; one of several that Taylor bought and raised. Kings Town has always been his real home."

"Any idea what happened to Silver after you released him at Spyglass?"

"That were the only thing I could do, sir!" Gunn cried, going into a fit of scratching. "Like I told ya, I owed him."

"Calm down, Ben. You did what your conscience told you to do." John rephrased the question. "Do you figure Silver might have made his way back to Jamaica?"

"Yer askin' things I don't rightly know, Cap'n. Silver might be dead, or he might even be somewhere here in America. My guess is that he's over in France or Spain where the King's Men can't find him."

"But how about Kings Town?" pressed John. "Any chance he might have gone back?"

"Not likely, leastwise not fer more than a quick visit."

"And why's that?"

"Why, he had a price on his head!" Ben gave his traveling mate a questioning look. "John Silver's smarter than ta be stickin' 'round right in the middle of a British Colony."

"Did he ever contact you after Spyglass?" Gunn considered the question carefully for half a minute.

"Ben?" added Captain Jones before the old man could answer. "If you'd rather not say, that's understandable."

"It's not that, sir. I was just tryin' to remember back."

"And?"

"Haven't heard a thing of him in New York or Boston, sir, but just after we got back to Bristol with Flint's treasure, there was a rumor 'bout someone with a missin' left leg runnin' a tavern on the waterfront at Kings Town." Ben gave John a wink. "But you know how them rumors go."

By noon, John and Ben had reached the Rappahannock River and purchased a ferry ride across to Fredericksburg. After a quick stop at the Paul Tailor Shop for additional money and a fresh change of clothes, they were once again on the road toward the Dandridge estate.

"Robert was telling me three of Silver's pirates were marooned on Spyglass in '65."

"Aye, they was Tom Morgan, Dick Gaffney an' Morley Rowe. But they'd all be dead by now."

"But you spent three years there, and you survived?"

"Well," said Ben with a scratch, "it were actually longer, now that I seen the dates an' such. An' as for them three livin' even one year on Spyglass, I think not. With nobody lookin' over 'em, they'd be at each others throats in a day or two, 'specially since they knew about all that silver left in my secret cave."

The sun was nearing the western horizon when John reigned the horse off the road and behind a small hill.

"Why are we stopping, sir?" asked Ben as he looked around. "I thought we were going to spend the night at the Dandridge estate."

"I didn't tell you the entire story, Mister Gunn," said John as he climbed from the carriage and tied the horse to a small tree. "I'm not supposed to see Dorothea."

"Oh?" asked Ben. "Trouble between you and her father?"

"Well, that too, but John Silver isn't the only one with a price on his head."

"Master Ormerod told me about your trouble in Tobago, sir." Ben hesitated, afraid he was going to overstep his bounds. "I don't wish to pry none, sir, but does her father know about the warrant also?"

"Yes, he does."

"So…what are we doing here?"

"I have to speak with Dorothea," said John. "I have to be sure she got my last letter."

"Has Mister Dandridge told her about the warrant?"

"I don't know." John suddenly felt foolish. "I just want to see her again, before we go to sea."

"How long do I wait before I come after you?"

"I shouldn't be long," said John as he strapped on his sword and started off through the woods. "If it gets dark and I haven't returned, bring the carriage to the estate. It's the first one you come to."

Ten minutes later, John stood behind the large oak tree he and Dorothea had sat under so many times that previous summer. John gathered up several small stones and began throwing them at Dorothea's window. After two successful hits, Dorothea stepped from the back door and walked across the lawn to his hiding place.

"Well, if it isn't John Paul!"

"Dorothea, I've just come from New York -- over two hundred miles to see you." He looked about, not sure what to do. "I have to explain some things."

"And as you do," she said coldly, "make sure there are no more lies."

"What's the matter with you?" John asked as he took the young girl by the shoulders, expecting his usual kiss. "What's happened?"

"You have a lot of nerve coming here!" she said as she pulled loose from his grip.

"What do you mean by that? Didn't you get my letter?"

"Of course I did, and that's why I'm so surprised to see you in Virginia. Won't your new employers be angry when they find out you've come here?"

"You know about them?"

"I know everything," she said as she pulled his letter from her skirt. "Why didn't you tell me about the warrant and the man you killed in Tobago?"

"The warrant?"

"Father also told me that when you're not in Fredericksburg, you go by a different name. Is that true?"

"I…there was a good reason for that."

"But you kept it from me. How could you do such a thing and then pretend to love me?"

"But that's exactly why I did it. I didn't want you to worry." John looked down at the letter she had now crumpled in her hands. "Is that my letter?"

"Yes, it is," she answered as she gripped it more tightly.

"Then you know part of what's going on," he said, relieved that she understood. "I've been sworn to secrecy, but when my friend and I reach Charles Town…"

"Charles Town?"

"I know my letter only speaks of Edenton, but things have taken another, most unexpected course. David and I were hoping to be given direct commissions in the Continental Navy, but…well, suffice it to say that what we're involved in is far…"

"Edenton?"

"Yes, Edenton, to see Joseph Hewes."

"John, I'm trying with everything in me to remain calm. Your letter says so little...just that your employers had sent you away. I want to understand what's happened between us, but you're making this very difficult for me."

"What's happened between us?"

"What's going on, John? You're wanted by the King for killing a man in Tobago. You've changed your name. You tell me in your letter that you've taken employment with a company in Philadelphia and that you must leave for the Hudson Bay immediately, and then you show up here saying that you're en route from New York to Charles Town on some secret mission."

"The Hudson Bay?"

"Yes, the Hudson Bay!" She paused as she remembered something else. "This letter's from Philadelphia, and you just told me you came from New York!"

"But I did just come from New York. I've never been in..." John suddenly realized what had happened. Dorothea's father must have somehow intercepted the letter he had asked Patrick to hand deliver, and Mister Jefferson's agent in Philadelphia had already sent a letter in John's name telling Dorothea that he was headed in the opposite direction. More letters would follow at one week intervals, each from somewhere between Philadelphia and the Hudson Bay.

"What?" she hissed. "Another lie on top of the first?"

"But it wasn't," he stammered. "I mean it isn't a lie. If you'll just give me a chance to explain."

"My father was right after all! He told me you were no good for me." John began to protest, but she continued. "Until yesterday when your letter arrived, I had hated my father for what he'd done to us. I suspected all along that he had something to do with you going away, but I didn't know why. Now that I understand everything, I never want to see you again."

"Please, Dorothea..."

"No more!" she hissed. "I'd appreciate it if you would leave now and never come back. That's unless you have no fear of the King's men."

"The King's men?"

"Father showed me this after I got your letter." She pulled a second piece of paper from her skirts and thrust it in his face. "He told me about his warning to you that Saturday we were to meet at the park, and now I agree with him. You're a very stupid man, John Paul!"

John unfolded the warrant. While Dorothea stood with her arms crossed, John read the charges against him for the first time:

WARRANT

EXTRACT from the Register of the Magistrate of Scarborough on Tobago, 12 October 1773.

Whereas; an accusation being pursued at the instance of the KING'S Procurator-General against one John Paul, Master of the merchant vessel Betsy, who had taken upon himself to escape the Island of Tobago aboard the Postal Packet Falmouth, and

Whereas; the Court, having declared this date that the aforesaid John Paul did on 11 October 1773, murder Jack Fry, an able bodied seaman and inhabitant of the King's possession of Tobago aboard said merchant vessel Betsy, does

Therefore, in justice to the English Nation and Her Colonies and according to the indications the Court hath received; that an Accusation and Warrant be drawn against him, that he may be proceeded against, according to the utmost rigor of the Law. Given Thursday the 14th of October, N.S., 1773.

Anderson
Greffier of the Court

"It's you they're after, isn't it?" she asked. "And you never intended to tell me, either!"

John considered his words carefully. "There was no reason..."

"That's exactly what Father told me you'd say!" she said, interrupting him. "What a fool I've been to think that somehow this wasn't true."

"But I can explain everything."

"What is there to explain?" She snatched the warrant from his hand and began to read the charges. "It says here that you killed a crewman and then fled Tobago under an assumed name." She looked up at him.

"Assumed name? The warrant said nothing..."

"My father told me," she answered with a glare. "Who was Jack Fry?"

"He was a mutineer. The man attacked me."

"And a jury wouldn't have believed you?"

"Not on Tobago, and besides..." John broke off with a huff. "It's too long a story for now. You'll just have to trust me that I was justified in not only killing the man, but also in my subsequent actions."

"Don't waste your breath!"

"But when you understand why I've done what I have, you'll forgive me. And after you do, I plan to ask your father for your hand."

"You're truly insane, John Paul!" She turned and began walking toward the house. Half way, she stopped and turned back to her vanquished suitor. "And as far as my hand is concerned..." She turned and continued to the house. As she reached the door, her father stepped from the house. John could see them speak, but couldn't hear their words. But when Dorothea pointed to where he was hiding, he knew it was finished between he and Dorothea. Before John could retreat, Nathaniel Dandridge was striding across the lawn toward him.

"Well, if it isn't John Paul, fresh from Philadelphia. Or are we going by our other name today?"

"That's none of your business!" said John as he grasped his sword.

"Oh!" Dandridge cried, holding his hands away from his sides to indicate that he wasn't armed. "The fugitive adds insubordination to his dishonesty!"

"Dishonesty?"

"That's correct, young man, or did you forget that a relationship can never be built upon a lie?"

"I'm not a liar, sir!"

"I'll say one thing, young man. What you lack in intelligence, you make up for with bravado."

"I have no desire to fight you, sir," said John as he pulled the sword half way.

"Then what do you desire, Captain Paul, seeing that I'm unarmed and my daughter will have nothing more to do with you?" John stood for a long moment, unable to answer the retired British Sea Captain. "Are you going to draw that sword or put it away?"

"I…" began John as he let the sword slide back into its sheath.

"Go away, John Paul. You're no longer welcomed here!" With that, Captain Dandridge turned and returned to the house where Dorothea waited. With one last look of defiance, Dorothea followed her father into the back porch and slammed the door closed.

Ben was waiting patiently as John arrived back at the carriage. He said nothing as John untied the horse and climbed up beside the old man. As John turned onto the road, Ben finally spoke.

"You don't look very happy, sir."

"I should have listened to Captain Steele. He told me that Mister Hewes didn't want me stopping anywhere. I wouldn't listen, and now everything's ruined."

"The way you were talkin' before we got here, it sounded like everything was set between you two. What happened over there?"

"It's a little complicated," said John as he laid the whip to the horse's back and they turned about toward the South. "It's over between Dorothea and me."

"Well, sir," said Ben quietly, "It hurts me to see you hurt this way, but maybe it's best." Ben scratched his arm pit nervously as he gathered his courage. "John Flint used to tell me somethin' that makes a lot of sense now."

"What's that?"

"Well, he was never married, you know, and fer good reason."

"And what was that reason, Ben," said John, losing his patience.

"Like John Flint used to tell me, wings aren't much use to a nestin' bird."

"What's that supposed to mean?"

"I've known many a female in my day Cap'n--and mind ya, this Miss Dandridge sounds like a winsome lass--but it's just that you aren't ready for marriage."

"What are you saying, Ben?" snapped John. "What's wrong with her?"

"It's not her, sir, it's you."

"Then what's wrong with me?"

"Well, sir," Ben continued haltingly, "she sounds to me like the nestin' type."

"And?" answered John with a note of agreement in his voice. "Go on man--spit it out!"

"Well, sir, I'll put it as plain as I know how." Ben began to scratch his scalp once again. "No offense to the lass, but she'd be pluckin' yer flight feathers to line her nest, an' them wings still gotta carry you too many places fer that."

John considered the old man's counsel for a moment. "I understand what you're getting at, Ben, but it could have worked."

"Had to get it off my chest, sir."

Alex and Ann Forrestal sat near the fireplace as Robert described the massacre of the Royal James crew at Spyglass. Captain Steele had beaten David for the second time at chess, and had just begun his third attack on the younger man when Mister Forrestal scooted to the front edge of his chair.

"Then the only reason you and your wife were spared by Flint was for your ransom value?" asked Mister Forrestal.

"I was worth a ransom to my father, sir," said Robert. "I also knew where the other two-thirds of the treasure was buried. Moira's only worth was that she was a woman. With her father dead, there was nobody left to ransom her, and John Flint and several of the others wanted her for their own purposes."

"Dreadful!" said Mrs. Forrestal as she set her teacup on the tray and stood. "Gentlemen, if you'll excuse Alex and me, it's past our bed times." As the men rose, she walked to the door and looked back at her husband.

"I'll be along in a moment, dear," said Alex. "I want to ask Robert a few more questions."

"It's after ten, Alex, and you know how crabby you get when you stay up too late." Alex gave her a defiant, almost child-like look and turned back to the Yorkman.

"How did you keep Moira for yourself, Robert?" asked Alex as he watched his wife turn and ascend the stairs. "You said it was just you and this Peter Corlear against the entire crew."

"John Silver told me to put my mark on her," answered Robert as he traced a cross on his left palm, "to show we were married; pirate fashion."

"Well," offered Alex, "since you and she are now happily married, it must have worked."

"No," answered Robert as he shook his head. "I was thrown into a ring of the cutthroats anyway, and forced to fight Billy Bones for her."

"And?"

"I had a clear advantage over Bones, for two reasons. First, he was three sheets to the wind, as the pirates say, and I'd done some Indian fighting. I gave him a bad cut to the face, starting at his right eye, and running all the way down the cheek to the corner of his mouth." Robert traced the knife cut across his cheek. "Next thing we knew, John Silver had us ushered aft to a waiting boat while he somehow set half the crew against the other half with knives."

"How wonderful!" cried Alex as he clapped his hands and sat back. "And here you are some twenty years later, on your way to dig up that same treasure you buried! It's such a marvelous story!"

"I appreciate your enthusiasm, sir. Let's hope our mission's still a secret."

"It is," interjected David.

"You sound very confident about that, young man," said Alex.

"Do you remember when I went into town the other night?" asked David. The old man nodded that he did. "My sole purpose was to snoop around and find out what people are saying about your twin ships."

The old man was nobody's fool. He reached across and tugged on a smudge of lip rouge on the lad's collar. "And what did you hear, David?"

"No less than a dozen different stories, sir, but not one of 'em named the treasure or the cannons."

"Good," said Alex as he turned to the Dutchman. "And that's exactly what they're supposed to believe, right, Jack?"

"Ya, Mister Forrestal," chirped the large Dutchman with pride. "All der stories I been tellin' dem boatwrights is workin' goot also, Mister Noble."

As they spoke, there was a knock at the front door. Mister Forrestal and his four guests fell silent as the servant opened the door and admitted John and Ben.

"Why, it's Captain Jones!" cried Mister Forrestal as he rose to meet his young friend. "We were beginning to worry about you."

"We'd have been here three days ago if we hadn't got stuck in Fayetteville. Did you get that storm through here also?"

"Only the edge," answered Alex as he studied the elderly man at John's side. "Correct me if I'm wrong, but this distinguished gentleman must be Mister Benjamin Gunn of Boston."

"Right pleased ta meet ya, Mister Forrestal," said Ben as his hand ventured forth nervously. "Cap'n Jones' been tellin' me all 'bout you, too."

"I'm sorry, Alex," said John. "We've spoken so much about you along the way, that I nearly forgot you two have never met."

"And since you already know Captain Steele," said Alex, "the only ones left are David Noble of Kings Town, and Captain Jack Van Mourik." The three men shared handshakes.

"Well, Mister Gunn," began Alex, "you're quite an interesting fellow, if half the stories David's been telling me are true."

"Stories?" asked Ben with a questioning look to the Jamaican.

"How, David, would you hear any stories about Mister Gunn?" asked Robert. "There are only a handful of men still living, apart from my wife and I, who know anything of Ben Gunn, especially his involvement with the treasure and the bloody events of two decades before." But before David could conjure a plausible explanation, Mister Forrestal interrupted.

"Gentlemen, we could tell sea stories all night, but I really need my sleep. I'm sure Captain Jones and Mister Gunn could use a bath and a comfortable bed, so why don't we all retire."

Captain Steele was quick to join Mister Forrestal as the old man limped from the room. As they passed Captain Jones, Henry gave John an icy stare.

"Mister Forrestal," Captain Steele whispered.

"Yes, Henry, what is it?"

"May I speak with you for a moment in the hallway?"

"You sound grim, Henry," Alex said as they took several steps forward, "like you're carrying a heavy burden."

"I am, sir," answered Captain Steele with another quick look back toward Captain Jones. "If you still want the Eagle to be a part of this mission, you and Mister Hewes will have to find a new master for either the Eagle or the Silver Cloud."

"I've noticed the hard looks you've been giving Captain Jones since he arrived. What's happened between you two?"

"We nearly killed each other after New York, just before he took his unauthorized side trip. I'll not be a proper choice as the man's protector."

Steele's words shook the old man to his marrow. "Henry, there's nobody else to do the job. I've no choice but to send you."

"What about Captain Johnson? The Swan's just as capable a ship as the Eagle. And besides, Michael was tellin' me a couple months back that he wanted to see some of this kind of action."

"The Swan's already well on it's way to New Orleans." The old man became desperate. "You have no idea how important this mission is, and how desperately I need you, Henry."

"Then why don't you tell me how important it is, sir! Everybody else around here seems to know!"

The old man rubbed his eyes like a person waking from a long sleep. With a groan, he asked Captain Steele to join him in the kitchen where they could speak without being overheard.

The smells of breakfast cooking in the Forrestal kitchen drew John and David down before the rest of the guests. To their surprise, Mrs. Forrestal stood at the pastry table in a white cotton dress, with flour to her elbows.

"Mrs. Forrestal," said David with a flourish toward John, "this unseemly character is none other than that fugitive of the King's noose, Captain John Paul Jones. John, meet the lady of this magnificent estate, Mrs. Forrestal." As John bowed low, he gave his impudent friend a burning sideways glare.

"Don't worry, Captain Jones," she said as she wiped the flour from her hands. "You and I are on the same side, and the King is on the other." She offered John her hand.

"Thank you, Ma'am. I'm very pleased to meet you." John sniffed the air and studied the little pile of white balls stacked on the pastry table. "Those look good. What are they?"

"They're sour milk biscuits," she said with a broad smile. "Alex keeps telling me I'm famous for them." As she continued to form the little rolls, Ben Gunn joined John and David, drawn to the kitchen by the same smells.

"And you, sir...?" she asked with a questioning look.

"This is Benjamin Gunn of Boston."

"Benjamin Gunn...?" she asked slowly. As with her introduction to David a month before, Mrs. Forrestal seemed somewhat distressed.

"Are you all right, Mrs. Forrestal?" asked David.

"Yes, David," she lied. "I didn't eat any dinner last evening, and I guess I should have. I'll be fine once I have something." She turned back to John and Ben. "Alex is having coffee on the back porch with Captain Van Mourik. Why don't you three join them until the servant calls you for breakfast?" As she spoke, she couldn't help but notice Ben's stare.

"Thank you, Ma'am," answered John. "We will." As he and David turned to leave, John noticed the old man studying Lady Forrestal. "She has that effect on all of us at first, Ben."

"Pardon?" asked Ben, realizing the other two were watching him.

"Why don't you two go on," said Mrs. Forrestal. "I think Mister Gunn wants to ask me something."

"As long as you're sure you'll be safe with the old pirate!" John said with a chuckle.

"I'll be quite all right, Captain Jones," she answered with a pat to his arm. "Go along now and tell Alex some more of your stories."

Ben was still studying her as she once again wiped the flour from her hands.

"Pray forgive me for prying, Ma'am," began Ben nervously, "but have ya ever been in Boston?"

"Yes I have, Mister Gunn, but many years ago."

"Did we meet there once?"

"In Boston? No. We've never met in Boston."

"But you seem so familiar, Ma'am." He studied her for several moments. "I'm almost certain..." She turned her back and began cutting out another batch of biscuits, but stopped and turned back to the old man.

"If you do happen to remember where we met, Ben..."

"Ma'am?"

"Nothing Ben," she said as she reconsidered.

After a large dinner, Mister Forrestal escorted his guests to the library for a brandy, and broke open a fresh box of Cuban cigars for those who had developed the habit. There was a large bundle of new charts lying on the desk, their seals yet unbroken.

"Oh, David," said the elderly ship owner, "Mister Martingale delivered these charts while we were down at the docks yesterday. If they're what I believe them to be, we'll all be anxious to see them."

David set his glass down and searched quickly through the rolled parchments until he came upon the two he wanted. Cutting the seals carefully with a letter opener, he spread them out before the others. John stepped close.

"These are wonderful, David!" said John. "Where did you get them?"

"Mister Forrestal has all his charts drawn up by Mister Martingale and his sons. His older son spends half the year at sea updating their master charts." David took a dry quill pen and pointed to the small numbers surrounding Buck Island. "If you look closely, John, these small numbers give the high and low tide water depths, while these other marks indicate the best anchorages for a ship as large as the Silver Cloud. And this line shows the channel to the West Beach."

"The only thing your map maker's left out is the location of the treasure," said Robert sarcastically.

"What's the matter with you, Robert?" asked John. "We need these charts, especially for the anchorages."

"But don't you see it, John? That mapmaker knows exactly where we're going! David's enthusiasm has probably cost us the secrecy we've sought so diligently to preserve."

John gave David a questioning stare. "He's right, David. You may have done a very foolish thing."

"Not true, gentlemen!" interrupted Mister Forrestal. "David had my mapmaker draw him charts of at least a dozen different small islands along the major shipping lanes. Martingale has no reason to suspect that this one is more, or less important than the rest."

"And exactly what did you tell this mapmaker?" asked Robert.

"I told him that Mister Forrestal had asked me to locate a small island where he could establish a warehousing and ship repair facility." David pointed at the map again with the large feather. "If you'll look at the legend, you'll see that Mister Martingale suggests that it may be too expensive to remove the coral reef from the northwest area of the island to widen the channel to the proposed docks." David searched the legend again. "And here Robert; read this!"

"Why don't you read it for us, David," answered the Yorkman.

"It recommends that Buck Island is not a good choice for the facility because of the lack of a fresh water supply."

"Hmmm," said Ben as he joined the others. "And did he make similar notations for Spyglass?"

"Yes he did, Ben," answered David. "He says Grand Turk would make an excellent island for a repair facility, except that it's too far off the normal shipping lanes to be practical." David pulled the second chart from beneath the one of Buck Island and turned it around so the old man could get a closer look. "That's where we'll anchor, Ben, at Captain Kidd's Lagoon." He gave the ex-pirate a gentle squeeze on his bony shoulder. "Provided we have time before we make the rendezvous." David gave John a questioning look.

"That's where young Hawkins an' the rest of 'em dropped anchor back in '64," said Ben, pointing to the lagoon next to Skeleton Island. "Be kinda pleasant to look on my old stompin' grounds again."

"And you will, Ben," affirmed Captain Jones as he laid the map of Dead Man's Chest on top again. "I'm almost certain of it!" He turned to Robert. "That's quite a reef, Robert. Exactly where did your great uncle put you and the others ashore?"

"We came in from the south in the long boats, using this break in the coral to reach the beach. He put us off just here." Robert's pen knife came to rest at the lower end of the thin strip of white paper measuring about a hundred yards from north to south and forming a thin crescent at the west end of the small island, "He picked us up again several days later at the same beach."

"Can you see the place where you buried the treasure?"

"Good try, John," said Robert as he looked up with a grin.

"Can't blame a man for asking," said John with a broad smile. "And besides, you should let somebody else know where it's buried, just in case something happens to you."

"Sorry. If I die, the secret dies with me. That's the way Mister Jefferson wants it and that's the way it shall be."

"Well, I don't like it!" John said in a low voice.

"Not to change the subject, John," interrupted Alex, "but I've been going over this list of preparations you gave me before lunch. We've already taken care of the bulk of the items, but you'll have to deal with the ship's surgeon and cook yourself." Alex tilted his head forward to peer at John over his spectacles. "And as far as the training and watch bills, I don't see how you're going to make any progress until you assign your friends here to their duties."

"I've been considering that. I have all of the assignments covered except for Robert and Ben."

"How about your cabin boy?" asked Robert sarcastically. "Might I be capable of that?"

John ignored Robert's jab and turned to Alex. "After we tour the Silver Cloud, I'll have time to meet with the surgeon and cook. Could you arrange that for me?"

"Why not right now?" asked Alex. "Since you appear to need a little more time to think about the officer assignments, you could make that inspection and be back before supper."

"I'd like that."

"If my guess is right, you'll catch Doctor McKenzie aboard," added Mister Forrestal. "He's been laying in his supplies since this morning."

The Silver Cloud was twice the ship John had expected her to be, and he expressed the same amazement David had over the hidden cannons and gun ports. After a thorough inspection of the gun and main decks, Alex led John aft.

"Mister McKenzie!" called Forrestal as they walked through the gun deck and into officer's country. "Are you there, sir?"

"Aye," came a thick Scottish brogue from one of the staterooms. "If your shoes are clean, you can enter. If not, I'd appreciate you speaking from the companionway."

"Our feet are clean, Mister McKenzie," John answered as he stepped inside the small cabin. "And before you pull your shillelagh for a crack at my skull, I'd suggest that you find out who it might be you're speaking to."

"Very well," answered the man as he pulled his head from a wooden box of odd shaped and gaily colored bottles. Adam McKenzie was a thin man of thirty, with sharp features and thick black hair brushed back over the ears.

"Mister Forrestal! Flog me sir, but I didn't recognize your voice."

"It's all right, Adam," said Alex as he ducked into the small stateroom behind John. "I've someone very important for you to meet." The Doctor's face began to beam as he anticipated his employer's next words. "This is the man we've all been waiting for. Adam McKenzie, this is the Master of the Silver Cloud, Captain John Paul Jones."

"Very pleased to meet you, sir!" the Scotsman said as he pumped John's hand several times. "Very pleased!"

"And I'm equally pleased to meet you, Adam." John pulled his hand free and turned back to Mister Forrestal.

"Alex, since we've found Dr. McKenzie onboard, why don't I speak with him now? I'll still need that talk with the cook tomorrow morning if you can arrange it."

"Very good, John. I'll have him at the house at ten." With that, Mister Forrestal excused himself and returned to his waiting carriage.

"I'm sorry for my comment about the shoes, sir, but some of these workers forget to clean the mud from their feet before they come in with my supplies."

"No offense taken, Adam."

"How may I be of service?" asked the doctor.

"I'd like to go over your list of supplies."

"Oh?" asked Adam with a worried look. "That may be more difficult than you realize."

"You do have a list, I trust?"

"I've a dozen lists, and therein lies the problem. I've divided it up between all these crates so I can take my inventory as I open each one." He looked around the cluttered room for a moment. "If you can give me ten minutes, sir, I'll collect them for you."

"That'll be fine," said John. "I'll be in my cabin when you're ready."

The master's cabin spanned the entire aft width of the ship and was nearly as long as it was wide. It had the smell of a sawmill where a pipe smoker once lived. John's hand went to one of the massive waxed overhead beams. He relished the rich texture of the hand-rubbed grain.

Much better than pitch and turpentine, he thought. A man can feel a ship's soul better through wax.

A massive table was positioned in the center of the room near the rear hatches, with a large chair at its after side, facing forward. This table was as long as a tall man and four feet across, doubling as the navigation table when the officers were not gathered about it for a meeting or their mess. At the starboard side of the room was the Master's bunk and toilet, while against the larboard side was a large oaken cabinet for the storage of his clothes, ships charts and other essentials of life at sea. Going on David Noble's recommendation, several sets of uniforms had been pre-pared and hung in the closet, along with an equal number of new shoes. John was busy trying on one of the coats when the doctor knocked.

"Come in, Adam," called Captain Jones as he laid the jacket across his bunk.

"Shall I leave these on your table?"

"Please, and take a seat while I look them over." John picked up the stack of papers and walked to the windows for better light. "I'd like you here in case I have any questions."

"As you please." McKenzie eased himself into a chair as his new captain paced back and forth along the row of larboard windows with the medical inventory. At the third sheet, John gave a low groan and looked up at the doctor. "Anything amiss, sir?"

"Where'd you come up with this list?"

"It's my standard kit, sir. I know what ten men need for one month and then I simply multiply the size of the crew and the length of the voyage. Mister Forrestal has provided me with those missing numbers. Why, is there something missing?"

"Did Mister Forrestal tell you what we'd be doing on this mission?"

"Just that we're headed for the Antilles chain. Nothing more."

"Did he mention anything about pirates?"

"Yes he did, sir, but that list provides more than enough supplies for any injuries we might expect."

"I'd agree with you," answered John, "if this were only a merchant voyage."

"It's not?"

"No." John scanned the remaining pages quickly and then seated himself at the head of the table. "For now, I can't tell you where we're going or what we'll be doing when we get there. But you'll have to double the number of battle dressings you have listed. And we'll need a full supply of apothecary chemicals and extra..."

"It sounds like we're going into battle."

"I hope not, but it's a distinct possibility." John pushed the stack of papers across to the doctor. "Can you increase your supplies to a fighting ship's inventory?"

"Aye, sir, but it'll take me a few more days. I have my battle list at home."

"Order what you need, and as quickly as possible."

"Yes, sir," answered the Doctor. "Will there be anything else?"

"Yes, one thing more. I'm a stickler for personal cleanliness. I want you to teach the men how to keep themselves clean."

"I'll order an extra supply of soap and rubbing alcohol, sir."

"Good," said John. "You may..."

"How do you feel about swim calls, sir?" asked the doctor, interrupting Captain Jones.

"Swim calls?"

"If you let the men swim once a week, they'll be a cleaner and happier crew."

"Let them swim?" Jones considered the idea with a tilt of the head. "I'll go you one step further, Adam. I'll make swimming mandatory."

"You can do that if you're so inclined, sir, but why not let the men think they're working for the weekly swim?"

"I don't follow you, Adam. As I see it, the only issue here is that they maintain a certain level of personal cleanliness. If I order it, it'll be done."

"Yes it will, sir, as it should be," answered the Doctor impatiently. "But think of the good morale you'll create by letting the men earn the right to swim? They'll work harder and keep the Silver Cloud twice as shipshape if it's for a reward rather than to avoid a flogging."

John stared at the man for a moment and wondered why the doctor wasn't a ship's captain. Perhaps, he thought to himself, if I'd have treated the crew of the Falmouth Packet more like McKenzie's suggesting, they wouldn't have jumped ship.

"I like your recommendation, Adam." John stood and led the man to the cabin door, where he hesitated.

"Is there something else, sir?"

"Just one thing," answered John thoughtfully. "If you ever see me doing anything you believe to be detrimental to our crew's morale, tell me. I don't want officers who agree with me just because I'm their captain."

"If you're serious, sir, then you can count on it."

The next morning after a late breakfast, John sat in the library with Alex Forrestal, going over what seemed to be an endless list of questions.

"John," said Alex with a huff of mild frustration. "I don't intend to get picky, but most of what you ask has already been taken care of by my fitters and ship's company. If..." He was interrupted by a lean man in his mid-thirties, standing in the doorway. The man fidgeted like Ben Gunn.

"Ah," said Mister Forrestal, thankful for the chance to disengage the young Scotsman, "the ship's cook! And ten minutes early, besides."

"I were told you wanted to see me, Mister Forrestal," the man said in an apologetic tone followed by an impish smile. "What ever it is, sir, I didn't do it, an' it ain't my fault." It was a tired joke; one the Irishman had used often. Captain Jones rose from his chair and turned to face his former crewman. "Cap'n Jones!" the Irishman cried.

"In the flesh, Albert."

"But I thought you..." the man stammered. "Are you comin' on this 'ere 'venture with us too?"

"Yes I am."

"I'm ship's cook!" Albert said with pride as he took a step forward, but checked himself with a sideways glance at Mister Forrestal. "You hirin' on as one o' the officers?"

"You might say that," answered John with a smirk. He enjoyed playing practical jokes on Barragan. "So tell me, Albert, have you told the crew yet that they'll have to hold their bread up to the sun before they eat it?"

"That's not fair," cried Barragan. "There was weevils in that flour from Kings Town, an' they only hatched out cause o' the warm weather."

"I'm only toying with you," said John in a fatherly tone. "It's good to have you on the crew."

"Yeah, you an' me again, just like when we sunk the Walrus!"

"David Noble's coming along also," said John. "Concerning the Walrus, we only disabled her."

"I been tellin' the rest of the crew we sunk her, sir," said the Irishman with a worried look. "You don't mind, do ya?"

"The officers know the truth, but I'll let you tell the rest of the crew whatever you wish."

"Thank you, sir," said Barragan with a broad smile.

"Well, Captain Jones," interrupted Mister Forrestal. "It's obvious you know Barragan better than I do, so I'll leave you two to discuss your business. When you need me again, I'll be with Mrs. Forrestal in the kitchen." The shipbuilder pushed himself upward from his chair with a wince of pain and limped from the room. By habit, the old man had learned to inhale every time he put his weight on the painful hip, just in case he needed to curse.

"How'd you get a spot on this cruise, Cap'n Jones? I thought ya had to be somebody special to sign on."

"You could say I knew the right people. But let's talk about me later. Last I saw of you was when I went off watch the night before you and the others jumped ship."

John spoke with an accusing tone as he gestured for the man to take a seat across the table from him.

"I feel bad 'bout that, Cap'n, an' I'd rather not talk 'bout it, if ya don't mind."

"But I do mind," said John sternly. "We'll be at sea for the better part of two months, and I don't want to set any part of the crew against me like I apparently did you three after Charles Town." John leaned forward. "Why couldn't you and the others wait a few more hours to reach Dahlgren?""

"Well..." The Irishman squirmed as he formed the words. "It were yer treatment o' the crew after Charles Town, sir, 'specially Clark."

"Go on."

"Well, it didn't lay well with us what ya did about Carini gettin' hit by that ball. It weren't fair."

"Fair had nothing to do with it! Clark disobeyed a direct order to man the mains'l sheet. That put the rest of us in jeopardy and I couldn't allow his act to go unpunished and then expect to maintain discipline for the rest of the trip."

"Cap'n," the cook began slowly, "ye can have strict articles, but when ye make a judgement, stick to the thing, right or wrong. An' when ya do decide to punish a man, do it quick an' get it over with." Barragan waited for the younger man to answer.

"Is there more?"

"Aye."

"Go on. Get it off your chest, here and now, Albert."

"Well, it's like this, sir! Before Charles Town, you seemed ta understand why Clark disobeyed yer order. You had him an' the rest o' us believin' he was off yer hook. Then ye waited three days an' flogs him out o' the blue anyway, just like he'd done somethin' else!" Barragan stopped to catch his breath. "Ya lost our loyalty that day, Cap'n Jones. We four just couldn't trust ya no more."

"Four?" asked John. "Mister Noble, also?"

"Aye, sir, but he wouldn't jump ship with us."

"So he knew your plans and didn't tell me!" John spat. "Did he say why he stayed with me?"

"Something 'bout a mission you two had..." The Irishman's eyes brightened. "He was talking about this here secret voyage of ours, weren't he?"

"Now that you mention it, I believe he was." John sat back as the implications of this new revelation became clear. "Wouldn't surprise me if Mister Noble's known about this secret voyage since we were in Kings Town."

"When did he tell you 'bout it, sir?"

John didn't answer, but returned to their former subject. "Your advice about giving orders and disciplining the men is well taken, Albert. If you see me getting out of hand once we're at sea, I'd be obliged if you'd come to me about it."

"I'll do that, sir."

"Tell me something else," asked John. "What happened to you three after Matchotic Creek, and how'd you get hired as our ship's cook?"

"Not that much to tell, sir," said Albert as he rubbed his nose from side to side. "Clark an' Etinger headed south toward Richmond to find their families while I went north, up to a place called Alexandria. Couldn't find my people there, so after a month in the sawpits, I got me a planker's job at a small yard back down in Dalgren. When the ship we was makin' was finished, I was out o' work. Word come up that they was hirin' plankers on these here two ships in Mister Forrestal's yards, so I made it down the coast quick as I could, an' got hired on."

"As a planker?"

"Not right off. Had to put in my time in the sawpits again, just like before. After that, they promoted me to carpenter's mate."

"And how, pray tell, did a carpenter's mate become a cook?"

"It were the other men, sir," continued the Irishman. "Food was God-awful bad an' I bore up to the other men's complainin' as long as I could. I finally told 'em I'd done some cookin'. Well, before I knew it, word got to the foreman, an' next thing, I'm the yard cook. Then when I hear there's able-bodied seaman positions available on these here special privateers, I applied. But bein' as late as I were, all they needed was a ship's cook."

"Who said the Silver Cloud was a privateer?"

"Well, nobody an' everybody." Barragan leaned forward. "Figure it out, sir. Why else would they be hidin' all them cannons behind that fake plankin', 'cept to fool other merchantmen?"

"You're close, but not correct." John pushed his chair back and walked to the far end of the table where a jumbled stack of papers lay. "The reason I called you here was to ask a few questions about our provisions."

"Anything you want to know, you just ask me."

The two talked for more than an hour and a half, until Mister Forrestal reappeared to announce that coffee was being served in the parlor.

"Thank you, sir," said John to his host. "The cook and I have finished what we needed to discuss, so I'll be with you in a moment." Barragan welcomed the opportunity to get back to his chores, especially the changes Captain Jones had suggested.

"Then I'll be seein' ya onboard when we set sail, Cap'n Jones?" asked the Irishman as he stopped at the door.

"Yes, Albert. You will."

"An' if anybody asks fer me vote, I'll tell 'em you'd make a right fine first officer, sir."

"Thank you. I may need that vote of confidence one day before this mission is concluded."

CHAPTER 9

One hundred miles to the south of Charles Town and fifteen miles inland from the Atlantic Ocean lies the small village of Savannah, Georgia. The land lying within the present boundaries was, previous to the year 1733, a wilderness. In 1732, this harsh ground was granted to James Oglethorpe by King George II for the purpose of creating a settlement for England's poor and those who had been imprisoned for debt. Although its growth was slow, its morals were unusually high; one of its first regulations was the absolute prohibition against the importation of Negroes and the use of rum. In 1743, after nearly nine years of rule as their first Governor, James Oglethorpe left the Colony of Georgia and returned to England. His absence created a moral vacuum which was quickly filled by the pirate Captain, John Flint.

For over a decade, Flint and the merchants of Savannah enjoyed a prosperous and sinful relationship. Flint provided the merchants with inexpensive goods, while the merchants provided the pirate and his crew with a safe port and total immunity from the law. In '65, John Flint turned over his ship to his first mate, Billy Bones, just days before the former died of liver sickness. Bones took the ship to sea on several raids, and then while hauled down for repairs in the Bahamas, Bones ran off to England with Flint's treasure map. Sixteen months later, most of the Walrus' crew followed John Silver and the Bristol Expedition to Spyglass Island to retrieve Flint's third of the treasure. A young and aggressive apprentice of John Flint by the name of Joshua Smoot traveled to England, took command of the Walrus and sailed her back to Georgia. Although his true origins were uncertain, several of the older inhabitants of Savannah believed him to be the bastard son of John Flint. The merchants of Savannah were thrilled to see the Walrus return. To show their gratitude, they granted title to the Oglethorpe estate to Captain Smoot, much to the consternation of the colony's new Governor, James Wright.

High Tortuga, as Smoot named his new home, sat alone near the edge of Canston's Bluff like an old man crouched against the weather. It gave Smoot an unobstructed view of his newly acquired American Clipper, the Hesperus. He would stand at times for as much as an hour, just watching his great ship swing about it's anchor in the gentle currents of the Savannah River.

Fishbone Smoot, as he was called for his habit of picking his teeth with the rib bone of a barracuda, was in his mid-forties, and looked like he'd been thrown out of hell for meanness. But for a thick mustache, he was clean-shaven, with tar-black, shoulder-length hair pulled back in a tight braid at the back of his neck. He had a hawkish nose, deep-set eyes, and a mouth full of crooked teeth, all but hidden beneath his great bushy mustache. A light-colored scar ran from the corner of his mouth to just above his right ear, where it became lost in the forest of hair at his temple. When he sailed, he wore a flame red coat all cobwebbed over with gold filigree.

"Damn you, Wright!" yelled the angry pirate at the younger man. "Why the hell do ya keep pretendin' it'd be such a bloody crime to deal with me? Once ya sign me Letter o' Marque, I'll be just as respectable as any o' yer other pirates! An' ya know I'd be bringin' ya twice the swag as yer other captains!"

"My signature wouldn't change you a farthing, Smoot, and you know it better than me!" said the Governor without turning from the salt-streaked window. "You're nothing but a cutthroat, brigand and pirate, and that you'll be until you meet your Maker!"

"Aye," agreed Smoot, "I'm a pirate through an' through. But 'tis only yer signature on this piece o' parchment what keeps me that way." Smoot pushed the document and the ten thousand pounds in crisp notes across the table toward the Governor's drink. "Yer other twenty Captains are pirates too, except they have your Letter!"

"Keep your blood money!" said the official as he turned about. "I don't care what you offer. You'll never see my signature on a document with your name, except to order your execution!" The Governor pointed at the pile of money. "That isn't the price of a commission anyway!"

"Oh?"

"That's the thirty pieces of silver the priests paid so they could kill our Lord! And if I accepted it, then I'd be no better than they when the innocent begin to die at your hands!" He took up his hat and satchel and walked to the door.

"Where are you goin'?"

"Back to Atlanta," he said as he opened the front door to the light rain that blew up the hill. "My business here is finished, and you can count yourself fortunate that I even came. Now that I've repaid the debts I owed to those money-hungry merchants who protect you, I hope to never see your evil face again, except with the hangman's rope pulled tight against the side of your throat!"

"I'll get that Letter of Marque, one way or another, Governor Wright!" Smoot warned. "You can lay to that!"

"One way or another?" the Governor echoed as he stopped and turned in the open doorway. "You aren't so presumptuous or so stupid as to think you can threaten the Governor of Georgia, are you, Smoot?"

"Oh, it's much more than a threat," said the pirate with an evil chuckle. "I can promise that you'll sign my Letter, and you'll do it without the ten thousand pounds, too."

"And you, Captain Smoot, can expect a visit from the local constable for that...promise, as you call it!"

"Send yer constable, an' see what good it does. Seems like I 'member Constable Gilmore bein' one o' my closest friends and wealthiest accomplices in Savannah. Ha! Ha! Ha!"

As the Governor stormed from the hilltop mansion toward his waiting coach, he brushed past a youth with carrot-orange hair and green eyes. The light rain which had fallen most of the morning had soaked the lad to the bone as his unshod and half-frozen feet carried him up the windswept pathway toward the mansion.

"Well! Well!" Smoot bellowed as the lad stepped through the open door and shook the water droplets from his coat. "Rip me jib if it isn't me old mate, Henry Morgan! Have a seat boy, an' fill yer scupper with a noggin' o' fine Jamaican rum!"

Smoot fetched a clean glass from the sideboard and filled it to the brim.

"Thank ya, Govn'r," said Morgan as he took the small cup and then stopped to blow the weather from his nose and give a dog-like shake of his head. Water droplets rained about him for several seconds before he took a large mouthful of rum. "Ah," he sang out as the warming liquor reached his stomach. "In the words o' Darby McGraw, rum'll do a man's innards good every time!" Morgan laid his satchel aside and took the seat across from his former captain. "Who was that fancy gentleman what almost put me on me backside?"

"That, me lad, is the man who'll make Fishbone Smoot a respectable privateer."

"That was the Govn'r of Georgia?"

"Aye, an' I've a plan what'll twist his arm more 'n it's ever been twisted 'afore." Smoot refilled Morgan's cup. "But tell me, Henry, have ya come back so soon to pay me my ten pounds?"

"Ten pounds?" Morgan protested. "What're you talkin' about, Govn'r?"

"Our wager, lad!" Smoot said as he filled his own cup. "They say the loser's memory's always the shortest, an' I reckon it's true by the likes o' yers."

"But I didn't lose the wager yet!"

"You welchin' on me?"

"No!"

"If yer not welchin', then why've ya come back from the shipyards after just two months?"

"I'm here to strike a bargain with ya."

"What, fer the name ya been wantin' to carve on the Walrus? Ha! Ha!" Smoot stood and walked to a stack of mail on his desk. After a quick search, he held a letter to his nose and inhaled deeply. With cat-like swiftness, Morgan circled the desk and snatched the letter from the old pirate's hand, and ran to the far side of the room.

"Got a girlfriend, Govn'r?" Henry mocked as he smelled the light perfume that escaped from the folded parchment.

"Damn you, Henry!" yelled Smoot. "Give me that letter!"

"An' if I don't," snickered Morgan as he sniffed the folded paper a second time, "what ya gonna do 'bout it?"

Before Henry could recoil, Smoot had leaped over the desk and pinned the lad's right hand to the floor with his knife.

"I should take off yer hand here an' now!" whispered Smoot as a trickle of blood ran from under the blade and onto the floor.

"Belay!" cried Morgan as he twisted to free himself. "I be needin' that hand fer diggin' up the treasure!"

"What treasure?" demanded the older man as he snatched back his letter.

"That's what I'm here fer, Govn'r!" Morgan looked about the large room to make sure nobody was listening and continued in a quieter tone. "I'm here to strike a bargain with ya 'bout a treasure what'll easy pay the ransom o' three kings."

"Three kings, ya say?" Smoot studied the young man through narrow eyes as he stood and laid the letter on his desk. "And just where, pray tell, does this ransom o' three kings lie?"

"Nothin' doin, Govn'r!" answered Henry as he wrapped his injured hand in a piece of cloth. "Not till we strike our bargain first."

"What sort of a bargain did ya have in mind?"

"I want five shares o' whatever we bring back."

"Five shares?" Smoot yelled, bringing a cringe from the slave hiding behind the dining room door. "I only get five shares meself!"

"That may be, Govn'r, but my share's gonna be the same as yers, or you an' yer crew can find yer own treasure."

"And how much money will these five shares bring you, Henry?" Smoot was a rogue, but he was a clever one. He knew Morgan was figuring on a split with over a hundred and fifty men, and he knew enough of his arithmetic to calculate the size of the treasure by Henry's part of it.

Henry smiled. "Not till ya agree to me price."

"I'll have to speak to the crew," Smoot lied, "but you gotta give me some kinda hint first. They'll be wantin' to know if the work's worth it."

The youth leaned back and folded his arms behind his head. "Let's say I'd never hafta work again fer the rest o' me natur'l life, if I didn't want to."

"Hmmm..." Smoot was interested, and would say anything to get more information. He could always kill Morgan when the time was right. "Tell ya what. If me crew agrees, and mind ya they're not..."

"Don't give me that bilge!" countered Henry as he came forward and hit the table with his half-empty glass. "Your crew does exactly what you say, ever since the Turk was killed two winters ago!"

"Okay!" Smoot gave up trying to deceive the lad. "You can have yer shares, but..."

"All five?" Morgan interrupted as he reached across the table for the bottle.

"Aye, all five, just like me." Smoot leaned forward and spoke slowly. "But, if we set sail and this turns out to be another of yer lies, I'll have yer heart fer supper!"

"It's no lie, Govn'r. You an' me, we be goin' to get the Treasure of Dead Man's Chest."

Smoot grabbed Morgan by the collar and pulled him close. "Show me yer chart!"

"I don't have none, Govn'r," cried Morgan as he pulled himself loose. "There's only one man what knows that, an' he's settin' sail from the Forrestal shipyards in a fortnight."

"In a fortnight?" Smoot asked as he rubbed the afternoon stubble on his chin. "Besides you an' me, how many know where they're goin'?"

"It's a well-kept secret," answered Henry. "Only the four or five of 'em what hatched the plan knows."

"And just how, pray tell, did you find out about it; if it's such a big secret?"

"One o' the crew, a big Dutchman with enough pride fer a dozen men, told me," answered Henry. "Took me a half sovereign o' rum to loosen his tongue, but he told me enough. All we have to do is beat the Silver Cloud to Dead Man's Chest and watch when they start diggin'."

"And will this Silver Cloud be sailin' alone?"

"Not sure of that, Govn'r. There's a rumor that the fourteen gun privateer Eagle, the same one what's bringin' down the Yorkman, is supposed to depart for Christiansted several days before the Cloud. I'm not sure of it, but it's my guess they be goin' ahead to make sure the way's clear."

"The Yorkman?"

"I think he's the one who knows where the treasure's buried."

"His name, Henry!" demanded Smoot. "What's his name?"

"Nobody's sayin', Govn'r," answered the young pirate. "They only refer to 'im as the Yorkman." Smoot began picking his teeth with the barracuda bone as he hummed a familiar ballad. "You think he might be the one what's mentioned in the ballad, Govn'r?"

"It has to be Robert Ormerod!" Smoot fell into deep contemplation. After several minutes, Morgan broke the silence.

"Yer not worried 'bout the Eagle, are ya, Govn'r?"

"Not on yer life!" He wiped the bone clean on his sleeve. "I was just thinkin'. If we could beat the Eagle to Saint Croix..." He stopped and gave the lad a poke in the chest with the bone. "Ya know, Henry, it sure would be a help if you could get yerself back on the crew of this Silver Cloud. What da'ya think?"

"Not a chance. Cap'n Van Mourik--he's the one what leaked the whole thing to me--may be proud, but he's not stupid. Won't take him long to start askin' me where I've been this last month, an' then he's sure to remember tellin' me 'bout the treasure."

"Then I'll just have to arrange fer a couple of me best men to get on that crew."

"But I tolt ya that the crew's already full up. Been full from before I left the place."

"I have a man what knows how to create the openin' he needs," said Smoot with a chuckle.

Henry filled his glass for the fourth time and set the bottle next to the letter. "What's with this letter, Govn'r? Got yerself a sweetheart since I been gone?"

"This, my young friend," answered Smoot as he picked it up, "is a letter addressed to our esteemed Governor; a letter he'll never receive." Smoot ran it under his nose again and breathed in deeply. Then with a wink of his eye, "This, an' a short side trip on our way to Dead Man's Chest, will get me that privateer commission I been wantin'."

"Where'd you get it? You sink another postal packet?"

"Aye!" Smoot answered proudly. "Ya can get a lot o' information that way. Learned it from John Silver hi'self, I did."

"Hope it were worth more 'an a new rudder this time."

"Watch yerself, Morgan," said Smoot as he waved his blade in front of the youth's face. "A man could lose more than his tongue fer half the insults I be lettin' you throw at me. Besides, the Turk was in charge that day, not me."

It was a morning of excitement at the fitter's docks. Two Dutch merchantmen stood tall and proud in the warm morning sun with their virgin canvas and pungently fresh paint playing games with the crew's nostrils. For those who had come aboard secretly at four in the morning and now sat impatiently below decks, the pungent linseed oil fumes had an almost anesthetic effect. To the uninformed--if such a thing were possible in the small town named for one of England's Kings--this was just another launching; not unlike the hundreds the townsfolk had witnessed during the preceding eighteen years. The only remarkable thing about these two magnificent vessels was that they were identical, from their fittings to the black and red paint that concealed their gun ports. And even more unusual were their names. They were both called Silver Cloud. That was Jefferson's idea. He said it was the only way Captain Jones could make it back through the blockade. The crew of the treasure ship was busy making ready to get underway while Captain Jones and his officers stood next to the Forrestal carriage.

"Gentlemen," the grey-haired ship builder began from the comfort of his carriage, "you'll find your orders in this sealed packet. I would request for security reasons that you refrain from opening it until you're well underway and beyond the last British man-of-war." He handed Captain Jones the leather case.

"May I ask what it contains, sir?"

"Captain Van Mourik's beginning to fidget, John," answered Alex as he pointed at the large Dutchman several paces to lee, thereby dodging the Scotsman's question.

"He's worried about the tide," answered John, "and how long it's going to take us to reach the shallows off Hadrell's Point."

"Ya!" echoed the large Dutchman. "If we don't get der Cloud movin' quick like, den we be forced ta go da long way, right past da toe o' Sullivan's Island an' dem British frigates, ya?" As the Dutchman pointed eastward, the other two could see the outline of three lesser-rated men-of-war at anchor between the island and the great sand bank stretching across the harbor to Fort Johnson.

"Then be on your way, my good Captain, and may the Good Lord be with you."

"Thank you, sir," said John as he lifted his hat in salutation.

"John," added Forrestal, "would you hold up a moment?"

"Sir?" asked John as Van Mourik strode across the dock beyond earshot.

"I'm not angry with you about last night. You've a legitimate concern. You'll simply have to trust me that you'll receive the rendezvous instructions in plenty of time. I can't tell you who'll get them to you, or how, but Mister Jefferson and the others have made ample provision for any eventuality."

"Even the man's death?" John spoke the words very slowly and with all the force he dared--just short of angering his superior.

"Yes, John, even that."

"Well, I certainly hope so, for all of our sakes."

"The Good Lord's in charge of 'our sake's, as you call them, young man. If He sees fit to bring those cannons to our shores, then no power in this world, will thwart His will. But if He chooses otherwise..."

"I wish I could share your faith, sir," said John as he pulled his sword several inches from its sheath. "This is where I put my faith." John let the sword slide back with a ring of brass against steel. "When you remember us in your prayers, sir, ask that our aim be true and that our hands not waiver when we hold our weapons in battle."

"That I will, John. That I will." Mister Forrestal reached forth and gave his young agent a fatherly handshake of farewell. "Go now, and if you'll allow me to twist the words of your lawyer friend from Virginia, may the good Lord give you and the Colonies liberty, and not death."

"When the second Silver Cloud sails to Jamaica," John said as he looked across at his ship's twin, "who will be at its helm?"

"We haven't decided yet, except we know it'll be a skeleton crew. Mister Noble will have to find additional men in Kings Town."

"For the other officers and myself, I thank you and your lovely wife for everything, Mister Forrestal."

As Captain Jones marched aboard his new ship, the bosun piped the crew to attention. David stepped forward with a brisk salute and asked for his Captain's instructions.

"Pipe the men to their stations for getting underway, Mister Noble," commanded John.

"Don't you want to talk to them first?"

"After we clear the harbor and the three British frigates off the bar," answered

John as he studied the crew.

It wasn't difficult to recognize the three classes of men who made up the crew of this new fighting ship. The thirty Dutchmen wore the brown uniform of their fatherland and stood behind Captain Van Mourik. The second group was the largest; the American sailors. They numbered eighty and wore loose-fitting blue and white striped shirts and light canvas breeches; best suited to the arduous work at sea. The final group was the Mountain men, all of them in buckskin and numbering forty.

"Aye, aye, sir!" answered David with another salute, and then turned his attention to the deck before him.

"All hands to stations for getting underway!" he cried, followed by the bosun's detailed commands to the various line hauling crews. For several seconds, the deck of the Silver Cloud resembled a street riot, with men running in every direction. Several men dropped down the various companionways while most climbed, cat-like, into the rigging. After a few minutes, word returned that all was ready.

"The men are at their stations, sir."

"Very well, Mister Noble. Cast off and set a starboard reach for Hadrell's Point."

Before David could relay the command, the bosun barked out the order to set the gallants and royal tops, followed a moment later by the order to cast off all lines. Like enormous white wings, the Silver Cloud's virgin sails unfurled to capture the rising south wind. The taut canvas strained at the rigging, pulling the disguised warship gently from its dock to leeward. The tide was good, and within an hour the Silver Cloud passed Hadrell's Point. Captain Jones called his officers to his cabin.

There were five of them, all standing just inside the grand cabin's door. Captain Van Mourik stood to the left, with Robert Ormerod and the ship's surgeon at his right shoulder. Behind them and slightly to the right stood the young Jamaican, David Noble and his new companion, the ancient pirate-turned-businessman, Ben Gunn. The leather packet lay open on the desk behind Captain Jones.

"Captain Van Mourik," began John. "You'll be my second officer. You'll be in charge of the watch schedule and seeing to it that the men are kept busy with their duties. I'll also expect you to conduct daily gunnery drills once we've gained the open sea." The Dutchman nodded. "And if we encounter any of the King's ships, it'll be your special duty to assume temporary command of the Cloud, along with the Dutch crewmen. I'll expect you and your men to put on a convincing show for the inspectors while the rest of us hide below."

"Aye, Captain Jones. Dat what we be here for, ya?" answered the large man.

"David, as I told you the other day, you'll be my first officer. And if you're willing, I'd like you to assume the responsibilities of ship's navigator." The young Jamaican nodded his approval and acceptance of the assignment. "I'll work with you for the first week or so, until you feel secure in your duties." The older men gave David their congratulations and then returned their attention to the Captain.

"Adam, as ship's surgeon, you'll be in charge of not only the men's physical health, but indirectly, their morale. Identify, if you are able, the natural leaders among the crew and get to know these men well. And, find out the potential trouble-makers. Listen to the rumors and complaints and advise me before we have a problem. I've had some bad experiences in the past and can't afford them on this mission." John gave David a quick glance.

"I've been tending to the men for several weeks while they've been waiting for our departure, sir," said Adam. "They already trust me."

"I don't want you to betray any confidences, Adam. I just want to know the climate below decks at all times."

"Understood, sir," replied the surgeon.

"Robert, since you're the only one on board, besides Ben, who's ever seen Dead Man's Chest, I'll make you my tactician. I'll expect both you and Ben to keep out of harm's way as much as is humanly possible. We can't afford to lose either of you, until we retrieve the treasures." Robert gave John a questioning look.

"Is something bothering you, Robert?"

"You make it sound like we're expendable once we take you to the treasures."

"I know how it sounds, Robert," said John. "The treasure is our mission and the two of you are only special until we know where the treasures lie." John turned to Ben. "Mister Gunn, I'd appreciate it if you would assist Adam with morale, and identifying the good and bad elements among the crew. I believe you have a God-given talent with men."

"Thank you, sir," said the old man with a knuckle to his forehead.

"Your other duties," continued John, "will be to oversee the food preparation and to teach the landlubbers the courtesies they must render to myself and the other officers." Ben's nerves were agitated by the weight of these new responsibilities, causing him to itch in several places at once.

"We have several very capable ship handlers aboard, both in the officers and the crew." He scanned the five men before him for a moment. "Captain Van Mourik, even though I've chosen David as my first officer, it does not mean that I think any less of you or your many years at sea. Our mission will call for the combined knowledge and skills of every one of you." John looked to each of the others in turn. "For that reason, I'm placing a special burden upon Jack and asking that he train each of you to be capable first officers. Can you do that for me, Jack?"

"Ya, Captain Jones!" the Dutchman blurted out. "I make dem right fine sailors. You see!"

John snapped the latch on the leather case and then looked up at his officers. "I'm sure all of you have many questions for me, but they'll have to wait until supper. David, I'll expect to be called when the crew's assembled on the main deck."

The morning sun was high in the sky as the Silver Cloud cut through the murky waters south of Charles Town. The British seemed to have no interest in the Silver Cloud, or if they did, they never made any attempt to close with her. A fifteen-knot southwesterly fit well with the course Captain Jones had selected. In accordance with his sealed orders, he set a course of 155 degrees, which would take the Cloud along the eastern edge of the Bahamas and into Puerta Plata. There, if all went according to plan, all of the cargo would be off-loaded, except for that which hid the cannons. From Puerta Plata, the Cloud would make no other ports until it had reached Dead Man's Chest.

"Bosun!" barked Van Mourik from the quarterdeck. "Call der men to order!"

"On deck! Attention!" came the Bosun's cry as John and his First Officer came topside.

Within seconds, the little knots of conversation about the deck were untied and 150 sets of eyes were turned to gaze for the first time on this unknown Captain. The only sounds were the groaning and snorting of the new timbers under the driving force of the wind.

"This is Captain John Paul Jones," the Bosun sang out, "an' he's got some words to tell us 'bout the treasure hunt we be on."

A rumble of excited conversation ran the length of the deck.

"What your Bosun says is true," began Captain Jones. "After a short stop at Puerto Plata, we're headed for a small island off the north coast of Saint Croix to recover possibly the largest treasure ever taken from a single Spanish galleon."

A voice cried from high above in the crosstrees. "Is it the Treasure of Dead Man's Chest, Cap'n Jones?"

John flashed a questioning look at David and got the usual 'not me' gesture in return. "You have heard correctly, but..." A cheer rose from the men and then another one of the crewmen called out.

"An' how we gonna share it, Captain? The usual way?"

John was becoming angry, but realized that in the absence of the truth, men will fabricate any story to fill in the gaps. It was obvious the crew knew most, if not all of the plan, and it would do no good to deceive them further.

"You've assumed wrongly about its purpose. You're a hired crew, not pirates or privateers. Each of you has agreed to a certain wage, and nothing more. The treasure is not to be shared in the usual manner, unless we..." A wave of grumbling passed over the deck. Captain Jones raised his voice. "Unless we find extra treasure, that is, above the million and a half needed by the Colonies."

"Extra treasure?" called one of the men in the rigging. "How can there be any extra unless it were planted there at the first?" Several others joined with similar questions.

"Bosun!" demanded Jones.

"Shut yer gaps if ya want'a hear the Captain out!" After a long moment of grumbling, the men fell silent again.

"I have standing at my side one of the four who buried the treasure twenty years ago. He tells me that its estimated value was just over one and a half million pounds at that time. He'll count the treasure after we get it aboard, and appraise it at today's value. There's certain to be extra."

The crew cheered.

"And if our schedule allows it," continued Captain Jones with a look to Ben Gunn, "we'll attempt to retrieve part of the other third of the treasure from Grand Turk Island; that portion the group out of Bristol failed to take ten years ago. Any extra, above the million and a half, will be shared among the officers and crew," said John as he squinted into the rigging, "in the usual manner."

"And what about pirates?" It was the man in the rigging again.

"Mister Forrestal has sent the privateer Eagle ahead of us to insure our path is clear. Captain Steele will be standing off Dead Man's Chest when we arrive."

"What about liberty at Puerta Plata?" called one of the crewmen on the main deck.

"My first officer will answer your questions later below decks." John signaled Von Mourik to take charge and then descended the companionway toward his cabin. David was at his heels.

"Captain Steele's still on the Eagle?" asked David.

"Of course he is. Why would you think otherwise?"

"Because Mister Forrestal said he refused to sail with you again. Something about trouble in New York." John stopped in the companionway.

"There was trouble during that trip, but I didn't know he tried to beg out of this mission. The man's being paid very well."

"Are you and he speaking?"

"No, and I have no intention of doing so unless circumstances require it." John turned and walked aft. "If we need his assistance for something, I'll send you or one of the other officers in my stead."

David held the list of rules the Bosun had read before they had gone topside.

"You seem troubled," said John as he pushed through the massive door and stepped into his cabin. "Something wrong with my rules?"

"Can I speak frankly, John?"

"Yes, you may," answered John with a guarded tone. "You may be my First Officer, but you're still my friend. Be advised, however, that I'll not tolerate insubordination, even from you."

"All you have on this list are crimes and punishments." David stepped into the cabin and pushed the door closed. "A dozen lashes for being late to watch. Two dozen lashes for fighting, and a half dozen lashes for whistling?" David paused for a moment and stepped toward his new captain. "Do you honestly intend that if the men are in a good mood--good enough to whistle--that they be punished?"

"I didn't want to get into this with you," said John as he paced his cabin with measured strides, "but since you brought it up, I'll explain a few things. First, any set of rules is, by its very nature, a negative document. That much you'll simply have to accept. My rule against whistling is easy enough to explain."

"I wish you would, because I don't see it."

"I welcome good cheer from my crew, as much as any other Captain would. I've gone to great lengths and made several compromises with Captain Van Mourik and Doctor McKenzie for that very purpose. But because of the ship's great size, many of the orders must be given by bosun's whistle, and none of us can afford the confusion the occasional good-natured whistling might create. As for the rest of my rules--and there are few compared to most ships--each one is there for a purpose."

"But this crew. They're..."

"Very special," John said, finishing David's thought. "Every man, be he Dutch or American, was handpicked by Joseph Hewes; chosen for talents which go far beyond their ability to fire a weapon or sail a ship. They were also chosen because they're brave men; proven in battle several times over."

"And that's exactly my point. You don't need to tell men of such high calibre not to cheat or fight each other."

"You're missing one major point," said John. These high calibre men are to be confined to a very small and restricted world for six to eight weeks, without female contact or any of the other outlets for venting their built-up anger and frustrations. We've already had one minor fight over berthing, and we've only been underway for part of one day. Since there are very few rewards to keep the men in line, I am forced to resort to the threat of punishment. And without that threat, their petty bickering will surely turn into anarchy and even mutiny in a matter of days."

"But what about the treasure?" asked David.

"You put too much weight upon that!" said John as he strode about his cabin. "The promise of treasure has never insured proper discipline on a ship; quite the opposite. If I were to relax my discipline and withhold the lash--which you obviously find so repugnant--you'd see our special crew at each other's throats long before we reach Dead Man's Chest, especially the Mountain men!"

"I think you're wrong."

"You can think what you please, but your lofty appeal to reason and man's good nature, and your mistaken philanthropy, wears very thin aboard a warship. You'd be surprised at the good a few well-administered lashings would do for most land-lubbers."

"But it seems so cruel."

"It's not a matter of cruelty! If a little blood doesn't flow from a deserving back now and then, I can assure you that a whole lot of blood will flow from those same men's veins when they perish in an undisciplined battle. Your complaint should not be against the just punishment of a disobedient subordinate, but rather against the faulty judgement used in the administration of that punishment."

"I don't wish to beat a dead horse, John, but these men were selected for their courage, and..."

John slammed his hand on the table. "Enough! You don't understand the meaning of the word!"

"Courage?"

"Yes!" John stopped to gather his thoughts. "Courage isn't some inborn quality of man. It's a trait we learn through hours and hours of training and discipline." John walked to the windows and gazed back toward Charles Town. "It's the dominion of willpower over the natural instinct of fear and panic. It's the ability of men to reload and fire even when being rushed upon by a screaming enemy, or with iron and lead balls flying amongst them. That's courage!"

"But where's the respect and compassion? These sailors share our hatred for England."

"Your lack of experience wouldn't balance the respect and friendship you have for the crew with the necessary discipline and justice they require." John realized he was making very little headway with his stubborn friend.

"David, I don't have time to argue the point further. Suffice it to say that this mission is much too important for me to experiment with this crew, simply to satisfy the unproven whims of my First Officer. Our backers have provided them with as much comfort as possible, including a share in the excess treasure. But even with that, there are always a few men who wouldn't be happy in Heaven, and it's for those we have these 'barbaric rules', as you perceive them. Trust me when I tell you that I know how to keep this crew working as one body and with a singleness of purpose. If at any time you disagree with my methods, keep them to yourself and speak to me in private. By the time we make it back to Charles Town, you'll see that I was right."

"I know I'm young, and but for the Falmouth Packet, I lack sea experience. Yet..."

"The Falmouth Packet!" interrupted John. "I made a great mistake during that trip."

"Aye!" agreed David. "The Walrus nearly sank us that day!"

"But do you realize why?"

"Isn't that obvious? They were bigger and faster than us!" David could see his Captain wasn't going to endorse his estimation of the event. "You're talking about something else, aren't you?"

"Yes I am," answered John, "and I won't allow it to happen on the Silver Cloud. I experimented with that crew; precisely what you propose I do with this one."

"Experimented? I thought everything went well until..."

"My mistake was that I treated them like friends, rather than as the crewmen they signed on to be. It didn't cause a problem until that lucky shot took off Carini's arm and Clark ran to his aid, rather than obey my order to man the sheets. We all could have been killed for Clark's refusal to obey my order."

"But his friend--his best friend--was dying! You can't expect men to ignore an injured or dying mate, no matter how well they're trained."

"But that's where you're wrong, David, fatally wrong. And that's why I had to flog Clark."

"Nearly two weeks after his offence?" asked David slowly. "The crew wasn't too happy about that."

"And I'll be the first to admit my error," said John slowly. "But therein lies a second lesson. Never lose control of your men in the first place, because in the act of recapturing that control, you may very well create a mutiny."

"You really believe you lost control on the Falmouth Packet?"

"I'm certain of it. The men were quick to obey an order they agreed with, or for which they could see a personal benefit. But when it came to the blind obedience required during battle, my control ended. Had the situation been slightly different that day, you and I would not be speaking thusly in the Master's cabin of this fine man-of-war." John had been wrestling with something since his talk with Barragan, and figured this was the most appropriate time to breach it.

"David, when you refer to the Falmouth Packet, it's always the crew against me." There was an uncomfortable silence.

"I was always on your side," David said quickly."

"And that's why you stayed with me at Machotick Creek?"

David gave his Captain a questioning look. "What are you implying, John?"

"I had a very interesting talk with our cook."

"Barragan?"

"Aye. He believes you would have jumped ship with the rest of them, except that you told him we were on some sort of mission."

"And you think he was talking about the treasure and the cannons?"

"That's what I'm asking you," said John slowly. "Did you know about all of this before we left Kings Town?"

"We both knew about the cannons, John, and as for the treasure, there's not a seaman in the Atlantic who hasn't heard of the Treasure of Dead Man's Chest."

"You're avoiding my question, David." John rephrased it. "Did your father select me for this mission?"

"That's ridiculous!" answered David as he forced a smile. "Think about it, John. Why would I follow you all the way to Virginia and work in that sweaty tailor shop for over a year? Believe me—if I knew about all of this, I'd have told you in Jamaica."

John sat down across the table and considered the puzzle.

"Then you didn't know about the shortage of cannons?"

"Neither of us knew that before we talked to those two fellows in Richmond?"

"Then you stood by me..."

"Because I wanted a commission, John, just like you."

CHAPTER 10

On the 24th of May 1775, the privateer Eagle dropped anchor in Christiansted, a quiet port on the north shore of Saint Croix. Since '71, the small port had lost much of its share of the thriving slave, sugar and rum commerce which followed the trade winds between England and the new world.

With her cleaner lines and earlier departure from Charles Town, the Eagle was well ahead of her ward, the Silver Cloud. There was only one other vessel in the harbor large enough to be worthy of the title 'ship', and this black and red monster with the gold trim was flying a French flag. Captain Steele surveyed her lines carefully for a clue to her identity, but the cut of her stern and the low angle of the afternoon sun made it impossible to read her name. Even if he had been able, the name had already been changed to Le Tiburon; the French words for The Shark.

"Cap'n Smoot!" cried the impatient youth at the bolted cabin door. "She's 'ere Govn'r, just like I tolt ya she'd be!" Morgan gave a series of urgent raps to the heavy oak door with the butt of his cutlass. "The Cloud'll be here shortly!" The youth sprang away and up the companionway to the top deck where he took two vicious cuts at the heavy Caribbean air with his blade and yelled once more down the companionway.

"Cap'n Smoot!" The lad dropped again to the dark passageway and pressed his ear to the cool oak door. "Are you up, Govn'r?"

"Aye!" bellowed Smoot as he pulled the door open. Morgan fell headlong into the Master's cabin. Smoot pulled away from the nude native girl who held fast to his left arm and stepped over the prostrate lad. "Which one is she, Morgan?"

"It's the Eagle, Govn'r," Morgan said quickly as he struggled to his feet and watched the native girl jump back into bed. Captain Smoot gave the lad a cuff to the head as he climbed the ladder into the bright morning sunlight. Once on deck, Morgan brandished his cutlass toward the newcomer as she tacked into the bay. "She's the escort I been tellin' ya 'bout."

"Well-well," said Smoot as he pulled on his shirt and laced it shut. "Looks like ye'll be earnin' them five shares after all."

As they watched, the Eagle luffed her main and jib and dropped her larboard anchor, putting her approximately 300 yards seaward of the Walrus. An hour later, when two thirds of the crew would have normally gone ashore for liberty, a lone ship's boat with but three men aboard, pulled slowly past the stern of the Walrus toward the cargo docks.

"They're checkin' us out, Govn'r," whispered Morgan as the boat passed within earshot of Le Tiburon. Smoot called out something in French and got the appropriate answer from Captain Steele. "It worked." whispered Morgan. "They think we're frogs."

"Aye, Henry. That they do."

"Aren't ya forgettin' somethin', Govn'r?" asked Morgan with a squint and an outstretched hand.

Smoot gave the boy an angry stare for three seconds and then pulled the agreed prize from his pocket, holding it just beyond Henry's reach.

"It's only fittin', Govn'r, since ya made me pay ya the ten back in Savannah." Morgan's eyes were fixed on the shiny gold coin which promised another night of good grog and female companionship.

"That was a fair bet, Morgan, and you lost." Smoot flipped the coin high into the air toward the mizzenmast, sending Morgan down the deck in a mad scramble toward a waiting scupper hole. When the boy returned with his prize, Smoot was deep in thought.

"Somethin' wrong, Govn'r?"

"I was just countin' on most of the Eagle's crew bein' ashore tonight in them taverns, that's all. We'll just have to change our plans a little to make up fer it."

"Well, they gotta go ashore some time," offered Morgan as he bit his newly won prize to test it's metal. "And when they do, we'll take their ship, won't we?"

After three days, not a soul besides those same three men had gone ashore. At exactly 1000 hours in the morning, the Captain and two of his seamen would pull to shore in the ship's boat and return two hours later with supplies. Then again at 1600 hours, the same three men would make their second trip, returning four or five hours later. Try as they might, Smoot's spies couldn't find out a thing from the seamen who stayed at Drake's Dock while their Captain was about his errands. Only that Captain Steele was buying supplies and negotiating for the sale of his cargo.

By the afternoon of the fifth day at anchor, the Eagle's crew was clearly ready for any diversion. As her Captain's boat passed abeam Le Tiburon for it's afternoon run to Drake's Dock, Captain Smoot gave the signal for his own launch to set out from the docks toward the Eagle.

"Mister Todd, sir!" shouted the Eagle's watch. "We've a boat full o' ladies approachin' from the larboard beam!" The first officer closed the logbook and walked quickly toward the rail where the agitated young seaman stood pointing. "There, sir!"

"They're still so far out," said the first officer as he studied the boat. "What makes you think its ladies?"

"Look how they're pullin' them oars an' meanderin' about the bay, sir," said the excited seaman as he pointed into the setting sun. "That's gotta be ladies or children, an' they're too big fer children!"

Most of the other sailors topside were quicker on their feet than the first officer, and were already crowding and shoving for a spot at the rail.

"Back away there!" commanded the officer. "Make way!"

The liberty-starved sailors barely heard his orders for their hooting and hollering at the approaching Women. The shifting breeze brought the full impact of the lady's sweet fragrances across the water, up over the bow and along the ship to the thirty-five waiting noses. The perfumes were mostly cheap, but the sailors were more interested in where the lotions had been applied than with their value. Todd was a man of similar desires, but duty to Captain Steele and their mission prevailed.

"You there!" Todd called out in a stern voice while the crew watched the boat circle to the East side of the Eagle. "In the boat! Stand off and state your business!"

A very bovine blond stood carefully to her feet and shaded her eyes with a woven cane fan. It wasn't that she was actually better endowed than her companions, but rather that she had paid her dressmaker better than the rest.

"Captain Steele sent us," came the bubbly voice. There arose a cheer from the crew for their Captain. When the yelling finally subsided and two sailors were fished from the warm water, Todd continued his interrogation of the visitors.

"And what evidence of that do you offer us, young lady?"

"This, sir!" The entire crew sucked in its breath as one man, as the young lass reached slowly between her generous bosoms and extracted a small rolled parchment tied with a crimson ribbon. The eleven other ladies giggled as thirty-five lusty sailors exhaled together and let out a second cheer; this time for the yet-nameless lass in the low cut dress.

"Not so fast, MacPherson!" Todd caught the eager seaman by the rope which held up his britches as he attempted to leap the rail.

"By yer leave, sir," protested the dangling seaman. "I were just goin' fer the note!" There was another round of laughter and catcalls from both vessels.

"Well, go ahead then." Todd released the rope and the youth, cheered on by his mates, leaped to the bottom rung of the ship's ladder with the agility of a spider. "But mind you MacPherson, touch nothing more than our Captain's note."

"Quick 'afore 'tis cool, Mac!" called one seaman above the cheers, while another was heard to offer a month's wages for the prize.

Todd knew that if he wasn't extremely careful, he could lose the entire crew on the spot. MacPherson was back in a moment with the note between his teeth. Todd read it to himself:

> "Mister Todd:
>
> I have reconsidered the present situation and have decided the men deserve some female companionship. Since they cannot come ashore, I've decided to send several women to the ship. Please take these ladies aboard for the evening, along with the refreshments they convey. I may be detained ashore with Mister Lewis longer than usual, but I expect to be back before the ladies are gone. If not, have them escorted to the dock no later than midnight.
>
> H. Steele
> Captain: Privateer Eagle

Mister Todd studied the signature for a moment. There was something different about it, but his baser nature prevailed; confronted as it was by the temptation awaiting him at the water line.

"Bosun! Bring the ladies aboard!"

The crew exploded in cheers and praises for their Captain and First Officer. Within minutes, the ladies were on deck with their six casks of rum, and as quickly disappeared below decks. The first two mugs were brought to Mister Todd and the Bosun. The men who would have to wait topside for their turns with the women made a sport of outdoing one another in toasting their absent Captain and throwing their dirks at the mainmast.

"I'm sure our Captain would appreciate your enthusiasm," said Todd to the twenty odd waiting men, "but the women are to be put ashore no later than midnight. And mind you," he added, "I'll see to it personally that any man of you caught fighting will find himself in irons in the morning."

Within an hour, the strong drink had done its job. Every sailor to a man, was fast asleep long before the women were to be returned to Christiansted. The ladies, who knew nothing of Smoot's purposes, or the sleeping potion he had put in the rum, were returned senseless to their brothels.

Without a single inhabitant of the small port town noticing, the crew of the Eagle was taken to an empty sugar warehouse at the West end of the wharf and put into irons. As the sun rose the next morning above the quiet Caribbean, a new crew was being selected to man the now-empty privateer Eagle.

The weather had been kind to Captain Jones and the Silver Cloud, putting them into Puerta Plata two days ahead of schedule. Except for a short delay near Andros Island when they were stopped and inspected by the forth rate British Man-of-War King James, they encountered no other shipping. As the Silver Cloud plowed through the late morning waves toward Saint Croix, Joshua Smoot and Henry Morgan walked about the deck of the privateer Eagle, surveying their new ship.

"Are ya sure," asked Morgan as he skipped across the deck of the Eagle after his Captain, "that Privy's the best choice fer the Walrus? I'd be more then..."

"Watch yer tongue, Henry," Smoot hissed as he ran his hands along the tiller, "'cause I'll cut it out fer questioning my decision, an' Pritchard'll do the same if he catches wind of you callin' him that."

"Sorry, Govn'r," gulped Henry as he touched his mouth, but if I heard rightly, it were Privy at the helm when that little postal packet took off yer rudder near Charles Town last spring."

"Aye, it was Pritchard, all right." Smoot gave the lad a quick glance, wondering at his intent. "You got a problem with him?"

"Well, maybe I be missin' somethin' 'ere, Govn'r, but I 'ear tell he's not so good in battle." The youth ran a calloused finger across his wet nose and dried it through his shoulder-length orange hair. "What if he gets the Walrus sunk or somethin'?"

"What's that to us?"

"But the crew? They'd miss out on their share..." The lad turned to look at his Captain and was met with a toothy grin. "Ya don't care if they die, do ya?"

"As I see it, Henry, if Pritchard an' his men can get the treasure, then we all split it up, just like normal. But if they get themselves sunk in the try, that's just bigger shares fer you an' me." Smoot's gold tooth flashed as his bushy black brows danced on his forehead. "Now that we got this fine Virginia privateer with her fourteen guns and the crew I got listed on this paper, we can take your Silver Cloud all by ourselves."

Morgan strained his neck to get a better look at the names. But since he couldn't read anyway, it didn't much matter.

"But..." Morgan began to protest, and then checked himself.

"The Cloud's gonna' think we're their protectors, Henry, and we'll play our part, just as they expect. We need the manpower from the Walrus to help get the treasure, but after that, I'd be willin' to help the Cloud sink Pritchard an' the rest of them fishbait troublemakers."

"Troublemakers?"

"Aye." Smoot turned about and rested his backside against the rail. "Back when I was a lad like you, I noticed how Captain Rip Rap was always tradin' his troublemakers away to John Flint. Didn't take me long to figure out what he was up to."

"Oh?" asked Morgan, "And what was that?"

"Well, my quick mind sprung on the thing right off," the elderly pirate bragged. "Rip Rap would send all the scoundrels and cutthroats over to Flint in exchange for the good followers; most o' the ones impressed into service. Ended up, the Walrus was havin' a mutiny 'most every day while the Royal James ran like one o' the King's own." He gave the boy a knowing wink. "That, my boy, is how I chose the twenty-eight men we're takin' with us on the Eagle."

"I got a question, Govn'r."

"Yes?"

"Well," queried the lad as he scratched something crawling through his hair, "if Rip Rap traded away all his troublemakers fer good followers, why'd he trade you an' John Silver away?" As the boy spoke, the old seaman's hand went to his knife.

"Go on," Smoot hissed, "make yer point?" The lad was at an angle where he couldn't see the dirk, so continued.

"Well, here we are sayin' Privy an' his troublemakers can go down with their..." The lad's eye caught the half-drawn dagger. "I..."

"Yes?"

"Well, I guess ya gotta have a little of the troublemaker in ya, or ya don't make as good a Captain as you been, Govn'r." The knife went back into its sheath and Morgan swallowed in relief. "When we splittin' the crew, Govn'r?"

"I'll be readin' the list to the men as soon as we return to the Walrus. As soon as they get settled aboard, we'll be takin' the Eagle for a cruise 'round Dead Man's Chest. Give us a chance to see how she feels on the wind an' scout the lay o' the land."

The Eagle was a splendid craft. She was quick at the helm and had the latest 'sharp' hull; designed like the new Walrus and the faster French corvettes. Her two masts were raked aft to improve her upwind abilities, and she carried half again the sail of most other ships of equal tonnage. She was a war ship from stem to stern, but built in the lines of the agile racing sloops at Oxford. Her thirty crewmen had no difficulty adjusting to her special needs.

"She's better 'n the Walrus, Henry!" cried Smoot as he ordered her tiller to lee for the tack back to the windward side of the little island.

"Aye, Cap'n, she's a real fine lady all right!"

"As sweet a lady as Governor Wright's daughter!" Smoot and Morgan walked to the bow and leaned against the windward rail as the Eagle's sails filled for the larboard reach back to Christiansted. Smoot studied the line of coral and the thin band of white sand called Rip Rap beach as they passed the western tip of the island.

"Have ya ever been on the Chest, Henry?"

"No, Govn'r, only heard tales 'bout it from the old crews what stopped at Tortuga when I were but a pup."

"Then you know nothin' o' the reef, other 'n what our chart showed?"

"You got me there, Govn'r. You figgerin' the Silver Cloud'll be puttin' in on the south side?"

"That's what I'd do if I were them. But then, we don't know where Rip Rap put his grand nephew ashore with the treasure."

"Does Privy know how many men to put ashore tonight?"

"It's all been arranged," said Smoot as something caught his eye. There, paralleling Saint Croix on a starboard tack was a large merchantman with new white sails. "Morgan!" Smoot said as he pointed. "What do you make of that?

"It's the Silver Cloud! She's 'ere, sir!"

"Are you certain?"

"Aye Govn'r--there's no mistakin' 'er. I carved most o' her decorations an' painted half her colors."

"Well then," said Smoot with an air of the theater, "we'd best get to playin' our part. Tell the men to break out those colonial outfits for the crew and tell the helm to set a course to join with the Cloud."

Two leagues to the northwest and driven by the steady afternoon trade winds, stood the majestic Silver Cloud. She was half a day ahead of schedule.

"Captain Jones!" said Robert. "I must insist you reconsider. Just because we haven't seen any pirates yet doesn't mean they aren't waiting for us on the island."

"You're being an old lady again, Robert. If our secret were out, don't you think we'd know it by now?" John strode to the rail and spun on a heel with spread arms. "Where are they? Do you see any other ships?" No sooner were the words out of his mouth than the foretop watch called out the familiar words, "Ship on the larboard bow!"

"David, get my glass!" John commanded as he shaded his eyes to see the intruder.

"Is it them?" asked David as he handed John the spyglass.

"We'll know in a moment." One quick look confirmed his hopes. "It's the Eagle!" John spun about to the Yorkman.

"See, Robert. I told you our secret was safe."

"Just the same, I'll not lead anybody to the treasure until I'm certain."

"Damn it, man!" cried John as he strode to the center of the deck and pointed into the rigging. "We have lookouts in the crosstrees! Nobody can get near us without being spotted, and we have enough firepower to sink a ship twice our size. If we send everybody but the gun crews, we can have the treasure dug up and back aboard within five or six hours. And as I keep telling you, if we were to be attacked, it won't be until we start digging."

"Just the same," said Robert, "it'll be my way or none." John looked about the quarterdeck at the officers and men on watch. They were obviously curious as to how this little drama would play out.

"We had best finish this discussion in my cabin," said John in a whisper. "David, go find Mister Gunn and meet us there."

David had never seen John this upset, except during their heated discussion about crew discipline the day they had departed Charles Town. He found Ben in the galley helping with the noon meal. As the two made their way aft, David brought Gunn up to speed on the argument between the Captain and the Yorkman, and cautioned him to keep quiet.

"Ah, Mister Gunn," said John as David and the old man entered the Master's cabin. John and Robert were already sharing a glass of scotch over one of the charts Alex Forrestal had provided. "Take a seat and pour yourselves some of Scotland's finest." The air was thick with tension as Captain Jones began.

"Gentlemen, we've had a long voyage and we're very close to our goal." He reached his right hand across the green felt toward the Yorkman. "Robert, I'd like to apologize for my outburst a few moments ago. You're right to be cautious concerning the treasure."

"Thank you, John." Robert was surprised with John's change of mood and accepted the offered hand. "I'm acutely aware that you three, and the whole crew for that matter, are anxious to bring the treasure aboard and be on our way as quickly as possible. But I've seen how pirates work. They may not use a whole lot of intelligence in their life-styles, but when it comes to treachery, there's none to match them."

"I can vouch fer that, Master Ormerod," added Ben with a glance at David.

"You said you had a plan, Robert," said John. "Now's the time to tell us, before we get to our anchorage."

"As I was saying on deck, we can't be too careful. Even with lookouts, we won't see any pirates until they attack."

As Robert explained the details of his plan, Ben Gunn turned the chart about on the table.

"Beggin' yer pardon, Captain Jones," said Ben, "but where do you plan on leavin' the Cloud while we're ashore?"

"We'll drop anchor at this opening in the reef." John pointed with his dagger as he looked to Robert for confirmation. "Isn't that where you said your great uncle put the Royal James when he put you ashore?" Robert nodded that he had.

"And while we're ashore," asked David, "who's to watch the Cloud?"

"We'll be leaving Captain Van Mourik and all of the gunners," answered John. "The winds'll swing the Cloud about to expose her starboard cannons to seaward. Between our long guns and the Eagle patrolling the deep waters outside the reef, no ship would risk an approach."

By dusk, the Silver Cloud had rendezvoused with the Eagle and dropped anchor a musket shot from shore, and just forty yards outside the island's protective coral reef. As expected, the winds pushed the camouflaged frigate about its anchor into the perfect position to give any approaching vessel a ten-gun broadside. As the sun set beyond the port of Christiansted five miles to the Southwest, final preparations were underway for the mornings assault on Dead Man's Chest.

The sun was still far below the eastern horizon when the last of the Cloud's boats skidded onto Rip Rap Beach. Its crew of twelve marched across the sand toward the rest of the shore party, each man carrying a mixture of cutlasses, pistols and shovels. Thirty-four gunners remained aboard the ship under the command of the Dutchman, Jack Van Mourik.

The beach had been named Rip Rap by Andrew Murray's crew; for that was the pirate's favorite brand of snuff. And although the small beach was shunned by most seagoing brigands, Captain Rip Rap found the privacy of this small stretch of coral sand to his liking. It was here that Robert Ormerod and his fiancée, Moira, along with her father and the Indian fighter, Peter Corlear, had been set ashore with the treasure twenty years before.

As the morning sky began to show its first flush of pink, Captain Jones turned to the Yorkman.

"Let's get to it, Robert. Where's the treasure?"

"We're not moving off this beach," scolded Robert, "until both of the lookouts are in position and have given their signal."

"Damn!" John huffed as he pulled his sword and began hacking at an obnoxious looking cactus at the upper edge of the beach.

"What was that?" whispered Ben Gunn with a hand cupped to his good ear.

"What was what?" demanded Robert.

"I thought I heard a man scream, sir," answered Ben as he peered toward the newly-silhouetted hill above them. Several of the Mountain men also heard the man's cries, and had instinctively moved to the tree line for cover.

"What's going on?" cried Captain Jones as he ran back to where he had left Robert.

"Up there," said the Yorkman with an arm outstretched toward the single hump a quarter mile east. "I told you there'd be trouble."

The screams of a man in full flight could now be heard by all hands, leaving no doubt that they weren't alone on the Chest. With a wave of his sword, Captain Jones deployed the men to positions of defense; most of the sailors to the tree line with the Mountian men, and the three gunners to man the single swivel gun they had brought ashore.

"There he is!" yelled David, pointing at the disturbed bushes. It was clear the poor soul wasn't following the path he and his comrade had used to ascend the hill. A moment later, he crashed onto the beach and spun loose from the tangle of vines.

"What in God's name?" cried Robert as they all watched the man stumble about for a moment, and then take off running past the boats and into the water beyond. "I've never seen a man that scared in my life!"

"The other one must already be dead," said John quietly, "and I owe you another apology."

"Save it," answered the Yorkman as he studied the hill for the watchman's attackers, "till we see how many there are."

By now, the watchman had finished thrashing about in the water, and had walked up behind his Captain.

"Sorry 'bout that, sir, but I never felt nothin' hurt that bad before."

"How many were there?" demanded Captain Jones.

"Just one, sir," the seaman said as he looked about the beach at his mates, their tools and arms at the ready. "There weren't but me an' O'Toole."

"Then what in God's name were you running from?"

"I wasn't runnin' from nothin', Cap'n. Just before we reached the top, I tripped against some sort o' tree with white ooze runnin' down its bark. Stung the hell out'a my skin wherever it touched!"

"Then the other watchman's all right?"

"Far as I know, he is." With that, the dripping seaman walked across the beach and headed up the trail to resume his duty. As he entered the bushes, the 'all clear' signal rang out from the other watchman. "See?" the young man called back to Captain Jones. "There are no pirates up there."

"Seems my apology was a bit premature," said John with an air of contempt. "Do you still believe we're going to be attacked?"

"We're still going to do it my way, attack or not." Robert walked away to the north end of the beach and climbed to the top of a rock. From his vantage point, he could see both sides of the island for a distance of half a mile. Finally satisfied, Robert turned back to the hundred-odd men gathered below him.

"It's there," he said as he pointed to the north coast of the island, "near Dorsal Rock."

The northern two-thirds of Dead Man's Chest was dominated by a grassy plain covered with waist-high grass and an occasional bush which reached to a man's shoulders. A half-mile from Rip Rap Beach stood Dorsal Rock, a volcanic hump of black stone fifty feet long, twenty feet wide and a dozen feet high. It was so named because it resembled the back of a dolphin as it broke the surface for a breath of air. It was an excellent spot to bury a treasure. Ten minutes at a quick pace brought the shore party to its western end.

"This is it?" asked John as he spun about to survey the surrounding land.

"There's none better," answered Robert as he pointed to various areas about the mound. "There were only four of us, and we had to find a place close to the beach where we wouldn't be surprised."

As the shore party watched, the Yorkman walked away to the eastern end of the mound. After what seemed to be an endless contemplation, he strode off to the south for ten paces, and then turned abruptly to the west. At the fourth step, he stopped and drove his sword into the fertile topsoil.

"Here!" he called out to the crew. "This is where we dig!"

The Mountain men smelled it first, that unmistakable acrid odor of unclean men.

"Something's wrong, John," whispered David. "Look at our fighters."

"Aye," John agreed as he watched the men drop their shovels and back toward the mound.

"Robert!" called John. "Look there--to the tree line!" John pointed with his sword at the flashes of reflected sunlight. "It seems we have company after all."

"Listen up!" shouted Captain Jones from where Robert's sword stood in the earth. "As most of you know by now, we've a large group of men hiding at the tree line several hundred yards to the south. Now that the treasure's location has been revealed..."

It was too late for making plans, for out of the trees came approximately fifty hairy sea dogs, running at top speed and screaming like men just released from hell. Each carried a cutlass and a brace of pistols slung about his shoulder. A hundred yards from the mound the pirates broke into four separate groups; two diverting laterally into flanking positions, while the remaining two groups charged directly toward Robert's sword. At fifty yards, Captain Jones barked his command.

"Fire!"

Buck Island is just over two miles long and one mile wide. The shallow waters which surround her irregular coastline are guarded by a narrow band of coral with but one entrance, and that on the south side near the western end. It was near this single opening that the Silver Cloud had anchored the previous night.

She had been left with a skeleton crew; just enough men to man the guns should another ship approach. If all went well ashore, she would be back to the safety of deep water by late afternoon.

The sun was still low on the morning horizon when the battle on the north shore began. From the Silver Cloud, the sound of the musket fire could easily have been mistaken for the popping of green wood in the galley stove; but the cook was ashore and his fires were cold. Jack Van Mourik and most of the gunners lay peacefully asleep in their hammocks about the deck. Only two of their mates remained awake, pacing quietly about the quarter deck and forecastle.

It was the forward watch who heard the musket fire first. Within minutes of his call, all hands except the old Dutchman were climbing into the rigging. If they were lucky, they might be able to see the action from the upper yards.

Seamen are a hard lot; they always were and they always shall be. After months or even several weeks at sea, as these men had been, a man thirsts for the solid earth under his feet and a chance to find himself any diversion from his shipboard duties. It is unheard of for a man to knowingly trade away his chance to go ashore. But, the ship's carpenter from Savannah had done just that the day before by trading his noon watch for the dogwatch. Not even the young seaman who had been the object of the trade, and was now engaged in the gun battle on the northern shore, gave it a second thought. If the rest of the crew had been sharp, they would also have noticed that while they climbed as high as possible into the rigging, the carpenter climbed only a short way up; not nearly high enough to see over the island's low ridge to the battle which was raging on the grassy flats of the north shore. With their attention thus engaged, they failed to notice when the seaman dropped to the deck and made his way forward to the anchor chain.

None had missed him, not even the gunner's mate who had offered him a hand to one of the yards. And likewise, no one saw him lower the bucket into the jade-green waters, retrieving it full a moment later. A quick glance into the rigging assured the carpenter that his absence and strange actions had gone unnoticed. With the swiftness of a cat, the traitor wet the deck from gunwale to anchor chain in an irregular pattern of drips and footprints.

It was perfect, he thought as he dried his feet and replaced the bucket and rags in their place. Just like Smoot would have done it! With a quick glance upward, he pulled the large metal bolts that secured the anchor chain to the deck. Nothing moved. He had calculated correctly, that the chains own weight was sufficient to keep it from paying out until the first morning breeze pulled at the mighty ship. It wouldn't take much; perhaps as little as the negligible swells which crept around Cottengarden Point and across the three miles of open water to set the great ship in motion. And once the chain began it's run across the deck, nothing could stop it.

Before the ship made it's first lurch, the traitor was high in the rigging again, balanced atop the main t'gallant yard next to the same gunner's mate who had given him a hand up earlier.

"What on earth are they doing?" asked David as they watched the confusion among the approaching pirates. What had appeared at first to be a well-planned flanking maneuver in support of their main attack, was quickly losing all headway. "It's as if they forgot what they were up to...or had lost their leader."

"If my guess is right," offered Robert, "it's quite the opposite." Robert had seen the Walrus' crew in action before.

"The opposite?"

"Yes, David, the opposite. I believe John will agree with me, that they've too many leaders." He looked to John and received the expected nod.

Each group, consisting of ten to fifteen men, seemed confused about which way to go, or which tactic to use next. Visible infighting broke out in the pirate's right flank first with shouts and then with a discharged musket. Within minutes, their main force had moved forward far enough that the little group of bickering pirates was now completely isolated from the rest. Before they could figure out what had gone wrong, two of their number were cut down by musket balls, leaving nine more. Six of these dropped their weapons and fled for the trees behind them, a young lad ran toward the main body of pirates and the remaining three turned and ran toward the water in a desperate attempt to avoid the thick musket fire from Captain Jones' crew of Mountain men. These three fell dead in the sand.

As Captain Jones and Robert climbed to the top of the mound for a better view of the battlefield, David and the bosun led two separate flanking forces about the pirates, keeping low and out of sight in the tall grass. At every ten paces, David and the bosun turned to watch for Captain Jones' signal, but before they were in position, one of the fleeing pirates from the aborted flanking maneuver ran headlong into David, knocking the young Jamaican flat. Thus, surrounded by twenty men, the poor pirate, a boy of no more than fifteen, was too startled to do anything but let out a faint cry as David's sword passed upward through his naked stomach and into his heart.

"They be all about us, mates!" cried one of the pirates as he stood and wildly fired both of his pistols at David's men. The rest of the pirates stood and began firing in panic before breaking and running for the tree line. When the last musket was fired and the final sword was wiped clean of dishonest blood, eighteen pirates lay dead or dying on the north plain of Dead Man's Chest.

"Bosun!" the Captain barked as he returned his sword to its scabbard. "Sound the order to reassemble!"

"Aye, aye, Cap'n!"

Within ten minutes, all the bodies had been found and dragged to the beach for viewing. Of the six survivors, only three were in any condition to talk, and only one seemed at all willing. Leaving David in charge of the other prisoners, John, Robert and Ben Gunn escorted the man to the east end of the mound for questioning.

"Before we begin on this cutthroat," said Robert as he took hold of John's elbow and led him away from their prisoner, "there's something I must tell you."

"Oh?" asked John.

"The treasure," Robert began as he pulled his sword from the earth, "isn't here."

"What!?" yelled John. Everyone within earshot turned. "What do you mean, it isn't here?"

"It's on the island, John, but not where I planted my sword."

"You risked the lives of my crew for..." John paused as he realized what Robert had done. He whispered, "You knew we'd be attacked!"

"I was almost certain of it, and I didn't want the treasure's location revealed while there was still a chance."

"Couldn't you have told us?"

"Of course I could", agreed Robert. "But if the men knew they were defending empty dirt instead of gold, do you suppose for a moment they would have fought quite so gallantly?"

"No," answered John as he surveyed the battlefield, "I suppose not."

"May I assume that you're not angry with me?" asked Robert.

"No, I'm not angry with you, Robert. I would ask, however, that from now on, you be honest with me."

"As you wish, John," said the Yorkman as he turned back toward the pirates. "Shall we see what our prisoners have to tell us?"

The breeze from the southeast had freshened to five knots; more than enough to pull the great anchor chain from the ship. Several of the men in the uppermost rigging noticed the movement first, but none but the traitor realized what had happened until it was too late. As her keel ground to a stop on the line of submerged coral, the great vessel shuddered, throwing one of the seamen from a yardarm to the shallow sea below.

"What was that!?" yelled the gunner's mate standing on the yard next to the traitor.

"Look! The Anchor chain's gone!" cried the traitor in feigned dismay as he pointed down at the bow. "We're on the reef!"

As quickly as they could, all thirty-one of the sailors slid the sheets to the deck, as if this effort could undo the harm already done.

"What is dat?" blurted Captain Van Mourik as he awoke from his sleep and rubbed a dirty hand across his swollen face. He gazed about the deck, trying to remember where he was.

"We're in trouble, Dutch!" McCoy was the senior gunner and didn't respect the overweight Dutchman enough to address him by his proper title. "Someone's come aboard and released our anchor chain and we've drifted onto the coral!"

Without waiting for Van Mourik to remember his instructions from Captain Jones, McCoy gave the order to fire three cannons.

"What's that mean!?" asked Robert as the last report reached them. "And what's the Eagle doing on this side of the island?"

"I told Van Mourik to fire three cannons if he had any trouble," answered John as he looked toward the Eagle. "And as for the Eagle, I must assume Captain Steele heard the musket fire and figured we needed help." Captain Jones made a quick survey of his men.

"Robert, I want you to remain here with six of the Mountain men to protect our wounded and guard those prisoners. The rest of us will return to the ship. They can't be under attack, or there'd be more cannon fire." John spun and looked to the Eagle once more. "The man may hate me, but Henry Steele would never abandon the Silver Cloud if there were an enemy within sight. We'll just have to wait until we can talk to Van Mourik."

After ten minutes of running, Captain Jones and his hundred men rounded the last row of trees, giving him a clear view of his ship.

"Can you tell what's wrong?" called David from several yards behind John.

"It's hard to say for certain, but I believe the ship's listing slightly." A moment later Captain Jones came to a stop on Rip Rap Beach. What met his gaze confused him greatly. There was now no doubt that the Silver Cloud was on the reef, but he was more puzzled by the strange activity at her waterline.

"This is all I need!" said John under his breath. "Another mutiny!"

The sky was clear the morning the Silver Cloud had been set aground. By the time her shore detachment had run the mile to Rip Rap Beach, the sun had risen high enough to cast its rays across the mighty ship's upper rigging. There was no doubt about it. She was beginning to list to larboard, exposing her starboard underbelly to the sea.

Smoot's plan had worked perfectly, even though much of it was simply dumb luck. While the musket fire from the north shore had been the signal for the traitor to release the anchor chain and for Smoot to sail away to the north side of the island, the three cannon shots were the signal for a third ship--the Walrus—to set sail from the south end of Saint Croix.

Smoot tried to take credit for the tide being just right when the anchor chain was released, and if Henry Morgan were a speck more gullible, he'd have convinced the lad that the Cloud leaned larboard by his doing also. This was Smoot's greatest stroke of luck, for had she leaned toward the open sea, then her ten seaward-facing cannons could have been brought to bear against any would-be attacker.

Captain Jones had no reason to suspect that the Eagle's abandonment of the Silver Cloud was other than to assist with their battle on the north shore. It was exactly what he would have done had he been the protector, rather than the protected.

McCoy was beginning to lower the first of two cannons over the side and into the bow of a waiting ship's boat when the shore party arrived back at Rip Rap Beach. The small craft sank nearly to her gunwales as the heavy six-pounder settled amongst the powder kegs and shot. As McCoy shoved off toward shore, Captain Jones and his first officer stopped at the waters edge.

"What on earth?!" asked John rhetorically.

"Is that even our crew?" asked David.

"Oh, there's no doubt about that. That's McCoy at the first boat's helm." John studied the ship carefully. "The question you should be asking is whether they've turned traitors."

"What's happening?" puffed Ben Gunn as he made his way through the tight line of crewmen to his Captain's side. His age and many years behind a desk in Boston had slowed him considerably.

"See for yourself, Ben." John pointed to the slow moving boats at the Cloud's water line. "While we were gone, it seems our loyal gunners decided to put the Silver Cloud on the reef and steal our cannons."

"But that doesn't make any sense, Cap'n," said Ben as he struggled for breath. "What could they hope to accomplish?" The old maroon didn't get an answer, for his Captain and First Officer were now busy launching one of the larger boats with a crew of eight armed men.

"Are you coming with us?" John called to Ben as he climbed into the boat.

"No, Cap'n," Ben puffed. "I'll wait here with the others. There's sure to be gunfire, an' I'd just be in yer way."

Midway between the crippled Silver Cloud and Rip Rap Beach, eight flintlock muskets leveled on the five gunners as they pulled toward the beach in the first boat.

"Heave to, Mister McCoy!" called Captain Jones from twenty yards away. "What traitorous folly is this?"

"Traitors, you call us?" The startled gunner ordered his men to ship oars and then threw the tiller to starboard to stop his boat. "Are you daft, Captain Jones?"

"No," John yelled back, "I'm not! And if you lack a good explanation for these bizarre actions, your life will be forfeited here and now."

"Captain, you have it all wrong!" one of the other gunners cried out. "We're not traitors!"

"Then why's my ship laying on the reef with a dozen of my gunners stealing two of my cannons?" John swung his pistol arm about and pointed toward the beach. "Were you planning on cutting us down with grape shot as we returned with the treasure?"

"Captain Jones!" McCoy bellowed at the younger man. "Before ya make a complete fool o' yerself, ye'd best hear what happened aboard the Cloud."

"And that is?" asked John as he pointed his pistol back toward McCoy.

"Someone came aboard during all that shootin' across the island and released our anchor chain. None of us saw him because we were watching your battle."

"And how do you know it wasn't one of your own men?" asked David.

"The deck was still wet where he came over the rail, sir. By the time the chain finally began slipping from the hawspipe, the man was back in the sea and long gone."

"Hmmm," said John as he considered. With a gesture, his men lowered their muskets. "And what about these two cannons and all that ammunition?" Four casks of powder and a score of balls lay in each boat's bottom, along with the other equipment necessary to carry on a protracted land battle.

"That's how I explain it, Captain Jones!" McCoy stood and pointed seaward, past the Silver Cloud, to the ship approaching from the southeast. "By the time that ship gets here, the Cloud'll have listed too far larboard to use her seaward guns!" McCoy pointed to the northwest. "And without the Eagle to protect us..." McCoy gritted his teeth as he looked back at the fat Dutchman watching from the Cloud. "I had to make a decision, Captain!"

A chill ran from the base of his spine to his neck as Captain Jones surveyed the intruder. It was more than coincidence that had brought this third ship to Dead Man's Chest. John strained his eyes to make out any markings on the large French Corvette as it crossed slowly toward his stricken ship.

"Take a look at her colors, David, and see if it reminds you of another ship we've encountered."

"Hmmm..." said David as he took the spyglass. "She must have..." David turned to his Captain and back to the approaching ship. "My God! That's the Walrus!"

"I'm afraid so, David."

"What are you talking about, Captain?" asked McCoy. "Do you know her?"

"I do, McCoy. Winter of last year Mister Noble and I were attacked by that ship several leagues south of Charles Town. Before her crew could board us, we got lucky and managed to tear her rudder clean away with one shot of barstock."

"Lucky, you say?" said David as he gave John a light shove. "You were aiming for that rudder!" John suddenly realized why McCoy was taking the two cannons ashore. He glanced quickly at the island and at the approaching pirate ship.

"McCoy, get those cannons ashore and to that cliff," he said, pointing slightly east of the beach. "We're in for a battle!"

"They must think we already have the treasure," said David.

"No doubt about it." agreed John as he took back the spyglass. "Our gunfire on the north shore was obviously the signal to release our anchor, and the Cloud's three cannons signaled the Walrus to begin her attack." John thought for a moment and continued. "I wish there was some way for them to find out we haven't dug up the treasure yet."

"Why don't we release the prisoners?" suggested David.

"Why should I do that?"

"Because they know the treasure's not dug up yet."

"You're right!" said John as he studied the cliff along the island's south shore. His eyes finally rested on a small prominence just below the ridge.

"And we won't have to feed or water them, either" added David.

"It's a long shot," said John as he signalled his crew to turn about and row to the beach, "but maybe one of those cutthroats will signal his mates on the Walrus before they get within range."

"Look, John," said David as he pointed across Rip Rap Beach. "There's the Eagle, and they've come about. Maybe they can get back around the reef before the Walrus gets here!"

"Not likely with these winds. Our only real hope is to get these cannons into position." John looked back toward the Silver Cloud. "I trust the remaining gunners know enough to move all the swivel guns to the starboard gunwale." McCoy heard the Captain's comment.

"Aye, Captain," he called back, "they know their jobs."

Pulling the 800-pound cannons through the sand and up the hill to the cliff took a just over an hour. The small wooden wheels were designed for the hard planking of a ship's deck, not the soft sands of Dead Man's Chest. It took most of the crew and a half dozen dead heads buried along the way to move the heavy weapons. Without the block and tackle McCoy had brought along, they'd have never finished the arduous task. As they finally twisted the second cannon about to face down toward their stricken ship, the Walrus set up for her first attack run.

"She's within range of the Cloud, sir," said Mc Coy. "I don't know what she's waitin' for."

"Smoot's waiting because he believes the Cloud's unarmed," answered Captain Jones as two of the Walrus cannons fired, their balls falling short of the Cloud. John put a hand on McCoy's shoulder. "Steady now, McCoy, and make this count."

Aye, Captain," answered the gunner as he sighted down his barrel at the Walrus. "On yer command, sir."

"Fire!"

CHAPTER 11

The report of the Silver Cloud's three warning shots rolled across the sea in all directions like distant thunder, bringing Henry Morgan down the Eagle's companionway and to his Captain's door.

"Did ya hear it, Govn'r?" cried Henry Morgan as he banged on the heavy oak door with the hilt of his cutlass.

"Did I hear what?" bellowed Smoot from inside his cabin. The middle-aged pirate had just begun a breakfast of biscuits and gravy with his two prisoners. He excused himself as he walked to the door, wiping his face clean with a fine French napkin.

"There's cannon fire from the Silver Cloud, Govn'r! They gotta be tradin' iron with the Walrus!" Smoot pulled the door open in the youth's mid-sentence, catching the lad's foul breath in his face.

"I've had it with you, Morgan! Didn't I tell you not to disturb me when I'm with..." Smoot paused to think. "You're wrong about them cannons. Them three shots was a signal, not a battle. I'd say they just now lost their anchor and went up on the reef." Smoot placed a large hand on the boy's face and pushed him backwards toward the ladder.

"Get topside an' come about for the south shore. We been gone long enough." Smoot turned to rejoin his breakfast guests, but stopped and turned back to the carrot-topped lad. "And I swear, Morgan. You bang on my door one more time with that damn cutlass an' I'll have yer heart for supper!"

Before the Eagle had reached the western tip of Dead Man's Chest, the Walrus was positioning herself for her first broadside, seemingly unconcerned by the occasional small iron balls flying through her rigging. At one hundred yards abeam, she shivered all but her fore t'gallant for steerage, and coasted to a near halt in the calm sea. Expecting little, if any opposition, Captain Pritchard brought his forty-gun ship as close to the coral as was safe, putting it well within the range of the yet-unseen shore battery atop the hill.

"Gunners!" called Pritchard. "They be unarmed, mates, so take yer time strippin' off her plankin'!" At Captain Pritchard's order, two of her cannons threw their ten-pound balls at the Silver Cloud's exposed underbelly, but as Smoot had expected, Prichard's first two shots fell short of their mark.

No sooner had the splashes fallen back into the calm water and the deafening roar of the exploding powder lost itself across the blue sea, than there was what appeared at first to be an echo from the cliffs above Rip Rap Beach.

The first of McCoy's two rounds smashed into the bulwarks just above the Walrus' number three starboard cannon, killing two men instantly and sending their mates into a temporary panic. The second ball followed the first by five seconds, hitting the mizzen topmast a glancing blow, tearing away several inches of wood just above the crosstrees, and then continuing through the luffed mizzen royal in a shower of splinters.

"What the hell!?" cried Pritchard as he looked about for the source of the attack.

"There!" cried one of the gunners, pointing to the cliff where the white puff of smoke and loud report originated. "They got a cannon on the cliff!"

By the time Pritchard had located the cliff battery with his spyglass, McCoy had reloaded, sending a third ball to the Walrus' hull just above the waterline amidships, punching a three-foot hole in the planking. Pritchard turned to the helmsman.

"Come about!" As the great ship began its turn to larboard, Pritchard turned back to the gun crews. "Fire as you bare!" One by one, and in two's and threes', the twenty cannons began firing on the Silver Cloud. But since the ship was well into her turn, only the first three cannons hit their mark. As the Cloud's shore battery reloaded for their next volley, the gunners aboard the crippled ship continued peppering the Walrus with muskets and larger balls from the eight swivel guns. Two of the one-inch balls found their mark, killing one and wounding a second man aboard the Walrus..

Smoot had seen enough. "Morgan!" he yelled at the boy in a voice louder than needed. "Trim yer sails for more speed and begin firing at the Walrus!"

"At the Walrus?" Morgan was confused. "Don't you mean the Cloud?"

"No. Not till we know for sure where that treasure is."

"But we do!" protested the youth, pointing back toward the North shore. "It's next to that mound!"

"Not necessarily," said Smoot. "When I see the chests of gold and silver with my own eyes, then I'll be convinced. Until then, we're still playin' the Cloud's protector, just like they expect us to."

"Do ya think Privy'll know to set sail and run when we start firin' on 'im?" asked Morgan.

"Take a look, boy," said Smoot as he handed Morgan the glass. "They've already hauled the wind to get away from those cannons on the cliff. Our attack'll only be for show."

By the time the Walrus had sailed beyond range, she had put three holes in the Cloud while taking seven hits from the shore battery. She had a small fire burning in the forecastle and nearly a dozen of her crew lay dead or injured. As the Eagle began throwing balls from the other side of the Western reef, the Walrus had come about and was tacking toward the safety of Cottongarden Point at the Eastern end of Saint Croix.

"McCoy!" called Captain Jones from the ledge thirty feet above the cannons. "I want you and the other six gunners to remain here while I go down to assess the damage.

If you see the Walrus turn back for another attack, fire a warning shot." Captain Jones trotted down the dusty path to the beach. David and Ben Gunn had just dropped into one of the ship's boats and were now pulling toward the beach. John called out to them.

"Did they hit the Cloud?"

"Yes," called back David.

"How bad is it?"

"Two of their three balls penetrated the hull, John!" called Ben. "One close to the bow and the second one amidships."

John waded out to meet them as their boat skidded onto the sand. "How long do you think it'll take for repairs?"

"The one at the bow is high enough that we can leave it alone," said David, "but the other is at the waterline! I'd say at least two days, if the pirates leave us alone."

"I think they'll be more than busy with their own repairs," said John with a look to the fleeing Walrus. "They're on fire and I believe we hit their mizzen mast."

"Good!" said David as he looked about at the Eagle. "I'm glad we had the Eagle along."

"Aye," answered John. "I must admit that I've misjudged Captain Steele."

"Oh?" asked Ben.

"If it weren't for him, we'd have likely lost the Cloud altogether."

"Does this mean things will be better between you two?" asked the old man.

"To a point, yes," answered John. "But if you're asking whether it heals all the wounds; no, it doesn't."

"I'm sorry to hear that," said the David. "It does us no good for you two to be at odds like this."

As John, David and Ben stood watching their injured ship list further and further toward shore, Robert trotted onto the north end of the beach with the six Mountain men.

"Is it bad, John!" he called. John turned about to the approaching Yorkman.

"Bad enough! There's a large hole amidships at the waterline." John took several steps toward Robert and stopped. "How'd it go with the prisoners? Did you get my message?"

"It's done, just as you ordered."

"Did they believe you," asked John, "that the treasure wasn't there?"

"Aye," answered Robert, "once we let 'em dig where I had stuck my sword, they did. And they promised to signal the Walrus if we'd let 'em go."

"Good," said John as he stepped into a waiting boat. "I'm going out to the Cloud to assess damage. While I'm gone, David, make sure the gun crews on the cliff are provided with food and water, and some shelter from the sun. It's going to be a long day."

Within a half hour, John and Captain Van Mourik were inside the crippled ship's lower decks inspecting the damage.

"That looks bad," said John as he pulled away several loose pieces of oak from the large hole in the ship's side."

"As I tolt Master Noble, we took three rounds to de hull, Cap'n, an' there's some damage to her innards besides." Van Mourik spread a sheet of paper on the deck and pointed to the areas of greatest damage.

"Damage to the innards?" asked Captain Jones. "How much?"

"Here and here," answered Van Mourik as he pointed to a lower deck beam and stanchion. "I tolt David we can leave der hole in the bow alone, but we'll have to move her to Rip Rap Beach ta fix dis one, ya?"

"Can you have your temporary patches in place before the next tide?"

"That'd be about 1900 hours, Cap'n," answered the large man as he considered. "Aye, she be ready to float clear of da reef by den."

By late afternoon, the hole at the Cloud's waterline was covered with a temporary patch of canvas and tar, and by sunset, just as the Dutchman had predicted, the sea had returned far enough that three of the ships boats began pulling the great ship free from the coral and into the deeper waters of the channel. By midnight, the Silver Cloud was secured near the high water mark of Rip Rap Beach and readied for hauling down.

"The carpenter tells me the permanent repairs could be completed in three days," reported John as he walked under the stretched canvas of the officer's pavilion, "provided there's no more trouble." He poured himself a cup of tea and looked back at his crippled ship.

"We figured as much," answered Robert as he mixed a spoon of sugar in his cup. "Was that the 'something important' you had to tell us?"

"No, it wasn't," answered John. "Today's encounter with pirates, both on the north shore and their attack on the Cloud, has put this mission into a completely different light and forced a decision upon us."

"A decision?" asked Robert.

"You," pointed John, with his finger close to the Yorkman's face, "could have been killed this morning."

"So?" Robert answered as he looked at the others. "Any one of us could have been killed."

"But you're still the only one who knows where the treasure's buried. If you're killed, we won't get the treasure and the Colonies won't get their cannons."

"I'm aware of that risk," said Robert slowly. "But Mister Jefferson gave me explicit orders to tell nobody, including you, Captain Jones, until we had shovels in hand."

"He didn't even trust me?"

"That's why he didn't ask for a map," said Robert, trying to soften the blow. "Once it was put to paper, anybody who could manage to get their hands on it could get the treasure."

"Beggin' yer pardon, sir," said Ben, "but Captain Jones is right. It doesn't matter any more what Mister Jefferson told you. You have to tell the rest of us."

Robert took a sip of his tea as he considered the old man's admonition.

"You shouldn't have to ponder this, Robert," added David. "You have to tell us where it's buried."

"John," asked Robert finally, as he gave hisCcaptain a comforting squeeze on the forearm, "do you have that chart of the island with you; the one we used when we selected the anchorage?"

"Aye," answered John as he went to his bunk. It still bothered him that Jefferson hadn't trusted him, but he knew the statesman was correct in taking the measures he had. "Here it is," John said as he spread the chart across the table and placed a lamp at each end.

The chart showed the outline of the island with the reef and beach at the west end, but none of the island's interior detail. Robert dipped a quill in John's ink well and drew a heavy meandering line across the island from East to West. Then, near the center of this first line, he drew a second one, perpendicular to the first and running halfway toward the northern shore.

"It's here," Robert said as he placed the point of the pen at the juncture of the two lines. "Right at the head of this valley. We figured the trees and bushes would grow the best there."

"Can you be more specific?" asked John.

"Yes I can. When you reach the point where the valley disappears into the ridge line, come back down exactly twenty paces to the Manchaneel tree...the one our lookout encountred this morning." Robert looked up at his three friends. "Unless new ones have sprung up from it's roots, the treasure lies directly under it's trunk."

"When do we go, John?" asked David as he jumped to his feet.

"Not so fast," said John as he considered. "If we bring the treasure down before the Cloud's ready to sail, we'll have pirates on us like lice on a maroon." Everyone looked at Ben as he stifled an itch.

"They'll be all over us no matter when we dig it up," offered David.

"Aye," countered John, "unless we take further precautions."

"Further precautions!" objected Robert. "We've nearly every able-bodied man on watch as it is! When half of them head up that little ravine with shovels, every cutthroat in the Virgin Islands will be watching!"

"Not if my plan works, Robert. Since we already know they'll be watching our every move, why not turn it to our advantage?"

"Our advantage? asked David.

"Aye," answered John. "We'll create a diversion."

"Like a fire or something?" asked Ben.

"A little more complicated than that, Ben." John lifted one of the lamps and let the map roll closed. "I intend to send out two or three digging parties a day with empty boxes. They'll be instructed to select a spot in the trees or along the coast and dig a large hole. Then, after they refill the hole, they'll return to Rip Rap with the same boxes."

"I may be a little slow, sir," said Ben, "but where's the sense in that?"

"I see it," said Robert. "After three days of digging false holes, the pirates won't know when we dig up the real treasure."

"Exactly," said John.

"You said there were several other things we might do," asked Robert. "Something besides your diversion?"

"Yes," answered John. "One of us can pay a visit to Captain Steele to let him know what's going on." John turned to David. "That will be your job."

"But shouldn't you go?" protested David. "You're the Captain."

"Aye, but I doubt the man would even allow me aboard."

"Hmmm," agreed David. "When do you want me to go?"

"Tomorrow morning, just after breakfast? We can send out a couple of shovel crews this afternoon, and another in the morning while you're at the Eagle. I'd like to hear Steele's reaction."

"And what if I run into trouble on the Eagle?" asked David. "What signal should I give you?"

John threw back his head in laughter. "Wave your handkerchief in the air, David. Ha! Ha! Just in case they've all turned into pirates."

"Right, John," answered David in a sober sulk. "It's yellow."

❀   ❀   ❀

Perhaps it was the Silver Cloud, crippled as she was and hauled down on her larboard side. Or maybe it was the knowledge that they were being watched from the hills and their mighty ship was disabled. Whatever it was, every man in camp could feel the heaviness of spirit as he went about his duties.

At Captain Jones' direction, the tents had been erected along a single line running north to south, just above the high water mark. Armed watches with battle rattles were placed near the end tents and two others stood watch aboard the hauled-down ship. Further up the beach, almost to the tree line, three sails were held aloft by upright oars and stretched taut so as to create shaded work pavilions for the carpenters and the ship's officers. Oil lamps here and there flickered out their meager light throughout the night as the fresh planking was sorted and measured for rough shaping.

It was three in the morning, and neither John nor Robert had been able to sleep. Somewhere aboard the Silver Cloud, a lone sailor sang a familiar verse from a sea ballad to the accompaniment of his concertina.

> *A curse on the jewels, the pearls an' the gold,*
> *A curse on the pirates what's honor was sold.*
> *A curse on the Yorkman what refuses to tell,*
> *Of the treasure laid by - may he rot in hell."*

John swung his legs out of his cot and walked across to the small stove. The tea was still warm.

"He's singing about you, isn't he?" asked John with a look to his friend.

"Aye," answered Robert as he sat up and looked about the camp. "But the way things have gone so far, I've a bad feeling the whole crew may taste of that curse before we get off this island."

John filled two cups and handed one to Robert. "You made the right decision to tell us. Heaven knows. It could just as easily have been you who took that stray ball at the mound this morning."

Robert didn't answer as his mind wandered to the treasure. The secret had been his for over twenty years, and it had given him a sort of power. A large secret will do that, especially when it deals with money. And it gave him a tremendous sense of security also, knowing that any time he needed it, he could sail to this--his private island bank account--and take away what he needed.

"What is it, Robert? You look a hundred leagues away."

"Oh, I was just thinking." He downed his tea and threw the last quarter inch of liquid and wilted leaves into the dark night. "Remember the other day when I asked you how you learned about me and the treasure?"

"Yes?"

"I don't mean anything personal against the lad," said Robert, "but doesn't it strike you as a little odd that it was David who told you?"

"Who else, if not David?"

"Look at it, John. His father owns the cannons and David knew all about me and the treasure?"

John stroked his chin and considered the chain of events between Kings Town and Edenton.

"The only part that bothers me is that he knew it all along, but kept it from me until I was desperate."

"Exactly!" said Robert, leaning forward.

"And you think David had the whole thing calculated from the first?"

"David," Robert agreed, "or his father. How much do you know about Charles Noble?"

"Not very much. I only met the man a week before David and I sailed for the Colonies. The few times we spoke, we only discussed my ship and it's provisions."

"I'd like a talk with David, provided you have no objections. I have a distinct feeling he's not telling..."

Robert fell silent in answer to John's raised hand. The young Captain seemed to bristle like a threatened dog.

"What is it, John?"

"Listen. Something's wrong." Captain Jones stood and looked across the camp to the north. A group of men had assembled and were speaking in agitated tones. John could only make out a word or two, but it was enough. "Somebody's been kidnapped!"

"There!" pointed the Yorkman as he joined his Captain. "Someone's running this way!"

As they watched, a powder monkey named Gilcrest ran down the line of tents, under the Cloud's masts and haul-down tackle, and then straight toward John and Robert's pavilion.

"What's happened, Alan?" Captain Jones shouted. The lad was still thirty yards out when he started crying something about men missing. But then, just before reaching them, the boy fell face down into the sand.

"Who's been taken, lad!" demanded Robert as he jerked the boy upright and gave him a shake.

"The pirates got 'em, sir!" The excited youth thrust a piece of parchment at the Yorkman.

"Who'd they take?" demanded Robert as John took the paper and pushed past them to the lamp. The message was crude and most of the words were misspelled, but there was no mistake about what had happened.

"They've taken Ben Gunn and our carpenter!"

"What?" Robert snatched the paper from John's hand. "Damn it! How in God's name..?" As Robert reread the message, a group of two dozen armed men began to assemble between the ship and their pavilion. David was among them.

"David!" called John. "Does anyone know where they are?"

"On the beach, north of the mound," answered David. "One of the men heard screams and went out to look. He said there were three campfires at shore's edge."

"Three fires..." Captain Jones echoed. "That means there's at least fifteen of them." John strapped on his sword and jammed two pistols in his belt.

"Are you going with us?" asked David.

"Aye, David!" barked the Scotsman. "Those are my men out there."

After a few words with Robert, Captain Jones and his first officer lead their twenty-man rescue party northward, out of camp. With lanthorns trimmed to a flicker, the darkness quickly swallowed them from sight.

"I know this is probably stupid of me," whispered David as the rescue party began to cross the grassy plain toward the mound, "but aren't they going to be waiting for us?"

"Aye," answered John. "They've probably dug up every inch of earth about the mound and didn't find anything. I'm hoping they want to strike some sort of bargain for those two."

"But what if you're wrong and they just want to kill as many of us as they can?"

"Then we'll fight until we have to swim for it."

"Swim for it?" David protested. "Are you crazy?"

"Not at all." John had been scanning the horizon to their left for the last several minutes. "Take a look out there, just inside the reef."

As David and the others watched, John raised and lowered his small lanthorn three times. A moment later, a similar lanthorn was raised from behind the rail of one of the ship's boats.

"Who's that?"

"It's Robert with three of our boats. I hope you're wrong about the ambush David, but if not, at least we'll have a way of escape."

"Will they make it to the north side in time?" asked David.

"They will if we have to swim for it."

As a man grows older, more things change than the color of his hair and the number of creases in his face. Out of necessity, he becomes wiser and more cautious about nearly everything. This aging process, and the desire that things come a little slower and easier than they did when he was young, happens to landlubber and seaman alike. So it is with ship's masters, and the art of driving a ship at night in strange waters. Although the brightness of a full moon will reveal his position to an enemy sooner, it is much more comfortable to have it than not. Thus, was the full moon given the name, Commander's Moon.

It was one of those special moons which rose from the eastern tip of Dead Man's Chest the night Ben Gunn and the carpenter were kidnapped. Captain Jones and his rescue party crouched in the shadows of the mound, a hundred and fifty yards from the three campfires. Nothing moved for ten minutes.

"Do you still think it's a trap?"

"I'm certain of it, David," John said as he glanced seaward. Robert's three boats were approaching their rescue position.

"Shall I pass the word for the others to move up?"

"Aye," whispered John, "but I want them going..." Before he could finish the sentence, there was a scream from beyond the smoldering campfires, followed by a second from the south, toward the hills. The rescue party bristled to a man as a flurry of angry whispers swept through their ranks.

"Damn their souls!" swore Captain Jones. "If they've killed either of our men..."

"At least we know one is still alive," insisted David.

"Don't count on it," answered John. "Anybody can scream out as if he's being tortured."

Captain Jones ordered the lanthorns trimmed and left at the mound. As the moon passed from behind a cloud, Robert's three boats were suddenly silhouetted against the horizon.

"Men!" Captain Jones began in a loud whisper. "We're going to be totally exposed from the moment we leave these rocks until we return to their cover. Pair up with a mate and follow Mister Noble and me by two's. Until I give the order, I don't want any of you to break ranks, regardless of what you see or hear. Is that understood?"

There was a muffled response from the men as Captain Jones continued.

"If we're attacked from the treeline, I want you to return to the mound and use your muskets to best advantage, being sure to watch your flanks. I hope you can all swim, because you may have to if things go bad for us."

"Don't worry," assured David. "They'll swim if it means their lives."

"Then let's get to it!"

Like a flood of ants at a picnic lunch, the rescue party poured over the rocks toward the sea. At the high water line, they turned eastward toward the now-dark campfires and their two kidnapped shipmates. Two of the fires had died completely, with the third putting up only a faint flicker as the breeze fanned its last bit of fuel. From all indications, the camp had been abandoned for some time, but one man's cries continued to come from its general direction. The rescue party's pace quickened to a trot as they passed the end of the mound.

"Can anyone make out who that is?" whispered Captain Jones.

"Can't tell for sure," answered David, "but I want to believe it's Ben Gunn."

With only a hundred feet between them and the pirate's camp, there came a blood chilling cry from their right; from the tall grass where several of the pirate's had fallen the previous morning.

"Save me, mates! They're cuttin' off me legs!" came the mournful cry, followed by another long scream which trailed off as if it were the poor man's last. Before Captain Jones could stop them, four of his seamen had broken ranks and were running in the tortured man's direction, intent upon his rescue. But no sooner had they entered the tall grass than a dozen muskets fired, cutting the four down in their tracks.

"To the water line!" commanded Captain Jones.

"Help me, Captain Jones!" came another cry from the same area. "Help me, Mister Noble!" came another. "Help us, shipmates!" came a third call, followed by a barrage of mocking laughter.

"They've tricked us!" whispered David with an oath as he dropped to the sand next to John.

"Aye, and we've paid dearly for it, too!"

The rescue party lay for half an hour at the high water mark, watching and waiting for the inevitable attack. The taunting calls for help and the cruel laughter continued for a short interval, and then stopped abruptly.

"What now, John?"

"There's nothing to do but go back, unless you still have a notion our mates are still alive."

"Go back?" protested DAvid.

"Aye," answered John. "Isn't it clear to you what's happened?"

"The only thing that's clear to me is that two of our mates are still out there someplace. For decency's sake, we owe it to them to be sure. If we don't..."

"I suppose you're right," admitted John. "Get me two volunteers. We'll give the camp a quick check before we go."

"I'll go!" whispered one of the seamen. It was Gilcrest, the powder monkey.

"And I'll go with him," added David.

"Very well, but go with caution. They'll be watching your every move."

"Don't worry," whispered David with a hand on the lad's shoulder.

As David and the powder monkey moved off across the sand toward the campsite, there was a clatter of oars being shipped and a boat skidding onto the sand to the west, announcing the arrival of Robert Ormerod and the extra men. After a moment, the Yorkman dropped onto the sand next to John.

"What's happening?" asked Robert as he followed John's gaze to the east. He had heard the earlier gunfire and the screams for help, and figured the rescue had been accomplished by now. "What are you watching for?"

"David and one of the powder monkeys are checking the pirate's camp. I'm certain they've already killed Gunn and Sanders, but I owe it to the crew to be certain."

"Then you haven't found them yet?"

"No," answered John. "We don't even know for sure they're in the camp."

"Then what was all that gunfire?"

"Unfortunately," answered John, "they lured four of my less experienced men away and killed them."

"Damn! One thing's for certain," added Robert, "they knew exactly who to kidnap."

"How do you figure?"

"Think about it. They know why Mister Gunn's with us. They needed him to find out where he hid the silver bars on Spyglass."

"I figured that part, but why a carpenter?"

"They don't intend that we ever leave this island," continued Robert. "How better to accomplish that than to kill off the men who know how to make the repairs?"

"If you're correct, then Sanders is done for." As they spoke, a call came from the pirate's camp.

"Over here, Captain Jones!" cried David. "They're both here in the sand, and there's at least a dozen dead pirates."

"Are they alive!" called John as he and Robert, and the rest of the rescue party ran to join them.

"Aye, but they're both quite senseless."

The smell of burnt flesh hung heavy over the bodies. At the center of the camp, laid together between the three fires, were the unconscious bodies of Sanders and Gunn. Ben was naked to the waist and lay on his face, with a small puddle of blood in the sand where it had run from his mouth and nose.

"Ben!" whispered Robert as he turned the old man onto his back. "Ben, can you hear me?"

"Oh God...I hurt so..." the old maroon whispered through bloody teeth. "I didn't...oh, Master Orm...they tried..."

"Save your strength, Ben," ordered Robert as he cradled his friend's head in his hands. "I'm just thankful you're still alive."

"I don't think he can hear you anymore," said John. "God only knows how long they've tortured him."

"How's Sanders doing?" asked Robert.

"He's alive, but just barely. They must have laid the cat to his back for most of the night."

The back of the man's shirt had been split open from waist to collar and his torn flesh was caked in a mixture of blood, sand and ashes.

"Robert," said John, "put these two in your boat and return to our camp as quickly as you can. They need medical attention and I'm afraid they wouldn't survive being carried that far."

"You're not coming with us?"

"Not just yet, at least not until we have a look about their camp."

"Did you see something else?" asked Robert as he searched the tall grass for the pirates.

"I'm not sure," answered John. "Something isn't right here."

As Robert and his men carried the two injured men away, Captain Jones and David made a survey of the camp. There had to be an explanation for the strange happenings of the night.

"Odd, isn't it," said John as he walked along the line of dead pirates, "that they'd collect their dead and lay them out like this?"

"You think the pirates did this?"

"Who else would have? Count them. These are the twelve we killed this morning."

John noticed something different about the five bodies at the center of the line. While the arms of the outboard seven were at their sides, the center five had their arms spread in various positions, like the hands of so many clocks. John kicked at one of their feet.

"Take a look at this."

"What?" asked David, lifting his lanthorn above his head.

"Do you know semaphore?"

"No," answered David. "Why?"

"Well if I didn't know better, I'd say these five were signalling the letters C-O-L-J-S."

"Is that supposed to mean something?" asked David as he knelt next to one of the bodies.

"Probably not," answered John. "But it just doesn't make sense for them to collect their dead mates and lay them out this way."

"These aren't the men we killed, John."

"They're not?"

"No." David brought his lanthorn close to one of the dead men's faces. With his free hand, David wiped the man's bloody throat with a finger. The blood was fresh and the body was still warm. "This man's been fresh killed. They must have got into a fight before we got here, and their mates laid out the dead ones to confuse us."

"Either that," added John, "or Captain Steele was over here earlier."

"I don't think he had anything to do with this," said David as he checked three more of the dead. "He couldn't have known our men were kidnapped. And besides, he'd have brought Gunn and Sanders back to us. No, this was done by somebody who hates the Walrus crew as much as we do."

"But who?"

"My guess is that we've another ship of pirates out there somewhere," answered David. "Somebody else wanting to get their hands on that treasure."

"If that's the case," said John, "then Captain Steele needs to know about it as quickly as possible."

The rescue party stepped onto the north end of Rip Rap Beach just as the sun's first rays streaked upward across the dark morning sky. The ship's doctor had been tending to the two injured men for a half hour when John and David returned from the north shore. Robert was waiting for them.

"How's Ben doing?" called John as he and David climbed down from the rocks at the edge of the beach.

"He's some nasty burns," answered Robert as he turned and matched strides with his Captain. "The poor soul was unconscious most of the trip back. He's lucid now, but he kept raving about Long John Silver."

"Long John Silver?" asked John. "What did he say?"

"Nothing I could put together," answered Robert. "Ben's carried a heavy burden these past eleven years."

"Oh?"

"He's the one who freed John Silver from the Hispaniola at Puerta Plata. The pirate was to be tried and hung the next day."

"That would certainly account for the hallucinations," said John. "But he'll be all right, won't he?"

"McKenzie says he'll be up and about within a week."

"And Sanders?" asked John.

"Died in the boat before we could get him back. The surgeon said he lost far too much blood for his size. And you were wrong about his back."

"Oh?" John stopped just short of the surgeon's tent. "Then it wasn't the cat-of-nine-tails after all?"

"No," answered Robert. "They cut something in his flesh; something I've told the surgeon to show to no one but you."

"A message?"

"Worse," answered Robert quietly. "It's a map."

As they entered McKenzie's tent, the pungent odor of fresh blood nearly made them wretch. The body of the ship's carpenter lay under the piece of sailcloth he had been carried upon, with the dark red blood and caked sand scattered about the surgeon's table.

"May I help you, Captain Jones?" asked the surgeon as he rose from Ben Gunn's side.

"Yes you can, Adam. But first, how's Ben doing?"

"They burned his lower legs pretty bad with their irons, sir, but he'll recover."

"Good," answered John as he lifted the corner of the sailcloth. The blood and sand had been washed away from the dead carpenter's back. A very accurate outline of the small island had been cut with the man's own chisel. The ridgeline and the two small valleys that radiated toward the north were there also, cut just to the left of his spine.

"There, John," said Robert as he pointed to the crescent shaped puncture wound between the seventh and eighth ribs. "That's what I wanted you to see."

"I figure it punctured his heart, sir," said McKenzie as he looked up from Ben's wounds. "He'd have died anyway, even if I'd got to him sooner."

"Adam?" asked John. "Is Mister Gunn well enough to speak with us for a few minutes?"

"I'd rather he didn't," McKinzie answered. "He has several deep burns to dress yet, and I'm afraid of gangrene if it's not finished soon."

"I can talk with you, Captain Jones," protested Ben. The old maroon raised himself onto an elbow. "These burns aren't nothin' anyway," he said as he raised the temporary dressing with a wince. "Look at that! From my ankles all the way to my knees."

"I'll give you ten minutes with him, Captain Jones, but please no longer." With that, Adam excused himself and walked from the tent.

"It's obvious they tortured you, Ben," began Robert. "Can you remember whether you told them anything?"

"I didn't tell them nothin', sir," said Ben. "Every time they burned me, I'd pass out stone cold."

"Then how do you explain this map on Sander's back, and the spot where they stabbed him?" asked John. "If you didn't tell them anything, how'd they manage to get so close?"

"That was just a lucky stick, sir. They cut the map first, an' then tried to make me finger the treasure. When I refused, they stabbed him dead and took to torturin' me again with their irons." Ben was in great pain, but the thought that his employer and his Captain didn't believe him hurt worse.

"Do you know anything about all those dead pirates at the edge of the camp?" asked Robert.

Ben shook his head. "Last thing I 'member before wakin' up here is my legs bein' burned. I never seen any dead pirates."

"Thank you, Ben," said John with a pat to the old man's shoulder. "We'll leave you to Doctor McKenzie's care for now. Do what he says so we don't lose you also."

"Aye, Cap'n Jones," answered Ben as the two left the tent. The doctor was waiting for them.

"He is going to be all right, isn't he?" asked Robert.

"Yes, but I'm surprised his heart didn't give out from the pain."

"He's a strong man," answered Robert, "very strong." With that, the two officers turned and walked quickly toward their pavilion.

"What do you think, John?"

"We'll just have to wait and watch. He might have told them, but considering..."

"Considering what?"

"Think about it," answered John. "It's obvious they never intended to kill Ben."

"Agreed," answered Robert. "Go on."

"How'd they know to take Ben in the first place, unless someone told them about the silver bars on Spyglass?"

"You think there's a spy on the Cloud, don't you?" asked Robert.

"It's a possibility, but we've very little to go on at this point. It may simply be a case of loose talk."

"You think it's one of the officers, don't you?"

"I wish there were another explanation, Robert, but..."

"But what?" Robert stopped walking and waited for the younger man to notice and do likewise. "I hope you don't think I'd..."

"No, Robert, I've never doubted your loyalty," answered John as he stopped and turned. "If I'm correct, about it being one of the officers, then Captain Van Mourik would be my first suspect."

"You think Van Mourik's in league with the Walrus?"

"He's not a spy, Robert, but he is a chronic braggart."

"Mmmm," said Robert. "And that's why he's conspicuously absent from most of our staff meetings, right?"

"Right," answered John. "It's best for all concerned that we control what Van Mourik knows."

"But I heard you telling him our departure will be delayed for at least another week. Why would you confide something like that when you know he'll tell everybody?"

"Because it's not true, that's why. Ever since I realized he's incapable of keeping a secret, I've been telling him false information. I'm counting on that information finding it's way to the pirates."

As they spoke, David approached from the sawyer's table. "I'm ready to meet with Captain Steele!" he called to John. "Anything you want me to talk with him about, Captain Jones?"

"I want to know if he killed those twelve pirates last night," began John, "and I'm certain he'll want to know about the digging parties."

"Should I tell him when we expect to load the treasure and depart?"

"If he asks, yes," answered John. "Send someone up to the battery and have them fire one shot to call the Eagle to anchorage."

CHAPTER 12

"Henry!" Captain Smoot bellowed from his stateroom door. "Henry Morgan!"

"Aye, Govn'r?" answered the orange-haired youth as he slid one of the mainmast stays to a light-footed landing on the deck next to the companionway. "You heard it too?"

"Of course I heard it!" Smoot spit back sarcastically. "Fetch Captain Steele!"

"Aye, aye, Govn'r!" Morgan was down the hatch and past his Captain in a flash, his trusty cutlass slicing the dark air ahead of him as he traversed the passageway toward the middle hold. The prisoner sat on the deck in his manacles with a single whale oil lamp hanging from the overhead.

"Finally come to kill me," came the raspy voice of Henry Steele, "or does Smoot need me at breakfast again?" His water had run out hours before, and he was already feeling the effects of dehydration.

"T' kill ya!" lied Morgan. "Smoot's sick o' feedin' ya, an' sent me to do ya in!" Morgan put the tip of his blade to Steele's throat and pressed it into the flesh. "But first he want's you to answer a few questions."

Minutes later, Henry Steele was pushed roughly through the door of the master's cabin and forced to his knees. Joshua Smoot sat tilted back in the imprisoned Captain's chair with his boots resting on the fine cherry table. The vulgar cutthroat pried at his teeth with a very large barracuda bone to extract the final remains of his breakfast.

"Ah," Smoot sang out, "if it isn't the pride of the Colonial privateers 'imself!" He flipped the bone into the air and flashed a toothy grin at Steele as it fell into his empty water cup. "Me an' the crew was wonderin' what that single cannon shot might mean. You wouldn't happen to know now, would ya?"

"You're going to have a visitor," replied Steele coldly.

"That were me very guess," said Smoot, as he eased the chair down onto all four legs, "wasn't it Henry?" He stood slowly and pushed past Morgan to the starboard windows.

"Aye, Govn'r," Henry lied. "Them was yer very words."

"And I suppose you want my help?" asked Steele defiantly. No sooner had his words left his parched throat than the old pirate's dagger pierced the decking between his knees.

"Not especially," Smoot answered with a raise of his right eyebrow. "It seemed to me more appropriate to present yer head to 'em on a platter, since they'll find out we're pirates now anyhow."

"But they don't have to find out," blurted Steele before he realized what he had said.

"They don't?" Smoot walked around the table and stood over his prisoner for several seconds. "Might ya be offerin' yer services to me, after all?"

"I might be willing to help you," said Steele slowly, "if you'll agree to release your other prisoner."

"We're making bargains now, are we?" laughed Smoot. "And just who do you suggest I release her to?"

"Face it," growled Steele. "They all know what I look like. You need me to convince them the Eagle's still their protector, especially if it's Captain Jones or that man from New York."

"Oh, Captain Steele," Smoot said with a frown. "You disappoint me somethin' fierce. If it's either o' them two, they'd make a much better hostage than you. If it's anybody else, then with all the things I learned from you these last five days, I should have no trouble foolin' 'em into thinkin' I'm you. An' like I said, if I can't fool 'em, then I'll just kill 'em. Ha! Ha! Ha!"

"Then why the hell have you kept me alive this long?" yelled Steele. "I must have some purpose!"

"Some purpose?" mused the pirate as he sucked at his teeth. "Aye, ya both do. Actually, the girl's worth more to me than you."

"What'll it be then? Do you promise to release her if I cooperate?"

"Why don't we wait to see how well you do. Then..."

"Cap'n Smoot!" cried Morgan from his place at the larboard window. "Ya better come see this!"

"What is it, Henry?"

"Look there, Govn'r, just below where they set up their shore battery."

"Why I'll be!" sang out the old pirate. "They've dug up the treasure in broad daylight!"

"Aye," agreed Morgan as he pulled his cutlass and began moving toward the shackled prisoner. "An' now there's no reason ta keep this one alive no more, is there?"

"Belay that!" cried Smoot as Morgan's blade was rising above Steele's head. "You can kill him, but not before we hear what our visitor has to say about the Silver Cloud's departure!"

"But..." cried Henry, as if he'd been marooned without cause.

"Lower yer weapon, boy, or by the powers ye'll die with him!" Smoot gave Henry a shove and then looked down at his prisoner.

"Now, regarding our other special guest," Smoot continued. "I'll consider your proposition. Play your part well and maybe both of you will survive this affair."

"But you said..!" cried Morgan.

"I don't care what I said, Henry. Remove Captain Steele's chains and see to it that he's washed and dressed in his finest clothes."

After several tacks, the Eagle dropped anchor at the break in the reef, near where the Silver Cloud was attacked the previous morning. It was taking far too long for Steele to get prepared, and Captain Smoot was becoming impatient.

"Morgan!" Smoot bellowed from the quarterdeck. A mass of orange hair popped from the forward companionway.

"Did you call me, Govn'r?"

"I wasn't calling yer sister! Where the hell's Captain Steele? The Cloud's boat is halfway here!"

"He's comin' now, Govn'r!" Morgan said as he leaped to the deck and stood with his cutlass drawn. Captain Steele climbed slowly onto the deck behind him, blinded momentarily by the bright sunlight. As he hesitated to gain his bearings, Morgan began kicking at the backs of his legs.

There was a flurry of arms and a flash of steel. Before Morgan could counter the attack, Steele had twisted the lad's cutlass from his hand, thrown the lad to the deck, and had pressed the blade to his throat.

"Kick me one more time, you worthless urchin," hissed Steele, "and you'll go into hell without your head. I'm a dead man anyway, and I'd love to take you with me."

"Morgan!" yelled Smoot. "You're out of place!"

Captain Steele released his grip of the lad's hair and threw the cutlass over the rail. Morgan watched his favorite toy spin through the water and come to rest between two coral heads. He gave his attacker a dark scowl.

"Well, Captain Steele!" said Smoot. "Are we ready for some play acting?"

"I'll play my part well enough," replied Steele.

"If they ask who I am," instructed Smoot, "you say I'm your first officer. Tell 'em that I replaced your other first officer when he was taken sick with canine madness in the Bahamas."

Steele gave Smoot a defiant glare.

"Careful man! You can rough up the lad, but cross me once and not only will you die, but the good lady in chains as well. And mind you, hers won't be a quick death. My men can make killin' her downright fun."

Smoot leveled his spyglass at the approaching boat and studied it's occupants. Something about the young officer tickled a memory.

"Morgan!"

"Aye, Govn'r?

"Take a look at that man at the tiller."

Morgan adjusted the instrument to one eye, and then the other. "Why, that's the one what knew 'bout me killin' Captain Claw back on Tortuga!" Morgan lowered the glass. "Do you know 'im?"

"Aye, it's Charlie Noble's boy."

"Charlie Noble?" Morgan screwed his face sideways as he thought. "Isn't that the Kings Town merchant what traded you the Walrus in '73?"

"The same." Smoot took back the spyglass and gave the small boat another close inspection. "That boy used to sit and listen to John Silver and me trade sea stories." Smoot turned about to Captain Steele. "Looks like you'll be on yer own," said Smoot as he grabbed Captain Steele's beard and gave it an angry twist. "Think you can handle it, without putting yourself and your cell-mate in jeopardy?"

"I can do anything I set my mind to," answered Steele, pulling free of the pirate's grip.

"Of course you can!" cried Smoot with a slap to Steele's back. "But just to make sure you keep yer word, I'll be hiding just a couple spans away with a cocked pistol."

"Ahoy, Eagle!" came a call from the approaching boat. "Permission to come aboard?"

"Permission granted, Silver Cloud!" answered Captain Steele as Morgan dropped down the forward hatch and Smoot stepped behind the mainmast. "How go the repairs on your ship?"

"Going well, sir!" replied David as his line was cast aboard the Eagle and his boat was hauled to the ladder. "If nothing else goes wrong," he said as he climbed to the Eagle's deck, "we could refloat her in two or three days."

"That's excellent," said Steele as he extended a hand of welcome.

"Mister Forrestal told me all about you and your fine ship," said David, "and I'm sorry now that I didn't take the time to come aboard when you were still at his docks." David gave Steele a salute of respect.

"I hope his report on me wasn't all bad."

"On the contrary, sir. He tells me Mister Jefferson hand-picked you and your entire crew for this mission."

"So I've been told," agreed Steele. "But tell me, why did you summon us?"

"For several reasons, sir." David looked about himself at the crew for the first time and was struck with how rough they appeared. Not your usual privateer crew, he thought.

"And those would be?" asked Steele.

"I'm sorry," David said as he collected his thoughts. "Captain Jones wants to know what happened to the Walrus."

"Last we saw of her," answered Steele, "she was headed around the eastern tip of the big island. Like the Silver Cloud, she's probably hauled down on a beach somewhere for repairs."

"We figured as much," said David with a smile. "Our gunners put several good ones through her hull and our gunner says he damaged her mizzenmast."

"Aye," agreed Steele. "What else did Captain Jones need to know?"

"Last night, two of our men were taken from our camp and tortured," began David. "When we found them, there were a dozen freshly killed pirates laid out in a line like chord wood. We wondered who killed them."

"Hmmm," said Steele, looking at the mast where Captain Smoot hid. "Captain Jones thinks I did it?"

"He was hoping so," David said as Captain Steele shook his head.

"Could it have been a mutiny among the Walrus crew?"

"We thought of that, but it doesn't figure they'd lay them out that way. It's almost like whoever did it was trying to tell us something." David paused. "We think there's another ship out here someplace."

"Another pirate ship?" asked Steele.

"No telling until we spot her. Captain Jones wants you to make a circuit of the island as soon as you can, and report back to him."

"We'll do it," answered Steele with a look to the men carrying boxes and shovels below the cliff, "just as soon as the winds freshen."

"I see you've spotted our third digging party," said David as he turned to watch with Captain Steele.

"Third?" asked Henry.

"We started yesterday after we got back from the north shore," bragged David. "You had to have seen the two we sent out in the afternoon."

"Sorry, David, but we missed them. Have you dug up the treasure yet?"

"No, not yet."

"Then what are those men carrying along the shoreline?"

"That's Captain Jones' idea so we can fool the pirates."

"Fool the pirates?" asked Henry with a quick glance toward where Smoot was hiding.

"Aye! He's sending out three or four of those crews daily to bury and dig up empty boxes. One of them will be carrying back the real treasure, but not even I will know which one."

Smoot heard every word from his hiding place. He stifled a curse.

"I suppose Captain Jones will want us to keep the Walrus away when you dig it up?" asked Steele.

"Well...yes, provided he knew when that would be," said David as he thought for a moment. "And mind you, I'd tell you if I knew. It all depends on how soon the Cloud's repaired." David looked to the island as he considered. "But there might be a way."

"Oh?" asked Steele.

"As you know," began David, pointing to the crest of the hill, "we've two cannons on that cliff yonder. Captain Jones won't leave without taking them with us.

"I don't see why not, seeing as how..." Captain Steele fell silent as he realized what he was disclosing to Captain Smoot.

"Of course we need them, sir. That's the whole reason for retrieving the treasure; so the Colonies can purchase my father's cannons." David turned back to Captain Steele and continued. "I'd say that when you see those two cannons moved down the hill, then you can be pretty certain the treasure's already on the Cloud and she's ready to float. That's when you want to begin watching for the Walrus."

While David was explaining about the cannons, one of Smoot's crewmen had been moving behind the lad, his eyes fixed on the brightly colored kerchief hanging from the young man's back pocket. With a quick but indelicate jerk, the yellow square of cloth was out of David's pocket and behind the pirate's back. Noticing the tug at his trousers, David spun about to catch the man.

"Hey!" the lad cried as he reached for his property. "Give that back!"

"No!" answered the pirate with a schoolboy's impudence. At that, the man began tying the kerchief about his unkempt hair, pirate-fashioned.

David made another lunge at the bandana, but the pirate twisted away and hid behind two of his mates.

"Captain Steele," the lad pleaded.

"Give it back," barked Steele, "this instant!"

The pirate gave a quick glance toward the mainmast and back to Captain Steele.

"Give it back or I'll have you flogged!" demanded Steele.

"But it's so purdy!" cried the pirate as his face contorted with frustration. "Here then," cried the dirty man as he flung the kerchief in David's face, "an' a curse on the thing!"

The argument on deck was more than Henry Morgan's curiosity could stand. As carefully as he could, the young pirate poked his head from the hatch for a quick look at their visitor. But a quick look was all it took, for in that split second before Morgan could duck away, David's eyes caught sight of the red hair and green eyes of the Charles Town carpenter.

"Captain Steele," said David, as a flash of heat raced across his neck and upper back, "is anything wrong?"

"Wrong?" answered Steele as he looked about to see what his young visitor had seen. "I don't believe so."

"Captain Jones..." said David as he began wiping his face with the yellow kerchief, "...wanted me to offer you some supplies. That is, if you're low on anything."

"You can tell my good friend that we have everything we need, unless he'd consent to sending across some rum."

"Rum..." David knew these two Captains hated each other with a vengeance, and for Steele to talk this way confirmed his suspicions. "I'm sure he'd do that for a good friend like you."

"Was there anything else?"

"No," answered David. "That was all Captain Jones wanted me to tell you."

"Then convey my respects to your fine Captain, Mister Noble, and tell him I look forward to our reunion at Charles Town."

"Thank you, sir. I will."

As quickly as he could, David was over the rail and into his waiting boat. As the oars took their first bite at the sea, Captain Steele found Smoot's hawkish nose in his face.

"So..." hissed the pirate. "My old mate, John Silver and Davey's father are trading their cannons for the treasure, are they? This is better than I ever hoped for."

"How so, Govn'r?" asked Morgan as he hopped up on deck.

"Don't you see it, Morgan? I was planning on sending Pritchard and the Walrus against the Cloud if they escaped from the Chest, but..." Smoot paused to consider the implications of the new revelation. "Fate has smiled on Fishbone Smoot. We won't have to risk sinking the Silver Cloud in deep water because the treasure's destined for the Noble warehouses."

"When do we tell Privy?"

"Not just yet," said Smoot as he watched the Cloud's longboat skid onto Rip Rap Beach. "Matter of fact, I don't believe it's in our best interest Pritchard ever knows."

"What?"

"If things go sour and the Silver Cloud escapes the Chest before the Walrus returns, we'll simply beat her to Kings Town and wait."

"You think you have it all figured out, don't you?" hissed Captain Steele.

"Ah, Captain Steele," sang the pirate. "I forgot all about you for a minute there, what with all this news of the treasure." Smoot walked to his prisoner. "What was all that chummy talk between you and Davey Noble?"

"What talk?"

"All of that 'best friend' bilge! Sounded like you an' this Captain Jones were brothers."

"He and I nearly came to blows about putting in at Virginia last month so he could visit a woman friend of his," answered Steele. "I just wanted the lad to know for sure we'd made up properly."

"If I find out you and Noble been tradin' signals..."

"And what if we were? You're planning on killing me now anyway, aren't you?"

"No," said Smoot as he toyed with the thought, "not just yet." Turning, Smoot ordered Steele returned to his chains and the sails set for the trip about the island.

Atop the hill, five gunners watched with mild interest as their first officer arrived at the privateer Eagle. They had heard the jokes about the yellow kerchief and had contributed their share of sarcastic comments about the young Jamaican's fears.

"Well, McCoy," asked the half naked lad straddling the larboard cannon, "what's your guess?"

"My guess?" answered the senior gunner. "Noble's either gone to reprimand Captain Steele for allowing the Walrus to attack the Cloud, or he's asking about all those dead pirates on the north shore last night."

"Steele's sure to ask about that digging party below us too," said the young gunner as he threw a small stone down the slope at his shipmates. "I thought this was bad duty, but digging holes an' carryin' empty boxes all day's a far cry worse. I just hope the effort isn't wasted on them pirates."

"Baker," answered the older man, "I don't think you could break wind without the pirates knowing about it." The three others on watch burst into laughter as one of them bared his backside toward the hill above them. "And Cooper's gonna take a lead ball in the butt if he keeps that up."

Baker pulled the spyglass from one of the other's hand and stretched himself prone on his cannon to watch the Eagle. For some time, Mister Noble simply stood amongst the others on deck and talked. But then...

"McCoy!" Baker cried as he thrust the spyglass at the senior gunner. "Take a look at that!"

"Damn! Do you suppose he just forgot and pulled it out by mistake?"

"It's hard to tell, Gunny. But I do know that Mister Noble was serious about it being the signal for trouble. What's he doing now?"

"He's still got it out and he's looking straight at us." McCoy lowered the glass. "Let's light our linstocks and take aim, just in case." A moment later, both the cannons were sighted at the Eagle's mainmast.

"He's leaving!" said Baker as he gave the senior gunner a questioning look.

"Could be a false alarm, but we've our orders."

"We could send Easton down the hill to find out," suggested Baker.

"Good idea!" agreed McCoy. "Easton! You heard Baker! On the double, man!"

The barefoot and half-naked youth took off down the path at a gallop. Captain Jones and the Yorkman were already waiting on the beach for the First Officer's returning boat.

"Captain Jones! Captain Jones!" cried Easton as he ran across the hot sand.

"What is it, lad?" called back John.

"McCoy wanted me to tell ya that Mister Noble pulled out his yellow kerchief. It might be nothin', sir, but..."

"Thank you, Easton," answered Captain Jones as he focused his spyglass on the Eagle. By now, the sleek privateer had set sail for her circuit about the island.

"Can you see anything amiss?" asked Robert.

"Nothing on the Eagle," answered John as he switched his attention to David's boat, "but David still has the kerchief out."

A few minutes later, David's boat pulled within earshot of the beach.

"John! Robert!" David shouted from his boat. "There's something terribly wrong on the Eagle!"

"What did you see?" called back Robert.

"I talked with Captain Steele, but everybody else is a pirate!" David ordered the oars raised as the boat skidded onto the sand.

"Calm down, man," urged the Scotsman as he helped his first officer from the boat. "What happened out there?"

"We've got to get Dutch and ask him about one of the men at Mister Forrestal's shipyard," David said as he began walking quickly toward their hauled-down ship.

"Hold it, David!" shouted John as he grabbed the younger man by the arm. "What did you see out there?"

"There was a carpenter with orange hair working on the Silver Cloud the day I arrived from Kings Town. He was supposed to be part of the crew, but disappeared the same day I met him. That man's now a crewman on the Eagle."

"So?" asked John.

"So?" cried David. "Think it through, John! How would he get on the Eagle, unless..."

"Unless what?"

"Unless they're pirates!"

"That's absurd! What did Captain Steele say?"

"He couldn't say anything! He was their prisoner!" cried David. "I'll wager my share of the treasure he's the only Eagle crewman left aboard."

"That's ill news, if you're correct," said John as he stared at the Eagle for several moments. "Where's Van Mourik?"

"He was taking a nap next to the Cloud," offered Robert.

"That worthless piece of Holland!" John swore. "Easton!" he called to the gunner's mate following on their heels. "Go fetch Van Mourik. Tell him to report to my pavilion at once."

"Aye, aye, Cap'n!" the lad called as he galloped off toward their crippled ship.

"David," asked John as the three began to walk, "how much do you know about Van Mourik?"

"As much as you do, John. Why?"

"Just thinking," said John. As the three officers reached the shade of their canvas pavilion, Van Mourik began lumbering across the hot sand. He was a revolting human, and had acquired the disgusting habit of tying a small towel to a rope about his waist to wipe the sweat from his belly. The towel smelled worse than he did.

"You want me, Cap'n Jones?" bellowed Van Mourik as he waddled into the shade.

"Mister Noble just got back from the Eagle and tells me he saw one of the carpenters you were working with at Charles Town."

"Who dat be?" asked Van Mourik.

"He was the one with the green eyes and orange hair," said David.

"Ja!" blurted Van Mourik as he took a swipe at his dripping belly with the towel. "Dat be Henry Morgan. A right fine carver, dat boy."

"What happened to him after that first day we met," demanded David.

The big man was confused. He was a good enough ship's master, but he lacked a quick mind.

"Dutch," said David, "it was the day Mister Forrestal gave you and Morgan the gold sovereigns."

"I 'member now! Me an' Morgan go out dat night to celebrate. Met me a woman with..." Van Mourik held his cupped hands in front of his sweaty chest and winked.

"Forget that part," interrupted David. "What happened to Morgan? I don't remember seeing him again after that day."

"Went off to Savannah, he did. Tolt me the sea were callin' to him again an' he knew a Captain down der who'd sign him on." Van Mourik tilted his head slightly. "What? Didn't he tell you he was goin', Mister Noble?"

"Why would he tell David?" asked John. The Captain looked to his First Officer. "Is there something here I should know?"

"Why, Mister Noble an' Henry go way back," answered the Dutchman. "They knew each other on Tortuga."

"I didn't know him, Dutch," protested David as he glanced nervously at John and Robert. "Not before that day I met you."

"Slow down a bit," interjected John. "Why do you think David knew this wood carver?"

"Well, sure he knew da lad!" said Van Mourik with a chuckle. "Told us stuff 'bout Morgan none of us knew. Somethin' 'bout the lad killin' a crab with a mangrove root when he was just a pup on Tortuga."

"Oh that!" said David. "Just a story I heard from a seaman in Kings Town. I only guessed it was Morgan because of his looks."

"We aren't concerned about the stories, Jack," said Captain Jones. "We just want to know what happened to Morgan after Charles Town."

"I already tolt ya, Cap'n. He went to Savannah."

"Did he say who the Captain was?" asked Robert.

"No. Only that they went way back."

John pulled Robert and David off to one side. "Do you suppose the braggart told Morgan about the treasure?"

"That's got to be it," whispered David. "Dutch let it out on the dock in front of Morgan, Forrestal and me, and a half dozen others. He called me the man who knew where it was buried. Morgan must have got the rest out of him that night when he was drunk."

"There's something else," added Robert.

"Yes?" asked the Scotsman.

"If Morgan wanted to go to sea so bad, why didn't he stay and sail up with us? He already had a place on the crew."

"I think it's obvious why he didn't," answered David.

"So!" said John as he looked across the hot beach to his injured ship. "Our ship's full of cannon shot and hauled down on an island that's crawling with pirates. We've lost our carpenter, and now we find out that the only ship sent to protect us is manned by pirates. What else can go wrong?"

"I know it looks bad," said Robert. "But..."

"There is something else," said David.

"What?"

"Captain Steele asked about the digging parties."

"And I suppose you told him?"

"If I'd have suspected they were pirates..."

"Then you did!" John paced out into the hot sun and mumbled something vile toward the Eagle.

"It doesn't matter, John!" called Robert. "David didn't know when we'd be digging up the real treasure, so neither does the Eagle."

John looked back at David for confirmation.

"There is one other thing," added David.

"Damn!" yelled John. He continued staring at the Eagle. "I've met the enemy, and he is us!" He looked back to his first officer. "What is it, David? Did you tell him where the treasure's buried also?" All the men within earshot turned to stare at their Captain.

"No," answered David. "But I did tell him that when we leave, we'd take the two cannons off the hill first."

"Oh, Lord!" said John as he spread his arms in the air and cried toward the heavens. "All they have to do is watch for the cannons to come down the hill!"

"Unless," added David sheepishly, "we can fool them with Quakers."

"We don't have any Quakers," argued John.

"I know," said David, "but some of the extra men, the ones not repairing the Cloud, could build a couple. They could be carried up the hill the same night we're ready to leave."

"Well, at this point," said John, "I'm willing to try anything!"

"Shall I assign some men to the project?"

"No David, not just any men," answered John. "This would be a perfect job for Van Mourik and some of his Woodshoes. Doesn't take much talent to carve a square beam round and paint it black, does it?"

Everything had been done that could be, but an uneasiness still gnawed at Captain Jones' insides; the type that tells a man that more trouble is waiting around the next corner. He sat for nearly ten minutes staring at the words he had just penned in the log, wondering how many more obstacles would be thrown in his path. Could Captain Steele be rescued, or was the man even worth the effort? Was there another pirate ship out there somewhere? And if nothing else came along to prevent it, could the Silver Cloud be floated and escape the island without detection? The odds of the mission being completed seemed to diminish with each passing hour. Out of the corner of his eye, Captain Jones caught a shadow on the sand. Without turning, he placed his right hand on the handle of his sword.

"Yes?" Captain Jones asked.

"Cap'n Jones?" It was the cook, Barragan. "Beggin' yer pardon, sir, but I gotta talk with ya."

"What is it, Albert," asked John as he twisted in his chair. "Need some help in the galley?"

"Oh no, sir," said the Irishman with a nervous glance back at the ship. "I got all the help I need, what with not much for the crew to do." Barragan was a talented cook, but he was possessed by a double portion of nervous energy and the need to get into everyone's business. The small towel in his hands began to feel the effects as he spoke, being twisted first to the right and then to the left. "I were just tellin' Strocco 'bout it, an' he said I should come right over an'..."

"Get to your point!" Captain Jones snapped. John always felt bad when he had to cut Barragan off in the middle of one of his lengthy explanations, but if he didn't, the Irishman would go on half the day before he hit his mark.

"It's the new carpenter, sir." Barragan twisted the towel until it broke into a set of spirals.

"Jamison?"

"Yes, Cap'n." Albert hesitated, not knowing whether he should have brought the subject up.

"What about him?"

"Well, sir," Barragan began as the small towel began to rip under the strain, "I been down watchin' the plankin', an'..."

"Damn it, man, will you get to it?"

Barragan huffed through his nose as he built up the courage to go on. "He's botchin' the job, Cap'n."

Captain Jones stood from his small desk and walked toward the edge of the shade where he could get a better look at the ship. "The work looked good to me."

"But it won't hold the oakum, sir."

"Why not?"

"The spaces between the planks is too wide an' there's no taper to 'em." Barragan took a step closer to his Captain and looked about for eavesdroppers. "I may be wrong 'bout him, sir, but it's almost like he's doin' it on purpose."

"That's a serious accusation."

"I know, Cap'n, but I can't figure it no other way." The cook stopped twisting his towel and stood a little straighter. "I asked him about it an' he got downright angry that I'd question his work." Barragan gave the ship another quick glance. "I just came from there, sir, an' it's 'xactly like I say!"

"Let's go take a look." Captain Jones took off at a fast march, leaving the cook several paces behind. "If what you say is true, then we're in deeper trouble than I thought. Especially if they've used all our spare lumber."

"There's enough lumber to redo the job, sir, but with the water supply like it is..."

"You needn't remind me of the water supply, Albert," said John as the cook caught up with him and matched strides. "I'm fully aware of our dilemma." As they approached the crippled ship, Barragan whispered to his Captain.

Cap'n Jones, don't get me in trouble with the carpenters. Okay?"

"It doesn't much matter what they think of you, Albert," John said as he stopped abruptly, with Barragan running headlong into his shoulder. "If the Silver Cloud isn't seaworthy, then we sink, hurt feelings or not!"

"When ya put it that way, sir, I guess..."

The two were met by Jamison, the new ship's carpenter. He had been lounging in the shade of the bow with several of the others, but jumped up and ran across the sand to meet his Captain.

"Good day, Captain Jones!" Jamison said with a knuckle to his forelock. "Can I be of service?"

"No, Jamison," answered the Captain. "You and the others finish your rest. I just want to take a look at your work."

"Aye, Captain, but if there's anything you need, give me a call."

"I will," said Captain Jones as he followed Barragan aft. It was a short climb up the scaffolding to the patch.

"Here, sir, take a look at how they done these spaces."

It was exactly as Barragan had described. The spaces were at least a half-inch wide, twice what they should be. Barragan pulled a twist of oakum from his pocket and pushed it between the planks.

"See there?" he said as the fibers pushed all the way through and into the space beyond.

"Damn!" Jones swore, as he ran his finger along one of the seams. The edges of the plank were neatly rounded and sanded smooth, but as nice as they felt, they were still wrong--just as Barragan had reported. "What will it take to fix it?"

"It'll make Jamison angry, sir, but he's either gotta lay extra planks inside, over each seam, or do the whole job over again. There's just no other way if ya want her to hold out the sea."

"Is there anybody else who can take over your cooking duties till we get off this island?"

"My cooking duties?" Barragan gave his Captain a long look. "You want me to take over the Cloud's repairs, don't ya?"

"Can you do it, like you did in Charles Town?"

"Aye, Cap'n."

"And if I give you all the men you need, how long until we can refloat her?"

Barragan studied the side of the ship carefully. "I'd have to pull these new planks off, back down to the ribs and new planks shaved to fit." Barragan looked forward to the second hole, the one above the waterline.

"Don't worry about that one, Albert!" said John as he pointed at the hull next to them. "Just this one! How long before we could float her?"

"Give me enough men to work around the clock, sir," Barragan answered slowly, "an' she'll be ready to float tomorrow night."

"A lot depends on this, Albert, so be absolutely sure before you make me that promise."

"She'll be ready, Cap'n."

As Captain Jones and Barragan climbed about the scaffolding to survey the needed repairs to the Cloud, one of the young gunner's mates was searching about camp for his Captain. Finally in desperation, the lad stood at the Captain's pavilion and yelled.

"Captain Jones!"

"Over here!" answered the Scotsman from atop the work platform. "What's the matter, lad?"

It was Easton again, and as he ran toward the ship, he was pointing toward the north.

"There's another privateer holding several leagues off the north coast, sir!"

"Oh hell!" the Scott cursed as he and Barragan scrambled upward over the Cloud's planking and onto the tilted deck.

"Albert," said Captain Jones. "See if you can make it across to the binnacle for my other spyglass."

"Aye, aye, Cap'n," answered the cook as he slid across the tilted deck. He was back in a minute with the device. Captain Jones studied the intruder for several moments as she began a jibe to come westward along the reef.

"Who is she, Cap'n?"

"I can't make out her name yet, but she's a Virginia privateer all right. She's a little older than the Eagle, but equal in sail and firepower. And except for her red sails..." Captain Jones fell silent as the stern came into view.

"What is it, Cap'n?"

"Have you ever heard of the Remora?"

"Once or twice in Kings Town," answered Barragan. "If you hadn't come along when you did, me an' Etinger were thinkin' of signin' articles with her."

John lowered the glass and gave the cook a long look. "Did David Noble or his father ever mention the Remora?"

"David's father was the one, sir. He was sayin' somethin' 'bout expectin' her in port soon an' not wantin' to give you as much flour an' salted beef as he finally did."

"Interesting," said John as he continued to study the Remora. "I wonder..."

The treasure of Dead Man's Chest had begun to live more in the world of legends and myths than in the world of reality. Each time the story had been served up, the teller would add another helping of gold and an extra spoon of blood and treachery, until even the oldest of seamen began to doubt its veracity. It was only the ballad that maintained the accuracy of the tale. And what a tale it was. There was hardly a man on the seven seas who hadn't sung its words as he hauled on the sheets, buntlines and halyards. And every jack man of them wondered after the treasure, hoping to somehow win a share of it. As each year passed, the chances of it ever being dug up diminished. But today, the Fourth of June 1775, Captain John Paul Jones led the digging party that would unearth the legend.

The repairs to the Silver Cloud had gone just as Barragan had predicted. The faulty planking was removed and replaced with wider pieces, and this time with the proper fit and taper. The shrill ring of mallets against hawsing irons that rammed the oakum between the planks testified to everyone on and about Dead Man's Chest that the Silver Cloud was nearly ready to float. Since it's arrival two days before, the second pirate ship had maintained a position about the island exactly opposite from the Eagle, a tactic that puzzled Captain Jones and his other officers.

After the midday meal, Captain Jones raised his glass in a toast to the Silver Cloud and her successful launching.

"Then she's ready?" asked Robert.

"Tonight," answered John. "There's a lot to do this afternoon if we're to be underway before sunrise."

John laid an unsealed letter on the table before the others. "This was left in my logbook."

"What is it?" asked Robert.

"It's our rendezvous instructions. We're to meet the second Silver Cloud at Tortuga, and by my calculations, there won't be enough time to stop at Spyglass."

"But the crew's counting on it," said David. "It was to be their bonus."

"I know that," answered John, "but there simply isn't enough time, and the additional risk is more than I'm willing to take."

"Couldn't we delay at Spyglass and make the second rendezvous?" asked David. "That way, we..."

"Please, please," said John, holding up his hands to quiet the young Jamaican's protests. "I've considered several options, and it simply won't work. The letter says that after Tortuga there may not be another rendezvous for several weeks."

"Do you believe that?" asked Robert. "Isn't it possible Jefferson put that in the letter just in case it fell into the wrong hands?"

"I have to believe it until I receive something which makes me believe otherwise. We have a time limitation. For all we know, the Colonies may have already begun fighting the British."

"Then can we at least tell the crew that we'll return to Spyglass for the other treasure, after we deliver the cannons?"

"I could," answered John, "but you know as well as I that if the war has begun, this ship won't be available for our use. And neither will any other ship which might serve against the British."

"Then there's no use arguing about it!" said David.

"I'm sorry, David, but that's just the way it is. Our immediate goal is to load the treasure and get the Cloud away from this accursed island without detection." He paused as he scanned a list of duties he had penned on the back of the rendezvous letter. "We'll be splitting the crew in thirds, with one group staying here at Rip Rap to make preparations to float the ship. The other two groups will climb the hill to dig up the treasure; with half the men at the shovels while the rest spread out with muskets."

"What about Ben?" asked Robert. "He deserves to see it dug up."

"You're right, of course," answered John as he turned about to the doctor. "Is Ben well enough to go with us?"

"I'll assign four of the men to carry his bed," answered Adam.

"Then let's be about it," ordered John with a broad smile.

Within half an hour, forty-five men stood amongst the waist-high brush and cactus looking at a twenty-five foot high Manchaneel tree. When last seen by Robert and his wife, the tree was a mere sapling, three feet tall and no thicker than a man's wrist. Twenty years and the torment of hundreds of storms had taken their toll on the once-straight tree. Its trunk was now nearly two feet thick and resembled a twisted collection of slimy sea creatures, oozing their caustic sap downward into the earth to mingle with the treasure.

"That's the one," whispered one of the sailors. "That's the one what burned me eyes the other day." But only the men to either side of the sailor heard him, for every other man's attention was focused on the Scotsman and the other officers.

"Men!" called Captain Jones to quiet their mumbling. "You're about to unearth the largest treasure ever buried in one location. It's going to be difficult work, but I can assure you that it'll be worth every drop of sweat and every ounce of blood it demands. The weapons this treasure will purchase may be the one thing which frees the Colonies and your loved ones from the death grip Mother England holds upon them."

"Robert, would you indicate the perimeter of the treasure?"

"That Manchaneel tree," Robert began while pointing at the aged guardian, "is the center of the treasure. We need to clear the brush and dig our hole for a distance of five paces in all directions from its trunk. Once all the gold is exposed, you'll switch places with the men with muskets and they'll carry it down the hill."

"Let the work begin!" commanded Captain Jones.

"Right!" cried the Bosun. "You 'eard the Captain! Lay yer backs to it, lads!" A cheer rose from the seamen as they attacked the brush. Within ten minutes, the large tree stood naked in the center of a thirty-foot circle of bare red dirt.

"Sir?" It was the Bosun. "Do you want we should cut down the tree?"

"Only if we have to," answered Captain Jones with a look to Robert. "Somehow I don't feel it would be fair to kill the old soldier, especially after guarding our treasure for all these years. I'm sure it'll have to lose a few of its roots, but let's go easy on it for now."

When Robert and his three conspirators had buried the treasure, they laid a cubit of earth atop it. Twenty years of decaying vegetation had added another foot of rich soil over the uppermost containers. At the end of the predicted two hours, all the treasure lay exposed to the late afternoon sun. Here and there, where a workman had torn a canvas bag, fifty and seventy pound gold ingots reflected the sunlight as brightly as the day they were cast by the Spaniards in the smelters near the Aztec mines.

"I had no idea there was so much, Robert," said John as he drank in the spectacle before them. "I can understand why it took you five days to put it here."

"Funny," chuckled Robert, "how things worked out, after all these years."

"Fate is a fickle mistress," mused John. "If I could entice her to insure the success of this mission, I'd be willing to offer most anything she wanted."

"Careful," cautioned Robert. "She may be fickle, but she has an insatiable appetite for human pain. You may not be able to bare the price she might require of you."

While Robert spoke his words of warning, two of the seamen placed a large chest before him and the other officers. Ben Gunn brightened as he pushed himself up into a sitting position on his stretcher. He gazed awe-struck at the chest before them.

"Master Ormerod!" cried Ben. "That's the other chest o' jewels John Flint raved about the day we escaped from Savannah!" The large iron lock that had protected the chest's contents from the dirt fell away at Ben's touch. As he twisted its last rusted fragments from the hasp, David gave the lid a tug.

"Oh, my God!" gasped John as he and the others looked upon the chest of cut and uncut jewels.

"This is all extra, Master Ormerod!" cried Ben as he reached deep within the jewels as a child will run his fingers through a bag beans.

"What are you saying, Ben?" asked John. "What do you mean that these are extra?"

"He's right, John," said Robert as he looked down upon the jewels. "I had no idea what was inside this chest until now." He looked back up at John. "This is all extra...above the million and a half we figured."

The sun was now two hours above the western horizon, a perfect angle for it's rays to set the jewels afire in an aurora of radiant splendor. There were diamonds the size of walnuts and rubies that would choke a cow. Several leather pouches of black and white pearls lay about the edges of the open chest. At its center, nearly hidden by the free stones, was a circle of gold discs, each standing upright.

"It's the King's crown!" whispered Ben in reverence as he pulled the object from the chest and looked up at Robert for recognition. "It's just like the one on Spyglass I told you about."

"There's another one like this?" asked John with a look to Robert.

"There is," answered Ben as he raised the crown in the air for all to see. After a moment, he lowered it slowly over his head. "But that other one's nothin' as big as this one."

The crown was oval in shape, with the head band nearly a quarter inch thick in solid gold. Atop the two-inch band were alternating crosses and sun-shaped discs, eight in all, and each set with a cluster of rubies and emeralds. It was so large that it dropped past Ben's ears and rested on his shoulders.

"Ha!" laughed Robert, "You're a royal sight, indeed!" Ben blushed and set to scratching several imaginary lice as he returned the crown to the chest. As Ben continued to caress the jewels, one of the seamen handed Ben a scrap of paper. The old man took it and carefully unfolded it, as the entire crew of diggers watched.

"What have you there?" asked John.

"It's..." answered the old man as he began to shake. "Oh lordy! It's a death curse!"

"A death curse?" asked John as he stepped close to read the words.

"Aye!" cried the old man as he dropped the note and backed several feet away. John picked up the parchment and read out loud.

"Beware the fires of Hell. He who first touches this treasure shall die within a fortnight and burn forever in the Lake of Fire."

"I'll never live to see America!" cried the old man as he continued to hobble away from John and the note.

"Calm down, old friend," said Robert as he took the note. "You're not going to die."

"But it's a death curse, Master Ormerod, an' it's on me!"

"It's only words, Ben. There's no power in words written on a scrap of paper, except for what you allow it to have."

"That's easy fer you to say, 'cause they aren't on you!"

"But I can remove them," said Robert as he tore the paper in eight pieces and threw it into the wind, "because, Ben, I wrote them twenty years ago."

Ben's mouth was frozen in a gasp of terror as he watched his death sentence flutter away in the stiff breeze that whipped up and over the ridge line.

"The curse is gone, Ben," laughed Robert. "I'm afraid I'll be stuck with you for at least another decade." At first it was only one man, but within seconds, the entire crew was laughing at the old maroon.

"Enough of this!" said John as he turned to the diggers. "I want each of you to lay down his shovel and go find your partner and take his rifle. We've a treasure to move and we're running out of daylight.

Shortly after sunset, a stream of treasure-laden seamen begun to flow down the easy slope from the still-standing Manchaneel tree toward Rip Rap Beach, resembling a hive of leaf-cutter ants returning with their harvest. By keeping close to one another, there was no need for the telltale lanthorns that would alert the Eagle and Remora that the treasure was finally moving.

It became quickly apparent to all but a few of the men that the cannon attack on the Cloud had actually worked to their advantage. With the great ship hauled down on the dry sand, it would cut the loading time to a fraction of what it would have been had the ship remained at anchor outside the reef.

By midnight, the entire treasure was secured in the hold under the tobacco and sugar recently purchased at San Juan.

"Jack," asked Captain Jones of the chubby Hollander. "Is everything ready?"

"Ja," answered the Dutchman as he wiped himself dry with the little towel. "Another half hour at most, Captain Jones, an' we'll have da tide fer easin' her down into the water."

"And the cannons?"

"De ver aboard just before der treasure," answered Van Mourik, an' them two Quakers is in der place on the cliff, ya?"

"Good!" said John as he looked to the lanthorns on the cliff.

As the tide lifted the twenty-gun frigate from the white sands of Rip Rap Beach, thirty-six of the crew's strongest oarsmen put their backs to the task of pulling her hull clear of the shore. At Captain Jones' order, Van Mourik's crew began to let out on their blocks and tackle, being careful to keep the ship from righting itself too quickly. An accidental slip during this delicate operation would not only allow the massive hull to bury its keel in the sandy bottom, but the whipping action could actually break one or more of the masts. A ship aground at high tide is a ship lost forever.

Before the tide had begun to drop again, and before the full moon had come up to expose their activities, the great ship was pulled beyond the reef and northward, away from the anchored Eagle.

"Bosun!" shouted the young Jamaican from his station at the quarterdeck. "Hail the boats in!"

"Make sure those men are sent below for a good rest," added John, "and a double ration of water, Mister Noble!"

"Aye, aye, Captain," the youth answered enthusiastically. David's joy was shared by the entire crew. They were finally back at sea, and the treasure was safe in their lazarette.

Pirates have never been a very disciplined lot, especially when it comes to staying awake on watch. And so it was that the Silver Cloud was able to slip undetected past the Eagle and into the open sea. Henry Morgan was the first to notice when he was awakened by a hungry gull landing next to him in the rigging.

"Cap'n Smoot!" he yelled as he slid a buntline onto the deck below. The sun had not yet broken the eastern horizon, but there was plenty of dawn light in the sky to silhouette Dead Man's Chest and the vacant white sands of Rip Rap Beach.

"They're gone, Govn'r! The Cloud's got away, an' the Remora with her!"

"Damn yer eyes, Morgan!" bellowed Smoot as he crashed his way half-naked along the companionway and up the ladder to the main deck. "You knew they were ready to sail! You heard the mallets!"

"But it were dark, Govn'r, an' look!" cried Morgan as he pointed. "You tolt me to keep a weather eye fer 'em to move them two cannons off the hill, and look! They're still there!"

"Dark, my rear!" growled the old pirate as he pulled on his shirt and strained his eyes to locate his fleeing prize. Several leagues to the west floated the Silver Cloud under full sail, with the red sails of the Remora silhouetted against her. "You were sleepin' on watch!"

"No I weren't, Govn'r," the lad lied with a hurt to his voice. "They was just too sneaky for us." Morgan thought hard. "They must'a been floatin' her off the beach at the same time I were watchin' that line o' torches below the cliff."

"An'' I don't suppose you noticed them movin' their camp fires to the east sides of their tents," spat Smoot as he pointed.

"Moved their...? Why would they do that?"

"To throw the Cloud into darkness, that's why! Maybe I should'a let you skipper the Walrus after all." Smoot looked about toward the far end of the larger island. "Which reminds me; where the hell's the Walrus? If the Cloud can be repaired in three days, then so can the Walrus!"

"But they took a hit to their mizzen, Govn'r, not countin' all them shot holes to her hull an' the fire in her focs'l." Morgan kept his distance from his irate Captain as he continued to defend Pritchard. "And they'd also hafta pick up their men from off the Chest 'afore they could begin to take up the chase anyway, so there's that besides."

Smoot didn't hear the lad's last excuse, for out of the corner of his eye he caught sight of something astern. The first rays of the sun streaked across the glassy sea to splash against the sails of a large American clipper just emerging from behind the Chest. Morgan spotted her also.

"There she is, Govn'r! Right on time, just like I said she'd be!"

"And it's a good thing for you she is," the older man huffed, as if it were really Morgan's fault.

"Make ready to set sail, Henry!"

The lad began barking orders to the waking crew, his favorite pastime. "Think we'll be able to catch her before sunset, Govn'r?"

"Of course we will, but it really doesn't matter."

The lad paused from his First Mate duties and looked back at his Captain. "Pardon?"

"You forget, Henry, that I've still got a man aboard the Silver Cloud."

"Sail Ho!" came a cry from somewhere in the Silver Cloud's upper rigging. "Two more sails on the stern at five leagues!"

"Damn them!" whispered John.

"Well," said David, "at least we got back to sea without a fight."

"Aye," agreed John as he studied the Remora through his glass. "But I expect they'll be nipping at our heels before the day's out."

With every inch of sail the frigate could hoist, the Silver Cloud gained valuable distance between herself and all but the Remora, which had watched her midnight escape and dogged her at every inch of headway. But by mid-morning, the wind had shifted to larboard, giving the Eagle, with her stay sails, and the Walrus, with her greater length, the advantage. By noon, it was clear they were closing the gap. As Captain Jones paced nervously about the quarterdeck, he noticed a man in shirtsleeves standing at the aft companionway, shading his eyes against the late morning sun.

"What is it, Adam? You look like a bear just ate your best fowling dog."

"May I speak with you alone for a moment, sir?" the doctor whispered. Doctor McKenzie was by nature a soft-spoken man, having been born to an aristocratic southern family and trained at the School of Surgeons in Boston. John sensed something was very wrong and tried to assure the young man.

"There's nothing Mister Ormerod and my First Oofficer can't hear, Adam. What's troubling you?"

"Something's wrong with those men from the boats."

"Go on."

"Well, at first I thought it was just the heat. But they've not gotten any better, no matter how much they rest." McKenzie wiped the sweat from his face with a sleeve. "It could just be a coincidence, sir, but it's like they all caught falling sickness at the same time."

"How many of them are affected?" asked Robert.

"All of them," answered the surgeon slowly. "Every last one."

"Is anybody else sick?" asked Captain Jones.

"A few, sir; maybe half a dozen at most." McKenzie was ashamed that he couldn't be more certain what was happening. "It might be the remitting fever, Captain, but then..."

"What do your books say?" asked Robert as he stepped close with David.

"That's what's so confusing, Mister Ormerod. It's a lot like the fever, but there's too much belly pain."

"Did they come aboard sick," asked David, "or did it start after they got below to rest?"

"They seemed fine when they came aboard, sir, except for being tired and thirsty."

"Find out what you can, Adam, and get back to me," said John." The surgeon turned to leave.

"And I'll authorize a double ration of water for each man," said John, "if you need it. If it's the remitting fever, they'll need a lot more than normal."

"The water!" shouted McKenzie as he spun about. "It has to be the water!"

"Damn!" John cursed loudly, bringing a chill to all within earshot. "David, go with the Doctor and inspect the casks." John turned to the Bosun. "Bosun! Pipe the crew to quarters!"

Within three minutes, nearly a hundred men stood about the deck shading their eyes as they waited for their Captain's message.

"Pipe down there!" barked the Bosun. "Cap'n Jones has some words for ya!"

"I assume you all know by now that a large portion of the crew is sick," began Captain Jones. "Doctor McKenzie suspects that the water supply has been tampered with."

A murmur ran across the deck and up the mizzenmast to one of the top men. "We must have a traitor aboard, Captain Jones!" the man called down.

"We don't know that for sure!" called back Captain Jones. "Doctor McKenzie will be reporting back to me as soon as he inspects the casks. Until we know for sure, I don't want you to drink any water."

"What about water taken from the main supply before we sailed?" whispered Robert. "If someone poisoned the main casks this morning, the topside water shouldn't be contaminated yet."

"You might be right," answered John. He turned back to the assembled crew. "Master Ormerod has suggested that there may be a supply of good water aboard. If any of you drew water prior to our sailing this morning, I want it turned over to Dr. McKenzie for testing." John turned to Captain Van Mourik. "Take charge, Jack, and dismiss the men. If you need me for anything, I'll be in the hold with the Doctor. I want to see those water casks."

A few minutes later, John found David and the Doctor and his two assistants atop one of the massive casks. "Have you found anything?" John's voice echoed through the hold.

"We've a traitor all right!" called back the Doctor. "And he's done a thorough job of it."

"What do you mean?"

"Look at this." Adam threw a moist handful of freshly cut wood shavings to the deck beside his Captain. "Our saboteur has drilled a hole in the top of every cask. I won't know for sure until I test each of them, but I believe it's safe to say that they're all poisoned."

"Damn him!" John turned and stared aft between the casks as he pondered their situation. "I've ordered all hands to turn over their personal water supplies to you. Is there a way to test it?"

"Once I know what he used, yes," answered Adam as he scraped together a small sample of white powder and placed it in a folded piece of paper. "It's going to take me a while, but with any luck, I have an antidote in my supplies."

By noon, fully half the crew had been stricken with stomach cramps and burning throats. Activity aboard the Cloud had been reduced to the bare minimum in order to reduce the need for water.

"Excuse me," said Doctor McKenzie as he pushed into the Master's cabin. John looked up from his meal.

"It's strychnine," reported Adam.

"Is there an antidote?"

"I looked it up in my medical books and it calls for emptying the stomach, and then drinking charcoal and permanganate of potassium..."

"I don't need to know all the details, Adam," said John impatiently. "Do you have what you need to make them well?" Adam didn't answer. "Well?"

"The saboteur knew exactly what he was doing, Captain."

"Which means?"

"He knew it would take a lot of water to save these men's lives, and that we would have to find a fresh water supply."

"How much good water do we have?" asked John.

"Fifty, maybe sixty gallons at most, sir," said Adam shaking his head. "That's only going to last through tomorrow."

"I was afraid of that," answered John thoughtfully as he unrolled a chart of the Caribbean. "Would you do me a favor and ask David and Robert to join us? We've several important decisions to make."

"As you please, sir," the doctor answered. "But might I have a half hour to check something first?"

"A half hour?"

"I just remembered something from school about rat poison. That should give me enough time to test my theory on a couple of the sick men."

At fourteen hundred hours, Doctor McKenzie was followed into the Master's cabin by David and the New Yorker.

"Have a seat, gentlemen," said Captain Jones as he gave the doctor an inquiring look. "Well, Adam, did your theory prove well?"

"Yes it did, sir. It's a crude poison, just as I suspected. My theory was that sugar-based alcohol might counteract its effects, or at least give some relief."

"And?"

"I was right!"

"Then we aren't going to lose any men?"

"Not a man, provided we can get to that supply of fresh water before noon tomorrow." The Doctor pulled a note from his pocket. "But we did lose two pigs and a half dozen chickens."

"Hmmm," said John as he thought. "Do you think the poison had time to get into the animal's flesh?"

"Probably not, but why do you ask?"

"Well, since the cook has to slaughter three or four pigs every day anyway, we haven't really lost anything."

"We can't eat them," said David in an apologetic tone.

"Oh? And why not?"

"Because I had them thrown over the side, that's why."

"You what?" roared Captain Jones as he sprang to his feet.

"They were dead, sir. I figured they weren't worth eating, and we couldn't have them on deck rotting.

"You fool!" yelled John as he turned and looked aft into the ship's wake. "Don't you realize what you've done?"

"It's water we're short of," argued David, "not food."

John spun on the younger man. "You've just told Joshua Smoot and those other two ships that their plan has worked!"

"What?" asked the young Jamaican.

"He's right, David," added Robert. "You gave the best possible signal to Smoot and the others that he's succeeded in poisoning our water."

"Is there anything we can do about the animals?" asked David in the hope that maybe the ship could go back and find the carcasses.

"No! It's too late to go back," answered John angrily. "It's more important that the crew gets fresh water than worrying whether the pirates know about our dilemma." John stared into the wake for a minute before turning about.

"John," began Robert, "you know my position on the cannons, so I may as well not mince words. If the pirates can force us to pull close to a river mouth, then they'll try to sink us in the shallows where they can retrieve the treasure at their leisure. I say the loss of life is part of the price the Colonies must pay for the cannons and the freedom they will bring."

"That's no choice!" cried the Doctor. "That's murder! I say to hell with your cannons! Sink or float, without a new supply of water, and a lot of it, half the crew will be dead by noon tomorrow!"

"But you said alcohol will counteract..."

"Aye, Captain, but not without several gallons of fresh water per man! We've no choice but to find a river!"

Before Robert could answer the doctor's objection, there was a knock at the door.

"Come!" shouted Captain Jones.

One of the Bosun's mates stepped through the door and stood at attention. Several others remained in the passageway, one of them wearing chains.

"We caught him, sir, and it's just like you told us. Smoot put him aboard in Charles Town, and he's the same one who cut our anchor chain."

"How'd you find him?"

"We looked for the water. It was in his sea chest, under a false bottom. Wouldn't 'a found it but for the wetness around the chest. We also found this." The man held up a leather pouch with white powder smudged along its top edge.

"I'll take that," said the doctor.

"Who is he?" asked Captain Jones.

The large Bosun's mate pulled the door open and grabbed the prisoner by his chains. "It's the carpenter's mate, sir. The one who took over the ship repairs when Sanders was killed the other night."

Jamison was pushed to the center of the cabin where he scanned the officers defiantly. He had been beaten badly, but none of the officers objected, not even the doctor.

"Did you ask him about the Remora?" asked Captain Jones.

"We did, but he refuses to talk."

"Well..." began Captain Jones, "perhaps a few days in irons up in the hot sun will loosen his lips. Chain him to the main mast and give him all the water he needs."

"But, Captain Jones..." protested McKenzie.

"We have six casks in the hold, Adam. Surely we can afford a few gallons for our prisoner."

Jamison's mouth opened and a weak cry came forth. It sounded more animal than human.

"Do you want to say something, Jamison?" asked Captain Jones as he bent and put his ear near the man's mouth.

"I've seen the Remora workin' around Jamaica and Cuba, takin' their share of ships."

"Then they are pirates!" said John as he stood.

"Aye, sir, as best as I know. But they're not workin' with Captain Smoot."

"You know that for sure?" John asked.

"Aye. Smoot's never worked with the Remora."

"And what about Captain Steele?" asked David. "What's Smoot planning to do with him?"

"He couldn't know that," offered Robert in the man's defense. "He hasn't had any contact with Smoot since before Charles Town."

"Robert's right," said John as he looked to the Bosun. "Take him below and lock him up."

"And the water, sir?"

"All he wants from the main casks," John answered as he glared at the traitor. "How's the Bible put it? An eye for an eye?" John watched his cabin door as the traitor's cries died away to the bowels of the ship. "Adam, when Jamison finally begs for the poisoned water, give him one ration of our good water."

"But why?" protested Robert. "He intended that we drink the bad water!"

"It's because we're better than he is, Robert." John walked to his table and looked at the chart again. "I'd like to return to our former conversation, gentlemen. Are there any more suggestions?" Doctor McKenzie was the first to respond.

"We don't have the luxury of a choice," demanded Adam with an angry look at the Yorkman. "We have to trade the treasure for our lives."

"We can't give up the treasure!" shouted Robert. "Even if we did, they'd kill us afterward they got it!"

"How do you figure?" asked McKenzie. "What possible advantage would there be in harming us after they've achieved their aim?"

"You really don't understand pirates, do you, Adam?"

"All I understand, Mister Ormerod, is that these men's lives are our most immediate concern. If we don't get fresh water, and very quickly, most of the crew could be dead from thirst in two days! And the rest'll be so weak they won't be able to fight off the lightest attack. Smoot's going to get the treasure either way. It's our choice whether we come through it alive or dead!"

"Horse feathers!" shouted Robert. "They've no choice but to kill us! They know that as soon as we turn over the treasure to them that we'll get the water we need, and then we'll come after them!"

"Then what do you suggest, Robert?" asked John.

"There must be a river with a deep anchorage nearby." Robert stepped to the table and turned the map about.

"But if we anchor, we're sitting ducks!" cried John. "Why in the world would we do that?"

"Because we have no choice!" answered Robert as John began to protest again. "Hear me out, John. Smoot is too smart to sink us in deep water where the treasure would be lost forever, but the moment we reach the shallows, as the good Doctor suggests, he'll put us on the bottom and kill every last one of us. Our only refuge lies in deep water."

"But why not drive the Silver Cloud into a river?" asked Adam. "We could throw buckets over the side and have all the water we need while the gunners hold off the Walrus."

"Because it doesn't matter to the pirates if we're sunk in a river or at a shallow anchorage!" Robert studied the map as John walked to the window and looked aft at the three ships that trailed the Silver Cloud. "Here!" shouted Robert as he pointed. "Pilsbury Sound!" John returned to the table. "It'll still be very risky, but the water here is deep! We can make a series of slow passes to load and offload the boats, and still have the ability to fight!"

"I like it," said John as he turned to his First Officer. "David, set a course for Pillsbury Sound." John turned back to the Doctor. "Adam, your job will be to distribute the uncontaminated water in the most beneficial manner until we get a fresh supply."

"Thank you, Captain Jones," answered the doctor as he looked to Robert. "Robert, permit me to apologize for my harsh words. I don't really believe you have no concern..."

"Apology accepted," said Robert. "The treasure is my primary concern, but a healthy crew is also important."

"How's Ben doing, Robert?" asked John.

"So, so, John. Adam did what he could for the burns, but Ben's age is working against him."

"He didn't drink any of the poisoned water, did he?"

"Fortunately not," answered Adam. "But I'm afraid that with the infection and the lack of water, he may not survive."

"Oh, Lord," said John as he turned to Robert. "You and he are so close."

"He's like a father to me, John." Robert waited until David and the doctor had left, and then turned back to John.

"When the Colonies finally go into battle against the British, thousands of men will die quiet, obscure deaths. If I should lose Ben Gunn to his burns, his will be one of those quiet deaths. Never-the-less, I'll consider his loss one of the most courageous of all."

"Aye," agreed John as he picked up his glass and pitcher of water. "I think I'll pay Ben a visit."

CHAPTER 13

By the time the course change had been passed to the helm, John reached Ben Gunn's cabin with the water. He tapped gently at the half-opened door. There was no answer, so John pushed it open with his backside and stepped inside.

"Ben?"

"Come in, Cap'n Jones," said the elderly man just above a whisper. "Maybe you'll give me a straight answer."

"A straight answer?"

"Aye," said the old man as he pushed himself up onto an elbow. "Van Mourik treated me like I was daft when I asked him about the ship's change of course."

"He didn't want to worry you," answered John. "And I'm surprised you could feel it. We only changed course ten degrees."

"Meanin' no disrespect, sir, but I've been at sea more years than you been suckin' the good Lord's air." Ben gripped the rail of the bunk and swung his legs over the side with a groan. "Can't ya feel a course change yet?"

"Yes, I can," answered John as he poured the old sailor a tin cup of water. "That's what I wanted to speak to you about." John pulled a stool close to the bunk and handed the old man the cup. "We've had a meeting, and decided our only option is to make for a river mouth on Saint John where we can refill our water casks."

"Which river were ya lookin' to use, sir?"

"From my charts, it looks like Pillsbury Sound is the best choice."

"Van Mourik told me about the poison," said Ben as he drank the cup empty and gave his Captain a questioning look.

"You look perplexed. What's bothering you?"

"Well, not to suggest you don't know what yer doin', sir, but won't we be sittin' ducks?"

"Yes we will, but we've no choice. It's either Saint John for water, or we lose everything."

"But we do have a choice, Cap'n." Ben lowered his feet to the floor as he pushed himself upright. "If you'll help me to yer cabin, there's something you need to see."

A few minutes later, Ben sat in one of the padded chairs in the master's cabin. The chart of the Antilles was still on the table. Taking a set of dividers in his hand, he pointed to a river near the eastern tip of one of the islands.

"There," said Ben, looking up at theCaptain. "There's your choice."

"I don't follow you, Ben."

"And neither will the Walrus or the Eagle," said the old man with a wink. "The map doesn't show it, but about a quarter mile up river, there's a deep fresh water lagoon 'bout five hundred feet across."

"But we'll be trapped, Ben. We won't be able to get back to the open sea."

"If the tide's right, we will."

"Hold it, Ben." John took a closer look at the chart. Ben's island was several leagues more distant than Saint John. "I've already been through this discussion with the other officers. Why would you say this river's a better choice when it's no different than putting in at Saint John?"

"Because it is." Ben scratched his head and gave his Captain a wry smile.

"You're still not making any sense," said John as he cast an uneasy glance at the old man. "Are you sure you're feeling all right?"

"There's nothin' wrong with me, Cap'n, an' it makes all the sense in the world...fer them what knows the secret, that is. That's why they call it Deception Lagoon."

As Ben explained his plan, the block and tackle was being lowered into the hold to raise the first water cask. While David and Jack Van Mourik emptied the contaminated water over the side, Doctor McKenzie began rationing the few gallons of good water that remained.

"So you figure the tide's our only real concern?" John asked Ben as the doctor paused at the open door.

"Aye, an a prayer to the good Lord that our friends on the Walrus don't know 'bout it."

"Excuse me, sir," said Doctor McKenzie as he eased the door open, "I have some bad news."

"Oh?"

"We've lost one man, and two others are doing very bad." The Doctor began to back out into the companionway when he noticed Ben sitting at the table. "Is that you, Mister Gunn?"

"Aye, 'tis me, sir," said Ben as he twisted in his chair.

"I didn't expect to see you up and about this quickly."

"Ben was just showing me something very interesting on the chart," said John. "He assures me that if we bypass Saint John by about twelve hours, we can get fresh water and escape the pirates without the risk we'll take at Pillsbury Sound."

"Twelve hours?" Adam slammed the door closed and strode to the table. "Pardon my language, sir, but that's too damned long!" He stared at John for a long moment. "I just told you we've lost one man! The other two could make it to Pilsbury Sound, but no more!"

"I've made my decision!"

"Then I'm making mine!"

"And what is that supposed to mean?"

"It means, Captain Jones, that I'm making an official protest of your conduct to our employers when we reach Charles Town! You asked if we'd lose any men, and I assured you we wouldn't. But that was based upon your assurance that we'd sail directly for Pilsbury Sound! Every man that dies from now on will be on your head!"

"Hold your tongue, Mister McKenzie!" barked John at the insubordinate officer. "I believe you have an assignment topside. If any of the men die, I agree with Robert. It's a small price the Colonies must pay for liberty."

Doctor McKenzie stood eye to eye with John, too angry to speak. He wanted to swear at this heartless man, but restrained himself and moved for the door. As he pulled it open, he hesitated.

"Was there something else?" asked John with an icy stare.

"If it comes to it, Captain, which of the officers die first?"

"What?" asked John.

"You heard me, and you know exactly what I'm getting at."

"So that there's no question," hissed John, "why don't you tell me...exactly what you're getting at!"

"Obviously you and I get enough water to live, because we're important!" He pushed the door closed and walked toward the far end of the table, next to Ben. "But what about Mister Ormerod and your young Jamaican friend? If it's only the mission that matters, then I don't see why we need those two any longer." Adam placed his hands on the old man's shoulders. "And what about our old friend here? Is he expendable also, or does he get to live until he shows you where his silver's hidden on Spyglass?"

John couldn't answer. As painful as his words were, the doctor was correct. After several moments, John walked to the door. As he pulled it open, he drew his sword.

"Unless you intend to lead a mutiny against me, Mister McKenzie, I would appreciate you leaving my quarters this instant."

"I'll leave, sir, but I don't understand how you can sleep at night."

"That's my problem, not yours!" Adam walked to the door and stopped. "Was there something else?" asked John. As the doctor opened his mouth to speak, Ben Gunn began shouting.

"Salvation!" John and Adam turned as the old maroon struggled up from his chair and hobbled toward the larboard windows. "The Lord's delivered us from death!" The two were confused as they looked out the cabin windows where the old man was pointing.

"What is it, Ben?" asked John. "What do you see?"

"Look there! On our windward bow!" The old man pointed. "My prayers have been answered!"

John took a step toward the old man when the cabin door burst open. David was out of breath and clearly distressed. John turned.

"What is it?" demanded John."

"You didn't see it yet!?" asked David.

"It's the Lord!" cried Ben again. "He's sent us His salvation!"

"We've a rain squall a half mile on the larboard bow!" said David. "I've ordered the spare sails spread on the deck! If we adjust our course a bit and set up catchalls, we might be able to fill most of the small barrels." Captain Jones moved to the larboard side of his cabin and peered into the setting sun.

"By God, Ben, I believe you're right!"

It took little maneuvering to intercept the squall, and by the skillful employment of all able-bodied hands and most of the extra sail cloth spread between the standing rigging, all of the topside water casks were filled, plus half those on the gun deck. The water tasted of old canvas and dust, but it was wet, and everyone got their fill.

"It's still not enough, Captain," the Doctor complained as he counted the casks, "but it might get us to your other island."

"I'll take that as a vote of confidence, Adam," answered John. "Seems the Lord intends that we succeed on this mission after all."

"I believe you're right."

"I'm depending on it, Adam."

"But without that rain, we'd have lost a score of our men for sure; antidote or none."

"You're so certain of that?"

"Yes I am," answered the Doctor coldly. "The best antidote in the world isn't going to work on a man in water shock." The Doctor gave his Captain a stern look. "You were very lucky this time, Captain Jones. Very lucky."

The gray cliffs at the eastern tip of Ben Gunn's island stood out of the dark waters of the Caribbean like a row of bank buildings in downtown London. As the Silver Cloud approached the craggy rocks close abeam and then began to parallel its face, the Eagle turned larboard to keep herself between the treasure ship and the Walrus.

"Morgan!" bellowed Captain Smoot as he searched the rigging. "Where is that son-of-a-sea-hag?!"

From the trail of dead animals in her wake, Smoot knew the Silver Cloud was in trouble and would have put in at a river for the night, but to the best of his recollections, there were no rivers near the row of cliffs. Sliding one of the buntline sheets, Morgan's calloused feet dropped lightly to the lower gaff spar where he could answer his Captain without all the shouting.

"I'm here, Govn'r!" answered Morgan. "Just above ya."

As Morgan waited for his Captain's reply, the Eagle edged forward by a hundred yards, far enough to make out a narrow crevice in the cliff face just beyond the Cloud's bowsprit.

"Take a gander at that, Morgan!" said Smoot with an outstretched finger. "What do ya know 'bout that crack in the cliff up yonder?"

"Nothin', Govn'r, 'cept it looks like some sort o' river mouth."

From their oblique angle, it didn't look large enough to take a ship, especially one of the Silver Cloud's beam.

"Don't figure, does it, Henry?" said Smoot as he continued to study their prey.

"What's that, Govn'r?"

"That they'd choose this place for water, unless..."

"Unless?" Morgan studied the situation for a moment. "Beggin' yer pardon, Govn'r, but unless what?"

"Unless they're figurin' we wouldn't risk sinkin' them in this deep water; like we would if they were next to a shallow beach."

While they watched, the Silver Cloud's running lights began to disappear into the darkness.

"Would ya look at that!"

"They're goin' into that crack! What are they up to, Govn'r?"

"Isn't it obvious?" called Smoot without looking up. "Their water's all gone an' they must think they'll find refuge up that narrow river."

"Ya really think they'd risk it?"

"Must be somethin' damn important in there."

"Cap'n Smoot! Look there!" While their attention had been fixed on the Silver Cloud, they had failed to notice that the Remora had broken from the loose formation and was departing to the north, around the point.

"Now that don't figure neither," Smoot said, "unless they decided we got the Cloud fer sure this time." He called topside and ordered his second-in-command to the deck.

"I think we do, Govn'r," said Morgan as he landed beside his Captain. He'd learned long ago that it went better for him to agree with anything Smoot said.

"You said we lost our edge back at the Chest, Govn'r, but I knew all along you had another plan."

"Tell me about that river mouth, Henry. How far in could ya see from up there?"

"Hundred yards at best, Govn'r," answered Morgan. "No more."

As the two pirate ships dropped their anchors and began to swing about their chains in the easy current, the Silver Cloud was swallowed by the darkness of the narrow passage. Within ten minutes, she had disappeared behind the second bend, leaving the faint reflection of her stern lanthorn as the only suggestion that the dark river waters had ever been disturbed by man.

"Do ya have a plan, Govn'r?" asked Morgan.

"A plan?"

"Aye," answered the boy. "We gonna follow 'em in, or what?"

"I'm thinkin', Henry, I'm thinkin'," answered Smoot as he surveyed the cliffs. "One thing's certain. We got 'em trapped fer as long as we want. An' that gives us the advantage."

"Aye," agreed the youth, "but they know they're trapped, too."

"What's that s'posed to mean?"

"Well, the way I figger it, if I were trapped with that same treasure in my hold an' two ships standin' guard at my only way back to the sea, I'd be lookin' to bury it before I was attacked. That way, I'd have somethin' fer dealin' me release later--if I were captured, that is."

"Hmmm," growled Smoot as he realized the lad was right. "My sentiments exactly." Smoot looked seaward at the Walrus and back to the cliffs. "We'll have to attack them tonight then, before they get a chance to off-load it."

"By land or by water?" asked Morgan as he pulled his new cutlass from his belt. The thought of finally getting to cut a man excited him.

"Both!" answered Smoot as he looked at the shoreline to either side of the river. He pointed his spyglass to a short strip of sand on the left.

"But first we'll have to put some men on top of those cliffs." He lowered the glass and pointed. "We'll land a half dozen men there, and another half dozen somewhere on the other side." Morgan studied the other shore.

"Don't look so good on that other side, Govn'r."

"And we'll send fifty of the Walrus' men up the river behind 'em," Smoot said, hardly hearing Morgan's advice. "Order my boat over the side. I need a war counsel with Captain Pritchard."

"Did you say fifty of the Walrus' men up the river, Govn'r?"

"Aye, that I did."

"But you an' me'll be goin up with 'em, right?"

"Wrong! We'll be stayin' right here on the Eagle. Somebody's gotta be here to meet the Cloud if she tries to make it back to sea."

Morgan was disappointed with Smoot's plan, and shoved his cutlass back into his belt with a curse.

"I've somethin' to get from my cabin," said Smoot to the disappointed lad. "Have that boat ready when I get back topside."

"You leavin' me in charge o' the Eagle, Govn'r?"

"Aye, if ya think yer up to commandin' a ship at anchor, that is. Ha! Ha!"

"That I be, Govn'r! That I be!" answered Morgan with pride. The lad recognized the insult, but it didn't matter much, since he'd get to play Captain for a while.

A few minutes later, two of the ship's crewmen waited at the waterline in a small boat. Smoot backed down the ladder with a new bottle of brandy slung from his belt. Ezra Pritchard had a weakness for the expensive liquor and would do most anything for it. Within a few minutes, Smoot's boat had crossed half the distance to the Walrus.

"Ahoy, Walrus!" Smoot bellowed at the three-masted clipper. "I'll be needin' a counsel with Ezra Pritchard!"

"I'm here!" came the raspy reply. "Will it be tonight, Joshua?"

"Aye, Ezra," answered Smoot, "it'll be tonight!" A few minutes later, Smoot pulled himself up the ladder to be swallowed up by the hundred-odd cutthroats who infested the Walrus.

It felt good to be back aboard his old ship. His crew was equally glad to see their real Captain, and reached out to touch him like orphans toward prospective parents. Pritchard pushed his way through the press of bodies with a string of profanity that would make any sailor proud.

"Where's the rest of the men?" asked Smoot.

"There ain't no more. We lost 'bout a third of 'em on the Chest."

"Damn!" bellowed Smoot. "I was countin' on more!"

"What'cha got in mind, Captain? You plannin' on followin' the Cloud up that crack in the cliff?"

"Aye, an' the sooner the better."

"I seen yer crew puttin' yer other boats over the side before ya came across, sir. Ya plannin' on doin' it all yerself?"

"Not at all," answered Smoot. "My men will go to the top of those cliffs yonder. As soon as they're in place, they'll give us a signal. Then you'll send fifty of your men up the river in boats."

"That's kind'a risky, isn't it?" asked Pritchard.

"Hell yes it's risky! But we got no choice."

"But you don't like fightin' at night."

"You don't need to remind me of that, Ezra," said Smoot as he watched the cliffs. "If we wait, they'll have time to set up their defenses and bury the treasure again, and we can't risk that."

"Hmmm," answered Pritchard. "Then I best give the word to man our boats."

"Aye, but it'll take my men 'bout an hour to gain the heights. An' since we got some time on our side, we can go below and kill this bottle of brandy I brung along fer good luck."

Before they could take their second drink, a very disturbed seaman burst into their cabin.

"Beggin' yer pardon, Cap'n Smoot," the seaman apologized, "but Morgan's callin' fer ya from the Eagle. Says it's mighty important, sir."

"Damn that boy! Probably wants to know which direction to coil a rope or somethin' stupid like that." He gave Pritchard a disgusted look as he rose to follow the seaman. At the door, he paused. "Don't you be touchin' no more o' that brandy till I come back, Ezra. I know its waterline."

The deck of the Walrus was busy with battle preparations as Smoot made his way to the starboard bow.

"Ahoy, Eagle!" called Smoot. "Is Henry Morgan there?"

"Aye, Govn'r!" the youth called back. "Look to the cliffs!"

"The cliffs?" Smoot said to himself as he turned about. "How'd they get up there so quick?" he called across the water.

"Them ain't our men, Govn'r! The bon fires belong to the Cloud's men."

"The hell you say!" swore Smoot, first to himself and then repeated it again and again more loudly, until all the men on both ships could hear his ravings.

"What is it, Captain?" asked Ezra from the companionway. "What's goin' on up here?"

"Look there, Ezra!" shouted Smoot. "The Cloud's beat us to the cliffs!"

"And the raiding party?" asked Pritchard. "What do you want I should tell my men?"

"They're my men, not yours!" barked Smoot as he stormed about the deck. "I'm goin' back to the Eagle. In case we don't talk again, I've two orders for you. I want fifty men up that river at first light. If you can't defeat the Cloud inside the river, then I want her boarded when she returns to sea."

"You gonna help?" asked Pritchard, realizing Smoot had put the whole thing on the Walrus crew.

"I can't, you fool!" bellowed Smoot. "They still think I'm on their side."

"But…" Pritchard began to protest, but fell silent as Smoot pulled his sword.

"You heard my orders, Privy!"

"Mister Noble!" called Captain Jones. "Order the sails furled and the long boats over the side!" As his first officer hurried to comply, John walked forward to where Ben Gunn stood at the windward rail, just aft of the cathead.

"There it is, Cap'n, just like I told you."

"And you're sure the Cloud will make it through?"

"Flint told me the old Walrus made it through, and she was at least another span wider than the Cloud."

"Well," said John as he studied the narrow opening, "I hope for our sakes John Flint was telling you the truth, because I don't like this at all."

"Don't worry, Captain," assured the old man. "We'll be in an' out by early morning."

"There's something else I don't like, Ben."

"The Remora?"

"You noticed, also?"

"Aye," answered Ben. "Doesn't make any sense they'd give up the chase like that, unless…"

"Unless?" asked John.

"Unless they also know the secret of the lagoon." Ben glanced aft to see the Remora disappear around the point. "There were a lot more men on the old Walrus that Flint could have told besides me."

"And you think one of them might be on the Remora?

Ben gave his Captain a worried look. "I hope not, sir."

By the time the Walrus and Eagle had anchored near a line of coral half a league from the river's mouth, the Cloud's boat crews had attached themselves to her dolphin striker and had their massive ship moving smoothly into the narrows. The rock walls were a mixture of gray and black slate, with long shadows falling downward from each outcropping like the torn fringe of a witch's skirt. Every sound, from the officer's orders and the jabbing and scraping of the pikes against rocks, to the creaking of oars in their locks, echoed back at them from the cold, wet stone. A deep despair crept across the deck and into every man's soul as the sea was choked from view by the tomb-like narrows that had swallowed them.

As Captain Jones and the old maroon considered the situation, Robert Ormerod struggled topside with a steaming teapot and several cups.

"Robert!" called John quietly. "Have you a moment to spare Ben and me?"

"Of course!" answered Robert. "As a matter of fact, I had a recommendation to offer you, in addition to this cup of tea."

"Oh?"

"Shouldn't we be doing something about protecting our backsides?"

"I was just discussing that with Ben," answered John. "I thought of trailing another longboat of sharpshooters, but..."

"If they follow us, I'd agree," said Robert. "My idea was to put a few men off on these rocks to set up an ambush."

"Possibly," answered John, "but not here. There just isn't enough cover. And if they're overrun, they'd have no way of getting up river to the Cloud."

"Might I suggest something, sir?" John and Robert turned their attention to the old man. "If I remember anything about Joshua Smoot, it's that he's a cautious man. If he'd been in charge of that attack back on the Chest, you'd have had a much harder time of it."

"We'd have had a much worse time of it if they had any leader," agreed John. "What do you think Smoot'll do tonight?"

"My guess," answered Ben as he surveyed the cliffs to either side of them, "is that he'll put men on the high ground before he sends his boats up the river. And since he likes to attack at first light, he'll have to put men on the cliffs tonight."

"Then we'll just have to put a few of our own up there first," said John.

"It'll take at least six, or maybe eight men on each cliff to make it worth while," said Ben. "And that's gonna hurt us bad with so many still sick."

"I know," said Captain Jones as he walked away to the larboard rail. After a minute, he returned.

"If everything was in place, one man should be able to keep a couple fires and half a dozen lanthorns burning."

"Aye," answered Robert. "But they'd have to get all the wood and other supplies up the hill first."

"How about this?" suggested John. "If we send half a dozen men up each side with the wood and lanthorns, then one of the weaker men could maintain the fires while the rest return to the narrows to wait in ambush for the Walrus' boats."

"And when he sees the fires, Smoot'll think we've put a dozen men on each cliff!" said Ben excitedly. "Maybe we won't have to contend with an attack after all!"

"Would you put the contingents together for me, Robert? asked John. "We'll hold the ship up just ahead where the cliffs begin to drop away."

"Consider it done, John." The New Yorker grabbed a nearby bosun's mate by the sleeve and disappeared below. Ten minutes later, two large piles of scrap lumber had been piled on the deck, along with lanthorns and extra containers of whale oil. The boat crews sat quietly with their oars propped against the rocks, holding the Cloud against the river's easy current.

With their last-minute instructions delivered, the seven men were set ashore. The eighth man, the one who would remain to tend the fires, carried only his weapons and enough food and water to get him through the night. As Ben had suggested, the second group of men were set ashore to larboard a short distance further up the river.

By Captain Jones' estimation, the boat crews had pulled the Cloud nearly half a mile up the river when it finally fanned out into a lagoon nearly sixty yards across. Like the narrows, the lagoon was very deep, with a thirty-foot waterfall dumping several thousand gallons every minute into it's depths. As the boat crews loosed their lines, David ordered the anchor dropped. At the same time, two of the large water casks were hoisted over the side with all their bungholes uncapped.

"I don't see it, Ben," said Captain Jones as he scanned the north shore of the lagoon.

A thick underbrush had crept from the nearby tree line to the water's edge where it sucked at the life-giving liquid. And but for a short strip of rocky beach to the right of the falls, there was no useable shore at all.

"You said there'd be a way out of here," John insisted.

"Aye, Captain Jones," answered the old man as he searched the same shoreline. "It's gotta be there someplace. If only we had more light."

The night in Deception Lagoon was as dark as the ink on the King's Warrant which had driven John Paul Jones from Fredericksburg. Without an explanation from their Captain, the crew's fear and mistrust had grown with each bend in the narrow river. Captain Jones had got them through some desperate situations in the previous week, but for all the gods, nobody could figure how he'd get them out of this one. They were obviously trapped; landlocked in a small freshwater lagoon, and every man knew it was only a matter of time before the pirates would send their raiding parties up the channel and over the hills to take the treasure, and as many lives as they pleased.

Before first light, an impatient Captain Jones stood outside Ben Gunn's cabin, listening for the old man to stir. There was no sound. "Ben!" John whispered as he tapped lightly on the door. "Ben, are you there?"

"No, Cap'n Jones, I'm not," came the answer from behind the Scotsman. John turned about to find the old man up and fully dressed.

"You're already up!"

"Couldn't sleep, sir. And after tellin' ya there was a way out'a the lagoon last night an' me not bein' able to show ya, well, I figured I'd have her spotted before you came for me."

"Well?" asked John. "Did you find it yet?"

"Not yet, sir, but the sun's comin' up and there's just enough light to see the shore. I think we'll be able to see something now." Ben turned and climbed back to the main deck, with Captain Jones at his heels.

The old man's dressings had been removed, exposing the results of his recent torture. A neat row of diamond-shaped burns ran up the outside of each calf from ankle to knee.

"Your dressings," said John as they stepped onto the main deck and the early dawn's light. "You've removed them."

"Aye," answered Ben as he twisted his right leg outward toward the younger man. "Sorta fashionable, in't it?"

"Fashionable?"

"The perfect scars fer a storyteller, says I," said Ben proudly as he strode aft to the taffrail. After a long moment, he pointed.

"There it is, sir!"

"What am I looking for? I don't see anything."

"Look there, at the waters."

"The waters?"

"Don't ya see it?" Gunn continued to point. "Right there, just this side of the white rock." Captain Jones stepped to the rail and studied the water. "There, sir! Look how the water's bein' sucked under them vines!"

Ben was right. Even though the sun hadn't crested the hills, there was just enough light in the sky to see the unmistakable swirl of a strong current pulling angrily from under the mass of vegetation. This was their escape route--the one John Flint had told Ben about some twenty years before. As the two studied the newly revealed channel, David Noble called from amidships.

"Captain Jones! Ben! I was on my way to wake you. What's going on?"

"We've found the second river, David! How long would it take to put the hand crews ashore to begin cutting?"

"They're all asleep," answered David, "except for the men loading the casks. I suppose we can put 'em to work right away and then let them break for chow by sections."

"It'll have to be so," said John. "We've several hundred yards of cutting to do before we can get back to sea, and Smoot won't be sitting on his hands while we're at it."

As they spoke, a volley of musket fire echoed up from the river, followed by the cries of men. Just as Ben had predicted, Smoot had begun his attack at first light.

"David, get Doctor McKenzie up here on the double. I need to know how many able bodied men we can deploy."

"Aye, aye, Captain!" David bounded away to the ladder and disappeared below decks.

"I'm putting more men on the cliffs, Ben," said John. "It won't take Smoot long to discover our deception when he realizes he's getting so little fire from above."

"What about more men down the river?"

"It won't be necessary. The dozen we left in ambush have good cover, and plenty of arms. Besides, they're fighting men who have to row against a current and fire their muskets. They'll do fine, at least until we can clear the vines and move the Cloud into the other river."

Most of the vines were a very soft kind of water plant that yielded easily to the sharp cutlasses and persistent pike poles. By mid-morning, the work parties had refilled the six large water casks and the channel had been cleared.

"Mister Noble," said John quietly to his First Officer. "It's time to recall the men from the river and the cliffs."

"Aye, Captain?"

"And once you've done that," added John, "order the anchor weighed and have the Cloud pulled into the river." The young Jamaican saluted and sped away to comply.

"You're not going to wait until it's cleared to the sea?" asked Robert.

"It will be," answered John. "By the time David can get the marksmen back and our boat crews have maneuvered the Cloud into the current, the cutting crews should be near the surf line. With any luck, we'll be at sea and under sail again by noon."

The second river was slightly wider than the first, but without the hundred-foot cliffs to either side. Using the same technique as before, the Silver Cloud was piked between the two shores at a walking speed, with hand crews on both shores to man the restraint lines. The morale of the crew had been resurrected, especially as the unmistakable sound of the nearby surf became louder and louder with each step. David had joined the starboard shore crew but ran to meet a seaman returning from seaward.

"What's the matter?" called John when he noticed the agitated seaman pointing down river and yelling at David.

"We've some shallows about two hundred yards ahead, just before the beach!" called David. "We may have some trouble getting through unless we can wait for high tide."

"We can't wait!" answered John. "As soon as our sharpshooters are back aboard, I want the Cloud moving again."

As the mighty ship inched forward toward the shallows, Captain Jones watched from the forward rail. They had been able to see the river's bottom all along, but now the boulders were closer to the surface, almost as if someone had rolled them there to form a dam. Then, as if his ship had been seized by the hand of an angry god, the Silver Cloud came to a sudden and frightening stop. The shore crews paused to look to their captain.

Before he could think what to do next, the river had made it's own decision. There came a terrible rolling and scraping sound from below, followed by an uncomfortable lurch forward. The river's waters had stacked up behind the Cloud's stern until it finally pushing her up and over the rolling boulders and on toward the waiting sea.

The Good Lord was on their side that morning for within minutes, the Silver Cloud had coasted into the low surf and had spun about on her hauling lines to face the beach. And none too quickly, for no sooner had the work crews been taken aboard and the order given to set sails, than three boats full of Smoot's men emerged from around a bend in the river with curses and musket fire.

"Shall I order up a broadside, sir?" asked David.

"I'm tempted, but I think not. Seeing us escaping like this is punishment enough."

The Cloud's great sails dropped from the yards like petticoats, each one filling with the gentle southerly breeze that rolled over the low hills of the island. Within minutes, the ship gained steerage and pulled through the surf and into the open waters.

"By the time those boats get back to Smoot," said Captain Jones, "we'll be out of sight."

"And we'll be done with pirates for good!" said Ben. The rest of the officers joined in their Captain's moment, but it was short lived.

"Sail astern!" shouted the top watch. "It's the Remora, sir, and she's under full sail!"

"Damn!" whispered Captain Jones as he searched the deck for his gunner.

"McCoy! Man the starboard cannons!"

CHAPTER 14

There was no sense in running from the Remora. Captain Jones had learned long ago that in a battle for position, a square-masted brig was no match for one of these agile Virginia privateers. Within minutes she would easily close with the Silver Cloud and maneuver into a position to attack the larger ship from either the stem or stern. He had only one option.

"Gentlemen," he began, "we've a golden opportunity before us which we simply can't afford to pass up. I don't expect we'll ever find our three pursuers separated like this again, so I intend to engage the Remora." John turned to his First Officer.

"David, pipe the crew to general quarters and clear the decks for action. I told McCoy to keep the siding in place, but I think it's finally time to show our guns."

"But..." David began, and then checked himself. "Aye, aye, Captain."

The deck came alive. Whereas half a dozen teams of men had been pulling at the sheets, there were now over sixty men running over the deck to their well-rehearsed battle stations. Captain Jones stood with his hands on the starboard rail as his ship cut smoothly seaward into the deeper water that he would need for maneuvering. With predictive certainty, the Remora continued on its intercept with the Cloud.

"I can't figure her," said John.

"The Remora?" asked David.

"She obviously knew about this second way out of the river, yet didn't tell the Walrus or the Eagle." John rubbed his chin and realized that he had forgotten to shave. "And there's something else."

"Oh?"

"Why didn't she attack while we were still in shallow water, when the men from the Walrus were at our backs?"

"Maybe she's not who we..." David checked himself again. "They must have figured they could take us by themselves, regardless of position or assistance from those other men."

"I don't know what's gotten into you, David. You talk as if you know something." John looked at the fast approaching ship and back to his young friend. "Do you?"

"No, sir. It's just that there's something strange about her. You feel it too, don't you?"

"We all do, but until we know better, she'll be treated exactly like the others." John looked forward to where McCoy was waiting for an order. "You've an order to give, David."

"Yes, sir," answered David slowly. "Gunner!" he called forward.

"Aye!" came the excited reply.

"As soon as she's in range, I want one round put across her bow."

"Should I take off a foot or two of her bow sprit, Mister Noble?" asked McCoy with a chuckle from the other gunners.

"No!" answered David with a nervous look at his Captain.

"Make it close, David," said John from under a shading hand.

"But we don't want to provoke them, do we?"

"Give the order, Mister Noble," said John coldly. "I wouldn't ask for the round unless I wanted to provoke them."

"Make it close, McCoy!" ordered David.

The Gunner gave a quick salute and dropped from sight, followed by a muffled cheer from the bowels of the ship and the roar of a six-inch cannon. And then as all hands watched with certain expectation, a column of water leaped into the morning sky from under the Remora's bowsprit, showering her foredeck with brine.

"Well done, McCoy!" called Captain Jones. "Now we'll see what she's made of."

"They won't fight us," said David just above a whisper.

"Won't fight us, you say?" asked John. "How can you know that, unless..." John was interrupted by a hail from the Remora.

"Ahoy there, Silver Cloud!" The voice was strong and deep, with an unmistakable Scottish brogue similar to the one that John had been working so diligently for the past year to lose. "Daniel Archer here! Have I permission to come across?"

"Aye," answered Captain Jones, "but be warned that we've another ten cannons trained on your vessel!"

"Thank you, sir," came the reply, "but you'll not be needin' any fire power against us."

As the two called back and forth, a six-man boat was already lifting from the deck of the Remora to transport Captain Archer across. "I've a gift for you, Captain Jones; a gift that'd tempt a Papist out'a his hassock."

"You know my name, sir!" John called. "Have we met?"

"No, we haven't, sir, but we do have a mutual friend!"

"I'm anxious to learn who this mutual friend is, Captain Archer!" John moved closer to David's side as he exchanged shouts with the Remora. "Make haste, Captain Archer, for we must be underway!"

"David," John whispered, "you've some explaining to do."

David remained silent.

"You've known about the Remora all along, haven't you?"

"No I haven't," lied the young Jamaican. "I didn't suspect anything until just now, just like you."

"That's a lie! You knew something when I ordered you to put one across her bow!"

David fidgeted with his sword as he searched for the right words. "I thought it possible that my father sent them to protect his investment."

"Your father, you say?" John set his jaw and faced David squarely. "I have tremendous difficulty with that! If he had, you'd have told me the day we first spotted the Remora." John took a long breath. "What did you tell your father about our mission?"

"I told him about Mister Jefferson sending the Eagle, that's all. He must have figured to protect his interests by doing the same."

"Damn you, David!" John's outburst caught the attention of all hands on the main deck, including that of Robert Ormerod.

"Damn you, David?" echoed Robert as he climbed the ladder to the quarterdeck. "What's the lad done now?"

"We may have another traitor in our midst, Robert!"

"You don't mean young Noble?" asked Robert as he clapped a hand on David's shoulder, "do you?"

"Yes, I mean David. That's unless he can do some quick explaining."

"What's up, lad?" asked Robert.

"David's known about the Remora from the first; even before she joined us at Dead Man's Chest."

"Is that true?" asked Robert. "Did you know?"

"Not for sure, sir."

"Not for sure, my eye!" protested John. "You knew enough to tell me they wouldn't fight back!"

"Well, yes...sort of," David stammered, "but..."

"Then you know who sent them, don't you?" asked Robert.

"Out with it!" hissed John. "Tell him before I throw you in irons with the other traitor."

"I really..." David looked back and forth at the two. "I don't know for sure. As I was telling John, they...I mean, my father didn't discuss it with me."

"They?" asked Robert. "Who else is in on this?"

David looked down at John's half-drawn sword.

"John," David began, "do you remember the old innkeeper when we first met?"

"The white-haired man with the articulated wooden leg?"

"Yes," answered David.

"Articulated wooden leg?" asked Robert.

"He's David's uncle!" answered John.

"David," asked Robert before the lad could offer a defense. "Is it by any chance his left leg?"

"Yes, it is."

John had heard enough. "Gentlemen, I think we can stop playing games." With his sword now fully drawn, John touched his first officer on the boot with its point.

"What's your uncle's real name?" demanded John.

Before David could answer, there came a lusty greeting from the main deck forward.

"Greetings, gentlemen!" shouted Captain Archer through his red beard. "Greetings from my employer and your protector, Long John Silver!"

"I didn't know he sent them!" begged David. "I only guessed it from how the Remora's been acting."

"He's telling ya the gospel, Captain Jones!" called Archer as he climbed over the rail and onto the main deck. "Neither Silver nor Davey's father told him a thing about me or my ship." Captain Archer pulled a sealed letter from his waistcoat and handed it to Captain Jones. "This should explain everything."

Captain Jones took the letter and read aloud.

To my predictable and most cooperative friend, Captain Jones:

First, allow me to congratulate you for accomplishing what hundreds have tried and failed. You have brought to me the legendary Treasure of Dead Man's Chest.

That may stick in your craw, good sir, but we're all winners in this exploit; the Colonies will have their cannons, you and David will get your commissions, and Charles and I shall have our long awaited rewards. Please don't feel bad that you've been used. There was no other way to accomplish what you and your comrades have done.

Until we meet again—and that shall be sooner than you think— I am your true friend and admirer.

Long John Silver

John handed the letter to Robert and returned his sword to its scabbard.

"So that sweet old innkeeper, Jack Bridger, is the infamous pirate, Long John Silver?" said John. "Why, I expected someone much more..."

"Like a bloodthirsty cutthroat?" Captain Archer asked, finishing John's thought as he pulled the bottle of Scotch Whiskey from a pouch slung from his shoulder.

"Well," answered John, "at least somebody who looked like a pirate."

"Don't let his looks fool you," interrupted Robert as he scanned the letter a second time. "He's a pirate all right, and he'll be one 'til the day he dies."

As Robert spoke, Archer offered the bottle to Captain Jones.

"What's this?" asked John.

"It's Captain Silver's special way of saying thank you, Captain Jones. He told me he promised it to you when you were in Kings Town the winter of '73. It took him until now to locate just the right bottle; one from the distillery near your birthplace in Scotland."

"Yes it is," said John as he read the label, "and I'll thank Mister Silver personally in a few days."

"Tell us, Captain Archer," said Robert, "what can we expect from John Silver when we reach the rendezvous? Are we to be killed?"

"For the treasure? Why no, sir!" Archer had hoped the bottle of spirits and his good humor would relax his hosts. "Silver may be a pirate, but when he gives his word on a thing, he'll never go back on it. Pirates can be some of the most honorable men afloat. You'll get your cannons, as long as he gets his treasure."

"No tricks then?" asked John.

"None, sir!" affirmed Archer. "There'd be no point to it." There was a moment of uneasy quiet as the two Captains studied each other. Finally Captain Archer spoke.

"I'd think my saving your two men on the north coast of the Chest would have convinced you of my good intentions, Captain Jones."

"So that was the Remora!"

"Aye, that was us!"

"It would have helped if you'd left us a message on one of the bodies," John complained.

"Hell, man," Archer cried, "I did!"

"Oh?"

"Didn't you see the semaphore?" Archer was sure someone in the Silver Cloud's crew would have picked it up.

"Those letters?" asked John.

"Aye, the letters!"

John looked to David. "What were they?"

"There were five of them," answered David. "I believe they were O-C-J-L-S."

"No!" interrupted Archer. "They were C-O-L-J-S." Nobody ventured a guess, so Archer continued. "They stood for 'Compliments of...'" He paused as he saw the Yorkman's expression change.

"Compliments of Long John Silver!"

"Ah!" chirped Archer. "I knew there was a clever one amongst ya!"

"If you wanted us to know you were responsible," said John, "then why didn't you just spell out your ship's name?"

"And tell the men from the Walrus also?"

John considered for a moment. "No, I suppose you did all you could."

"And that's the only way John Silver would have it," added Archer.

"You talk as if the old man's among us," said Robert.

"I am, Robert," came a familiar voice from behind Captain Archer.

"My God!" gasped Robert as he pushed past David and John to watch the old pirate climb through the open rail.

"Not yer God, Robert," Silver chuckled as he pulled his bulk onto the deck, "but certainly yer benefactor."

"Gentlemen!" sang out Captain Archer as he moved to Silver's side, "may I introduce the unofficial Governor of Kings Town, and my employer, Long John Silver?"

"John Silver!" hissed Robert.

"Sorta tears the scab off the wound, doesn't it, Robert?"

"Aye," hissed the Yorkman, "and with a dose of salt and vinegar for extra sting."

To Captain Jones, John Silver was the crude but friendly innkeeper from Silver Jack's Tavern on the wharf at Kings Town. But to Robert, who had watched the man kill at least seven of Murray's men during that final battle on Spyglass, he was the vilest of cutthroats.

"Aren't I a vision of heaven in my new waistcoat and fancy articulated leg?" sang the old seadog with a slap to his left thigh.

"More like a vision from hell," hissed Robert, "you thieving cutthroat!"

"Thieving cutthroat?" Silver echoed with feigned surprise. "You wound me, Robert."

"But that's exactly what you are! A thief and a cutthroat."

"And I suppose you and my little brother are respectable merchants?"

"Of course we are!"

"Wrong!" laughed the old man. "We're all cut from the same cloth; you, Charlie an' me. The only difference is that your lines follow a slightly different pattern. We both deal in valuable goods and we both ask the highest price the market will bear. As I see it, the only place we truly differ is that I take a slightly higher percentage of the swag than you."

"But you're still a pirate!" said Robert. "You and your kind kill for the goods you take!"

"And what if I were to purchase a Letter of Marque like those Colonial pirates you deal with?"

"Nothing would make you..."

"Or what if I were a Spaniard? Would you still hate me as much?"

"A Spaniard?"

"Aye, a Spaniard. Ten years ago when we were at war with them, I heard you blew up at the mere mention of the race." Silver took a long breath as he waited for Robert's answer. "Stumped for words, Robert?"

"Calm down, you two!" commanded Captain Jones. "We've more important things to accomplish than settling old scores."

"You're finally going to get the treasure, aren't you?" asked Robert, ignoring the young Captain's rebuke.

"And did you ever doubt I would?" asked Silver with a toothy grin.

"Yes!" answered Robert angrily. "I figured you'd be shoveling coal in hell by now, provided the Devil would allow you into the place."

The thought of tangling with Satan, one-on-one, amused the old pirate. His lips curled back in a wry smile, revealing the row of large white teeth.

"Enough!" cried Captain Jones as he gave Robert an angry stare. "We have more important matters, I say."

"Such as?" demanded Robert, turning on the younger man.

"Such as why John Silver's on the *Remora* rather than the cannon ship," said John, "and what we're going to do about the Walrus and the Eagle?"

"I'm on the Remora because of the treasure."

"But that wasn't your mission!" insisted Captain Jones. "You were supposed to meet us with the cannons!"

"I have men who I trust to do what I've told them to do, Captain Jones," hissed Silver, "unlike your Mister Jefferson."

"What do you know about Jefferson?" asked Robert.

"Nothing directly."

"Then explain your statement," demanded John.

"It's his choice of Captains for the Eagle. How could he allow Smoot to get close enough to disable the Silver Cloud like that?"

"Smoot's not on the Walrus, Uncle Silver," said David. "He and Henry Morgan are on the Eagle, or at least they were when we departed the Chest."

"A lad with green eyes and flame-red hair?" asked Silver. David nodded. "Well, I'll be a maroon's armpit!"

"You know Morgan?" asked John.

"We met briefly, ten years ago on Tortuga." Silver looked back toward the South and the point that hid the anchored Walrus and Eagle from view. "Smoot's been playing your protector, hasn't he, Captain Jones?"

"Aye."

"Interesting," said the old pirate as he continued looking to the jagged rocks. "You know of course, that he'll sacrifice the Walrus and it's entire crew if he has to in order to take your ship."

"That's why I want to get under way as quickly as possible," insisted John. "Would you please return to your ship?"

"Smoot doesn't know we're using two Silver Clouds, does he?" asked Silver as he stroked his beard.

"Not unless Morgan figured the thing out before he ran off to join Smoot," answered Robert as he regained some of his composure.

"Good!" said Silver. "That means there's a chance he'll wait until we off-load the treasure at Kings Town."

"I believe he'll attack before Kings Town," said David.

"How do you figure, Davey?"

"You know the man better than I do," said David. "He figures we're trapped in Deception Lagoon. When his men return with word of our escape, he won't take it well."

"I think David's right," agreed John, "but not in deep water."

"He is," added Silver, "and I wouldn't be surprised if it were deep water."

"Then all the more reason to be underway," affirmed John.

"Wait!" cried Robert.

"What now?" asked John.

"If you've been manipulating John and me as long as you claim," began Robert, "then you must know something about that anonymous letter of introduction...the one telling about Captain Jones' visit...that I received from the Committees of Correspondence in early March."

"Aye," answered Silver as he turned to John, "and I was at the Dandridge estate the day you and Dorothea planned your little picnic."

"That was you?" asked John, somewhat confused. "But, why?"

"To deliver a copy of the King's Warrant to the girl's father and make a suggestion how he might get rid of you."

"You bastard!" cried John. "How dare you?"

"How dare I?" asked Silver as he retreated a step. "Would the Americans be getting their cannons if I hadn't?"

"No," cried John, "but..."

"And would you and David be getting your naval commissions if I hadn't?"

"The only reason you did any of it was to get my treasure!" cried Robert. "Only God knows how many lives you've affected by your greed!"

"And there's a lot more to come, my friends," sang out the old pirate as he turned toward the opening in the rail, "a lot more."

"One more thing before you go, John Silver," said Robert.

"And what would that be?"

"What do you know about the two men who kidnapped my daughter six years ago?"

"The two men..?" As Silver fumbled over his words, Robert pulled a pistol from his belt.

"You remember, Uncle Silver," said David, not noticing the weapon. "You told us about it in Kings Town the same night..."

Before anyone could react, Robert had raised the pistol to within ten inches of Silver's chest and squeezed the trigger. Everyone on the quarterdeck gasped together, expecting the fatal shot to fell the old man. But in his haste, Robert had forgotten to cock the flint.

"Damn your soul to hell!" cried Robert as he pulled back on his pistol's lock and aimed at the old man. There was a moment of confusion as David reached out to deflect Robert's aim. The pistol fired and John Silver cried out as he fell to the deck. Before the smoke had cleared, David was at his uncle's side.

"Uncle Silver!" David cried as he searched the old man for life. Certain that he was dead, David turned and looked up at Robert. "Damn you, Robert! You shot him! You've killed my uncle!"

"He killed my daughter!" said Robert as he poured more gunpowder into the barrel of his pistol.

"He never meant for her to be hurt!" David said as he shielded Silver with his own body. "He explained about the fire! It was an accident! When he found out what his two agents did, he had them shot!"

"Well that doesn't bring back my daughter!" hissed Robert as he rammed a lead ball down the barrel of his pistol.

David broke into a storm of tears and sobs. "Oh, Uncle Silver! How will I tell my father?"

"Tell him I died in a fight with Joshua Smoot," came a feeble whisper in David's ear. David sat up with a start.

"Uncle?" the lad asked with a nudge to the old man's ribs. "Are you dead?"

"Not quite, Davey," answered Silver as he blinked up at the men standing over him. "I think it's just my wooden leg he's killed."

"You'll die this day, you black-hearted snake!" cried Robert as he pulled back on the hammer and pointed the pistol down at Silver's heart. "Brenda's death will be avenged today!"

"Belay!" cried Silver as he held his hands out at Robert.

"No!" commanded Captain Jones as he wrenched the weapon from the Yorkman's hand. "You men! Take Mister Ormerod to the bow!"

"Thank you, Captain Jones," said Silver as he sat. "I'm in your debt."

"You're not in my debt yet, Mister Silver."

"Oh?"

"He's right!" called Robert as the four seamen forced him to the bow and held him fast. "I'll see to it that you're hunted down and hanged! Your debt to me comes first!"

"Leave my ship," John commanded to the two visitors, "before I release Mister Ormerod and allow him his revenge."

"But I wanted to talk to Ben!" begged Silver as he noticed his old shipmate emerge from the officer's companionway.

"Now!" ordered John with a look at Ben Gunn. "You and he can talk at the rendezvous."

"Rendezvous?" asked the old pirate as he hopped toward the rail. "What about the treasure on Spyglass?"

"I didn't think we had time," said John.

"The cannon ship is at the rendezvous as we speak, Captain Jones. My men'll wait, no matter how long it takes you."

"Very well," said John as he accompanied Silver and Archer to the ladder, "we'll go to Spyglass. Signal when you're ready to get underway."

"Before I go," asked Silver, "any special instructions for when Smoot catches up with you?"

"Just keep the Eagle out of range. I can handle the Walrus."

As John Silver turned about to descend the ship's ladder, several of the sick crewmen had been gathering on the main deck to get a look at the famous pirate. Captain Archer hesitated as he noticed their gaunt, tired look.

"Your men don't look well, Captain Jones."

"They aren't. We've had a traitor on board since we departed Charles Town. He not only cut our anchor, but when we put back to sea from the Chest, he poisoned our water supply."

"Could you use a few of my men until your crew's stronger?"

"Yes, I could," answered John. "I'd take a dozen topmen, if you could spare them."

"I'll order the exchange," answered Archer. "I can take your weakest men aboard the Remora until we reach Spyglass."

Within a half hour, the Cloud had taken on the Remora's crewmen and was underway for Spyglass. At Captain Jones' request, David and Robert were waiting in his cabin.

"Well," began John as he closed the door and walked to his desk. "As John Silver wrote in his letter, I've certainly been used."

"We've all been used," said David, "from the very start."

"From when you went back to Kings Town to deliver the five letters, you mean?" asked John.

"Oh no, John," insisted David. "He used us from the night we met at Silver Jack's Tavern in '73."

"Silver Jack's?" blurted Robert. "My God, John, the name of the place should have warned you!"

"You forget that I'd never heard of Long John Silver before I met you and Ben. I suspected something when Ben told me about Silver on our way to Fredericksburg, but I guess chose to ignore it."

"He had to ignore it," said David, "just like I had to deceive him." David turned back to his Captain. "John, be honest with us. Would you have thrown in with me if you knew a pirate was using us like this?"

"No!"

"And would you," continued David, turning to the New Yorker, "have agreed to lead John and me to the treasure if you knew Silver was involved?"

"Never!"

"And answer me one more thing," continued David to both older men. "Do the Colonies need those cannons?" Neither of them could argue with his logic.

"And now that you know it was Long John Silver all along, does it really change anything?"

"Not really," answered John.

"Speak for yourself, John," said Robert. "The moment we arrive at Charles Town, I'm issuing a warrant for John Silver's arrest. I'll not rest until he's punished for his crime against my family."

The Silver Cloud plowed through an endless parade of rolling swells, spawned in some far off storm toward the equator. A steady quartering wind from the south filled her canvas, pushing the great frigate ahead of the following sea. A school of sleek black and white dolphins played like a group of graceful school children upon the ship's bow wave, leaping to take a fresh breath of air or to capture one of the many flying fish startled into flight by the ship's stem. The deep pounding sound of far away surf breaking over an unseen reef, mixed with the complaining of rope and leather against mast and yard, created a symphony most pleasing to the nautical ear.

By dusk of that first day out of Deception Lagoon, there was still no sign of their two pursuers; the Walrus and the Eagle. The Remora, by request of Captain Jones, had stationed herself a league to windward; the best position for a quick rendezvous should her assistance be necessary.

As Captain Jones looked into the wake in quiet contemplation, David joined him at the taffrail. "It feels good doesn't it, David?"

"Aye," the youth agreed. "But I was truly doubtful we'd ever see open water again."

"Oh?" asked John as he glanced aloft to check the trim of the sails.

"You have to admit that Ben's escape route was a bit risky, John," said David, "even for you."

"It was a gamble I had to take, and I apologize for making the decision without conferring with you and the others. If it hadn't worked out the way it did, well..." John paused for a moment to think and rub off the accumulation of salt from his eyebrows.

"You're the Captain, and it was your decision to make." David turned about and studied the sea behind them. "How long do you figure before they'll catch us?"

"I'm surprised we haven't spotted them already," answered John as he looked about at the setting sun. "It's nearly dark, but I'll wager ten crowns the watch reports two sails astern by first light."

The evening was uneventful aboard the Silver Cloud, except that a rumor had escaped from the quarterdeck and had run through the ship like a fox with its tail afire. Scuttlebutt was what they called it, and this rumor predicted a battle with the Walrus the next day.

Captain Jones had insisted from their departure at Charles Town that all personal weapons be kept battle-ready at all times. There was no need for a reminder this night.

The young Scotsman sat down at his desk to consult his charts and bring his logbook up to date. It might be his last chance to record the happenings of the last several days.

At first light there came an impatient hammering at Captain Jones' stateroom door, along with the excited calls of one of the young gunner's mates. It was clear that his prediction of the previous evening had come true.

"How far astern are they?" asked John as he opened the door.

"Five to six leagues, sir, and Mister Noble says they'll be on us before noon!"

"Tell Mister Noble I'll be topside shortly."

"Aye, aye, Captain!"

By the time John had gained his position on the quarterdeck, the other five officers were assembled and awaiting his orders.

"Shall I sound general quarters?" asked David.

"Not yet, Mister Noble. I'm still convinced they'll not attack us in deep water."

"You're wrong, John," said Robert as he studied the approaching ships. "As much as I hate to agree with John Silver, I feel he and David are correct."

"I can't run a ship on feelings, Robert."

"You forget, John," said Robert with a long look aft, "that I lived with some of those beasts for nearly a month. I know how they think."

"And how do they think, Robert?"

"They're angry, and frustrated. They've failed in four separate attempts to take the treasure from us, and they think our next stop is Kings Town."

"But a deep water attack?"

"They don't have to sink us to take this ship, John."

"Well, I'm still certain you're wrong!" answered John as he looked to each of the other officers.

"Cap'n Jones!" cried Ben from the taffrail.

"What is it, Ben?"

"I think you'll change yer mind when you see this!"

"See what?" asked John as he walked aft and took the glass from the old man.

"Take a look at her flag, sir," said Ben. "It's red."

"Damn!" said John quietly as he lowered the glass and turned back to the others. "They've hoisted their 'no quarter' flag. Seems our Yorkman has predicted correctly once again."

The crew of the Silver Cloud had been in a state of readiness since they had departed Dead Man's Chest, so it took them only moments to begin transforming the hybrid ship into the man-of-war she truly was. The barrels of sand by each of the great masts were spilled onto the main and gun decks in preparation for the blood that might shortly flow over the planking. Doctor McKenzie and his two surgeon's mates descended to the interior of the ship where they began to lay out their medical tools and set two dozen cauterizing irons in a small stove prepared for the purpose. The bilge pumps were primed and a continual procession of seamen brought an assortment of ball, grape shot and bar stock, along with neatly tied flannel bags of black powder from the ship's bowels. It was no small task to roll away the casks of molasses and swing away and secure the interior facades which had hidden the twenty cannons from the inspector's eye, but within an hour the Silver Cloud had completed it's transformation. With the Walrus and the Eagle at half a league, the ship's gunner approached the quarterdeck to report.

"The guns are loaded an' manned, sir," said McCoy excitedly. "An' the men asked me to thank ya."

"Thank me for what?"

"Why," continued McCoy, "fer orderin' the attack against the Walrus and Eagle, sir!"

"It's not for their benefit, McCoy, but you can tell them I've accepted their gratitude anyway."

"An' will ya be wantin' ta make yer inspection now, sir?"

"Aye," answered John. "Lead the way."

A large smile broke across the gunner's face as he turned about and dropped to the gun deck and marched amongst the cannons and their half-naked gunners. The hatch aft into officer's country had been removed and a group of crewmen were crowded in the narrow passageway. Captain Jones gave McCoy a questioning look.

"That'll be the two cannons I ordered set up in your cabin, sir. I apologize fer disturbin' yer furnishin's, but we'll be needin' the aft fire power if the Walrus positions herself to fire on our rudder."

"No apology necessary, McCoy."

The gun deck had changed. Where there had been hundreds of barrels of molasses, there were now eighteen fine black cannons already loaded for action. The rammers, sponges and worming irons were laid in neat rows between the guns, with small arms enough for every man stacked neatly against the masts. A cask of seawater stood next to each cannon in case of fire, and the racks of cannon balls looked like so many strings of expensive black pearls.

"You've done a good job, McCoy," said John. "If Mister Noble's done as well topside, I'd say we're ready for anything they can throw at us."

"Aye, Captain," answered the gunner. "She don't have a chance against these fine lads o' mine; not a chance."

John stepped to the muzzle of the seventh larboard cannon. "This veneer. Will it hamper your aim?" asked Captain Jones.

Only for the first volley, sir. After it's blown away, we'll have a clear view of the Walrus."

"Good enough. And while we're down here, McCoy, would you show me where the doctor's set up his treatment station?"

"Aye, sir!" answered the gunner as he turned aft. "Accordin' to one of my mates, he's on the deck below us, just aft of the mizzenmast step."

"In the tiller room?" Captain Jones spun about and marched off toward the companionway, with McCoy at his heels.

"Aye?" the gunner called after him. "Did ya not want him there?"

"Not unless it's the only place left on the ship!" At the base of the ladder, Captain Jones swung about the great mast and stepped through a small hatchway. Several pairs of taut rope stretched down through the overhead and about pulleys to the great tiller. The doctor was giving his men a drill in amputations.

"Captain Jones!" said the doctor, looking up from his work. "You startled me.

We didn't expect you to pay us a visit this early."

"Why'd you set up here, Adam?"

"It looked like a good spot, sir. I figured we'd be out of the way, yet close enough to the gun deck and one of the companionways for quick access to both fighting decks."

"McCoy," asked the Captain while ignoring the Doctor, is there an open space forward where we could move the Doctor and his men--maybe in the area of the foremast?"

"Aye, sir, but..."

"Doctor McKenzie!" ordered Captain Jones. "Pick up your wares and move forward at once, away from the tiller area."

"But why, Captain?"

"I'll explain later when we assemble the crew on deck. As for now, move your men and equipment forward as quickly as possible." John turned back to his gunner. "I can find my own way topside, McCoy. Pass the word to the gunners that the doctor has moved forward."

"Aye, aye, sir!" answered the Gunner as John scaled the ladder toward the main deck.

By now, the sun was well into its slow arc skyward, bathing the ship in a sparkle of reflected light. Waiting for Captain Jones on the quarterdeck were his four other officers; Ben Gunn, Robert Ormerod, David Noble, and the Dutchman, Jack Van Mourik.

"David!" called John as he trotted aft. "Order the men piped topside for muster!"

Moments later, the shrill tune of the Bosun's pipe rang out over the ship, bringing the hundred odd hands to the main deck.

"Attention on deck!" called the First Officer to the orderly ranks of fighting men. "The Captain has a word for you before we go into battle!" As David finished, Doctor McKinzie arrived and joined the others.

"As I'm sure you all know by now, we'll be engaging the Walrus, and possibly the Eagle, in approximately one hour. Since we carry an enormous treasure, I don't expect either of our enemies to fire at our hull; at least not below the water line. Their strategy will be to disable the Cloud by taking off her masts, or by hitting her rudder." Captain Jones looked to the Doctor, to insure he understood about the tiller room. Doctor McKenzie nodded that he did. Captain Jones was satisfied, so continued.

"If they're successful in either of these tactics, they'll then attempt to board us. We can expect to lose several men to their cannons and musket fire, but I've fought the Walrus before and I believe with a little providential help, we'll prevail."

"Will we attack both of 'em at once, sir?" called one of the topmen.

"I'm hoping not!" called back the Captain. "The Eagle's been playing the part of our protector thus far, and I'm hoping they'll stand off and watch how the Walrus fares."

"And if we sink the Walrus," called another man from the deck, "what then, Captain?"

"Then it's off to Spyglass for the rest of John Flint's treasure!"

"Hooray for Captain Jones!" called one of the gunner's mates, followed by three cheers from the rest of the crew.

"And now my fellow Americans--to your battle stations! We've a of ship to sink!"

The watch had just struck 1400 hours on the ship's bell when the Walrus began her attack maneuver. She approached from slightly windward of the Silver Cloud's wake, thereby avoiding the nine waist cannons. As Captain Jones had predicted, the Eagle made a faint show of repulsing the Walrus by sending several balls through and around the attacker's sails, but broke off when the Walrus returned her fire.

"I was hoping for that," said John to his First Officer as they watched the Eagle break away to the south. "Smoot believes we're still fooled after all. And unless I've measured him wrong, he won't interfere again until he sees we're either disabled or taken."

"And the Remora?" asked David. "Do you think Captain Archer will do his part?"

"That's what John Silver's paying him for."

At two hundred yards astern, the Walrus altered course slightly to starboard to cross her prey's wake to lee.

"Robert!" called John from the taffrail. "Go to my cabin and supervise those two aft gun crews. I want the Walrus kept out of range of our rudder as long as possible.

Shortly after the Yorkman had dropped from sight, the first of the two stern cannons sent a round of barstock twirling through the Walrus' rigging, leaving a bone shaped tear in the flying jib and splintering a lower yard as it continued aft through the forest of masts, spars and ropes. But on she came, apparently unconcerned with the damage Robert's two cannons were inflicting upon her.

"She didn't return my fire!" shouted Robert from the gallery outside John's cabin.

"I noticed!" called back John, leaning over the rail. "My guess is that Smoot's ordered the Walrus captain to board without sinking us. The fool's probably taken that to mean he can't use his cannons at all!"

"The Walrus is moving forward, out of our range!" called Robert once more. "Do you want me to remain with these two cannons or come topside?"

"Come topside!" answered John as he watched the Walrus through his spyglass. "And have your cannons returned to the gun deck as quickly as possible." Two minutes later, Robert joined his Captain near the aft rail. John was still studying his attacker. By his count, there were more than fifty pirates along the rail; their sashes filled with flintlocks, daggers and cutlasses.

"What do you see?"

"I was correct, and this time I'll be ready for them!" answered John. "The fools didn't learn their lesson."

"Their lesson?" asked Robert.

"The Falmouth Packet...remember?" Robert nodded as John continued. "They'll attempt a boarding from our lee, if I allow it, that is."

"If you allow it?"

"Aye," answered John as he lowered his glass and pointed at the Walrus rigging. "Their canvas is set for speed, and they'll have to spill half of it to slow for a boarding maneuver."

"And?" asked Robert as he studied the Walrus.

"And they won't be able to," John said as he pointed into his own sails. "David and the best of our marksmen will rain down lead on the first man who touches a sheet."

"I'm not sure I follow you, John. What are you planning to do?"

"Once they've moved far enough forward, we'll cut behind their stern to leeward where we can bring our windward guns to bare on their hull. With any luck, we can sink the Walrus before she can reposition."

As the Walrus neared their beam position, a steady barrage of small arms fire rained from the Silver Cloud's rigging, keeping most of the pirates off the deck and away from the sheets. As John had planned, the Walrus' greater speed quickly drove her past her prey and into the open water beyond.

The Cloud's helmsman was a young Irishman by the name of Gill Poynter; a lad of nineteen years.

"Any moment now, Poynter," said Captain Jones with a hand on the helmsman's shoulder. "When I give the signal, I'll want you to bring the ship hard starboard."

"Behind her, sir?"

"Aye," John answered. "She can't board from windward, and we need a little more time."

"Mister Noble!" called Captain Jones. "Bring your sharpshooters down to join the gun crews to larboard! We'll be moving to her lee and I'll want your best broadside."

"By your order, Captain Jones!" answered David as he slung his rifle about his shoulder and slid a sheet to the deck.

"Now, Poynter!" shouted Captain Jones. "Hard to starboard!" The Silver Cloud seemed to bury its bow in the waves for a moment as her forward movement was cut in half and her massive bowsprit swung within twenty yards of the Walrus taffrail. For a brief moment, the eyes of the two Captains-- Pritchard on the Walrus and Jones on the Silver Cloud--met in a defiant stare.

"I'll have that treasure or die tryin', Captain Jones!" yelled Pritchard as he drew and fired his pistol at the Scotsman. The ball hit the young helmsman in the left thigh, dropping him to the deck. Captain Jones grabbed the spinning wheel and yelled back a cryptic reply.

"If you know me by name, then you'll remember the Falmouth Packet also, and how she took off your rudder near Charles Town winter of last year."

"That was you?" cried Pritchard in disbelief.

"Aye, and I'll do worse today!" John turned to his First Officer as a new helmsman relieved John at the wheel and the injured man was taken below.

"I'll have that broadside now, Mister Noble!"

A moment later, the afternoon sky was filled with white smoke as a wall of iron crashed into and through the Walrus' hull. The two massive ships stood no more than a hundred feet apart, making every shot point blank. But still the Walrus held her fire and continued to fall aft.

"They'll be moving to our lee again, Robert, just like before. But this time I've a little surprise for them!"

"All sheet crews," called Captain Jones, "take up grappling hooks and small arms to larboard, for we've a hand fight before us! And since the cutthroats offered us no quarter, there'll be none given to them!"

As the critical moment approached, Captain Jones studied the Walrus' deck crew for the slightest sign of movement. It began with a signal from the pirate Captain to his first mate, and with the first mate calling to the several groups of half-naked men at the sheets. A moment later, the Walrus' sails began to slack to slow the ship for her turn behind the treasure ship.

Rather than risk having his helmsman misunderstand his order and turn the wrong way, Captain Jones took the helm. At just the right moment, he threw the Silver

Cloud hard to larboard, driving her directly into the path of the turning ship. A panic broke out on both ships as the bowsprit of the Walrus rammed over the Silver Cloud's larboard bulwarks amidships.

There was a tremendous shudder aboard both ships as the figurehead on the Walrus' bow shattered against the Cloud's rail. Nearly every man was thrown to the deck as the two entangled ships began to twist counter-clockwise in the blue swells. A dozen grappling hooks flew through the air and bit deeply into the Walrus wherever they could, permanently coupling the two together.

"My God!" yelled Robert in dismay. "What on earth have you done? Do you want us to go down with them?"

As Robert recoiled from the mass of pirates who began to scramble through their jib stays toward the Silver Cloud, a thunder of small arms fire erupted from the Cloud's deck. Those pirates not killed by the first volley, or by the jabbing pikes, quickly retreated to their own deck.

There was no point in Captain Jones or the new helmsman staying at the wheel, nor for any of the crew to remain at their sailing stations, for the two ships were locked together like lovers on the dance floor; the Walrus fastened amidships and perpendicular to the Cloud. With his sword drawn and flashing in the afternoon sun, Captain Jones rushed forward to join the attack.

"McCoy!" John called behind him. "Open their hull with bar stock until you've a hole large enough for a dose of burning coals and grape shot! I want her set afire, and her planking stripped from her ribs!"

One by one the great frigate's cannons belched out their fire and brimstone into the bow and flanks of the helpless Walrus. Helpless, because none of her main cannons could be trained forward more than ten degrees beyond the perpendicular. The only firepower she could return was small arms and the three swivel guns mounted on her forward rails.

It was a short and one-sided battle. While the larboard guns four through seven punched holes in the Walrus' bow and sent a hell of destruction through the length of her gun deck, guns one though three and the two remaining aft cannons raked the Walrus at her waterline. As the two great ships twisted in their grisly dance of death, the breeze began to carry away the accumulation of sulphurous smoke, revealing to the Silver Cloud's crew the destruction they had wrought on their enemy.

Like an executioner tearing flesh from his victim's ribs with the cat, the Silver Cloud's gunners peeled the Walrus' planking away piece by piece. Between each explosion of cannon and shattering of wood, the screams of pirates could be heard as they were either thrown or leaped from the holes opened along her waterline. As Captain Jones had ordered, cannons numbers four through seven were loaded with a combination of barstock and what McCoy called a hot load; pieces of burning oak and coal. Two of the loads hit their mark, causing several secondary explosions within the great hull.

Only the more seasoned sailors aboard the Silver Cloud had ever witnessed such human carnage. One of the Walrus' powder monkeys; a lad no more than ten or twelve years old, jumped from the purgatory that the Walrus' gun deck had become. It was to quench his burning clothes that he leaped, completely unaware that his left arm and part of his shoulder had been ripped away in the battle. Another pirate stood in one of the yawning holes on the windward side, holding his face. The way his hands wrapped about his mouth, it appeared as if he was going to call out to someone on the Cloud. But then he dropped his hands to his sides, revealing that his bottom jaw was missing. He stood for a moment longer and then toppled forward into the sea.

The dark waters now began to spill into the Walrus' stern, pulling her several yards lower in the water. As her bow began to rise and she backed away, the grappling lines began to tear loose from the Silver Cloud. Now, nearly free from the Silver Cloud, the Walrus' wallowed about in the surge of oncoming swells, exposing her main deck to the Cloud's cannons. These gunners reloaded with grape shot and methodically cut down every pirate who had run topside from the fires below.

"John!" cried Robert as he grabbed Captain Jones by his sword arm. "Haven't they had enough?"

"Not until they're sunk!" John answered as he pried the Yorkman's hand from his arm.

"But, have you no mercy?"

"It's justice, Robert, not mercy they've earned! If the tables were turned, do you suppose for an instant they'd treat us otherwise?" Robert said something, but it was drowned out by two more of the Silver Cloud's cannons ripping men from the Walrus' deck in a spray of blood, splinters of wood and broken bones.

The two ships had been coupled in battle for no more than six or seven minutes when the Walrus' taffrail sank into the cooling waters, extinguishing the fire which had erupted near her stern.

"Noble!" called Captain Jones from the quarterdeck. "Give the order to cut her free!"

The warm waters of the Caribbean are alive with sharks. At feeding time, these wolves of the sea are drawn to their prey by not only the smell of blood, but by low-frequency sound waves pulsating for long distances through the water. As the one-sided battle raged between the treasure ship Silver Cloud and the pirate ship Walrus, each crash of ball into and through the inner members of the Walrus' hull, and each thud and bump of her stores colliding with her bulkheads, sent out that unmistakable call to dinner. And long before the last grappling hook had been severed and the Walrus' great bowsprit had ripped itself loose from the Silver Cloud's rigging, the sea churned with the frenzied beasts.

The cannon fire had finished its ugly work, turning over the task of sinking the Walrus to her own ballast; the tons of stones placed years before in her bilges for stability. She was sinking rapidly now, slipping backwards below the swells more quickly with each passing swell. The thick smoke which had been pouring from her hatches and lee side ceased abruptly with a hiss and cloud of white steam as the sea rushed in. She was like a dying beast, crying out her agony in tremendous groans and heaving sighs as each compartment was flooded from stern to bow. As her ballast continued to pull her down, she pitched backwards until her mizzenmast lay back flat in the water and the bowsprit pointed skyward in a final salute to her defeat.

And then the Walrus was gone. The bone-chilling sounds of sucking and blowing, like a drowning cow, had stopped as her shattered figurehead and bowsprit descended from view, leaving only the tangle of rope and torn canvas as a mute testimony that a ship had once been there. But there were also the survivors; seven pirates clinging to the splintered planking and broken pieces of rail and yardarms.

"What about them, John?" asked David over their cries for help. "Shall I order the boats out?"

"I don't think there'll be time," answered Captain Jones. "But I guess decency demands that we do something."

"Time?" David asked. "I don't understand!" David fell silent as he realized that the survivor's calls for help had changed to terror. Up until the Walrus had sunk, the sharks had remained at a distance, as if the great ship was a competitor for the meal they had come to take. But with it's descent into the depths, the sharks closed in. The first three to venture close to the men were small, only six to eight feet long. But the forth shark was a giant. It's slate-gray pectoral fin stood two feet out of the water as it cruised straight for the three men clinging to a length of top rail.

"My God!" yelled Robert as he pointed. Before the great shark had made its attack, one of the dead pirates who had been cut in half and thrown into the sea by an explosion, suddenly popped to the surface, twitching and jerking about as if it had regained life and was back to cast a final curse upon it's enemy. As the pale face turned about for a lifeless gaze at the Silver Cloud, three large barracudas played a tug-of-war at the flesh of its arms and ribs.

"Help us, mates!" begged one of the pirates over the cries of his fellows. "Don't let us die like this! Don't let the sharks..." He fell silent to watch the large fin pass close abeam and then twist about toward him and his mate. There was a flash of white underbelly as the monster rolled to it's back.

It's said that what's in a man's heart will come out just before he goes to meet his Maker. If that's true, then this pirate was a Godly man, for his last words before the great shark pulled him below the waves came directly from the pulpit.

"My God! Oh sweet Jesus, save this poor sinner!" And then he was gone.

A deathly quiet fell over the Silver Cloud and the six remaining pirates as they stared at the spot on the splintered yard where the man had been a moment before.

"The boat, John?" demanded David. "Shall I order it lowered?"

"There's no point." As John spoke, two more of the pirates were pulled from the flotsam amidst screams and boiling water turned crimson with their blood. "Even if they deserved the least mercy, those sharks will have finished their task long before we could begin ours."

"But we can't just let them die that way!" pleaded Robert.

"No, I suppose we can't," said John as he turned. "David, I want four of our best marksmen to the rail with their muskets."

"But there are too many of them!"

"They won't be shooting at the sharks."

"You're going to shoot the men, rather than try to save them?" asked Robert.

"I have no choice," answered John coldly, "unless you want those poor souls to die like their mates." The four riflemen stepped to the rail as ordered, and at their Captain's signal, fired at the four pirates. The Yorkman turned away in horror as the four balls struck their marks.

The battle was over, with only two of the Silver Cloud's crew dead and three others injured. While the seabirds were fast at work cleaning up after their larger cousins' furious lunch, Captain Jones walked to the starboard rail where his friend from New York was losing his lunch.

"I'm sorry I had to do that, Robert. The sharks gave me no choice."

"Don't you think I know that?" answered the older man as he wiped his mouth with his kerchief. "It's just that..."

"It's no wonder," interrupted John, "that you made that promise at your wedding. You and Moira must have witnessed ten fold what we saw here today. All we can do is put it behind us and continue with our mission."

Within twenty minutes, the damaged rigging had been cut away; the salvageable lines and sailcloth were stowed while the rest was cast over the side. Following a quick look at his chart, Captain Jones reset the course for Spyglass Island, with the Remora a half-mile on their stern and the Eagle another quarter mile further aft.

The closer the Silver Cloud moved toward Spyglass, the more the old maroon, Ben Gunn, changed. He grew quieter each day and the scratching became more furious as he drifted back to that other world; the solitary life of guarding John Flint's third of the treasure. The transformation bothered Captain Jones deeply, but there was nothing to be done for the old soul.

CHAPTER 15

In 1764, when the brig Hispaniola departed Spyglass, three of Long John Silver's crew escaped capture and remained marooned for ten years, just as Ben Gunn had been up until that time. Without provisions beyond the meager tools Doctor Livesey had left for them, survival was difficult at best; the three subsisted mostly on roots, coconuts, and the sea creatures they could pull from the tide pools at the base of the Western cliffs. There were plenty of goats roaming the hills, but once their supply of powder and balls had been spent, they were forced to live from hand to mouth; no better than the animals they sought to capture.

It was during the fourth month of their second year on the island that 'Morley the Demented', as the other two had named their slow-witted mate, chanced upon Ben Gunn's cave. Here was hidden the part of Flint's treasure left in haste by Captain Smollet and the others for fear of another attack by the three.

Despite his slower wit, Morley Rowe was a cut above his mates, always looking for a nicer place to claim for his own. The old stockade had begun to smell like the bilge of a slave ship and Morley wanted out. He had searched the island for several months when he chanced upon Ben Gunn's second cave. It was deep and narrow, and high on the face of a cliff, accessible only by way of a narrow and heavily overgrown ledge. The treasure was hidden deep inside, far beyond the light of day.

When silver oxidizes it has a distinctive, sulfuric smell, and that's what drew Morley inside. By the light of a torch, the man found over three hundred silver bars weighing seventy pounds each, and a small chest of jewels containing a gold crown, the companion to the one now lying in the lazarette of the Silver Cloud. It was this crown that Morley foolishly brought to his shipmates just at sunrise that fateful day. Dick Walpole and Tom Morgan lay on their makeshift cots in the smelly stockade, scratching the body lice that Ben Gunn had so graciously left for them.

"Rise and pay homage to your king!" Morley blurted from the doorway in his most pompous voice. The bright morning sun shined through the door and into the eyes of the two drowsy pirates.

"Yer daft, Morley!" spat Dick as he raised himself on an elbow and chucked a stone toward the light. "Go back and talk to yer goats. Ha, ha, ha!" Tom and Dick could only make out Morley's silhouette and missed the object that adorned his head.

"Daft, am I?" he protested as he strode across the room and stood proudly between them. "If I be daft, then what do ye call this bauble on me head?"

"Where'd ya get that?" cried Walpole, springing to his feet.

"Yeah!" echoed Morgan as he grabbed for the crown. "Where'd that come from?"

"Why, it's the other part o' John Flint's treasure, it is!" said Morley as he dodged Morgan and strutted about the dark room with his new toy. "Ben Gunn must'a forgot 'bout this part."

As Morley finished his short circuit of the room and looked upon his two mates once more, he noticed that Tom Morgan had his cutlass drawn and was moving toward him.

"Not so fast, Tom!" warned Morley as he backed away toward the door. "Kill me and ye'll never find the rest."

"Oh, I won't be killin' ya, Morley," hissed Tom as he continued forward. "I were only fixin' to torture ya into sharing the treasure with yer two mates, as is proper when ya sign articles." As Tom continued his press, Dick sat down on his cot in confusion.

"If ye want yer share, Dick," warned Tom, "then take up yer weapon an' join me!"

"But I don't know what to do!" cried the third maroon. "Yer both me mates, not just you, Tom!" Dick Walpole had never been a man of decision. He was strong, and he was a faithful follower, the perfect combination for a pirate. But when faced with a decision, his timid nature took over and held him back as surely as irons hold their prisoner.

"Choose quickly, man!" shouted Tom. By now, Morley had drawn his cutlass in defense and had backed out into the bright sunlight. Since he had already been out in the light, his eyes adjusted quickly, giving him a temporary advantage over the other two. "Pull that cutlass now, Walpole, and stand by one of us!"

As the two argued over their loyalties, Morley seized his chance to flee. By the time Tom and Dick had realized he was gone, Morley was down the hill and across the swamp, halfway to Captain Kidd's Lagoon. It was a simple matter to follow their prey, for rather than choose the rocks and dry ground where his tracks would be concealed, Morley plodded through the mud and knee high grass, cutting a trail even he could follow. As his two pursuers neared the short stretch of beach, Morley's voice peeled out at them in panic.

"Ye've ganged up on me again, an' that's not fair! An' besides, it's my treasure by rights!"

"By what rights?" called Tom from a hundred yards away.

Morley had backed himself to the water's edge, right where the first boat from the Hispaniola had landed more than a year earlier. He held his cutlass in one hand, and the crown in the other. His pursuers skidded to a halt thirty feet up the beach.

"By the right of me findin' it, that's what!"

"You go first, Dick," whispered Morgan with an assuring hand on Walpole's back. "He trusts you the most. And besides, I'll be right here at yer shoulder."

With a push from his mate, Dick stumbled several steps forward and stopped.

"Don't make me hafta cut ya, Morley," begged Dick as he glanced over his shoulder to make sure Tom was still there. "You know I'm the best with a cutlass, an' besides, we should share the treasure three ways, shouldn't we?"

"Of course we should!" whispered Tom as he gave his timid mate another shove. Then, calling over Dick's shoulder, "Tis better it be shared by all three of us than fer us to hafta kill ya and split it in twain!"

Morley circled up the sand to the high water mark as the two advanced upon him. At six paces, he replaced the crown on his head and switched his cutlass to his left hand. With his right, he drew his cocked pistol and aimed it at Walpole's head.

"That'll be far enough, Walpole!" Morley hissed. His two pursuers stopped, frozen in their tracks, with Walpole leaning backward against Morgan's pushing hands.

"That pistol's empty!" Tom whispered in Dick's ear. "He ran outta powder last fall, same time we did!"

Bolstered by Tom's words of assurance, Dick ventured one more step forward.

"I'll give ya that one step, Walpole," said Morley as he pointed his flintlock at the man's foot, "but yer next'll be yer last." Morley raised the pistol and pointed it between the coward's eyes.

"Don't believe him, Dick!" whispered Tom with a shove. "He's just bluffin'!" There was an explosion of white smoke and two screams, one from an injured man and the other from a greedy pirate.

Out of the sulphurous cloud came Tom Morgan, swinging his cutlass like a madman. Morley stumbled several paces backwards into the water, threw the spent pistol aside and met his second attacker with the cry of a cornered animal. The rusty blades clattered together for several confusing moments amidst a tangle of grunts, growls and profanity. When the brief battle was over, the three pirates lay senseless on the beach, each with blood pumping from his wounds.

The King of Spyglass lay atop a pile of rotting seaweed for three days, while a herd of small crabs competed for the delicious meal that the right side of the pirate's head had provided. The cutlass blow hadn't killed Morley, but it had taken his right ear completely off as it cut deeply into his skull. When he finally regained consciousness, it was to a world entirely different than the one he had so recently left. Whereas the problems of his past were hunger and itching from the body lice, this new world was filled with pain and double images; a confusing carnival which spun about him with every movement of his body.

Lifting himself slowly from the seaweed so as not to retch, a searing pain shot through the right side of his head. It felt as if Tom's blade were still embedded in his skull, when actually it was only the gentle afternoon breeze which happened to blow into the gaping hole the crabs had made of his right ear canal.

"Damn you!" swore Morley across the sand at his senseless mates. The fingers of his right hand were still wrapped tightly about the old cutlass.

"Ye've opened me head to the elements, ye have!" he cried as he waved the rusty blade toward them. The small herd of glutted crabs backed away a few feet to wait patiently for the pirate to lie down again so they could resume their feast of blood and inner ear. But instead, they scattered as Morley's cutlass slapped the sand amongst them.

"And damn you crabs too!" swore Morley as he struggled upright to stand for a moment before falling senseless back into the shallow water.

Ten years later, nearly to the day, the pirate Morley Rowe and Dick Walpole stood on Mizzenmast Hill as three ships glided toward Captain Kidd's anchorage a quarter mile below and to the east. Morley gave Tom a shake.

"There, Dick! That were me!" bragged Morley, pointing at the man in the Silver Cloud's fore chains. "I were the one what threw the lead line fer John Flint, I was! Ya can't be too careful comin' in through them mud flats, ya know. Only measured two fathoms at high tide, it did."

The Silver Cloud edged past Skeleton Island with only her t'gallants and spanker catching the light evening breeze. The water depths were relayed aft by three of the crew, while a man standing on the lower foremast yard signaled the helm when to turn.

As the massive anchor dropped into the black waters, Morley poked his mate once more in the ribs.

"I tolt ya, didn't I?" he whispered. "This should teach ya once an' fer all, ya bilge-lickin' swab!" He gave his mate another short shake for emphasis and then the two stood watching, using each other for support. The same wind that pushed the ships to their anchorage whistled into Morley's enlarged right ear canal, bringing with it the same pain he had felt nearly a decade before when he awoke on the rotting seaweed. As his mate watched the ships with his typical hollow stare, Morley drooled slightly.

A large blow fly which had orbited Morley's head three times finally decided the gaping hole would make a fine place to rest a spell and perhaps lay a few eggs. Morley took a swing at the insect just before it landed, sending it off for a moment. The six-tiered gold crown the others had voted to let him wear fell into the dirt between them.

"What's that ye say?" Morley blurted, as he set the crown back on its rightful spot. "How'd I know they was comin'?" He gave the slack-jawed coward another shake. "I tolt ya last night I can smell a ship at ten leagues, I can." He pulled Dick close and looked about just in case someone might be eavesdropping on their conversation.

"It be John Silver an' Jimmy Hawkins," Morley whispered, "comin' back to rescue us. I knowed they wouldn't be maroonin' us here fer good." He took another swing at the blow fly and adjusted the crown once more as he studied the largest of the three ships.

Rowe was by nature a very suspicious fellow. He never brought but one of his mates with him at a time when he foraged for food. To do so was to risk an open mutiny and the loss of his crown. And likewise, he never left them alone together in his cave, for he knew they would plot against him in a minute if he should. Rowe seldom got a full night's sleep for all their whispering and bickering, but there was no way around it except by sleeping between them, as risky as that might be.

"Ye best be thankful I brought ya out here with me to see our rescuers, rather than Morgan," said Morley with a superior tone. "Tom's a nice enough fellow when we're all together, but when you ain't around, ya oughta hear him talk about ya. If it weren't fer me, you'd have no friends at all, an' ya know that to be true, right?" Walpole said nothing, but his toothy grin signified he must agree.

"There!" shouted Morley as he pointed at the ships. "Didn't I tell ya they'd drop anchor right there? Why, that be 'xactly the spot where Cap'n Flint an' me put the Walrus." Morley looked Dick in the eyes, suspecting the other didn't believe his lie. "John Flint trusted me, Dick Walpole, an' don't you let Tom tell you otherwise."

By now, the Silver Cloud had swung about her anchor chain, with the Eagle standing at the mouth of the lagoon and the Remora another two hundred yards beyond in open water. The sounds of the Captain's orders, and the men going about their duties stirred a hunger inside Morley that he hadn't felt for years.

"Aye," said Morley as if he were sitting in a box at a fine opera house in London, "listen to the Bosun's commands! 'Tis music to me ears, it is." Walpole seemed to whisper something to Rowe. "To me larboard ear, then, thanks to you an' yer cursed cutlass!" Dick's head cocked sideways to study the two other ships.

"Them other two?" Morley answered. "Why they be rescue ships fer you an' Morgan, of course. John Silver knows us three never got along very well, so he had to send one fer each of us." As Morley turned his head a bit too quickly to look back down at the three ships, he had another of his frequent dizzy spells and fell sideways to the ground, with Walpole falling full length on top of him. Morley's dagger flashed in the afternoon sun.

"I warned you 'bout that, damn you!" swore the demented maroon at his mate. "This time ye've gone an' done it, and with yer rescue so close at hand, too!" Morley pressed the blade against Dick's windpipe, just above the Adam's apple. The two faced each other nose-to-nose as Dick's eyes seemed to plead for mercy.

"Oh sure!" blurted Morley sarcastically. "Go on, won't ya, usin' that same line on me! Fer all I know, ya never did have a wife or no four children ta feed back in Savannah! Ya think old Morley Rowe's a long gone fool, don't ya? My brains didn't slip out through no scupper." Morley glanced behind them, sure to find Morgan skulking about in the shadows somewhere; just waiting for the opportunity to jump Morley while he was down.

"You an' Tom think it's right funny to make old Morley fall in the dirt, don't ya?" Dick's head shook slowly from side to side.

"No?" asked Morley, sensing his mate was beginning to show true repentance for tripping him. "Well, since our rescue's so close, I might let ya off this one last time. But don't try nothin' tonight, ya hear?" Morley threw Dick backward against the cliff. "An' if I see ya talkin' with Tom 'bout me fallin' down, you'll have hell to pay."

As the two maroons replayed this oft-acted scene, the orange orb of the sun dropped quietly into the dark Caribbean waters to the west. Old seamen used to say that if you listened very carefully, you could almost hear the hiss as it was extinguished for the night. With the suns last pink rays reflecting off the high clouds, the three ships folded their wings for the long awaited sleep they so well deserved. Nightfall was also the signal for Morley and his mate to return to the protection of their cave on Mizzenmast Hill.

"Ye'll see," Morley said as he jerked Dick to his feet. "They'll come fer us at first light, so we'd best be about gettin' our things together."

As the two edged their way along the narrow ledge toward Ben Gunn's cave, Morley turned for one last look at his rescuers. But as always, the movement was just enough to confuse what remained of his mutilated right inner ear, throwing him and Tom against the cliff wall with a string of curses. The words wove an especially disgusting tapestry that floated like a magic carpet downward across the beach and over the glassy waters of Captain Kidd's Lagoon.

"Cap'n Jones!" said the stern watch in a whisper as he pointed toward the silhouetted hill. "There it is again, sir."

"You still think you hear the cussing, Clark?"

"Aye, sir, I'm certain of it."

"And you're sure it's coming from that hill?"

"Aye, an' it be as plain as you speakin' to me, it be." Captain Jones walked to the rail and listened carefully, but the maroons had retired to their cave for the night.

"Interesting," said John as he walked toward the companionway. Stopping, he turned back to the seaman. "Inform Mister Noble that I've retired to my stateroom."

"Aye, aye, sir, and..."

"And what?" asked the Captain as he hesitated.

"I were just thinkin', sir. If ya be needin' volunteers to go ashore in the mornin', I'd be in yer debt if I could be in one of the first boats."

"You're a good man, Clark. I'll have a word with the other officers."

"Thank you, sir," the lad said as he remembered something else. "Oh! An' you'll still be wantin' a call tonight at 2200 hours?"

"Yes, I will."

Captain Jones looked across the hundred yards of still water to where the Eagle pulled gently at her anchor chain.

"It's a perfect night for a swim."

Shortly after 2200 hours, twelve men clad only in their britches, slipped over the starboard rail of the Silver Cloud and into the warm waters of Captain Kidd's lagoon, putting them on the opposite side from the Eagle. Each man was armed with a cutlass and several daggers, which hung from sashes about their shoulders.

Silence was the order, but with the raucous singing and laughter coming from the Eagle, their detection was next to impossible, even for the single watchman who sat alone drinking on the privateer's bow. Strains of a familiar line-hauling song filled the sultry air:

> *"Buckets o' blood spilt in the hold,*
> *Flint accused Rip Rap, The treasure ye've stold.*
> *Ye took it to the Isle called Dead Man's Chest,*
> *Where ye laid it by fer half a score's rest.*

> *"Fifteen men on the Dead Man's Chest,*
> *Yo ho ho and a bottle of rum.*
> *Drink and the devil has done for the rest,*
> *Yo ho ho and a bottle of rum.*

By the time the drunken pirates had finished the song and repeated it for a third time, Captain Jones and his eleven men clung to the Eagle's planking. The singing continued, but the rum had slurred the words so badly that it sounded like most any other late night tavern song. Several men topside had begun to argue while three or four others slept. From the thumping and yelling, it was plain that at least two men were engaged in a fight somewhere on deck.

"I don't think anybody's on watch," whispered David.

"No," agreed John. "And from the sound of it, they're all forward, near the fo'csle." Captain Jones wiped the salt water from his eyes and made a quick head count.

"David," John began at a whisper, "take half the men to the larboard side and climb to the gunwale. Hold there until you see me come over this side." Turning to the rest of the men, he gave a final note of caution. "Remember, our primary objective is to rescue Captain Steele. If we can do that, and take the pirates alive--especially Smoot and that kid with the orange hair--then well enough. But if some of them die, then that's the price they'll just have to pay." He paused and looked about his small raiding party. "Any questions?"

"I've one," said Robert. "Why haven't they tried something before tonight? It's so odd that..."

"It only seems that way," whispered John. "They've had several good chances to attack us, but since we maintained the advantage, they must have decided to continue their masquerade until the treasure reaches Kings Town." John looked around at the others. "Anything else?"

"I've never done anything like this before," whispered David nervously.

"Neither have I," answered John, "but I think we have an excellent chance. We've the advantage of surprise on our side, and what's more, their only lanthorn is that one at the bow. It'll be nearly impossible for them to see us until we're upon them."

"Aye," added McCoy, "an' they be full o' the spirits, too."

"Go now, David," ordered John. "I'll give you a count of one hundred before we move."

Several minutes later, twelve pairs of eyes peered over the rails. As Captain Jones had predicted, all the topside crew was huddled about a single lanthorn forward, some sitting on powder kegs while the rest either laid on the hard deck or sat atop the two forward cannons. The fighting at the fo'csl was still going on, bringing the irate cry of Captain Smoot.

"Damn you two! Either kill each other, or be done with it!" The cutthroats burst into laughter and cat calls as they egged on the two combatants.

"Now!" whispered John, as he and his five men slid over the rail and began to creep forward. They were met by David and his team just aft of the main mast.

"Why are they fighting that way?" whispered David as the two pirates circled and slashed at each other's faces. "Why don't they let go and back away?"

"Because they can't," answered Robert. "Look closely at their left arms."

"My God! They're strapped together at the forearms!" cried David. "Why..?"

"They did the same thing on the Walrus twenty years ago," answered Robert. "It was Flint's way of settling disputes and providing a show for the rest of the crew."

"Then there's only eighteen to deal with," whispered John. "Let's take them now, while their attention's drawn toward those two."

By now, the two men had lost so much blood that they had sunk to their knees. Their cries of pain and curses had become feeble, almost inaudible whimpers when Captain Jones and his men descended upon the other eighteen. A confused moment later, eight of the pirates lay dead or dying. Of the remaining ten cutthroats, only three had the presence of mind to surrender without further bloodshed. The other seven leaped over the side and swam for shore, with two non-swimmers drowning within seconds. But the sounds of the short battle were just loud enough to bring Captain Smoot from his cabin in a rage.

"Damn you!" he shouted. "Do I have to kill ya meself?" Before him stood twelve men with cutlasses and daggers at the ready, clad in britches and silhouetted by the forward lanthorn.

"So it's a mutiny, is it?" Smoot hissed as he slashed at the two nearest men with his sword. "You fools! I told you we'd wait an' take the treasure after it reaches Kings Town; when we can take it without a struggle." He waited for one of the men to answer, but none did. "If ye've had a fo'csl council, then be men enough to tell me!" There was still no answer. "Very well. If ya intend to cut me down, then do me the decency o' lettin' me choose who I fight first, like is fittin' fer pirates." His eyes darted back and forth at the dozen men. "Where are ya, Morgan? Step forward, lad, and be the first to taste my steel! You owe me that much!"

"I'm up here!" shouted Morgan, "Tied up with the others!"

"Tied up! Then who..?" Smoot raised his sword hand to shade his eyes from the light behind John. "Who are you?"

"I'm John Paul Jones, Captain of the Silver Cloud."

Smoot's eyes flashed a combination of fear and hatred as he retreated a step. "And while your men sang and drank to their own destruction, I've taken your ship." The Scotsman took a step forward with an outstretched hand. "Your sword, Captain Smoot!"

Expecting what followed, John was quick to pull back his hand as Smoot slashed downward through the sultry night air. The pirate's descending blade cut deeply into the oak decking between the two Captains. At a signal from John, his men backed away to give the two combatants a clear deck.

"David," ordered John as he and Smoot circled each other like two wolves fighting for dominion over the pack, "take several men and find Captain Steele!"

"Aye, aye, Captain!"

"That's unless you've killed him," hissed John, "like the rest of his men!"

"Ha!" barked Smoot as his cutlass glanced off the younger man's blade with a clatter. "If cuttin' sugar cane on Saint Croix means they be dead, then dead they be."

"So you're not a complete barbarian after all?" said John as he defended himself against several more wild cuts from the pirate. In a moment of carelessness, Smoot's neck became exposed to Captain Jones; a perfect opportunity to decapitate the pirate. But rather than kill the scoundrel, John cracked Smoot upon the left side of his throat with the flat of his sword.

"Ahhhh!" cried Smoot, grabbing at his throat and looking at the fingers. There was no blood. "You bastard! Why didn't you kill me?"

"I'm not sure," answered Captain Jones. "Something tells me I should keep you alive." Smoot lowered his sword, and for the second time, John stretched forth his hand.

"I'll ask you just one last time, Captain Smoot. Will you surrender now, or must I kill you?"

"Since you put it that way, Captain Jones, I've no choice but to..." Smoot turned his sword at right angles as if to lay it in John's open hand, and then lunged forward with a vicious slash, just as he had done before. As before, Captain Jones was expecting the action and pulled his hand back to safety. But by coincidence, John had positioned his hand over the mainmast pin rail so that Smoot's downward blow cut away several ropes and one belaying pin, and with it two buntline sheets.

With a resounding slap, the starboard half of the spencer unfurled directly above the two combatants. Smoot, expecting rigging to come clattering down about their ears, ducked and made a quarter turn to his left, bringing his sword hand across in front of Captain Jones. There was a flash of polished steel and a high-pitched whistle as John's sword arced downward through flesh and bone. Captain Smoot had surrendered his sword after all, but with his hand still gripping it's hilt.

"My hand! My hand!" screamed the pirate as he fell backwards against one of the waist cannons and then dropped forward to his knees, watching wide-eyed at the fountain of bright red blood squirting from the severed limb. "You've killed me! I'm losin' me life's blood all over the deck!"

"Captain Jones!" called David from the aft companionway. "Look what I found!" David walked forward toward the light with Captain Steele at his left side. But behind him and to his right stood a young girl in her mid teens. She was a little shorter than David, five foot four at the most. Her dress was of a light cotton fabric, torn in several places at the hemline. Her shoulder-length blond hair showed the last traces of curls at the ends. She looked down in shame at her condition.

"Well, well!" said John as David took her hand and urged her forward. "It looks as if our little rescue party's netted us two prizes rather than only the one we'd hoped for!" John took a lanthorn from one of his men and brought it near the girl. "Who is she, Smoot?"

"What about me?!" screamed the bleeding pirate. By now, the pain had driven the pirate forward, with his forehead pressed hard against the deck. "Look at it!" he continued to scream as he gripped the stump. "My blood's leakin' down through the scupper!" John ignored the man's cries as he raised the lanthorn to the girl's face.

"And who might you be, young lady?" asked John. The girl wouldn't answer him.

"Smoot knows!" interrupted Captain Steele as he walked forward, rubbing his iron-sore wrists. He gave Smoot a kick in the side. "She was aboard before he took me prisoner at Christiansted."

"I'll ask you one last time, Smoot. Who is she, and where'd you get her?"

"She's nobody!" whimpered the pirate, turning his head on the oak planking to look toward the girl. "She's just a... pretty face."

"Did they molest you?" asked John of the girl. She shook her head.

"I can attest to that, John," said Captain Steele. "Nobody's laid a hand on her since they've come aboard."

"If that's true," said John with a sword prick to Smoot's shoulder, "then she must be somebody special. You must have expected a large ransom for her, or else you and your men would have..."

"John!" said Robert with a shake of his head. John pulled the light away and turned to Captain Steele.

"Henry, did she tell you anything?"

"She couldn't. Smoot kept us separated except for the occasional meal he'd force us to eat with him. Kept her locked in the cabin next to his own. I heard her threaten Smoot several times that her father would take revenge, but that's all she ever said."

"Well," answered John, "the sooner we can get her back to the Silver Cloud, the sooner she can begin to recover." He turned back to David, who was still holding the girl's hand. "Since you found her, David, I'll trust you to see that she's taken care of."

"With your permission," answered David, "I'll take her and Captain Steele back to the Cloud in the Eagle's boat, and send it back for you and the others in a few minutes."

"Do that," answered John. "We'll be busy here with Captain Smoot for a short while anyway."

"Is anybody going to do anything about my hand?" cried Smoot.

"Perhaps if you'll tell us who she is," answered John as he pressed the tip of his sword against the raw flesh. Smoot jerked the bloody stump away with a scream.

"Don't!" cried Smoot. "She's just...she's nobody special!"

"Hold his arm down," ordered Captain Jones. Once again, John pressed the tip of his sword against the open wound. "Who is she?"

"Ahhh!" cried Smoot. "I'll tell! I'll tell!"

"Well?" asked John.

"She's the Governor's daughter!"

"Governor Wright's daughter?" asked John with a look at the girl. "This is Jane Wright?"

"Yes, for God's sake!" cried Smoot. "Now will you do something about my arm?"

"And you figured he'd have paid dearly for her return, right?" asked John.

"I wasn't after the money!" answered Smoot. "I was gonna trade her for a Letter of Marque."

"And what if the Governor hadn't agreed?" asked Captain Steele. He and David were still aboard, waiting for their boat to be lowered into the water. "What then, Smoot?" added Steele as he bent down and grabbed a handful of tarred hair and twisted the pirate's head sideways. "You'd have eaten her too, wouldn't you?"

"Eaten her?" John held the lanthorn close to Henry's face. "What do you mean by that?"

"Smoot's a cannibal," answered Henry slowly. "I heard his men brag about it. They cooked and ate another girl they were holding prisoner. Miss Wright was forced to watch the entire thing."

"Is that true?" asked John slowly as he raised his sword above the kneeling pirate. "Did you and your crew kill and eat a human being?"

"Don't, John!" cried David with a touch to his Captain's arm.

The sword hung in the night air above the decadent pirate's neck, with only a speck of human compassion holding it back. It quivered with each of Captain Jones' heartbeats, poised for the downward slash which would take the animal's head off.

"He doesn't deserve one more breath of God's good air!" John hissed. "Not another breath!"

"But we're civilized men," argued David, "not animals, like him. You said it yourself! We're men of law, not of passion! He'll surely hang from the gibbet, but he deserves a fair trial first!"

John held the sword in the air for another moment and then drove it downward with all his might into the planking next to the pirate's bleeding wrist. "Burn his wound shut!" John ordered. "And burn it well!"

When Captain Smoot finally regained consciousness, it was in the brig of the Silver Cloud with irons on his ankles and left wrist. A single shot hole that hadn't been worth patching allowed the morning sunlight to stream in upon him and the other six prisoners. Among them was Henry Morgan, the carrot-topped carpenter from Tortuga. He was staring intently through the peephole at something.

"What ya be lookin' upon, Morgan?" asked Smoot weakly as a shudder of pain coursed through his bandaged right arm.

"The boats, Govn'r," answered Morgan. "They're goin' fer the rest of Flint's treasure."

"Jane?" called David quietly as he tapped her cabin door. "Are you awake?" There was no answer so he tapped a second time. The girl hadn't spoken the previous night, and she had spoken but sparingly since her abduction from the merchant ship Alan Booth twelve leagues east of Savannah two weeks earlier. Smoot had only attacked the merchantman to capture the Governor's daughter. The second girl was an afterthought; something pretty his men could play with so they wouldn't bother their Captain's personal prize. David waited several moments and called through the closed door.

"I brought you some breakfast. I thought you might be hungry." There was a sound from within the cabin, followed by the slide bolt retracting from its keeper. The heavy door swung open a few inches.

"Jane?" She still refused to answer, so he pushed the door with the side of his foot and looked inside. The sixteen-year old girl stood at her porthole with tears running down her cheeks. She held a bar of lye soap in her hand.

David sat the tray on the desk. "Barragan cooked you something special." She turned and looked at him and then turned back to the activity outside her porthole.

"They're going ashore for provisions and to get the last of John Flint's treasure. I'd be going along also, but I told Captain Jones that I'd rather stay on the ship with you."

"I want to go ashore," she said through her tears. "I want a fresh water bath and clean clothes."

"I don't know if that's possible."

"It has to be possible. I won't come out of this room except to take a bath."

"Captain Jones said you were to remain aboard." The girl turned and wiped the tears from her cheeks.

"You'll ask him for me, won't you, David?"

"Couldn't you bathe in salt water, like we do?"

"No. My soap won't work in salt water." She held up the white bar just as Ben Gunn stepped from the stateroom across the passageway.

"Good morning, Master Noble!" cried the old man.

"Good morning, yourself, Mister Gunn! You're doing better than I expected."

"Aye," answered Ben as he looked into the young lady's cabin. "Will you an' the lass be comin' ashore with us?"

David stepped back into the passageway and pulled the girl's door closed behind him.

"The Captain gave me explicit orders that she remain aboard."

"You'll miss all the fun, lad."

"That doesn't bother me as much as..." David hesitated as he glanced toward her door.

"What's the matter, sir? Something with Miss Wright?"

"Ben, you know this island, right?"

"I should! I spent more time on it than any man should have to!"

"Is there someplace where a body can take a fresh water bath?"

"Aye," whispered Ben with a nudge to the lad's ribs. "Were ya plannin' on makin' yourself clean for the little lassie?"

"It's Miss Wright who wants the bath, not me. Her soap's made from lye."

"I see," answered Ben as he scratched a memory from his scalp.

"I told her it was impossible," said David, "but..."

"It isn't impossible, sir."

"Oh?"

"There's a stream a hundred yards beyond Flint's stockade that runs into the swamp. It should be full this time of year and there's a pool large enough for a right fine bath. I expect the trail would be grown over by now, but if you skirt the swamp, you'll come upon it in due time."

"Thank you, Ben," said David as he turned aft toward the Master's cabin.

"If he gives his permission," called Ben after the young man, "I'd take along a couple o' weapons, just in case. Captain Jones tells me some of Smoot's men might have made it to shore last night."

Within a half hour of talking with his Captain, David and Jane were ashore with one of the last groups of seamen. Following Ben's instructions, they found where the stream dumped into the swamp and then followed it eastward to the pool. David made a quick circuit of the area.

"It looks safe enough," said David as he pushed through the last bushes.

Without a word, she laid her change of clothing across a rock and began unbuttoning her bodice.

"Uh..." David said as he looked about for a place to go. "I'll sit on the other side of that rock until you're finished."

Jane watched until he was out of sight, and then finished undressing. A moment later, she lowered her tired body into the cool clear water. As the soap began to cleanse her skin, the young girl started humming a familiar ballad.

"With all that commotion on the Eagle," called David from the other side of the rock, "I didn't get a chance last night to tell you about myself."

"No, you didn't," she answered as she rubbed the soap into her hair. "I did hear your Captain say something about Jamaica, however. Are you from there?"

"Born and raised in the place!" he called back. "My father's a merchant there, and if I do well, I suppose he'll turn the business over to me some day."

"If you do well?"

David faltered, not knowing quite what to say. "What I meant was that if I get the naval commission Mister Jefferson has promised Captain Jones and me, then father will probably give me a partnership in his business."

"And how could a young man your age get one of Mister Jefferson's commissions? Does he owe you something?"

"It's the cannons," he answered. "My father has a thousand of them, and..."

"You said your father was a merchant, not an arms maker."

"He is a merchant. He traded them two years ago for..."

The air about David seemed to come alive as a high-pitched scream pierced his ears. He leaped up and over the rock as Jane refilled her lungs for a second scream, this one louder than the first.

Across the pool on a flat rock at water's edge stood the objects of her terror.

"What are you doing here!" cried David. "Why aren't you helping with the provisions?" The five began cavorting about like they were carrying burdens and then one pretended to whip the others with a twig. Jane had ducked down in the water to her chin and waited for the men to go away. When it became obvious they had no intention of leaving, Jane cast a look back at her protector.

"That's it!" swore David as he pointed one of his pistols above their heads and fired. By the time the smoke had cleared, the five were gone, leaving the two teenagers alone once more. David watched the trees for another minute, and then sat down on the shore to reload his pistol.

"Ahem," said Jane as she remained crouched in the water. David looked up from his work. "Do you mind," she said as she pointed back at his rock. "I'm not quite finished?"

"I'm sorry," he answered as he scrambled to his feet and walked beyond the rock.

"Do you know which five they were?" she asked.

"No," he answered. "There's a hundred and thirty of us on board. Those five are probably on another watch."

"Will they be punished?"

"Aye, at least a dozen stripes each. They know better."

"Twelve stripes? Isn't that a trifle severe? After all, they've been at sea for a long time and they were only curious."

"They should have been working rather than watching you bathe. Besides, it's my job to watch you bathe."

"Oh?" she giggled as he blushed.

As he rammed a lead ball down the barrel, a man cried out from the direction of the stockade as he pointed at David and Jane.

"There they are! They're at the stream to the north of the stockade!" A moment later, Jane had ducked into the water and twenty men stood about the pool with pulled weapons.

"What was that shooting?" asked John.

"Five of our men were watching Jane bathe. I had to fire one of my pistols to drive them off."

"Those had to be Smoot's men," corrected John, "the five who got away last night. I didn't expect them to show themselves this soon, if at all."

"Well," added David, "they won't be back again because I put a ball right over their heads."

"You underestimate them, David," said Robert.

"Robert's right," added John as he looked to the girl hiding in the water and back to David. "See that Jane's taken back to the Cloud and kept there. She's too big a temptation for those five."

"Don't forget our men," added Robert. "They've been without women for longer than the pirates."

"Do I have a say in this?" called Jane from the stream. "This is the first time I've been off a ship in nearly two months. I insist you allow me to remain ashore!"

"No," answered John. "And no, you don't have a say in this."

"But, why can't I..?" She paused as she looked about at the two-dozen men watching her. She ducked a little deeper in the water. "Do you mind?"

"You men," ordered John, "may return to your duties!"

"Thank you, Captain Jones," she said as the men snickered and ambled away. "Now, concerning my remaining ashore; I'm certain I'll be quite safe if I restrict my movements to the beach and return to the ship before dark. David has two pistols and he'll be with me at all times." John considered as he looked to the tangle of vines and undergrowth beyond the stream.

"I wouldn't advise it, John," whispered Robert.

"Captain Jones," Jane asked haughtily, "need I remind you who my father is?" John considered for a moment.

"Very well," said John to the girl, "but only on the beach, and you must be back aboard the Cloud before dark."

"You're very kind, sir. I'll be sure to tell my father all about you."

"I pray my kindness isn't tested, young lady."

"It won't be, John," said David as he pushed his pistols into the brace that hung across his chest. "I won't let her out of my sight." As John, Robert and Ben turned to leave, Ben tugged at John's sleeve.

"When can I take you up to my cave, Cap'n Jones?"

"First things first, Ben. I want all the provisions aboard and the rigging repaired. There'll be plenty of time."

"But..." began the old man. Captain Jones put a friendly hand across the old man's shoulders as he led him away from the pool.

"The sooner everything's aboard our ships, the sooner we'll be able to go up and take a look at it, Ben." As the last of the crew left the pool, David took up his position of defense once more, unaware that the maroon, Morley Rowe was watching their every movement from the cover of the bushes.

Work went quickly that day on Spyglass, despite the heat and humidity. As the sun began to drop toward the western horizon, David joined Jane at one of the camp fires.

"Do you suppose," she said as she ran her finger across the back of David's hand, "that Captain Jones would mind if we took a short walk on the beach?"

"He said we could," answered David as he looked at the sun to estimate how much more daylight remained to them. "Besides, those five would never try anything so close to the rest of the men." As they began to walk west along the water's edge, Captain Jones called after them.

"Mind yourselves. You can predict most of what a pirate will do, but..."

"Don't worry, Captain Jones," Jane snipped as she took David's hand and pulled him away toward the setting sun. "I'll keep him out of trouble." John flashed a stern look at David. "He's a worrywart, isn't he?" she said with a giggle.

"He's our Captain. Every man, and woman, onboard is his responsibility. He has to worry when so much is depending on him."

"So much?"

"Didn't Captain Steele tell you about our mission?"

"He never had the opportunity. We were kept apart except when Smoot brought us together in his cabin to dine." As she spoke, she took his hand and interlaced her fingers with his.

"I don't know whether I should say anything..." began David.

"Of course you can tell me! I'm Governor Wright's daughter. I hear all the secrets eventually anyway." David stopped walking while he considered. As he looked about, Jane stepped in front of him and looked up into his eyes. Her innocent beauty overwhelmed him.

"David?"

"What?"

"You were going to tell me about your mission."

"All right, but you have to promise that you'll not let anybody else know I told you, especially Captain Jones."

"I promise," she said as she crossed her heart.

"There's over a million and a half pounds in Spanish treasure in the Silver Cloud's lazarette, and we've stopped here to pick up another 350 silver bars. From here, we sail to a secret rendezvous with a twin ship filled with a thousand cannons for the Colonies.

"Will you get a reward for doing this?"

"Thomas Jefferson has promised Captain Jones and me commissions in the Continental Navy."

"Is that all?"

"And a share of the treasure; whatever's left after we purchase the cannons."

"A share?"

"Adding in this new treasure, my part is roughly fifteen thousand pounds."

"How delicious," she purred as she wrapped her arms about his left arm and urged him forward toward the rocks at the end of the beach. Stopping under a rock ledge, they watched the sun drop by degree toward the sparkling sea. She gave his arm a tight squeeze. "Want to know what kind of a man I'll marry someday?"

"What?"

"First, he'd have to be a God-fearing man like you, with..." Jane flashed a glance at his face. "…with hazel eyes, black hair, and he'd be exactly…" She reached across and put her opposite hand on his head as she spoke. "This tall."

"Are you saying…?"

"Do you like me, David?"

"Very much."

"Enough to kiss me as the sun sets?" David took a quick glance at the sun and then down into her eyes. The reflection of the sea set them ablaze. "They say it's good luck."

"I've never…"

"Kissed a girl before?"

"I've… kissed lots of girls," he lied. "I've just never kissed one… at sunset."

"It doesn't hurt," she purred. "Just lean down and close your eyes."

As David's eyes fluttered shut, a black form dropped from the rocks above them like a panther, knocking them both down. David felt a whack on the back of his head. When he regained his senses a few minutes later, it was dark and Jane was gone. The only hint she had been on the beach was the single shoe left next to him.

"There he is!" came a frantic cry from up the beach. Captain Jones was the first to reach him.

"What happened, David? Where's Jane?"

"I don't know. We were about to…" he said with a blush, "…uh, head back when someone hit me."

"Damn!" whispered John as he looked about for Robert. "Why must he always be right?"

"Was it the pirates again?" called Robert as he ran up to the circle of men.

"I didn't see them," David said as he rubbed the lump on his head, "but who else could it be?" David stumbled to his feet and pulled his pistols.

"Not tonight, David," said John with a hand to the lad's arm. "I know you want to go after her, but there's no way to follow those men in the dark."

"Captain Jones!" cried Ben, pointing to the sand next to the trees. "Come here!"

"What is it, Ben?"

"I don't think it was Smoot's men. Look at this!"

"What did you find?" cried David, still weaving slightly as he followed the others to the old man.

"There was only one of them, Mister Noble, and he was barefooted." Ben pulled off his shoe and stepped next to one of the prints in the sand. "Look how deep his prints are. He musta carried her off on a shoulder."

"He?" asked Captain Jones.

"It's one of the three we left here ten years ago," said Ben. "I'm certain of it."

"You honestly believe a man could survive here for ten years?"

"Aye, Captain," answered Ben. "I did it for five."

"I don't care who it is or how long they've been here," cried David, now fully recovered. "Let's go find her before he has a chance to…"

"If she's going to be molested," said John, "then we're already too late."

"But we can't just stand here!"

"Back your sails, David," said Robert. "Other than search at Flint's stockade, we can't do a thing until first light."

"They won't be there," interrupted Ben.

"What are you saying, Ben," asked Captain Jones. "Why not?"

"I was up there shortly after we came ashore, Captain," the old maroon said. "Nobody's lived there in years; so long that there aren't even any body lice in the place. My guess is that if it's the three we left ten years ago," he said as he pointed at the dark silhouette to the north, "they'll have taken Miss Wright to my cave."

"Then that's where we look first," said John, "but not until dawn."

An hour before the sun's first rays streaked across the smooth sea and onto the gray slopes of Mizzenmast Hill, twenty armed men were already halfway along the narrow ledge, the only access to Ben's cave. At one point where the ledge was only six inches wide and required both hands to navigate, Captain Jones turned back to Ben.

"How did you manage to carry 350 silver bars up this path? They must have weighed fifty pounds each."

"Seventy pounds, Captain," answered Ben as he clung to the rocks to catch his breath. "I made me a chest sling and carried one bar at a time. Took the better part of five months, with the weather and all." He took a couple breaths. "I'd never do that again."

"Is there another place to hide the treasure?"

"Several, but none as good," huffed Ben. "I'd still use the same cave, but I wouldn't carry them bars up by hand."

"There's another way?" asked John as he looked about.

"I'll show you after we find out if the girl's up here."

While John helped Ben across the narrow section, David reached the plateau and ran ahead to the cave entrance. As he peered into the dark chamber, the sun's light silhouetted him in the irregular circle of darkness. As he felt about in the darkness with his cutlass, a rock fell from the wall and landed with a loud thump next to his foot, followed by a string of screams from the terrified girl; certain her abductor had returned for her.

The startled lass had been carried, tied and gagged, up the long trail. Halfway along, she had regained her senses, but prayed that unconsciousness would retake her. Except for the belt which carried his rusted cutlass, her abductor was naked and filthy, and smelled like a sick bear. She knew she had been carried next to a rock wall because her head had scraped and bumped the cold stones for what seemed like an eternity. By the time she had been thrown onto the bench where her hands were secured with old galley irons, blood trailed down through her hair and had soaked the right shoulder of her dress.

"She's here!" cried David as he rushed to the girl's aid. Thinking her abductor had returned, Jane continued screaming and jerking at her manacles until her wrists were wet with blood. As the light began to invade the musky cave, the skeleton of a man became visible across the table from her.

"Let me go! Oh, dear God! Please let me go!" The frantic girl continued to scream and twist in her rusty bindings until she was nearly breathless.

"Calm down, Jane," the young Jamaican coaxed her as he unbolted the manacles and took the sobbing girl into his arms. "It's me, Jane. It's David."

One at a time, the others reached the cave; first Robert, then John and finally Ben.

"Is she all right?" asked John as he stepped to the two.

"I think so," answered David as the other men arrived and lit their lanthorns.

"David," said John as he helped the two youths from the cave, "take as many men as you need and escort Miss Wright back to the ship."

"I'll be all right, Captain Jones," she said weakly as David dressed her injured wrists. "David will be enough."

"I'll take two men, John," said David. He didn't want to take another chance of losing Jane.

David picked his men, and the four of them left the cave. John watched them pass out of sight along the ledge as Ben tugged at his arm.

"You gotta come see this, Captain Jones."

"See what?" asked John as he followed Ben back into the cave.

"Look!" whispered Ben as he trimmed his lanthorn and held it high above his head. "It's all here! Every bit of it!"

The crevice leading to the treasure room was narrow and approximately ten feet long. It was exactly as Ben had described. First, there was the table made of ship's planking that the old man had moved, piece by piece from the stockade, with a bench seat to either side. At the near end of the room, next to the passageway, lay the single cot that Ben had built and used for so many nights before his rescue. Most of the cooking utensils and other necessities to make life tolerable were gone, but the treasure was still there.

Each silver bar weighed approximately seventy pounds, a convenient size for the mules to transport across the Isthmus from Panama to Porto Bello. But they were no longer stacked on a single cube, as Ben had left them. Instead, they had been rearranged to create a massive throne that now stood at the end of the ship's plank table. Seated at the table, in chains, was one of the objects of this royal jest; the bones of Tom Morgan, knit together with fine roots and palm fronds.

"He must have the other one with him," said John as he held his lanthorn close to the skeleton.

"That poor soul," said Robert. "He must believe they're still alive." He lifted the chains from the table and inspected the manacles. They were so oversized that left hand slid loose and fell onto the table with a clatter.

"Don't you say a word, damn you!" yelled Rowe from the end of the cave. As they all watched in disbelief, the naked maroon scuttled past the astonished men and placed the second skeleton in the spot where Jane had been sitting a moment earlier. With the dexterity of a turnkey, Morley slid the bony hands into their manacles. Then, noticing that Tom's left hand was free, he let out a guttural growl.

"I told you not to talk to them!" cried the naked man as he replaced the hand in the iron bracelet and gave the skull a backhand slap. "And look what they got you to do! That's gonna cost you dearly, friend Tom." His jail keeper duties complete, Morley removed his rusted cutlass and crawled slowly to the throne in all his nakedness. His backside was seemingly numb to the chill of the silver bars as he opened a small chest to his right and pulled something from its center.

"That's it, Cap'n Jones!" whispered Ben as Morley turned something about in his hands. "That's the mate to the crown we dug up at Dead Man's Chest! And that small chest he pulled it from holds the queen's ransom I told you about!" As they spoke, Morley placed the crown upon his head and surveyed his new court.

"I'm Morley Rowe," the naked man cried as he layed his weapon next to the chest of jewels, "the king of this 'ere island an' all the treasure you see before you. Touch it and my two subjects will rise kill ya 'afore ya can take yer next breath!"

As Captain Jones and the others stood in stunned silence at the strange spectacle before them, the maroon stumbled from his throne and clapped a hand over the mouth of one of his skeletons.

"Don't you listen to 'im!" the maroon cried to Captain Jones as he gave Tom

Morgan's bones a shake. "I never done them things to these two!" And then it was the other skeleton the demented man attacked with a backhand across his mouth. "They're lying, just so you'll rescue them before me!"

"Robert," whispered John, "assign a couple of the men to escort King Rowe to Flint's stockade for safe keeping. We're going to be busy with this silver for the rest of the morning and don't need him confusing things."

"Gentlemen," John said as Morley was dragged from the cave screaming and fighting, "there was more than enough treasure on Dead Man's Chest to pay for the cannons. With what's here, I estimate that we'll have nearly half a million pounds to split with the crews."

"The crews?" asked Robert.

"The Silver Cloud and the Eagle," answered John.

"What about the Remora?" asked Robert.

"Captain Archer and his crew will get their pay," answered John, "but it'll have to come from John Silver once they reach Kings Town." John turned to Ben.

"And now, Mister Gunn, if you'll show me what you were talking about a few moments ago; how you would have carried the treasure up here rather than the trail?"

"This way, Captain," said the old man as he handed his lanthorn to one of the others and pointed toward the cave entrance.

"Robert," said John as he stopped next to the two skeletons, "would you see that the treasure is stacked in a pile outside? If what Ben's going to show me has any merit, we may not have to carry the silver down that dreadful trail." Ben stood at a short distance waiting for his Captain to follow.

"Over here, Captain!" said Ben as he hurried off through a small grove of trees. "I didn't discover this until I had all the bars in the cave."

As he emerged from the trees, Captain Jones found himself looking over a hundred-foot cliff. A single banyan tree stretched it's massive branches in all directions, one branch thrust out over the cliff directly toward Captain Kidd's Lagoon and the three waiting ships. The remains of a rotted piece of rope hung twisted about the gray branch fifteen feet above their heads.

"There!" pointed Ben. "That's where I bent my block an' tackle to the branch. I hoisted the chest of jewels to the tree and tied it off. Then I threw a hook out and pulled it onto the edge.

John peered over the cliff at the jungle below.

"How hard would it be to get from the base of this cliff to the beach where we landed?"

"It's a five minute walk across mostly level ground," answered Ben. "A couple of men with cutlasses could clear it in a couple hours."

"If we hooked up the proper rig," said John as he looked up at the branch, "we could lower a half dozen bars at a time."

The work went faster than John had hoped. Within three hours after the new block and tackle had been secured to the banyan tree, the entire treasure had been lowered to the base of the cliff and had begun moving to the beach for transport to the Silver Cloud. At Captain Jones' order, the four boats began ferrying the silver bars out to the ship, along with the last of the provisions of fruit and animals.

Throughout the day, Henry Steel had isolated himself aboard the Silver Cloud, avoiding Captain Jones. As one of the last boats loaded it's cargo of silver bars aboard the ship, Captain Steele climbed aboard for the pull back to the beach.

"John," Captain Steele called as he approached the younger man, "may I speak with you?"

"By all means, Henry!" said John, pleased that the older man had finally decided to come ashore. "How's Miss Wright doing?"

"Much better," said Henry. "I was certain her encounter with that dreadful maroon would have put her back into that depression, but I believe the whole affair's actually done her good."

"It's my first officer who's done her the most good," said John as he gave the older Captain a wink.

"What's the Remora up to?" asked Henry as he watched the privateer tack up to the entrance of the small bay and then cut away. "I would think they'd need fresh water and provisions, just like the Eagle and the Cloud."

"I asked Captain Silver to avoid Robert Ormerod."

"Oh?"

"Several years ago, Silver sent two men to New York to bargain for a treasure map. When Robert refused, they took it upon themselves to abduct his small daughter and offer her in trade for the map. She was left unattended in a warehouse and the place somehow caught fire. The girl died."

"I see."

"Robert tried to kill Silver several days ago, and he'll succeed if given a second chance. I don't wish to provide that chance to him."

"Good thinking, John," said Henry as he began walking southward along the beach. "Will you walk with me?" John caught up and matched paces with the older Captain.

"John?" said Henry after twenty paces.

"Yes?"

"I'm not really sure how to put this, but..."

"But what, Henry?"

"Do you know what the Savior said about forgiveness?"

"Yes, I do," answered John, "but why don't you tell me what He said?"

"Jesus said that if someone offends me, I'm to rebuke him, and if that person repents, then I must forgive him." John stopped walking. He had hoped to avoid this conversation. After an uncomfortable moment, he spoke.

"I was a problem during that trip to New York, wasn't I?"

"To say the least."

"It's bothered me ever since. I..." John fell silent, hoping he had said enough to get the forgiveness he so desired of Henry. Henry said nothing, so John continued. "As much as it hurts my pride to admit it, you were right about me from that first morning at Edenton. I was wrong for undermining the orders you gave your crew, and for taking that little side trip to see Miss Dandridge. I had my priorities mixed, and I'll be the first to admit so. Can you find it in yourself to forgive me for my insolence and what I said about your wife?"

"Of course I can, John."

"Thank you," John said as he took Henry's hand. "You're a good man."

"And you as well, Captain Jones." It was the first time the older man had addressed John by his proper title. "Do you remember what Smoot said about my men last night, just before you took off his hand?"

"Yes. Something about them cutting cane on Saint Croix, wasn't it?"

"Do you think he was telling the truth?"

"I don't see why not," answered John as he paused to consider. "He was already in enough trouble over you and Miss Wright. He had nothing further to gain by lying."

"My thoughts exactly!" said Henry.

"You'll want to return to Saint Croix," John affirmed.

"Yes, I do."

"How many of my men will you need?" asked John, anticipating the older man's next question.

"I could do with twenty, but thirty would be better."

"Then I'll make it thirty, and if you want, those extra ten men could be some of our Mountain men. They wouldn't be much use sailing the Eagle, but they'd come in very handy after you get ashore at Saint Croix."

John looked back up the beach to where the landing parties were working. "The treasure'll be aboard in another hour or so. If nothing else goes wrong, I'll want to weigh anchor by the noon tide." John looked back at the other Captain. "I'll need your list of crewmen and supplies as quickly as you can put it together."

"I've already made them up. There are more than enough men who've told me they want to go back. All I needed was your approval." He pulled a list from his pocket and handed it to the younger man. "These are the names of the twenty men I was hoping for, along with the provisions we'll need. Smoot and his cutthroats ate up most of what we'd laid in for the voyage, so I'll need quite a few things. And if ten of the Mountain men are willing to join me, I'll be ready to leave shortly after you and the Remora."

"See Robert about the provisions and I'll pass the word for the men to transfer their gear."

As the two turned to return to the work at the east end of the beach, the ship's cook and Gilcrest, the powder monkey, approached.

"By yer leave, sirs!"

"What is it, Barragan?" asked John.

"Well, sir, a couple of the men was complainin' 'bout them two skeletons up in Morley's cave."

"What about them?"

"They think we shouldn't leave the island without givin' 'em a Christian burial." John looked at Henry and then up at the cliff.

"You honestly believe those two were Christians?" asked John.

"Probably not, sir, but the rest of the men still feel uneasy leavin' them cuffed to that table."

"How long would it take?" asked John. "We want to sail with the noon tide." Barragan considered as he looked at Mizzenmast Hill.

"We're both pretty quick on our feet, sir," said the Irishman, "so it shouldn't be more than an hour, at the most."

"Go ahead, then," said John. "But mind you, those five pirates are still out there somewhere."

"Thank you, Captain Jones," said Albert as the two rushed off toward the trail, "we will!"

"I don't want to interfere, John, but I hope those two aren't planning on carrying the bones back along that narrow path."

"You're right," said John as he looked once more to the cliff. "Is the hoist still rigged?"

"No. It was cut down twenty minutes ago when the last load was dropped."

"Where's the rope?"

"It should be at the base of the cliff with the rest of the silver." As John rushed off, Henry called after him. "Where are you going?"

"To take the rope up to the cave!" John finally caught up with Barragan and Gilcrest as they emerged from the cave. They had torn apart the two skeletons and had tied them in bundles for transporting back down the hill.

"Did either of you think to bring any weapons?" asked Captain Jones.

"No, sir," answered Gilcrest with a look to the older seaman. "We didn't think there'd be a need for it."

"It's my fault, Cap'n Jones," apologized the cook. "The lad asked me 'bout it, but I told him..."

"Well, you're probably right," said John as he walked to the edge of the cliff and laid the rope down. "Morley Rowe's tied to a tree at the stockade and we haven't seen those other five since they were peeking at Miss Wright yesterday." Using the rope and a cloth sack, both skeletons were lowered to the waiting crewmen below.

"Ya know, Cap'n," offered Gilcrest as he looked up, "if we could bend your rope to that one on the tree, we could slide down and be back to the beach in five minutes." The block had been cut away, but the single length of rope hanging from the banyan tree was still there.

"Good idea," said John as he dropped the last coils by his foot and looked about for a stick. There were none in sight.

"What ya lookin' for, Cap'n?" asked Barragan.

"We'll need a pole to hook the line over to us," said John as he looked out at the hanging line. "Take a look in Ben's cave. There might be something that would work."

"I'll take the cave, lad," said Barragan. "You look up by those trees."

As the two ran off, John walked among the tree's great roots.

"Perfect," he said as he broke off a four-foot root and returned to the edge. Reaching out, he caught the line and pulled it as close as it would come, but as it arced toward him, the end swung up and out of his reach. As he threw the root aside and turned to call after the others, there was a scream from the direction of the cave.

"Barragan?" he called as he drew his sword and ran through the trees. He was met by the five pirates; one of them holding Gilcrest by the shoulder. Barragan was on the ground in front of them with blood flowing from his throat.

"They killed Albert, Captain Jones!" the lad cried. "They was waitin' for him in the back of the cave!"

"Well, well," sang out one of the pirates. "Let the lad go, Deuce. Lady Luck's given us a bigger prize!"

"Are you all right, lad?" called out Captain Jones as he surveyed the five pirates. Only one of them was armed with a cutlass; the rusted one that had been taken from the naked maroon. The other four had only their dirks. John stood his ground as he watched the boy run along the path toward safety.

"I'm fine, Cap'n," cried the lad as he stopped a hundred feet down the path. "But I can't leave you here like this!"

"Keep going!" ordered Captain Jones as the five pirates began moving toward him. "Tell Captain Steele and the rest what's happened. Maybe they're planning on trading me for something—maybe a boat and provisions so they can sail away from this place!" The pirate with the rusty cutlass seemed to brighten at the suggestion and gave his leader a nudge.

"Don't let him fool ya, mate," scolded the leader. "We got better things to trade for than food and a stupid boat."

"Like what?" asked the one with the cutlass.

"Like that chest o' jewels an' the boat besides." All this time, John had held his ground as he watched Gilcrest move along the path. When he was certain the lad was beyond reach, he pulled and fired his pistol at the closest pirate. As the man fell to the ground clutching his face, John turned and ran for the cliff.

"He's gettin' away!" one of the pirates cried as he started to run after Captain Jones.

"No he isn't, you sod!" cried their leader as he followed at a walk. "There's no way off this hill but the path."

"But what about his rope?" asked one of the others.

"He doesn't have time," answered the leader as he walked to the trunk of the great tree and sat on a root. "Look!" he said as he pointed. "The rope they used to hoist down the silver's cut off beyond reach and the branch is too high for him to throw a loop."

The pirate was right. No matter how hard he tried, John couldn't throw his rope through the thick foliage and over the branch. The only other place to secure it was around the trunk and by now, the other three had joined their leader.

"Now, Captain Jones," began the pirate leader amongst the cat calls, "shall we all sit down an' discuss how we're gonna make this 'ere swap?" The rest laughed as their prisoner surveyed his predicament. "Why don't you be a good prisoner an' throw that nice sword of yers to me so we don't have to cut you up none?"

As John looked about, he remembered the tailor he had hired in Fredericksburg. It might work, he thought. In a gesture of failure, he pulled his sword from its sheath and dropped it over the cliff, handle first. Still holding the hoisting rope, he turned his back to his captors.

"What's he doin'?" asked the pirate with the cutlass.

"Nothin', you ninny," answered their leader. "He knows he's trapped, good an' secure."

As they argued, John tied a loose slipping noose in the end of the rope and made one last calculation. Setting his feet at the edge, he gave the stack of coils a kick, sending it over the cliff toward the workmen a hundred feet below. Then, with all the strength he could muster, John leaped into open space. As he flew toward the length of hanging rope, he twisted smoothly to his back and slipped the noose up over the end. Then, with a quick jerk on both ends of the noose, the hoisting rope was trapped, forming a sheet bend just like the old tailor, McCreedy, had done in the tailor shop two months earlier. Before the pirates realized what John had done, he had slid halfway to the jungle floor.

"What the..!" cried the pirate leader as he grabbed the cutlass from his mate and ran to the edge. It was too late to stop the Captain, but if he was quick, he might be able to kill him. With all his strength, the pirate made a swing at the rope, but it was beyond the cutlass by two inches. "Take me other hand!" he cried to his mates. After three vicious cuts, the pirate finally managed to cut the rope, dropping John the last fifteen feet to the ground.

"Captain Jones!" cried one of the crewmen as the rope fell about them. "Where the hell did you come from?"

"Never mind that for now!" answered John as he threw off the tangled coils and retrieved his sword. "Grab those last bars of silver and let's get away from here!" As he spoke, a storm of large rocks began to land about them, hitting one of the crew a glancing blow to the shoulder.

"John!" It was Captain Steele.

"Over here, Henry! Help me with this man!"

"What happened up there?" asked Henry as he hoisted the man to his shoulder. "Where are the others?"

"Barragan's dead, and the lad's..."

"Dead? Who..?"

"Smoot's men—the five who escaped from the Eagle last night," answered John as they hurried along the path. "As soon as we reach the beach, I want a dozen armed men. I'm going back up there."

"They're already on their way!" called Robert as he and Ben met the two Captains.

"Who's on their way?" asked John.

"David and McCoy," answered Robert. "They took ten of the Mountain men up the trail as soon as we heard your pistol report. Don't worry. They'll catch all of them."

"Unless..." added Ben.

"Unless what?" asked John.

"I never had cause to do it myself, but a desperate man might risk scaling the cliff face above my cave."

"I don't care how long it takes," said John as he turned to scan the cliff, "they'll pay for killing my cook!"

"But we've a rendezvous with John Silver," argued Robert. "If we're to reach him before dusk as planned, we'll have to depart by noon."

"I want those pirates in irons or dead trying! Only then will we leave."

"But if they make it over the ridge, we'll never find 'em," argued Ben.

John continued to watch Mizzenmast Hill, trying to see David and the fighters. "Then we'll maroon them if we have to."

By 1100 hours, the last of the silver and provisions had been loaded aboard the two ships. Both crews watched the trees and listened for gunfire, but there wasn't a sound.

"There they are!" called the watch from high atop the Silver Cloud's main mast. "They're on the trail near the cave!"

"How many?" called Captain Jones.

"It's just Mister Noble and the Gunner, sir," the watch called down, but then he pointed. "No...there's the rest of 'em!"

"What about the pirates?"

"I don't see 'em, Captain! It's just the dozen who went up!"

"They must have made it over the ridge after all, Ben," said John.

"Then we can get underway?" asked Robert.

"Aye," answered John, "the moment David and the others are aboard."

Within the hour, the disguised frigate and her two escorts weighed anchor. As they cleared the last line of coral, the four newly marooned pirates burst onto the beach, along with Morley Rowe.

"Look there," said John as he pointed aft with his spyglass.

"I thought you said you killed one of them," said Robert.

"I did," answered John as he handed Robert the glass. "The fifth one is Morley Rowe."

As the four officers watched, Rowe yelled something at the group of pirates, and then stormed off toward the pile of tools next to the stockade. A few minutes later, he was back with a shovel, searching about the beach for something. There was more yelling and shoving.

"He's trying to dig up his skeletons, isn't he?" asked Robert as he squinted toward the beach.

"He must think they're suffocating down there," added Ben.

"Or calling to him," offered David.

Morley began throwing dirt into the air by the shovel full. As he did so, one of the pirates rushed him from behind and grabbed the tool from his hands. There was more yelling, followed by the shovel being thrown to the water's edge. This infuriated Morley, who stumbled after it and fell headlong into the water from another dizzy spell. A moment later he was back up the beach and began digging between two of the pirates who now stood on the graves.

"He's certainly a persistent dog," said Robert.

"And I don't expect those others will take much more of it," said Ben.

"That's his problem," said John, "not ours."

"Is it too late to go back an' get Morley?" asked Ben. "Ten years is a long time to be marooned."

"That's plagued me also, Ben," said Captain Jones, "but look at him. He'd never adjust to civilization."

"Captain Jones is right, Ben," added Robert. "The fine people of Boston would put the poor wretch in a cage."

The last the crew of the Silver Cloud saw of the five maroons was the bizarre sight of Morley Rowe tied against a palm tree with his eyes covered. While he was thus constrained, the others dug up the graves and moved the two skeletons to a new location. It was the only thing they could do short of killing the King of Treasure Island.

CHAPTER 16

Lieutenant James Hawkins had been away from England and his fiancée for over fourteen months when the midshipman lost his life. Nobody understood why the Captain insisted upon the court martial at sea, rather than making for Kings Town or Havana. But at the well-intended advice of the Executive Officer, none of the junior officers questioned the action until it was too late. Mutiny is a hanging offense, and for the crew to object openly to an execution was to risk the same fate. Lieutenant Hawkins had wanted off the King James from before the incident, but it would be bad for his career to ask for a transfer at this sensitive time.

"Perhaps Christiana's father can arrange for my transfer so I can get off by the time we reach New Orleans," Lieutenant Hawkins mumbled as he penned the letter. "And if my orders come directly from the Admiralty, Captain Stevens would have no reason to take any action against me."

"Mister Hawkins!" called an orderly at the young officer's stateroom door. "Are you there, sir?"

"Yes," he called back. "What is it?"

"It's me, sir! Presley! You asked me to tell you the moment I spotted the next postal packet."

"Thank you, Presley!" There was sure to be a letter from Christiana. And figuring how long it took for mail to reach England, he might be off the ship by July or August. He quickly finished the paragraph he was writing and slipped the four pages under his desk pad.

The young officer emerged onto the main deck, still buttoning his tunic. Out of habit, he squinted up into the rigging to check the winds and then turned toward the quarterdeck.

"Permission to come aft, sir?" called Hawkins. The Executive Officer, Commander Foster, leaned against the rail and looked down at his youngest Lieutenant.

"Not until you're properly dressed, young man." Lieutenant Hawkins looked down at his misaligned buttons.

"Excuse me, sir," said the embarrassed youth as he turned away to straightened his clothing. "I understand we've a postal packet inbound."

"Yes we do," said the senior officer, pointing to the small ship to lee. One of the King James' boats was already returning with several large bags. As he watched, the welcome cargo was hoisted, hand over hand to the main deck where Captain Stevens waited. His was a special bundle of dispatches and letters, packaged separately from the rest.

"You seem anxious, Lieutenant," said Commander Foster with a chuckle. "Hoping to hear from that girl you left in Bristol?"

"Aye, sir," answered Jim proudly as he climbed to the quarterdeck. "We're to be married when I return to England."

"I saw her, James," said the older officer. "She's a right handsome young girl. I'm sure she'll make you a wonderful wife." Jim only half-heard his superior, as the letters began flowing to the waiting hands on the deck below them.

"If you're waiting to hear your name called, Jim, you'll be waiting all day. By Captain Steven's order, the officer's mail has already been segregated and will be handed out in his cabin.

"In his cabin?" said Jim with a note of frustration. "What kind of..?"

"I know," agreed the executive officer. "It's his new policy. He thinks that since he calls all the officers to his cabin to hear the new dispatches anyway, he might as well hand out our mail at the same time." As the commander spoke, several of the other officers began drifting toward the aft companionway.

"Do you think it has anything to do with this recent trouble, sir?"

"I'm sure of it," answered the older man in a guarded tone. "But if we cherish our careers, we'll keep our opinions to ourselves." He put a fatherly hand on the young officer's shoulder. "Shall we go below?"

By the time Commander Foster and Lieutenant Hawkins had reached the Captain's passageway, most of the other officers were standing about in small groups. The mail had been delivered, but the door to the Master's cabin was still closed.

"Watch yourself, Jim," warned Foster in a whisper as the door opened.

"Enter and stand at ease, gentlemen," mumbled the Captain as his aide laid the large satchel of letters and packages on the table. Lieutenant Hawkins pushed his way to the front and strained to see if one of the four letters that slid onto the table might bear his name.

"As usual," began the Captain, "we've received several important dispatches. None of them concerns the junior officers except this one from the Admiralty in Kings Town. It seems we're not relieving the Queen Anne at New Orleans after all." He looked over his glasses at young Hawkins' attempt to read the names on the next two letters in the bag.

"Are you with us, Mister Hawkins?" said the Captain as he slapped the mail bag with his riding crop. Jim jumped as he pulled back his hand.

"Sorry, sir...I was just..." There were snickers from two of the other junior officers. The Captain continued.

"As I was saying," he paused to give Hawkins another look of disapproval, "we'll not be going to New Orleans next month as previously ordered." He scanned down the first page saying half words and mumbling phrases here and there as he went. "Ah! "Here it is." He stopped to adjust his glasses. "As of your receipt of this dispatch, trade between America and the West Indian Colonies shall be restricted to consumable and dry goods only. So as to insure that no weapons or..." He skipped down the page to another short passage. "...only those vessels which have been previously inspected and are returning to the American Colonies from those in the West Indies shall be allowed passage. However, under no circumstances shall any arms, ammunition or gun powder be allowed to pass." He looked up at his officers and removed his glasses. "It seems that an anonymous source in Kings Town has informed the Admiralty that a very large number of cannons and gun powder is being shipped from somewhere in the West Indies, and will pass Andros Island on its way to America. The King James has been tasked with interception and commandeering those weapons."

"Why us, sir?" asked Lt. Hawkins.

"The dispatch didn't say. I would assume, however, that we are the best qualified, since we probably inspected the same ships when they were en route to the islands." The Captain looked about his junior officers. "Are there any other questions, gentlemen?"

"Just one, sir," added Hawkins.

"Yes?"

"Well, a little over a month ago, I inspected a Dutch merchantman by the name of Silver Cloud near Abaco Island. They were transporting tobacco to Saint Croix and should have returned by now with molasses for our distilleries in New York. Must we inspect that one again?"

"Of course we will!" answered the Captain. "And she'll be allowed to pass as long as she has the proper papers and your seal in her gunwale. Is there a problem with that?"

"No sir," answered Jim, "except that..."

"Then there is a problem."

"Well, I was wondering if maybe another officer might inspect her when she returns."

The Captain laid the dispatch down and studied the young officer. "Get to your point, young man. Is there something about the Silver Cloud you failed to put in your report?"

"My report?"

"It was a Dutch crew, wasn't it?"

"Oh, they were Woodshoes all right! You should have seen their Captain! Disgusting man! Got so close when he talks that he spits all over your face." There were snickers from about the cabin, which encouraged the young officer. "It was like sitting under my old minister back in Bristol. The front two pews got baptized with spit every time..." The other officers burst into raucous laughter before Hawkins could finish. He enjoyed the attention. "And Van Mourik's smell! I've known swine..."

"That will be enough, Mister Hawkins!" barked the Captain. His voice was firm, but a smirk danced across his lips as he spoke. "I don't care what your personal problems are with this Dutchman. Since you inspected her the first time, you'll be the inspecting officer when the Silver Cloud returns."

The Captain took off his glasses and looked at his officers.

"Before my aide distributes your personal letters, I have a grave matter to discuss with you." He paused so that he could look each officer in the eyes for several seconds. "I have reliable information that there are at least two officers among you who have been plotting a mutiny."

A chill fell over the room as the young officers looked about at one another.

"I felt the same way when I first learned of this treachery, and have been forced by these two individuals to take extraordinary and drastic measures. Those of you who are yet innocent of this treachery will agree with me that my new policy is fair and necessary. I expect that the two mutineers will give themselves away by their protest of that policy."

"And what might that new policy be, Captain Stevens?" asked the Executive Officer coldly.

"Effective this date," answered the Captain slowly, "I will open and censor all of your personal mail prior to it being received of sent off the ship."

An almost audible wave of anger swept across the officers as nostrils flared and jaws tightened. The Captain waited for a full minute for the imagined mutineers to expose themselves.

"I will take your lack of objections as a vote of confidence, gentlemen, and that you agree fully with the new policy." He scanned each man's face as before, and then continued. "If there are no further questions, I expect you to return to your duties. You'll be notified when I've finished reading your mail."

The distance between Spyglass Island and the rendezvous point was no more than a half day's sail. Morale was higher than it had ever been on the great frigate. The excitement that their mission was nearly completed and that they were no longer threatened by pirates could be felt radiating from the very timbers.

"Land Ho! Land Ho!" shouted the top watch. Captain Jones strode quickly to the starboard rail and leaned far outboard for a look. Besides the Remora leading them by several leagues, all that was visible of their destination was the windswept cloud of moist afternoon air that had been pushed aloft by the island.

"Do you still think we can make the strait before dusk?" asked David as he handed John the spyglass. It was a bulky thing; the size of a man's arm and wrapped in the distinctive coach whipping of the Bosuns' mate's trade, with large Turk's heads adorning either end. John took a long look at the area below the cloud, hoping to see the masts of their twin ship.

"Aye," answered John as he lowered the spyglass, "and with two hours of light besides."

"Mast Ho! Mast in the straits!" called the top watch again.

"They're here!" said John with relief. "David, see to it that the crew's ready. I want to put as many miles between ourselves and John Silver as possible after we trade ships."

"The men were ready when we left Spyglass," answered David. He paused as a thought came to mind. "What part of the treasure are we keeping?"

"What part?" John gave David a questioning look.

"I would suggest we leave the silver bars for my uncle and take the more valuable parts of the treasure with us; the excess, that is." David hesitated. He could see by John's concerned look that he'd also recognized the logistical problem involved. "We stacked the silver on top of the gold."

"I didn't even consider that." John was disappointed in himself for the error. "I was planning on taking the silver with us since we'd already calculated the million and a half from what we got off Dead Man's Chest. We're going to have to recalculate and then adjust what we bring topside for transfer."

"If you'll give me the key to the vault, I'll find Robert and Ben, and begin the work," offered David. "And at the same time, we can begin loading the more valuable parts of the treasure into duffle bags for the transfer."

"Duffle bags?" asked John.

"To make it look like personal gear," said David. "No use tempting my uncle any more than necessary."

"Good idea," said John as he pulled the chain from around his neck and handed the key to his capable young friend. "See to it."

At 1530 hours, the treasure ship's massive anchor splashed into the turquoise waters between Little and Great Inagua Islands. As the bubbles spread out on the surface and then cleared away in a circle of light foam, the enormous iron and oak hook struck a coral head and settled into the white sand. The chain was allowed to slack another 25 yards before it was stopped and the shackles were driven through the enormous link. The great anchor rose on its side for a moment as one of the large flukes drove itself deep into the sandy bottom. The second Silver Cloud lay anchored 200 yards to the south and was already lowering a boat as the treasure ship began to swing about her chain in the easy current. The Remora, as John Silver had directed as he transferred to the gun ship, remained under full sail a league to windward. Captain Jones ordered all boats lowered and for the crew to make ready to begin moving across upon his signal.

"It appears they're more anxious than we are to trade ships and get underway," said John as he studied the men climbing down to the other ship' boats.

"We've finished our calculations and loaded all the jewels and a large part of the gold in the duffle bags," reported David. "Do you want the men to take it across in the first boats?"

"Not until we inspect and count the cannons," answered John. "Do you have a manifest of the treasure to give to Mister Silver when he arrives?"

"Yes I do," answered David, "and Robert's waiting at the lazarette."

"While Silver's occupied with the treasure, I want you to accompany me to the gun ship for our inventory. If everything's as it should be, I'll signal Robert with the flags J P J. That's when we'll begin sending the crew and our share of the treasure across."

By the time John had finished giving David his instructions, the gun ship's long boat had pulled to within earshot.

"David!" came a familiar voice. "Is that you?"

"Father?" answered the startled youth. "What are you doing here?"

"I'm here to count the treasure!" A moment later, Charles Noble's boat was secured to the ladder and he had climbed to the main deck.

"Welcome aboard, Mister Noble!" said John as he extended a hand of greeting. "This is a pleasant surprise, especially for your son. We expected John Silver to be coming across again."

"Again?" asked Mister Noble.

"He didn't tell you about our meeting before Spyglass?" asked John.

"No, but the old man keeps a lot from me," answered Charles as he gave his son a hug and handshake. "He did tell me about Mister Ormerod trying to kill him, but didn't say when it happened. I just assumed it was at Spyglass."

"We figured your brother would want to count the treasure personally."

"He's tired...says his new peg leg has made his back sore and he only wants to make the trip across once. He figured you'd want to count the cannons while I look at the treasure."

"Your son assures me that everything's ready for you, Mister Noble," said John as he gestured for the manifest from David.

"Will David be helping me?"

"No," answered John. "Robert Ormerod and Ben Gunn will assist you, unless..." John hesitated as he noticed the begging look David was giving him. "But then, David could help you with the count just as well."

"Could I?" asked David. "I'm sure Robert or Ben would be more than willing to go count the cannons. And besides, I know where everything is!"

"That would be fine," answered John. "Send Ben topside."

"Thank you, Captain Jones," said Charles.

"This is great!" sang David as he and his father walked aft. "We'll get to talk before you have to leave again." David's father began to say something, but was interrupted by Captain Jones.

"David, be sure to watch for my signal."

"You can count on me," answered David obediently. "The moment I see it, I'll order the crew to begin moving across." Several minutes later, Captain Jones and Ben Gunn were in the long boat pulling across the two hundreds yards which separated them from the gun ship.

David led the way aft toward the companionway, but stopped and turned to his father.

"I've missed you so much, Father," said David. "I wish there were a way you could continue with us to Charles Town."

"Well, David," said Mister Noble with a broad smile, "this is indeed your lucky day!"

"Oh?"

"I'm am continuing with you to Charles Town!"

"You're coming with us?" David asked as he looked back at his father. "But I thought you'd be returning to oversee the off-loading of the treasure at Jamaica."

"I've already discussed that with your uncle. I think after all these years I can trust my own brother," said Charles as he clapped a hand on his son's shoulder.

"Which reminds me, Father," said David. "After we inventory the treasure, there's someone I want you to meet."

"Is he someone you've written about?"

"It isn't a he, Father."

The eighty man crew of the gun ship was a mix of slaves, indentured servants and pirates. The slaves were the easiest to pick out, because their skin was black. The indentured servants looked much like the lighter-skinned sailors, except their clothes were hardly better than rags when compared to the regular crew's finer dress. As the two men stepped through the opening in the larboard gunwale, they were welcomed aboard by Captain Silver.

"Well," cried Silver with his arms spread wide, "if it isn't my old mate, Ben Gunn!"

"Top o' the day to ya, Captain Silver," answered Ben with a nervous look at John.

"Yer lookin' a far sight better than when they was burnin' yer legs on Dead Man's Chest," said Silver. "They healing well?"

"They still sting a bit when I sweat, Mister Silver, but other than that, I'm doing fine," answered the old man as he remembered something. "You were there that night, weren't you? It wasn't just a dream."

"Aye," answered John Silver.

"He killed all the pirates, Ben," added Captain Jones, "all twelve of them."

"There were only nine of them torturing Ben and that other poor soul, Captain Jones," said Silver. "Three of the dead were mine."

"Ben and I appreciate what you did for him, Mister Silver, but could we get to the business at hand?"

"What's the rush, Captain Jones? Ben an' I haven't seen each other for over ten years; not since he saved my life at Puerta Plata. That deserves a minute or two, doesn't it?"

"Yes," answered John, "but you can talk with him while I count the cannons, can't you?"

"Aye," chirped Silver, "that we can!" The old pirate pushed himself up from the mainmast pin rail and pointed toward the companionway. "After you, Captain Jones." He looked good at fifty-two years old, with the light breeze blowing through his white hair and decked out in his finest seagoing fare. Protruding from his left trouser leg was the new wooden rod that had replaced the wooden leg Robert had shattered several days before.

"That was some pretty piece of work the other night at Spyglass, Captain Jones."

"Our attack on the Eagle?" asked John.

"Aye. We heard the yelling and saw several men jump overboard. What happened to Joshua Smoot? Did he die with the rest?"

"He's alive," answered John. "He and the red-haired lad who calls himself Henry Morgan lie in chains in our hold with five of his crew. The rest of his men, the ones we didn't kill, escaped to Spyglass."

"You took him alive?" asked Silver through a squint.

"He surrendered his sword to me on the deck of the Eagle."

"Never!" barked Silver. "Smoot'd never surrender his sword! Gentlemen do a thing like that, not men of Smoot's cut."

"Well, he didn't exactly surrender it," said Ben with a wink at his Captain. "He was sorta forced to give it up."

"Ha!" laughed Silver uproariously. "I knew it! Smoot's a true pirate, he is!"

"I had to take his right hand off with it," added Captain Jones with a wry smile.

"Argh!" groaned Silver, as he rubbed his right wrist in sympathy. "An' ya say ya got the lad Henry Morgan too?" It had been ten years since he'd passed through Tortuga, but one doesn't quickly forget such a curious person.

"We do," said John.

"An' what might ye be plannin' fer the lad, Captain Jones? Is he to dance at the gallows with Smoot an' the others? "

"They'll all stand trial in Charles Town, for piracy and cannibalism."

"Cannibalism, ya say? Well, I can't say the passin' of Smoot'll be a loss to this 'ere world none. He were no damn good when we was mates, an' by yer measure o' him, he don't sound to 'ave changed a single spot since he were hatched."

"I spoke with him last night," added Ben, " and I can assure you he hasn't!"

"But hell," Silver added with an evil laugh, "we've more important business at hand than blowin' wind about the deck over them two." He stumped off toward a hatchway with the others at his heel and then gestured for Captain Jones to go down the ladder first.

"Not I," objected John. "This is your ship, at least until I've accepted the cargo."

"I get the feelin' I'm not trusted, Cap'n Jones."

"You're not!" said Ben.

"Now you've really gone an' hurt me, Ben Gunn, an' after all I done fer ya at Savannah."

"Please, gentlemen," huffed Captain Jones. "Haven't we flogged the subject enough?"

At the gun deck, John Silver stumped through the barrels of molasses and bags of sugar to the mizzenmast where he turned about. The facades with the sugar bags had been raised, revealing the twenty cannons lined up at the gun ports. They were a mix of long barreled twelve pounders and the shorter-ranged carronades of various muzzle sizes.

"Ain't that a pretty sight now?" Silver asked, spreading his arms as one would to show off his wife and children. "Like a church o' Papists lined up to torture a Baptist, they be," Silver crooned with pride. "But you be wantin' a look at the bilges, what? Nine hundred thirty-eight Scottish cannons make a fine ballast fer a frigate, Captain Jones."

The three men descended the ladders behind the old sea dog, deep into the bowels of the ship, finally stopping just above where the planking met the keel. There lay the other heavy weapons that had slept for nearly two years in the warehouse at Kings Town. As agreed, all the wooden parts had been removed so as to minimize the space each would occupy.

"We threw out all them rocks from Charles Town and be usin' yer cannons fer ballast instead, Cap'n Jones."

"That answers your earlier question, Ben," said John, "of why she wasn't lower in the water."

"And there be no ball or tools with 'em either," added Silver. "Just the cannons and the powder like yer Mister Jefferson ordered."

"There's no way that we can un stack them to make a full count, Mister Silver" said Ben with a look to his Captain. "Can Captain Jones trust you that they're all here?"

"Well, by the powers!" Silver barked. "If ye can't trust old Long John Silver, then ye can't trust Charlie Noble, neither."

"We can trust David's father, Ben," said John with a hand on the old man's shoulder. "If Charles says all the cannons are here, that's good enough for me."

"Ben," said Silver in his most distressed tone, "ye pain me to me marrow, ya do. Weren't it me what fixed it so's you an' the others could 'scape from the Walrus in Savannah? Billy Bones was gonna have you all killed, except for me steppin' in."

"Don't waste your breath!" spat John. "Your allegiance lies with the greatest advantage, just like a whore lies with the man with the largest purse. If it weren't for Robert and Moira knowing where the treasure was buried, you'd have joined the rest in killing them, and you know it!"

Silver lowered his head like a scolded child. "Do ya really believe I'd stoop so low, Captain Jones?"

"Massa Silver!" came a cry from the ladder above them. It was one of Silver's slaves. "Massa Charles' comin' back!"

"Well, mates," said Silver, glad to change the subject, "what say we go topside an' hear what Charley has to report!?"

As the three reached the main deck and the bright afternoon sun, Charles Noble and his son were just climbing to the deck from their long boat.

"Is it all there, Charles?" called Silver as he pushed himself up from the companionway.

"Every farthing, just as you said it would be."

"And the chest of jewels from off Spyglass?" Silver asked as he licked his lips and gave Ben a questioning look.

"I can answer that, Mister Silver," said Captain Jones. "Our bargain was the thousand cannons for a million and a half pounds in treasure. That's exactly what we're leaving for you on the Silver Cloud; that and the twenty cannons that came with her. As far as the jewels from Spyglass are concerned, they're excess and we're keeping them."

"Like hell you are!" Silver's eyes burned with fire as he dropped the pretended accent. "One word from me and my men'll scuttle the treasure ship where she stands!"

"No you won't," threatened Charles. "We made an agreement with them, and they've fulfilled their part of it, to the letter!" Charles had placed himself between the two Captains, doing his best to hold them apart. "They've delivered the agreed amount," Charles repeated, "and I'm satisfied." He turned to Captain Jones. "When can we begin exchanging crews?"

"Wait!" protested Silver. "I'll agree to hold to our side of the bargain, but there's one concession I'd ask of you, Captain Jones, just to sweeten the pot a bit, as they say."

"And what might that be?" asked John suspiciously.

"I want Smoot and the lad, Henry Morgan."

"I already told you where they're destined," protested John.

"Ah yes," agreed Silver. "There's no question those two have earned a date with the hangman, but Fishbone Smoot earned an obligation from me in Savannah that I've never had the chance to repay, until now." He turned to Ben. "You remember it, don't you? That last night when young Ormerod fought Billy Bones for Moira an' then cut his face? Smoot might have only been a pup at the time, but he was the only other one that stood by me against the rest." John Silver looked back to Captain Jones. "You'll have to pardon the sentiments of an old man, but I don't like the noose settling my accounts for me."

John wouldn't answer the old pirate's request, but rather stood with a defiant stare. Finally Charles intervened.

"Is it so important that Smoot and Morgan be hanged, Captain Jones? Isn't your mission to bring the cannons to the Colonies?"

"As much as I hate to admit it, Charles is right," said John. "Besides, every minute we waste here arguing about it is a minute of sea we won't be able to put between us and the treasure ship. For the sake of getting underway quickly, I'll agree to leave them chained in the treasure ship. But had we had more time..."

"And his other five mates?" asked Silver with a sideways glance at the young captain. "What need do ya have fer them?"

"He's right, John," added David. "Why don't we just leave them all in the brig and be done with it?"

John thought for a moment as he considered.

"All right, Mister Silver, you can have all seven! But not another word about the treasure."

"Agreed!" sang out the old pirate.

"Give the signal to begin the transfer, David," said John. "I want to be in open water before dark."

The signal to exchange crews was given, and within two hours, the gunship weighed anchor and set sail for the American Colonies. It was Captain Jones' plan to utilize the shallows as much as possible until they reached the relative safety of the coast of Spanish Florida. If attacked and sunk, this would give him the option of running the ship aground, placing the cannons in a position for recovery from land. Their loss to the Americans might mean the loss of the war, whereas their recovery by the British would make but slight difference, since the British fleet had no need for extra cannons.

The Trade Winds blew fair through the Bahamas, driving the cannon ship forward nearly two hundred miles each day. From the rendezvous, Captain Jones steered a course directly for the southwestern tip of Acklin's Island, passing close abeam its lush but rocky coastline. By late afternoon of the second day, they had crossed Crooked Island Passage and were nearing Deadman's Cay, two miles west of Long Island.

At David's request, Captain Jones had assigned Doctor McKenzie to Ben Gunn's cabin. It was only right that David and his father be able to share a room for the remainder of the voyage.

"Father," asked David as he closed the drawer under his bunk. "You never explained why you aren't returning to Kings Town with the treasure."

"It's a matter of business," answered Charles as he threw his son one of the fresh blankets the cabin boy had laid out. "We're making an offer to your Mister Forrestal, which, as Silver assures me, has the potential of creating the greatest shipping company in the Western Hemisphere."

"Then I must assume this package contains the details of that offer?" The package still lay on the desk where Charles had set it the day before. David picked it up and turned it about.

"Exactly my assumption," answered Mister Noble. "But beyond that, I don't know anything more than you. And nobody will until we open it in front of Mister and Mrs. Forrestal."

"Uncle Silver wouldn't tell you?"

"You know your uncle and how much he loves surprises. The only thing he'd say was that when the Forrestals open it, we're all going to be thrilled. And for us to be thrilled--and those were Silver's exact words--it must be something very important."

"Hmmm," said David as he laid the mysterious package down and ran his hands across the tightly bound oil cloth. "And you're certain we can't open it before we get there?"

"I'm tempted, David, just as much as you. But I gave your uncle my word, and my word is my bond."

"My God!" swore David. "The man has so many of us under his spell!"

There was a knock at the door.

"Mister Noble, sir?" It was the voice of one of the powder monkeys.

"Yes?" answered David as he opened the door.

"It's nearly time to relieve Captain Jones at the watch."

"Thank you, Billy. You can tell the captain I'll be up in a few minutes."

"Aye, aye, sir!" the boy answered and then ran off.

"You've turned into a true ship's officer, David. I'm proud of you."

"Thank you, father."

"And Captain Jones tells me that you and this girl you helped rescue from Smoot are...well, getting along smartly."

"I'm in love with her," said David proudly. "And if she'll have me, I plan to ask for her hand tonight."

"Well, congratulations! I might be a grandfather some day after all!"

"Not so fast. I still have to get married."

"Well from the scuttlebutt I hear about the decks, Miss Wright's ready to accept."

"I'll be off watch at 2000 hours, father. I might be able to tell you for certain then."

"I'm supposed to have dinner with Captain Jones at 1700 hours," said Mister Noble. "When we're finished, I'll come up and find out what she said."

"I hope I don't disappoint you, father, but either way, I'd appreciate your visit."

A few minutes later, David sprang from the companionway and bounded up the ladder to the quarterdeck. Captain Jones was at the taffrail, watching as one of the seamen checked the ship's speed and leeway. He couldn't miss his relief's noisy approach.

"Well, David," said John with a chuckle, "you seem anxious to take the helm. What's up?"

"I'm going to ask her this evening," whispered David so the deck crew wouldn't hear. "And I think she'll say yes."

"Your young lady's already on deck for her evening stroll as we speak." John indicated her location with a nod of his head. "I have dinner guests to freshen up for, so if you're ready, I'll leave you two alone."

"If you've nothing to pass on, sir, I'm ready to take the watch."

"Ah, yes. There were two things. First, we'll be changing course once we pass abeam Deadman's Cay. I want to head for the southern tip of Andros Island and then skirt its Western coastline as far north as possible. The second thing has to do with the British man-of-war that inspected us on our way to the Chest. We've some preparations to make just in case they're still there and decide to stop us. I'm meeting with all the officers in my cabin at 2000 hours. I'll need you there."

"Very well, sir," David said with a salute, just in case Jane was watching.

Captain Jones had been gone for no more than three minutes when Jane wandered aft, waiting for her usual invitation to the quarterdeck. Neither she nor David had realized that he seemed to always get the afternoon watch. It was perfect for them because they got to enjoy every sunset together. Captain Jones had planned it that way, not so much to get the two romantically involved, but rather to divert Miss Wright's thoughts from the atrocities she had witnessed at the hands of Joshua Smoot.

"Good evening, Miss Wright," called David in his most gentlemanly manner. "Have you noticed how beautiful the sunset is tonight?"

"Good evening yourself, Mister Noble." She chuckled quietly to herself as she accentuated the Mister. "And, yes, it is a beautiful sunset."

"Why so formal?" he asked with a frown.

"It's you who's being formal, David. You've been calling me by my Christian name ever since Spyglass Island, and now suddenly I'm Miss Wright again?"

"I'm sorry," said David uncomfortably. "I'm a little nervous this evening."

"Oh? Is Captain Jones after you about something?"

"No, it's just that..."

"Yes?" she purred.

"Why don't you come up on the quarterdeck?" asked David nervously.

"Well thank you, kind sir. I'd love to."

David was fascinated with the way she moved. Whereas a man walked from one place to another for no other purpose than to get there, Jane somehow made an art of it. It was almost as if she were stepping to a minuet, the way she glided along. Even her hands grasped the rail differently from a man. Before he realized it, she was standing with her back against his chest, watching the western sky change colors. The sweet smell of her freshly washed hair was overpowering.

"Are you sure you won't get into trouble for me being on the quarterdeck?"

"Quarterdeck?" He was confused. He knew she had been talking about something, but his mind had somehow missed everything but the single word.

"Won't Captain Jones be angry at you for having me up here while you're on watch?"

"Oh that!" he answered. "Don't worry about John. He may be my Captain, but he's still my friend."

Satisfied, she reached down and grasped his hands and wrapped them about her waist. The sun was now poised at the horizon, ready to make its nightly plunge into the sea. Its lower edge began to distort as it became one with the dark waters, but David missed it all together. He was only concerned with her scent and the closeness of her warm body to his own. They stood like that for several minutes when David leaned down and gave her a gentle kiss upon the right temple, just like the first one he had given her. As he did so, he noticed a reflection from her cheek.

"Jane, you're crying."

She wiped the tear away and sniffed.

"Does it still bother you; the things you saw when you were on the Eagle?"

"Of course it does," she answered, "but I'm not crying over that anymore."

"What is it then? Something obviously has you disturbed."

She turned about to face him and placed her hands on his shoulders. More tears had welled in her eyes and began to spill more quickly down her cheeks.

"I'm just so happy I met you, David, and that I'm finally going home."

"We're going home, Jane," he said with a different tone. She gave him a questioning look as he bent down and kissed her lightly on the lips. He straightened himself and spoke with all the conviction he possessed. "I'm going with you to Atlanta to ask your father for your hand in marriage."

"Oh, David, do you mean it?" She pushed him out to arms length and studied his face carefully. "Do you really mean that?"

"Of course I do. Ask Captain Jones."

"Ask me what?" called John from somewhere forward. They hadn't noticed that John had met Robert on the deck and hadn't gone down to dinner yet.

"Sorry, sir," stammered David, "I asked Miss Wright to come up to the quarterdeck. It won't happen again."

"Don't worry about it. You have the authority to invite anyone up there you please." John walked aft with Robert and leaned against the companionway cover. "What was it you wanted Jane to ask me?"

"Oh!" he said as he remembered. "She didn't believe I was serious about wanting to marry her." Jane pinched David's arm, making him jump.

"I'd say he's serious," answered John, trying to remain as serious as possible. "Why, just this morning he was asking me if I had the authority to perform a marriage at sea."

"And?" Jane asked with great interest. David couldn't believe she would be so bold.

"I told him I could, but that it would go much better for both of you if he asked your father's permission."

"Thank you, Captain Jones," she said, and then turned back to David. "Then it is true. You really do love me."

"I wouldn't joke about a thing like that." David gave her another kiss on the lips, not caring that the two older men were watching. He suddenly realized that the matter wasn't concluded, so he pushed her out to arms length. "You didn't answer whether you'd marry me."

"You didn't actually ask."

"I didn't?" David looked at John and Robert and back to Jane. "I guess I didn't after all." He cleared his throat and looked down into her eyes. "Jane, will you marry me?"

"Oh yes, my beloved. I'd be honored to be your wife!"

CHAPTER 17

"Mister Hawkins! Mister Hawkins!" cried the cabin boy as he knocked frantically at the junior officer's stateroom. "Mister Hawkins! Captain Stevens wants you on the quarterdeck!"

The young officer laid his pen aside with a huff and slipped on one of his freshly polished boots. He could finish the letter to Christiana later. "Probably wouldn't be another packet by for a fortnight anyway," he thought.

"Are you there, sir?" repeated the cabin boy.

"I'm coming, Jason, I'm coming!" He opened the door to the ten year-old. The lad was red-faced and sweating. "Good Lord, son, you really shouldn't run so in this weather. You're asking for heat prostration for sure."

"But, sir, the Captain..."

"The Captain's always in a rush. Go tell him I'll be along smartly. It's probably a question about my inventory of the weapons locker, or something else of an equally mundane nature. God but I'm tired of that!" The executive officer stepped into the passageway behind the cabin boy.

"Lieutenant Hawkins!"

"Yes, sir!" cried the junior officer as he jumped to attention. A stack of novels fell from the desk onto his second boot.

"You've a poor attitude, Mister Hawkins!" barked Commander Foster as he mounted the ladder to the main deck.

"Sorry for the delay, sir," begged Jim as he pulled on the second boot. "On my way, sir!" Jim grabbed his waistcoat and hat and followed the commander up to the main deck. As he squeezed past the Executive Officer, the older man seized him roughly by the shoulder.

"Look there, Mister Hawkins!" Commander Foster pointed to the south. "The Silver Cloud's returning! That's why the Captain has summoned you, not your weapon's report. Go now," he said with a shove, "and let this be a lesson to you!"

"Aye, aye, sir!" Jim gave a salute as he ran aft.

"Up here, Lieutenant, and stand at ease," barked Captain Stevens as he strode up and down the quarterdeck, his hands under the skirts of his coat. "It appears your Dutch friend is returning from Saint Croix with his molasses and sugar." The Captain scanned through the report Hawkins had filed regarding his first inspection of the approaching ship.

"Is there anything wrong with it, sir?"

"Nothing at all," answered the Captain as he handed the report to an aid and turned about to Hawkins. "I needn't remind you of the importance of this inspection, do I, Mister Hawkins?"

"No, sir!"

"Good." The Captain turned again to the approaching merchantman. "According to my dispatches, the cannons have not yet been found. If they're aboard the Silver Cloud..."

"I understand, sir," said Hawkins. "May I assume then, that I'm still to be..?"

"Yes you may," answered the Captain with a huff. "As I told you and the other junior officers, you'll be able to detect a deception better than someone who's never been aboard the Silver Cloud."

"Yes, sir," answered Hawkins, trying to sound as obedient as he could. "I'll go over her like a ferret. If she has the cannons aboard, you can be assured I'll find them."

"The Admiralty is counting on us, Jim. Take as many men as you need." Jim was surprised the Captain would call him by his first name. It was normally unheard of in the British Navy to do such a thing, especially during wartime. He saluted and excused himself.

As the Silver Cloud approached the low island, the H.M.S. King James rotated her luffed sails to catch the southwesterly breeze and set a course to intercept the merchantman. Within an hour, the two great ships stood to at a hundred yards. Lieutenant Hawkins had taken four armed Marines to assist with the inspection; the standard number for such an assignment. As Jim's boat neared the merchantman, he and the others could hear the sounds of a man being flogged somewhere on the main deck.

"Damn!" cursed Lieutenant Hawkins as his boat bumped against the Cloud's planking and one of the marines stood to climb the ladder. The young officer caught the man by the sleeve.

"Hold here until they've finished with that poor soul," Hawkins ordered. "God but I hate this ship!"

The beating had gone on for several minutes before they had reached the Silver Cloud's side, and seemed to be taking entirely too long to complete. The young British officer and each marine cringed with every cry from the man's parched throat. They had been required to witness the two recent hangings and many similar floggings aboard the King James, but none so prolonged. Finally the screams stopped, but not the lashes.

"I can't take it any longer!" cried the young officer as he stood to his feet. As Hawkins grabbed the ladder, the fat and sweaty face of Captain Jack Van Mourik poked rudely over the rail.

"Goot day, sir!" blurted the Woodshoe. "Hey, isn't dat Letenent Harkers down der?" Jim looked up at the man in anger and disgust. "Why...it is, it is!" The young officer hesitated halfway up the ladder, fearing to get too close to the hideous thing that reached down at him.

"I got some 'a dat goot rum you like!" shouted the Dutchman as he noticed his guest stop and retreat a rung down the ladder. "You comin' 'board or not, Letenent Harkers?"

"Not until you put an end to that lashing! My God, the man's unconscious!"

Van Mourik turned away and barked something in Dutch. The whine of the angry cat stopped.

What happened next was the Woodshoe's own idea for keeping the young Britisher out of the bilges. With the dexterity of a beached sea elephant, Van Mourik sucked a mouthful of bread from a moldy loaf he held. By the time he had leaned over the rail a second time, the bread was well saturated with saliva. Taking careful aim, Van

Mourik opened his mouth as if to speak. The chunk of wet bread glanced off Jim's right shoulder and landed with a plop amongst the disgusted marines.

"Is done!" Van Mourik chirped as he wiped his mouth with the back of his sleeve. "You come up now, ya?"

Jim hesitated as he looked to the marines for moral support. They sat with wide eyes and closed mouths.

"Here, take my handt, Mister Harkers!" said Van Mourik as he switched the bread to his left hand and extended his right.

"No thank you," said Jim. "I can make it up myself." Van Mourik acted crushed for a moment while Jim gained the deck and made a quick survey of the filthy ship. At Charles Noble's recommendation, several cages of pigs, goats and chickens had been left in the warm sun and none of the animal's droppings had been picked up. The dung and urine had been walked into the decking and tracked fore and aft to each companionway. This, combined with the appearance and smell of the dozen Dutch crewmen topside, made the Englishman want to turn and flee to the safety of his boat.

"How was Saint Croix?" asked Jim as he placed his left hand on the rail just above the ladder.

"Ah...Saint Croix!" answered the Dutchman as the senseless body of the prisoner was cut loose. As he slumped to the deck with a thump, the old Woodshoe began describing Christiansted harbor in his native language.

More by instinct than intent, Jim ran his finger into the dirt-filled grooves of the King's seal he had stamped there on his previous inspection. He glanced down at the deep impression, wondering why it seemed different.

It was different, but only slightly. When it had first been placed in the rail of the other ship, Captain Jones had ordered his smithy to copy the seal, knowing that the other Silver Cloud, the one carrying the guns, would probably not have the same inspection marking. True to Captain Jones' instructions, Van Mourik watched for the young Englishman's touch to the counterfeit impression and moved quickly to distract him.

"I not see ya fer der longest time, ya?" blurted Van Mourik as he moved in on the young officer with an extended hand of greeting. Hawkins forgot about the rail and stepped sideways past two of his Marines, moving beyond the Dutchman's saliva range.

"I don't have any time for visiting, Captain," Jim lied, "so if you don't mind, I'd like to get right to your cargo."

"If yer sure of dat," said Van Mourik with his best tone of disappointment, "den here!" He shoved the cargo manifest and King's order for the three hundred tons of molasses at the young officer. Thomas Jefferson and the others had done their work well, even down to the wax seals on the documents.

"Yes," insisted Lt. Hawkins, "I'm sure of that! Would you lead the way, please?"

"Oh, poop!" pouted the Dutchman as he threw the remainder of his bread at the pigs and marched off to the forward companionway. Stopping for a moment at the ladder, he began to beg his visitor a second time to have just one drink with him. Hawkins refused.

The gun deck had been prepared carefully for inspection, just as thoroughly as the main. The facades had been lowered and the crew's hammocks hung in such a way as to hide the hinges in the overhead. The molasses casks had been arranged to create two aisles, one to either side of the mainmast. And in order to prevent the inspector from leaving either aisle toward the rows of hidden cannons, the casks were pressed close together and stacked two deep with bags of muscovado sugar. As Lieutenant Hawkins walked quickly through the deck, he occasionally kicked a cask or stuck a sugar bag with his penknife, making sure none of them contained gunpowder. Van Mourik continued to beg the young officer to stay for a visit, but Hawkins ignored the invitation.

"I'll see your bilges now, if you please, Captain," said Hawkins as he stopped to read the manifest. As he looked up for the Captain's response, a noise from below caught his attention.

"What was that?" asked Hawkins as he took a lanthorn from one of his marines and leaned over the ladder. Something in the darkness below them had moved.

It was one of the remaining Mountain Men, dressed as a Woodshoe and being helped up the ladder by a mate. The man stumbled up the ladder with one arm across the other's shoulder and the other hand across his stomach. Lieutenant Hawkins looked at Van Mourik and back down at the two men. A stench worse than the animals on the main deck blew upward past the two as they hesitated on the third step below Lieutenant Hawkins.

"That man doesn't look very well, Captain Van..." began Lt. Hawkins, but before he could finish, the Mountain man vomited between Lieutenant Hawkins' feet, with some of the mess running down onto the ladder and dropping into the bilge.

The other crewman shook his fist at his Captain and yelled something in Dutch. Hawkins and his four marines beat a quick retreat up the ladder to the main deck and the open air, ignoring the rest of their inspection.

"My God!" shouted Hawkins as he strode to the rail and began to back down the ladder. "What are you feeding your men?"

"Den you won't be eatin' no lunch wid Cap'n Jack?"

"No, I won't!" yelled Hawkins in disgust as he threw the manifest and sugar order back up to the deck at Van Mourik's feet. He had intended to impress a second King's seal into the railing next to the first, but decided nobody would ever miss it.

"Oh," pleaded Van Mourik, barely able to hold back the laughter, "please tell Cap'n Jack you don't go now?"

"I'm sorry!" Jim said as his Marines shoved away from the disgusting ship. "We do indeed go now!"

As soon a Lieutenant Hawkins was back aboard the King James, he reported to his Captain.

"Well?" asked the skipper. "Anything unusual to report?"

"She's exactly what she appears to be, sir. A Dutch merchantman with three hundred tons of molasses and raw sugar for the King's distilleries in Charles Town; the same ship I inspected last month. The only cannons she carries are her four swivel guns topside."

"No large cannons at all?"

"None, sir. She wasn't even fitted with gun ports. We laid at her waterline for several minutes before going aboard. I made a close inspection of her planking. It was solid oak from rail to waterline."

"Hmmm," said the Captain as he tapped the Admiralty dispatch with his letter opener. "They've probably smuggled them around the other end of Cuba and up the west coast of Florida; maybe into New Orleans. If so, the Windsor'll most likely intercept them." He looked up at the young officer and realized he was muttering.

"I think you're correct, sir. Yes...I'm certain of it. They must have gone for New

Orleans." Jim was relieved that his commanding officer hadn't asked for any further details of the inspection.

"Have a boat take across our outgoing mail for the Colonies and tell your Dutch Captain he has my permission to continue."

"Aye, aye, sir!" Hawkins was glad to leave the pressure cooker, as the other junior officers called the Master's cabin. He rushed to his own room and sealed up the partially written letter to his fiancée, along with the four others he had been saving, and delivered them to the postal orderly. Within half an hour, the mail was aboard the Silver Cloud and once again the precious cargo of cannons was en route for America.

"What was that all about, Jim?" asked Lieutenant Montgomery Mason as Hawkins entered the two-man stateroom. The younger man was dressing for his 1600 watch.

"Have you ever inspected a Dutch merchantman, Monty?"

"No. Can't say as I've had the honor. Why?"

"If you're ever given the choice, don't do it!" Jim threw his waistcoat and hat across the room at his bunk, and then sat down at his desk to remove his boots. "Filthy people!" he said as he shook his head from side to side. "I think I'd rather be on a slaver than on a ship like that again."

"That bad?"

"Monty, you wouldn't believe it!" Jim threw one of his boots at the other officer, still dripping of seawater. "Look at that! I kicked my foot about in the water all the way back, but there's still vomit along the sole line! Ate the finish right off the leather, it did!" Monty held the boot with his fingertips and then let it fall to the floor. "One of the sailors wretched on the deck in front of me, and the others stank so bad of sweat and urine..."

"You forget, Jim, that I was there when you tried to beg out of the re-inspection."

"That's right." Jim shook his head again and continued. "That Captain! He has to get this close when he talks to you!" Monty backed away from his roommate's face thrust in his.

"If they're so disgusting," asked Monty, "why do we employ them?"

"Politics, Monty," said Jim as he pulled a clean boot on. "Politics and greed!"

"Well... on that sour note," said the younger officer, "I'll be leaving you for my watch."

"Filthy people!" Jim said again.

"Too bad you didn't remember the old man when you were over there."

"Remember the old man?" Jim asked, giving his roommate a quizzical look.

"Aye. He's always telling us to keep a weather eye for men we can impress into the service of the Crown."

"That sick sailor!" said Jim slowly as a broad smile broke across his face. "Ha! Serve the old man right to get vomited on now and then!"

"A dose of his own medicine!" laughed Monty.

As his roommate departed, Lieutenant Hawkins sat down to write up his inspection report, being careful to expound upon the thoroughness with which he inspected every deck, including the bilges.

Three hours later, there was a frantic knocking at his door.

"Enter!"

"It's me again, sir!" said the cabin boy who had called earlier that day. "You'd best get to the Captain's cabin on the double, sir. I've never seen the Skipper and Commander Foster so agitated!"

"What now?" He pulled on his other boot and waistcoat, just as several of the other junior officers ran past his door. By the time he had made his way aft, all ten of the others had assembled outside the Captain's cabin; speculating at the reason for this latest of so many panic situations.

"Does anybody know what's going on?" asked Jim.

"If you ask me," said one of the cadets, "I'd say the Captain's gone and..." Before the lad could finish, the two senior officers burst through the door and marched past the startled officers.

"Lieutenant Hawkins!" called Captain Stevens from halfway up the ladder.

"Sir?" Jim answered as he and the others followed up to onto the main deck.

"Mister Hawkins, would you tell me and the other officers what that is?" The Captain was pointing to the departing Silver Cloud, now twelve to fifteen miles to the northwest under full sail.

"Why, it's the Silver Cloud, sir! I just inspected her and then sent her on her way, as you ordered."

"Well, then," asked the Captain as he swept his arm in a great arc toward the southeast, "what's that?"

Less than three miles away was what appeared to be an exact duplicate of the ship he had just inspected, and following the same route.

"She looks like the Silver Cloud, sir," cried Hawkins as he spun about to the departing ship to make sure. "But that can't..."

"And what do you propose we do about her, Mister Hawkins?"

Jim was confused, and felt that Captain Stevens was setting him up for something.

"Shouldn't we detain and inspect her, sir, just like we did...that first one?" suggested Mason, wondering if the Captain had lost his senses.

"Thank you, Mister Mason," said the skipper as he looked into the rigging and shook his head, "for that inspired suggestion!" The Captain turned and stepped to within six inches of Monty's nose. "And since you seem to know exactly what to do, why don't you accompany your good friend to find out what the hell's going on here, unless that's too taxing for your young brain?"

"No it isn't, sir!" answered Mason.

"Shall I have the gunners man their cannons?" asked Commander Foster.

"We're a man-of-war, aren't we?" asked the Captain sarcastically. "Unless you'd like to meet them unarmed."

Commander Foster gave his Captain a questioning look.

"Select a dozen Marines to go with you, Lieutenant Hawkins," said Foster, "and if there's anything amiss, even a sick crewman, fire a warning shot."

"Aye, aye, sir!" answered the young officer as he took his roommate by the arm and descended for the main deck.

As the treasure ship approached within cannon range and began spilling her sails, the inspection boat shoved away from the windward side of the H.M.S. King James.

"What a day!" complained Lieutenant Mason as he released the tiller of the ship's boat long enough to wrap and buckle his sword belt about his waist.

"Don't blame me, Monty!" Hawkins said with a shrug. "As I see it, you got yourself into this one without anybody else's help." The twelve Marines acted as if they didn't hear the conversation between the two young officers.

"I've two more reports due before I turn in tonight," complained Monty, "and I'll no sooner get back from this stupid inspection and I'll have to take the forward watch!" He sheathed his sword and straightened his coat. "How do I look?"

"You look fine," answered Jim as he studied the merchantman. "If this is anything like my first inspection, your concerns for your uniform will be as the Good Book says; casting pearls before swine."

There were several strange things about this second Silver Cloud, besides the fact that her twin was no more than six hours ahead of her on the same course. The way she drove straight for the King James and then furled her sails and heaved to, almost as if she were asking to be inspected. Although none of them had yet articulated their concern, it filled the two young officers and their twelve escorts with a sense of doom. They had covered only a quarter of the distance from their ship when the Silver Cloud's upper rigging began to throw shadows across the small boat. As they neared this second Silver Cloud's lee waterline and the waiting ladder, Monty gave Jim a nudge.

"Something's very wrong, Jim."

"You feel it too!" agreed Hawkins as he turned to the Marines. "I want every man of you to be extra alert once we get aboard. I'm sure each of you realize that we're not here to simply inspect this ship's cargo, but her Captain and crew as well." The Marines nodded their understanding.

Lieutenant Hawkins climbed the ladder cautiously, being assisted over the bulwarks by two large Negro seamen. One by one, the marines began to follow, but much too slowly for Jim's liking. As he waited for the others, his hand went instinctively to the King's inspection seal in the rail. It had been impressed from the deck side of the bulwark, as was proper. But the other seal, the one on the first Silver Cloud, was impressed backwards, as if the man holding the iron were standing in mid air, outside the rail. And there was the small groove where a sliver of wood had been torn from the rail!

"What's the matter, Jim?" called Monty from far below in the boat. He was the last in line for the ladder, and there were still seven marines in the boat ahead of him.

"Do you remember the infection I got last month from the splinter under my right thumb?"

"How could I forget? You whined about it for a full week."

"Here's the spot that splinter came from," said Jim as he tapped the rail.

"But that can't..." Monty held his tongue as he realized what Jim had just discovered. It was clear that this was the ship Lieutenant Hawkins had inspected in late April. The one he had inspected earlier in the day was its twin, yet the crew from this ship was now sailing away to the north on that twin, toward the American Colonies.

Jim scanned the fifty-odd crewmen who had been collecting on the deck. None of them were Woodshoes, but rather Englishmen and Negro slaves, and far too many for a merchant vessel. Then he spotted the major damage to the far bulwarks. The gunwale was destroyed for a twelve-foot span amidships, with a nasty gouge in the decking at the center of the broken rail. He had seen this type of damage only once before. It had been caused by a collision at sea with another ship of equal size. As he wondered after it, a very tall Englishman dressed in some sort of officer's uniform approached him.

"Greetings, Mister Hawkins!" the man said with an outstretched right hand. Being a gentleman himself, Jim accepted the hand without hesitation, an act which he would soon regret.

"Greetings...ah, sir," answered Jim in a suspicious tone. He wished that more of his marines were topside, and that Monty was there also, for moral support if nothing else.

"You'll be wanting to inspect our cargo of course," said the tall man in a friendly manner, "but first, my Captain desires your presence in his cabin." Jim struggled slightly to free his right hand--his sword and pistol hand--but the other man held him firmly and began leading him aft through the other white-skinned sailors and black Jamaicans who infested this strange ship.

"Monty!" Jim called over his shoulder. "If I'm not back in ten minutes, come after me!" He wasn't sure whether his fellow officer had heard his cry for help, but he knew the Marines had. As he was pulled through the hatch below the quarterdeck and into the passageway leading to the Master's cabin, he realized a second anomaly.

"How do you know my name?" he demanded, as he once again tried to free his fighting hand from the tall man's grip. But his captor ignored Jim's protest as he knocked at the Master's door.

"Come in, Lieutenant Hawkins!" came a strangely familiar voice.

Jim's hand was released as he was pushed roughly through the door. He searched the cabin from starboard to larboard, finding only one man bent over the great table, pushing a line of farthings across a chart of the Caribbean toward a gold pocket watch. There was a course drawn from the Bahamas to the southern tip of Florida, and then straight to the Mississippi delta.

Jim stooped over slightly to get a look at the man's face, but to no avail. He was an old man, judging by the color of his hair; with large leathery features and skin burned as dark as mahogany by too many days in the sun. A single shove to the back by the tall officer sent Jim stumbling forward, into the table.

"Sir!" Jim protested as he grabbed at where his pistol should hang in its holster. "I'm Lieutenant James Hawkins of His Majesty's Ship King James. I demand to know the meaning of this treatment!"

The man at the table held up his left hand in a gesture of "Wait!" and then gave the coins a final push. Pleased that the last coin had touched the watch, he brought his hands together at the center of the chart. There was something familiar in the way he interlaced his fingers one by one. Without saying a word, the old man raised his head and gave the lad a wink.

At first there was no recognition. The ten years since their last meeting had changed the Captain as much as it had changed the lad. Jim stood not six feet away, but it might as well have been a hundred, for he still did not know who he was looking at. And then the old man spoke.

"Well scuttle me if it be none other'n me old ship mate, Jimmy Hawkins! Har! Har! Har!"

"Long John Silver?" Jim whispered in amazement and shock. Yet in a strange way he was thrilled to see his old friend again. In the confusion of the moment, he drew a small pistol from his right boot and aimed it at the old pirate.

"Aye, Jimmy, 'tis a sweet reunion, it is," crooned Silver in his best scupper talk, "exceptin' yer 'bout to put a ball betwixt yer old shipmate's eyes with the pistol he gave ya." Silver leaned back and laced his fingers behind his head. "Why is it? Seems every time I give a friend a weapon, it ends up bein' turned on me?"

Jim looked down at his hand. Sure to the old man's words, the pistol John Silver had given him the day they met in Bristol was cocked and pointed between the snow white eyebrows. For a moment he had forgotten why he was aboard this strange ship.

"Marines!" Jim cried out. "Arrest this man!"

The three men waited for nearly a minute before the cabin door pushed open. Without lowering his pistol, Lieutenant Hawkins turned his head for a quick look, hoping to see several of his marines. Instead, two more pirates had joined them and stood to either side of the tall officer. One was a young man about Jim's age, with carrot-red hair and emerald-green eyes. The other was in his late forty's, with his right hand bandaged tightly.

"Lower yer pistol, Jimmy," said Silver in a fatherly tone. "It'll do ya no good ta resist. An' besides, a fine lad what's life's been saved so many times shouldn't go shootin' the one what did all the savin' now, should he?" Silver's words had an almost hypnotic effect on the young officer. Against all his military training, he allowed the old pirate to reach across the table and remove the pistol from his hand. As Silver did so, the red-haired lad removed Jim's dirk and sword from their sheaths.

"There now," the old pirate crooned, "that's better fer us all." Silver studied the small pistol carefully as he lowered the flint to the half-cocked notch. "Ye've taken' good care of it, Jimmy, just like old Long John learned ya."

"How'd you know it was me!?"

"Why, Jimmy," answered Silver as he set the pistol in an open drawer, "I saw you through me spyglass as ye were pullin' across."

"But how did you know I was even on the King James!?"

"By yer letters," Silver scolded. "Haven't ya never heard of the Royal Navy mail?" Silver pulled three envelopes from the same drawer and then pushed it closed. "Which reminds me. I believe these are yours."

"Mine?" asked Hawkins as he took the letters. "These are from Christiana! How...?"

"I figured we'd be seein' each other sooner'n you could get 'em by postal packet, so I brought 'em along from Kings Town. Why, most of what makes it's way out to the Kings men-o'-war passes through John Silver's hands first. Didn't it seem a little unlikely yer ship'd get assigned back to the Bahamas so soon after it were ordered moved to Cuba?"

"You sent those dispatches to the King James!" Jim cried.

"Aye, an' the one about the cannons, also. A pretty piece o' forgery now, wasn't it?" crooned Silver. "Oh!" he added, "my congratulations on your recent promotion! I couldn't be prouder if you was me own son!" There was a short pause as Jim searched his mind.

"I was right! Those were your initials on my commission!" Silver gave the lad a toothy grin. "And you've got the cannons and powder we're supposed to stop!"

"Wrong, lad, by about six hours!" Silver answered with a chuckle. "I've got the treasure that Robert Ormerod hid twenty years ago on Dead Man's Chest! That other Silver Cloud had the cannons; the one your officers inspected and passed through earlier today."

"Oh, my God!" whispered Hawkins. "I was that inspecting officer!"

"Then ya disappoint me, lad."

"I'll take the responsibility for my error," said Jim, "but why would you send a dispatch out to the British about the shipment of cannons? I don't understand."

"I only told the King James, Jimmy."

"Did you intend that we discover them?"

"Didn't matter one way or the other," answered Silver.

"But why not just let them get through to the Colonies?"

"Because it added the authenticity I needed to fool yer Captain." Silver pushed himself up from his chair and stumped his way to the starboard window. Leaning his hip against the sideboard, he studied the British frigate as the two ships drifted closer. He turned back to his young friend. "Your Captain Stevens would be so excited over the prospect of capturing a thousand cannons bound for the American Colonies that he wouldn't think twice 'bout bein' ordered back to Andros Island, now would he?"

"But why the King James?"

"I wanted to see you again, Jimmy!"

"You're mad, John Silver!" cried Jim.

Smoot and Morgan burst into laughter.

"And who are these two?" asked Jim.

"Why that's none other'n Captain Fishbone Smoot, now missin' his right flipper, he is," said Silver as he made a hook of his index finger and wiggled it at Smoot. "True to his oath, he lost his hand rather than surrender his sword in a fight." Silver threw his dirk across the room. It stuck in the deck between Morgan's feet. "An' that's Henry Morgan from Tortuga. It were him what helped me with my sea chest a few days after Ben Gunn released me from the Hispaniola."

Jim eyed the two suspiciously as they joined John Silver at the starboard windows.

"Answer me somethin', Jimmy," said Silver as he kept looking across at the King James.

"What?"

"Seems I 'member you sayin' that once ya reached Bristol, ye'd never set foot 'board a ship again."

"I never intended to, but when all this trouble with the Colonies..." Jim was cut off as a series of ten explosions to starboard rocked the great ship.

"My God! What was that?" Jim shouted as he stumbled and then ran to the windows. Nothing could be seen for the white smoke that hung between the ships. "Why would they attack before my men and I could get off your ship!?"

"Har! Har!" laughed John Silver at the lad's mistake. "That were the sound I been waitin' fer, Jimmy. Take a look at yer fine man-o'-war now."

The King James hadn't fired upon the Silver Cloud, but rather the other way around. It was this supposedly unarmed merchantman which had leveled a perfect ten gun broadside at the man-of-war. And the destruction was nearly complete, for men were already abandoning ship by the time the smoke had drifted far enough away to see the damage. Both the main and mizzenmasts, and all their yards and tackle had crashed to the deck and into the water on the near side of the ship. There was no use for the panicked crew to try cutting the debris clear from the guns, because thick black smoke and flames were already billowing from all but the two forward gun ports. As the four watched, each with his own reaction, three secondary explosions in the gun decks sent a shower of chain plates and pieces of oak into the air about the two great ships. And as if the fate of the King James wasn't already obvious to all hands, the ship's drummer began to beat out the abandon ship order.

"You devil!" Jim screamed as he spun about on John Silver and grabbed at his empty sword sheath. "What have you done?"

"Why," said Silver in a pained tone, "I just paid back a long-owed debt to me good friend, Jimmy Hawkins, I did!"

"Paid back!?" cried the youth as he watched his shipmates leap from the burning ship. "What are you talking about? I never did anything like that to you!"

"Oh, Jimmy," whined Silver as he held a hand to his chest in mock pain, "ye wound me to the marrow, ya do. I'm not payin' ye back fer some hurt ya did me, 'cause yer right. Ya never did any such thing." Silver stepped to Jim's side and laid a large hand on the lad's shoulder. Jim pulled away in revulsion.

"This is fer tellin' Cap'n Smollet he could trust old John Silver to the care o' Ben Gunn while you four went ashore at Puerta Plata. Hell, boy! If ya hadn't done that bit o' fast talkin' fer yer old mate, he'd 'a been crab food ten years ago!"

"But you've attacked my ship!"

"Aye," crooned Silver proudly as he observed the wonderful job his gunners had done. "But I've saved yer life, Jimmy, an' that makes us square again, don't it?"

"You're insane!" cried Jim as he searched the cabin for another weapon. "I demand to be released, this instant!"

"He wants ta swim fer it with the rest, Govn'r," said Morgan with a sneer. "Why don't ya let 'im?"

"Because the lad comes with me, that's why!" hissed Silver. "If anybody swims, it'll be you, Morgan!" The young pirate backed a step away as John Silver turned back to his young friend.

"Ya might as well get used to these two, Jimmy, 'cause ye'll be seein' plenty of 'em for the next three weeks.

"Three weeks?"

"Aye, lad," answered John Silver, "at least until we reach New Orleans."

Following John Silver's chart, the treasure ship sailed due west for the passage between Long Key and Grassy Key, and then turned northwest to hug close along the western coast of Spanish Florida. At first, Jim refused to speak at all to Joshua Smoot or his young mate, Henry Morgan. But on the fifth day after the attack on the King James, he was drawn into Silver's discussion with the two concerning what had happened at Dead Man's Chest and Spyglass. It was a fascinating tale, and impossible to believe except for Smoot's freshly severed right hand and the treasure in the ship's specially built vault.

Jim was a privileged prisoner, with free run of the ship. John Silver tried to convince his young friend several times to take a turn at the helm, but Jim had refused, saying it would amount to treason against the Crown to do so.

As the Silver Cloud paralleled the western coastline of Florida some ten miles off Pavilion Key, the crew began to notice the first hints of an approaching storm. The weather front came upon their ship gradually, beginning with a darkening sky and a light rain. It was spawned somewhere in the Pacific Ocean near the equator, and had crossed land at the Yucatan Peninsula, gaining both moisture and power as it moved northeast through the Gulf of Mexico.

"She looks like a bad one, Jimmy," said Silver as he joined the young officer at the bow, "and I predict we'll be taking in the canvas to a storm reef by noon. I hope you feel different about helping us out, especially if this breeze takes the course I expect her to."

Jim acted as if he hadn't heard the old pirate, for he was adamant about not assisting the crew. He pulled the collar of the borrowed jacket high around his ears as he continued to study the nearby coastline and the roughening waters ahead.

"Tell me when you change yer mind, Jimmy," said the old man with a clap to Hawkin's shoulder. "When you do, you know where to find me." The old pirate stumped aft, leaving Hawkins alone with his thoughts.

It was a little before noon when the order was given to lower the yards for furling the massive square sails. Lieutenant Hawkins watched the sailors scramble aloft by teams, taking on one great sail after another. As soon as they had side-stepped along the footropes to their well-rehearsed positions, one would call below that they were ready. The Bosun would then call aloft to storm furl the sail. One by one, each of the great pieces of canvas was wrestled in and secured to their yards, leaving only two reefed topsails to fight the increasing winds.

Silver stepped away from the helmsman and called to Jim, spreading his arms in a gesture of invitation. "Come on, Jimmy! Come up on the quarterdeck with yer old shipmate!"

"Beg as you may, John Silver, I'll never join your crew, even if it were to keep this ship off the rocks!" called Jim against the wind as he stood several yards forward of the quarterdeck. "If you need one more crewman so badly, why don't you ask Captain Smoot to take the helm?"

"I would lad, but that missing hand's got his whole body afflicted with the chills."

"What about Morgan?" called back Jim. "He knows how to sail, doesn't he?"

"He does, but I wouldn't trust nothin' more valuable than a bilge rat to the boy." Silver paused to yell an order to several of the sailors who'd begun to secure the aft hatch. "I need ya, Jimmy! I want ya ta be a part of this!"

Lieutenant Hawkins stood for several minutes watching John Silver struggle to hold his position on the slippery deck, but the leather-covered knob at the end of the peg leg lacked the traction he needed against the wet deck.

"I'll be below in my cabin!" called Jim as he turned and dropped down the companionway. Several crewmen stood in the officer's passage as the Lieutenant stepped off the ladder and turned to walk aft. The men gave the young officer a queer look as he stepped toward them.

"What are you men doing here?" demanded Jim. "Why aren't you on deck where you're needed?"

"We were ordered below to move the two cannons from the Master's cabin back to the gun deck, sir," said one of them as the ship lurched, throwing Jim against the bulkhead.

The worst part of the storm was now upon John Silver's treasure ship. Jim had felt only one other this severe, and that time they were well to sea, rather than near a coastline. The water on the main deck had built to a point that the sea flowed in a steady torrent down the ladder and into the passageway where Jim and the three sailors stood. As he steadied himself against the aft mast, there was a tremendous cracking and ripping sound above, as one of the yards broke loose from the mizzenmast and crashed to the main deck. As he turned to climb the ladder, something cracked him on the head, dropping him into the cold water. That was the last thing Jim Hawkins remembered of the Silver Cloud before he was found adrift on the piece of broken deck.

CHAPTER 18

"Captain Jones," called Charles Noble from the main deck, "may I join you and my son on the quarterdeck?"

"By all means!" Captain Jones walked to the starboard ladder to meet the merchant. "Well, sir, what do you think of our Dutch Captain's performance back there?"

"If I were that young Lieutenant, I'd have been off the ship in half the time." He laughed and shook his head. "And that man who vomited on his boots! A trick like that could be worth money in the proper circumstances."

"This was the proper circumstance," said John with a chuckle. "It's a good thing your brother didn't meet up with that man-of-war; vomiting crewman or none."

"Ease up, Captain Jones. I know you're offended at the way he and I used you, but you'll have to admit that he's probably done more for the Americans than any other single man."

"If he'd have just approached me honestly, I'm certain we could have reached an agreement."

"I doubt that," answered Charles, "because even I was against the plan at first. But even if you had, do you honestly believe Robert Ormerod and your group of statesmen would have joined forces with a pirate."

"Not even for the sake of the Colonies?" asked John, seeing that Charles was probable right.

"No, Captain Jones, not even for that. The times and circumstances were right, but the people were not. John Silver did it the only way it could have been done."

"I suppose you're right." John walked to the aft rail and peered at the shrinking war ship. "If that Lieutenant Harkers only knew how close he came..."

"Hawkins," Charles corrected. "His name is Lieutenant James Hawkins. And if I'm correct, he's the lad who found Flint's map and was with John Silver on the expedition to Spyglass ten years ago."

"Oh?" John smiled as he continued watching the man-of-war. "Wouldn't that have been ironic if it were the other Silver Cloud, rather than us, that was stopped by the King James? John Silver and Jim Hawkins back together again after ..."

"It's an amusing thought, sir, but hardly possible. John Silver's smarter than to get within twenty miles of a British warship. And if his winds blow fair, I'd expect him to be off-loading the treasure in Kings Town within two days."

"And you trust that old pirate to split with you?"

"Of course I do! He's my brother."

"Brother or not," said John, "I've seen closer men than you turn on each other over a hundredth part of that treasure."

"Well, that's my problem, isn't it?"

"That it is, Charles. That it is."

It had been nearly six hours since the Silver Cloud had been inspected by the King James when the top watch reported the column of black smoke from the area of Andros island.

"I see it," called back Captain Jones.

"Top Watch!" called David. "Can you see what's burning?"

"It's too dark to make it out, sir, but my guess is that it's just a brush fire!"

"Well," mumbled John to himself, "it's none of our concern."

By dusk the next day, the Silver Cloud had reached Biscayne Bay and turned to parallel close to the coastline, just as they had done during their passage through the Bahamas. Further north, as they passed the occasional river mouth, the muddy waters which spilled into the Atlantic testified to the passage of a very large storm somewhere inland; the same storm which had crossed paths with John Silver and Jim Hawkins on the opposite side of Florida. Three days later, the familiar coastline of South Carolina began to pass abeam.

"Charles Town Light, one point off the larboard bow!" called the top watch. By now, every man was suffering from what sailors call channel fever; that restlessness which always sets in during the last few days before a long journey's end. And every man, including the officers, had pooled their money to bet on the day and hour they would first spot the lighthouse. The hundred and forty pounds went to one of the surgeon's mates, but nobody really cared who won the pool because their greatest reward was going home. It was as if the Lord Himself had reached down and touched the crew the moment the lighthouse was first spotted, for every man seemed to come alive. Within six hours, their feet would once again touch America and their arms would hold their loved ones.

Shortly after noon on the last day of June 1775, the Silver Cloud rounded close abeam Hadrell's point, and trimmed for the larboard reach to the Forrestal yards on the north shore of Charles Town. The only British ship protecting the harbor was a small frigate engaged with two privateers. The two smaller craft circled the frigate a short distance off Fort Sullivan, like a pack of dogs about an angry bear, effectively drawing the British attention from the Cloud. Several small fishing boats returning from the open sea joined the Silver Cloud on her larboard reach across the harbor toward her berth, creating a small parade for the returning ship.

Alexander Forrestal's carriage waited at the dock as the frigate shivered her timbers and threw across her first hawser.

"Welcome home, gentlemen!" called the elderly shipbuilder as he brushed away the helping hands of his footman and limped forward from his carriage.

"Thank you, Mister Forrestal!" answered Captain Jones as he trotted down the gangway to the steady planking of the dock, with the others at his heels. "It's good to be home." Alex gave John a handshake and a fatherly hug, followed by similar greetings to Ben and David.

"And who might these two be?" he asked as he approached David's father and the girl.

"This is my fiancée, Jane."

"Pleased to make your acquaintance, miss," said Alex as he kissed Jane's hand. "Where'd you find her, David?"

"It's a long story, sir," answered David as he gestured toward his father. "Mister Forrestal, this is my Father, Charles Noble."

"Charles Noble?" asked Alex slowly.

"You're wondering why I'm here," asked Charles with a grin, "rather than on the treasure ship?"

"Yes I am, sir. This is very unexpected."

"My brother, who is also my associate, asked me to come. He's taking the treasure back to Kings Town. I'll be joining him as soon as my business here is concluded."

"Your business?"

Charles held out the package to Mister Forrestal.

"Is that for me?"

"Yes it is, sir," answered Charles, "but my instructions were explicit that I present it to you and your wife together."

"Hmmm," said Alex as he studied the package. "If it's waited this long to be opened, I suppose a few minutes longer won't hurt." Alex turned to John. "Tell me about the cannons, Captain Jones."

"We've got them, sir," said John with a toothy grin, "every last one of them! And they're the most beautiful weapons I've ever seen."

"And do the carronades fire as well as we had hoped?"

"Aye!" answered John. "We fired several rounds at a shore target and my gunners couldn't believe how accurate they are. Hitting your mark is no longer a matter of luck."

"Especially when your enemy has T-boned you, and he's lashed to your rail," added Robert with a wink at John.

"Lashed to your rail?" asked Alex.

"Aye," answered John. "We sank the Walrus and captured the pirate Captain, Joshua Smoot."

"How delightful!" cried the old man. "And how about the treasure?" Before John could answer, Forrestal was searching the bay for another ship. "Where's the Eagle?"

"Captain Steele went back to Saint Croix with part of my crew, sir," answered John.

"What on earth for?"

"To rescue his men from a sugar plantation where they were made slaves by Joshua Smoot."

"What? Saint Croix? Smoot? Slaves?" Forrestal was too excited to comprehend anything at the moment.

"That's where we found Miss Wright."

"You found this lovely girl at a sugar plantation?" asked Alex as he took the girl's hand a second time and kissed it.

"We found her on the Eagle, sir, but..." John paused. "As David said, sir, it's a long and complicated story, best told over some good Scotch whiskey after dinner." As he spoke, John noticed a large group of men approaching along the dock. "Who's that, sir, and why are they looking at us so strangely?"

"Oh," answered the shipbuilder as he released Jane's hand and turned about, "those are my men. They're going to move the Silver Cloud up the river to one of my older yards to off-load the cannons. I've several warehouses where we'll store them until they can be distributed." The old man considered John's second question and continued. "Their odd look is because none of them expected you to get through the blockade."

"Blockade?" asked John with a look back toward the sea.

"That's right! You wouldn't know about Lexington and Concord because word of the battle didn't reach me until you were at sea. We're at war with England, John."

"I expected it, but not this soon. Did we get the cannons here in time?"

"Plenty of time," answered the shipbuilder. "But I want to know about this Pirate Captain. Is he aboard the Cloud?"

"No, he isn't, sir."

"He's not?" cried the old man. "But I was hoping..."

"It's quite a story, sir," said John. "We'll tell you all about it after dinner, along with the rest of our adventures." John looked about as Mister Forrestal's men began to board the Cloud. "But before I leave the ship, sir, I've a crew to see to."

"Don't worry about them," said Alex. "My men'll take charge of the ship and let your crew off before they move it. We've set up one of my warehouses for them to sleep in until they're paid off. You and the others can go back tomorrow morning for your things." Mister Forrestal led the six travelers to his carriage.

Ten minutes later, the carriage rolled to an easy stop at the front steps of the Forrestal mansion. Ann Forrestal had watched their approach and waited patiently at the top of the stairs.

"Is it the Silver Cloud, Alex?" she called down to her husband.

"Yes it is, dear, and we'll be having six guests for dinner!"

"Splendid!" she cried in anticipation of the wonderful sea stories the men would share. She looked quickly along the line of men as they stepped from the carriage and scaled the steps one by one. At the end of the line, a few steps behind Ben Gunn, came Charles Noble with the package under his arm.

"Alex," she asked as she studied Charles, "who's that?"

Charles Noble stopped several steps below the porch as Mrs. Forrestal walked forward to meet him. There was something about his face. It was the same peculiar cut of his nose and the way his mouth curled up slightly at the corners that had caught her attention several months earlier when she first met his son David.

"Oh," apologized Alex as his man-servant helped him up the steps, "forgive me dear. This is Charles Noble of Noble Shipping in Kings Town. He's David's father." Alex turned back to Charles. "And this is my wife and best friend, the first Lady of Charles Town, Ann Forrestal."

"I'm very pleased to meet you, Ma'am," said Charles as he climbed the last three stairs and took her hand. "David's told me so much about you and your husband, and the splendid time he spent with you in April."

"Thank you, Mister Noble," she said as she studied his face. "We enjoyed David more than he could know."

"Oh!" Charles remembered the package under his arm. "This is for you and your husband. My brother gave strict instructions that you open it together."

"For us?" She looked at Alex and back to Charles. "What is it?"

"I wasn't told." He handed the package to Mrs. Forrestal, and then added. "I've an idea it has something to do with our shipping companies, but that's only a guess."

She turned the package over several times.

"Your brother?" she asked as she studied the handwriting. "Who is he? What's his name?"

"He goes by Jack Bridger, but that's not his real nema, Ma'am. He asked that I not disclose his true identity until after you've opened it."

She began to pull at the knot, and then looked back at the four men waiting near the front door. Someone was missing.

"Where's David?" she asked, "Did he go back to Kings Town already?"

"No," answered Captain Jones. "He's with us."

"I thought he was following me," said Charles, looking back at the carriage. "David!"

"Coming, Father!" answered the youth as he stepped onto the cobblestone driveway. He turned back and reached inside the carriage. "I was just speaking with Jane." Taking David's hand, the young girl stepped to the ground.

"Who's the young woman, Captain Jones?" asked Mrs. Forrestal as she handed the package to Alex and descended several steps toward the approaching couple.

"She's Jane Wright, the daughter..." John began.

"You're Governor Wright's daughter!" cried Mrs. Forrestal as she ran to the girl. "My Lord, girl...we'd given you up for dead when word reached us that you'd been taken prisoner! How...?"

"We rescued her, Ma'am," said David. "You should have seen it!"

"You need a bath and new clothes, you poor dear," said Mrs. Forrestal as she compared Jane to herself. "You can tell us all about it later." She called to a servant near the front door. "Nelly! Warm a bath for Miss Wright and set out one of my dresses in the second guest room. Make it that light blue one with the lace...the one I wore to the Andersen's last month!"

"I appreciate your kind offer, Mrs. Forrestal," said Jane, "but I've just spent three weeks with these gentlemen and I insist on being present while they tell their stories, and especially when you open the package from Long John Silver."

"Long John Silver?" Ann said slowly as she looked back to Alex. "Oh my!"

"Well," said Alex, to break the chill that had momentarily engulfed them, "there's no point in standing about out here. Shall we adjourn to the library?"

"Aye!" agreed Robert. "And I could go for a glass of Madeira, if you have any, sir."

"That's a woman's drink, Robert!" said John as they were ushered to a large wood-paneled room. "You want a man's drink. Something like Scotch or Irish whiskey."

"Gentlemen!" interrupted Alex as he followed the two women. "I have any drink you could desire." He led John to an overstuffed chair next to the fireplace and pulled another up close beside it. "Sit here, John. While Edward gets your scotch, you can begin telling me your story. I've never met a real pirate, except once in New York at a dinner party when I was just a lad. Now, tell me all about this Joshua Smoot!" He reconsidered. "No! Start at the beginning--when you left here in the Silver Cloud."

"Well, as you know, we left Charles Town in early April and set course for..."

"I know all of that!" said Forrestal, patting John's arm like an impatient child. "Get to the exciting parts!" Ormerod and the others burst into laughter.

"Tell him about arriving at Dead Man's Chest, John," said Robert. "That's when things really..." He was interrupted by Mrs. Forrestal.

"Excuse my interruption, Mister Ormerod, but Miss Wright will never get to her bath and clean clothes unless we open John Silver's package." She scanned the room and spotted the package on the end table next to David. "Alex?"

"But Captain Jones was just about to tell me..." He stopped and gave the other men a look of husbandly despair. "We do have all evening for that, I suppose." Alex stood with a wince of pain and picked up the package. "Oh, one thing before I attend to my wife's request, Captain Jones."

"Sir?" asked John as Alex pulled two rolled and sealed parchments from his desk drawer.

"What's this?" asked John as he broke the wax seal.

"It's what you went on your adventure for. It's our offer of a permanent commission as a First Lieutenant in the Continental Navy."

"Then he's formed the navy!" asked David.

"Not yet, son," answered Alex. "There are a lot of details to be worked out yet, especially the necessary funding for ships. Personally, I believe it will be late in the summer or early fall. I'm not privy, mind you, to everything that Mister Jefferson is doing, but I do know about the ships."

"What's to happen to the Silver Cloud, sir?" asked David.

"She'll be fitted with a dozen more cannons and renamed the Raleigh," answered Mister Forrestal, "provided we get the necessary funding."

"What about all the privateers?" asked John.

"They're already fighting the British, Captain Jones, but Jefferson assures me that he'll find the necessary capitol for real frigates."

"Alex?" whispered Ann sternly. "The package?"

"Yes, Dear," he answered with a step toward the hallway. "But there was one other...oh, yes! Mister Jefferson has asked that as soon as you and David can manage it, that you meet with him in Philadelphia. He wants a full report of the expedition and he needs help in forming the navy."

"We can leave tomorrow, sir," answered John with a look at David.

"Let's not be too hasty," said Alex. "I want to hear your story before you tell it to Jefferson." John smiled broadly and raised Jefferson's letter in a salute to his host. "Mister Jefferson will have to wait awhile anyway, because I've an important appointment in Virginia."

"You're too late, Captain Jones," said Mrs. Forrestal as she steped to the sideboard and picked up a delicate letter. "This came while you were gone." Before John could open it, she continued. "Miss Dandridge accepted Patrick Henry's proposal of marriage not two weeks after you had set sail. That's Alex' and my invitation to their engagement party." John read the invitation silently. A tear spilled from his right eye, but the wounded Scotsman diverted it before it was noticed. He regained his composure and looked up.

"I'm...disappointed, but not surprised," said John as he glanced down once more at the document which testified to his lost love.

"That's all?" asked Mrs. Forrestal. "We were sure you'd..."

"I don't deserve her hand. Perhaps I never did."

"You underestimate yourself, Captain Jones," offered Alex.

"It's all my fault," said John as he handed the invitation back to Mrs. Forrestal.

"Oh?"

"You see, even though Dorothea's father forbid that I write, I sent a letter the day before David and I left to go see Mister Hewes."

"But nobody could blame you for that, John," said Alex.

"But there's more," continued John. "Mister Jefferson warned me against going to see her, and finally, Captain Steele tried to stop me from taking that side trip to Fredericksburg with Mister Gunn." John fell silent for a moment and then continued. "Nevertheless, I still have a moral obligation to pay a visit to Dorothea and her father to explain what they must perceive as very bizarre behavior on my part during these last few months."

Mrs. Forrestal cleared her throat, causing Alex to jump.

"If you'll excuse me, my good friends," said Alex with a glance at his wife, "my presents are required elsewhere." A moment later, John and his fellow adventurers were alone.

"John," said David, "I won't be going with you to Philadelphia, not right away, at least."

"But it's an order, David. We're to be officers in the Continental Navy."

"I'll have to follow you later," said David as he laid his letter on the table and took Jane's hand. "I've decided to go with Jane to Georgia as you recommended."

"But that advise was given only because you were insisting I marry you and Jane aboard the Silver Cloud. You're both young. You have plenty of time for a proper courtship and marriage."

"Please, Captain Jones," asked Jane, "can't you tell Mister Jefferson that David will follow you in a month or two...just long enough so he can decide? I want him to meet my father."

As Jane finished, John noticed the others were staring past them toward the main hallway. John turned about. Ann Forrestal was standing in the doorway with a letter in her hand. Tears were streaming down her face.

"What is it, Mrs. Forrestal?" asked John. "Are you all right?"

"I'm fine, Captain Jones, better than I've been in many years." Without taking her eyes off David, she walked across and placed her arms about his shoulders. After a long embrace, she kissed his cheek. "Welcome home, David." Then, without an explanation for her strange actions, she turned and walked to David's father and stood for several moments in admiration. After Charles and the others were thoroughly perplexed, she wrapped her arms about Charles' shoulders and gave him a long kiss on the cheek, just as she had done to David.

"Oh, Charles, my wonderful Charles!" After a moment, she stepped back and placed the letter in his open hand.

"This letter is addressed to you."

"I don't understand..." he began, but she put a gentle hand to his lips.

"Shhh," she whispered. "The letter will explain everything. Please, read it aloud. It's important that the others hear it also."

Charles unfolded the letter and scanned quickly through it's pages as Mrs. Forrestal and the others took their seats.

"This is the letter from..." He looked up at the elderly lady. "Do you know my brother?"

"I did for a brief time, when I was very young." She looked about at the others and back to Charles. "Please read the letter. It'll explain everything." Charles gave her a questioning glance and began:

My dear Brother, Charles:

By the time you read this letter, my wife and I will be well on our way toward our destination: a place of which I have never spoken. Yes, as you've suspected I would, I've taken the entire treasure. But in so doing, I have not violated my word to you. My promise, if you will remember back to that first night I met Captain Jones, was that you would receive compensation far beyond your dreams.

Your treasure is the most wonderful and fitting I could possible give to you, my beloved Brother, and it is infinitely greater than the gold and silver which now lies in the lazarette of the Silver

Cloud,

I had never told you the story of your youth, always waiting for that perfect moment that never seemed to come. It wasn't until I saw the name of Alexander Forrestal on one of the five letters David brought to you in April that I realized it was finally the right time.

Like you, I was purchased by James Taylor when I was just a pup. My mother, bless her soul, was a tavern maid and couldn't keep me. But unlike you, I had a double portion of the wanderlust running through my veins, and ran off to sea when I was nine. As I've told you often, that's how I lost my leg and ended up a cripple at ten years old. You'd have thought such a thing would have cured me of ever wanting to go back to sea, but at fifteen, I ran off to England on a merchantman. But before I left, our adopted father made several trips to Old Greystone prison, as we called the place, to purchase the release of a girl who'd been a pirate in Calico Jack Rackham's crew. The girl spent several weeks in our home trading sea stories with me until her father, William Cormac, came from South Carolina to collect her. I shipped out with them to Charles Town, and then continued on this same merchantman to Bristol.

It was during this voyage that I was befriended by the professor from Oxford University. He offered to educate me in exchange for my stories about Blackbeard, John Flint, and the other pirates I'd sailed with. As you already know, that's where I learned my cooking skills and the King's English. It was when I returned from England eight years later that I first met you. I began to notice that a letter came from Charles Town every two months, as regular as the sun. Being the nosey fellow I was, I found and read several of those letters. I kept my ability to read a secret from father, so it was very easy to keep abreast of all his affairs; him leaving the letters about his desk and all. The letters were all about you and the girl Mister Taylor had helped free from Greystone. One of the older letters explained the whole affair; how you were born in Cuba and were then sold to Mister Taylor in '20 for one hundred pounds, all at your grandfather's direction. Every letter contained ten pounds. I can only assume it was to keep our father quiet about your ancestry.

I began to look more deeply into the matter and succeeded in collecting the documents you have turned over to Alex and Ann Forrestal. Do you remember the trip I took to Havana in '38, the one upon which I wouldn't let you come? That's when I acquired the guest register and bill of sale for the infant child named Charles Noble. The Innkeeper sold you to James Taylor of King's Town for several times more than he had paid for me.

You were born to Ann Bonny and Jack Rackham in late August 1719, and named Charles Noble by the Innkeeper. When William Cormac—Ann's father—arranged for your sale to Mister Taylor, he paid the Innkeeper fifty pounds to tell your mother you had died in infancy, should she ever come back searching for you.

When old man Taylor died and left the shipping company to you, there was no longer the need for Cormac to send any more money. I lost contact with your mother, but not before finding out that she had married a wealthy shipbuilder's son by the name of Alexander Forrestal in 1725. Unfortunately, she was unable to have any more children after having your younger brother in Greystone prison.

So, brother Charles, except for the part Captain Jones kept to split with his crew, I have the Treasure of Dead Man's Chest, and you have your family. And wouldn't you agree that you're the richer for it? Our paths may never cross again until we meet on the other side; wherever that may be. Until then, dear Brother, I wish you and your new family fair winds and following seas for the rest of your days.

> *Long John Silver*
> *Pirate to the death*

"That's why you asked if I remembered you," whispered Ben.

Ann gave the old man a loving look and walked to David.

"Do you remember that first time we met, David?"

"You nearly fainted," he answered as she touched his cheek. "I must look a lot like my Grandfather."

Ann gave David a kiss on the cheek.

"Is this true, Mrs. Forrestal?" asked Charles as he lowered the letter. "Are you my mother?"

"Yes I am, Charles, and every word of John Silver's letter is true." She walked to where she had laid the guest register and opened it to the seventh of August, 1719, and pointed to an entry signed by the Innkeeper, Calico Jack Rackham and herself, followed by Jack's mark of a skull and crossed cutlasses. It was an agreement that Ann, who was heavy with child, would be kept at the inn until her child was born and she could travel again.

"See, Charles," she pointed to one of the entries, "Jack paid thirty-five pounds for my room and board. And look here!" She turned a dozen pages. "Here! The twentieth of August, 1719! It's the record of your birth!" In the open page lay a half dozen letters and documents John Silver had collected over the years, each one verifying a portion of the story. "And look here! This is your certificate of baptism, and here's the agreement and fifty pound receipt between Jack and the innkeeper that they keep and raise you as a God-fearing lad." She continued to leaf through the letters.

"You sold me?" asked Charles slowly, with a tone of betrayal in his voice.

Ann stopped turning the pages and looked up at her son. A new flood of tears welled in her eyes and spilled down her cheeks as her temporary joy turned back into the guilt she had lived with for so many years.

"I was a young girl; young and full of the devil. Jack and I returned to the sea and...well, we were caught within six months. After a short trial, the entire crew was sentenced to hang. I wanted to return for you, but..." She wiped the tears from her eyes and gave him a pleading look. "You can see it, can't you? It was best that

I didn't keep you."

"Answer my question," repeated Charles slowly. "Did you sell me?"

She shook her head as she tried to choke out the words. "I...I..."

"No, Charles," answered Alex as he led Ann to a chair. "Jack Rackham paid the Innkeeper and his wife to care for you until he and Ann could return for you. It was Ann's father who sold you."

"My Grandfather sold me?"

"Don't be too condemning, Charles," continued Alex. "He didn't want the scandal of having a bastard for a grandson, but he also didn't want to lose you completely. That's why he arranged for you to be purchased by James Taylor. Your Grandfather's name was William Cormac."

"Was?" asked Charles.

"He died eight years ago," added Ann, "and took his secret and my last hope of finding you, to the grave."

"Did Alex know any of this before today?" asked Charles.

"Yes, I did," answered the old man. "We had been married twenty years without a child. When we finally consigned ourselves to the fact that Ann was barren, she told me the whole story."

"I took Alex back to Cuba to look for you," added Ann, with a loving look to her patient husband, "but the innkeeper told us you had died shortly after Jack and I went back to sea. He even..." She broke into sobs at the thought.

"It's alright, Dear," said Alex as he put his arm around her and looked up at Charles. "The innkeeper took Ann and me to your grave. We stopped looking after that."

"Why didn't you come looking for me earlier?"

"Oh Charles," she sobbed, "I'm so sorry about that. You were a part of my life I wanted to forget. I never wanted Alex to know that his young bride had been a pirate or that she'd had two children out of wedlock." The tears were once again pouring down her cheeks in unbroken streams. "I know I should have come for you sooner, but..." She broke into deep and convulsive sobs.

The guest register was still open, so Charles leafed through the remaining papers. Everything was there, even the letter from William Cormac confirming Ann's marriage to Alex Forrestal and the letter in which Taylor promised to keep the whole affair to himself.

"Mother?" said Charles as he put his arm around her shoulder. It was the first time he had called any woman by that title.

"Yes, Charles?"

"What's my real name?"

"Well..." she said as she sat up straight and wiped away the tears. "My name was Bonny when you were born, but Jack Rackham was your father." She paused for a moment. "I suppose..."

"It'll be Charles and David Forrestal!" said Alex as David joined his new family.

"I suppose this means," said John as he watched the tearful reunion, "that between the two shipping companies, you won't need that naval commission after all."

"No, Captain Jones," answered Charles, "he won't. My son and I will be too busy serving the American Colonies through our shipping company."

"And we'll serve together," added Alex. "Between Jamaica and Charles Town, there'll be no greater shipping company in the Western Hemisphere!"

EPILOGUE

The Admiralty investigation of the near sinking of H.M.S. King James had gone on for two days and filled nearly seventy pages of testimony. It was late in the afternoon and the officers were tired.

Fairchild: I still don't understand how Captain Stevens could have been so unprepared; to be taken by surprise like that.

Hawkins: But he was prepared, sir. Every cannon was manned. Furthermore, he was so concerned by this second Silver Cloud's appearance that he doubled my inspection party.

Reynolds: Then why didn't the King James fire on the Cloud when she raised her gun ports?

Hawkins: At first I thought they had.

Reynolds: But surely you saw the Silver Cloud's gun ports as you rowed across from your ship. That should have...

Hawkins: They were too well camouflaged, sir, and they fired without raising the veneer that hid their guns.

Fairchild: They what?

Hawkins: Captain Silver explained it to me later. There were no covers, only a thin oak veneer which hid the guns from even the closest inspection. It tore away like paper in the first volley. Captain Stevens had no reason to suspect he was up against an armed ship.

Fairchild: There will be a ten minute recess while the Board considers its closing questions.

(The hearing reconvened at 1640 hours)

Fairchild: We have only two or three questions to ask before we conclude this hearing, Lieutenant Hawkins. Mister Stewart will begin.

Stewart: How did this Captain Silver know you'd be the inspecting officer, Lieutenant Hawkins?

Hawkins: I asked him the same thing, sir, with the thought that if I hadn't gone aboard the treasure ship, the King James might not have been sunk.

Stewart: And?

Hawkins: He knew that I inspected the first Silver Cloud when it was en route from Charles Town to Dead Man's Chest. He also knew that it's the

Royal Navy's practice that the same officer conduct the inspection upon a ship's return passage.

Stewart: He knew you inspected the Silver Cloud before? But how?

Hawkins: The mail, sir. He looked at nearly everything that passed through Kings Town. Once he discovered I was on the King James and that we had been ordered to the Gulf, he sent a false dispatch to Captain Stevens, ordering us back to Andros island.

Stewart: Hmmm. My last question has to do with your capture. Would you sum up your testimony by recounting the events following the storm?

Hawkins: Well, sir, as I told the Board yesterday, the last thing I remembered before finding myself in the water was when I turned to return to the deck to assess the damage to the rigging. And if you'll allow me to digress for a moment, that's one of the reasons I'm convinced the Silver Cloud sank.

Stewart: Please explain.

Hawkins: Think about it, sir. How could I have got from the inside of the ship and into the water while I was senseless, unless the ship broke up?

Stewart: True, unless Captain Silver wanted you to believe that.

Hawkins: Sir?

Stewart: Did he ever tell you why he kidnapped you?

Hawkins: He said it was to pay back an old debt to me, and so he could give me my share of the treasure.

Stewart: And what did you do to earn your share?

Hawkins: He didn't say I earned it, sir. It was for our friendship and my promise to testify on his behalf at his trial.

Stewart: Interesting. Let's get back to your shipwreck, Lieutenant Hawkins.

Hawkins: After waking up, I spent two and one-half days on my piece of wreckage without food or water. When the storm had finally passed, there was no sign of the Silver Cloud or her escort, the Remora. I was picked up by a fishing yawl at the latitude and longitude I told the Board yesterday, and was then delivered to a private residence on Sanibal Island. A family by the name of Wilkens nursed me back to health. Mister Wilkens knew I was a British officer by the inspection papers which I still carried in my trousers. After three weeks with this kind family, two men came to their home. They spoke with Mister Wilkens for most of the morning, and then took me by boat across the bay to Pine Island where I was kept for the next thirteen months with another family named Clayton. Like the Wilkens family, the Claytons were also very kind to me. It didn't take long before I had convinced them that I wouldn't try to escape; that I didn't want to return to the war. I was given pretty much free run of the island. On occasion, I even went to Saint James on the mainland for supplies with Mister Clayton and his two older sons. In late August of '76 while on one of these trips, I managed to elude my keepers. It was not difficult to catch a ride to Charlotte Harbor where I joined the crew of the H.M.S. Expedition under Captain Allister Eastman. I managed to return to England several months later. The rest you know.

Fairchild: That's a very interesting story, Lieutenant Hawkins, but I still have difficulty with the sinking of the treasure ship. Apparently, the thousand cannons did arrive in Charles Town, and it is true that a certain American Naval Officer; a Captain John Paul Jones, has given the British fleet fits for two years. But...

Hawkins: The treasure ship did sink, sir, five miles west, southwest of Cape Romano, just as I told you.

Stewart: How can you be so certain of that, Lieutenant Hawkins?

Hawkins: Think about it, sir. The piece of wreckage upon which I was found was the lower twelve feet of the mizzenmast and part of the main deck. I've thought it through many times and I'm convinced that the Silver Cloud couldn't have survived the forces necessary to tear a mast from her decking that way. Captain Silver couldn't have contrived such a large piece of wreckage, just for my benefit.

Fairchild: The man's a master of contrivance, Lieutenant Hawkins. He's capable of anything, even such a piece of wreckage. But you stated in earlier testimony that it seemed strange that there was no other wreckage or survivors.

Hawkins: That's true, sir, and it did bother me at first. Then I figured the thing out. Isn't it possible that I could have been thrown overboard early in the storm, and at some distance from where the Silver Cloud finally went down?

Stewart: Yes, that's possible.

Hawkins: (to Fairchild) And you, sir...can't you also agree that it's possible?

Fairchild: (The Commodore shook his head to signify "No".)

Stewart: I have one last question for you, Lieutenant Hawkins.

Hawkins: Sir?

Stewart: If you were unconscious, how do you explain not slipping from your piece of wreckage, especially in the storm?

Hawkins: I was tied to it, sir.

Fairchild: Tied to it? And you still believe the Silver Cloud went down in the storm?

Hawkins: Of course I do.

Stewart: That's impossible! If you were tied, then someone had to tie you there. I know you're only a Lieutenant, but even *you* must be able to see that someone wanted to be sure you survived to tell your story.

Hawkins: I wasn't alone on that flotsam, sir.

Stewart: You weren't?

Hawkins: One of the other crewmen made it to the same piece of wreckage and must have tied me on until I regained my senses.

Stewart: That does make a difference. Who is this other man and how may we find him?

Hawkins: You can't, sir, because he's dead.

Stewart: Dead?

Hawkins: We were still in the storm when I regained consciousness. He lay at my side, still clutching the end of the rope that bound me. The side of his head was stove in from a heavy blow. He must have had the presence of mind to tie one of his own arms to the wreckage before he lost his senses.

Stewart: Can the people who found you corroborate your story?

Hawkins: No, sir, because he slipped into the sea that first night.

Stewart: Very convenient.

Hawkins: Sir?

Stewart: Nothing.

Fairchild: We appreciate your candor, Lieutenant Hawkins, and the cooperation you have given myself and the other members of this Board these two days. The Admiralty will publish its official findings in due time. Officially, I expect the record to show that the ship that attacked His Majesty's Ship King James was sunk in a hurricane off the west coast of the Spanish territory of Florida. My personal, and unofficial opinion, however, is that your only purpose for being taken aboard the Silver Cloud was to provide this Captain Silver with the witness he needed so as to escape detection and pursuit by the Crown.

Hawkins: Sir?

Fairchild: From everything else you've claimed he's accomplished, it's certain that he could have made you believe anything he desired, even the sinking of his disguised frigate. As for the dead crewman on your piece of wreckage, it's possible he was already dead when he was placed there; killed when the Silver Cloud was damaged.

Hawkins: With all due respect, sir, I must insist that Long John Silver died at sea. He simply could not have...

Fairchild: Arranged for the storm?

Hawkins: Exactly! I can understand your interpretations of his other actions, but how would he create a storm?

Fairchild: My guess is that he had some other way of providing for your separation from the treasure ship. That storm was pure luck.

Hawkins: But you can't possibly know that for certain, sir. It's just as likely that he actually went down with his ship. With all due respect, sir, your line of questioning...well, it implies...

Fairchild: That I know something more? (pulls folded letter from file) I shouldn't be showing you this, but in October 1775, approximately four months after you were rescued, I received a most interesting letter from my cousin in Philadelphia where he's one of the principal stock holders in a very large bank. When I first read it, I knew it was important, but didn't know why until yesterday when you described Captain Silver and his treasure. Listen to this section of the letter and see if you don't come to the same conclusion as I have: "Something strange occurred last Thursday evening that I thought you might want to know. Thomas Jefferson and three other gentlemen made an after-hours visit to our bank and spoke with Mister

Harding for nearly an hour. The men had Jamaican accents, and the oldest of the three was wearing a mechanical left leg that made a snapping sound every time he took a step. The second, a man in his forties, was missing his right hand, and the youngest had red hair and green eyes. After they left, Mister Harding told me that they would return at midnight with thirty-eight oaken barrels. It was a King's ransom in gold and silver; approximately one and a half million pounds. The entire sum was deposited in one of Mister Jefferson's personal accounts. I asked who the other two gentlemen were and he told me that Mister Jefferson would not say." (Fairchild to Lieutenant Hawkins) Well, Lieutenant Hawkins?

Hawkins: I don't know what to say, sir.

Fairchild: Then I'll say it for you. (tapping letter) Here's your Captain Long John Silver, and here's his treasure. His plan would have worked perfectly except for this letter. He didn't die in that storm, Lieutenant Hawkins. Rather, he became a traitor against his King. It's apparent that the sisters Fate and Irony joined hands to play a cruel joke upon the Crown.

Hawkins: Cruel Joke?

Fairchild: You said it yourself, young man. It seems that Captain Andrew Murray's intentions were ultimately served; that the Treasure of Dead Man's Chest was used against King George III. (Pause) If and when Captain Silver contacts you next...

Hawkins: Sir?

Fairchild: Nothing, Lieutenant Hawkins. (to the board) Unless further evidence comes to light, I declare this hearing and the matters of the attack on His Majesty's Ship King James, the pirate Long John Silver, and the Treasure of Dead Man's Chest officially closed.

The End